MAGIC
CLUB

To Sandy & Gary —
Hope you enjoy this
story set in our
Grand Valley —

Harry C Br

April 20th, 2012

MAGIC CLUB

A Novel

Harry Clifford Brown

SANTA FE

Sunstone books may be purchased for educational, business, or sales promotional use.
For information please write: Special Markets Department, Sunstone Press,
P.O. Box 2321, Santa Fe, New Mexico 87504-2321.

Book and Cover design ›Vicki Ahl
Body typeface › Constantia
Printed on acid-free paper

———————————————————————————————

Library of Congress Cataloging-in-Publication Data

Brown, Harry Clifford, 1953-
  Magic Club / by Harry Clifford Brown.
     pages cm
  ISBN 978-0-86534-783-0
  1. High school seniors--Fiction. 2. Mountain life--Colorado--Fiction. 3. Grand Valley
(Colo. and Utah)--Fiction. 4. Psychological fiction. I. Title.
  PS3552.R68554M34 2012
  813'.54--dc23
                          2011050852

———————————————————————————————

WWW.SUNSTONEPRESS.COM
SUNSTONE PRESS / POST OFFICE BOX 2321 / SANTA FE, NM 87504-2321 /USA
(505) 988-4418 / ORDERS ONLY (800) 243-5644 / FAX (505) 988-1025

*I*n memory of Tom Stubbs, may he run and paint forever—
Ars longa, vita brevis.

He's invisible, a walking personification of the negative.
—Ralph Ellison, *Invisible Man*

. . . victory is an illusion of philosophers and fools.
—William Faulkner,
The Sound and the Fury

ACKNOWLEDGMENTS

The author thanks all the many friends who took the time to read the first draft—you know who you are—especially, Jim Fuchs, whose knowledge of astronomy was invaluable; Dick, Kerry, and Mark for a lifetime of misadventures and the eventful inspiration they've spawned; Jake, Chuck, and Tom and all past club members for allowing the glue of Magic Club to be applied to this story; Beth for introducing me to the inner sanctum of a Lakota sweat; Colleen and Ken for their constant encouragement; Fred Ramey and James C. Smith for their expert editorial eyes; and, most affectionately, Carolyn for encouraging me to write. And, finally, I'm grateful to the spirit and memory of Miss Darling, who not so gently appeared in a dream to dissuade me from changing her character's name.

◇◇◇

Author's note: The Mandarin Chinese, as spoken by the character Greg Woods, is alphabetized using Pinyin, the official system to transcribe characters into the Roman Alphabet in China and Taiwan. The pinyin system also uses diacritics placed over a letter for correct pronunciation. These tone marks have been excluded from the text for simplification purposes. It should be noted that the Chinese spoken by Greg Woods is marginal at best.

1

Miss Darling was a citizen of the universe. She had been an Egyptian princess and a tobacco farmer in Virginia. She traveled the stars at night and lived in a mud hut near a canal bank by day. She'd been one-third of a song-and-dance act in vaudeville. She was a cripple, a poet, a palm reader, a fortuneteller, her soul living in the last of its nine bodies. She was five-hundred-and-sixty-two years old. Miss Darling cast spells, threw curses, mixed herbs, wrote anti-war letters, smoked Pall Mall Menthols when she could afford them, and rarely, if ever, bathed. She boarded five Pomeranians—you don't own other creatures, she said, doing that can untoss the cosmic salad—one of which sported a dusty yellow, crocheted sweater over its pink furless body and all of which twirled in circles when they yapped, which was often. Miss Darling stood four feet nine inches and shrinking. Many people who knew her and most who sought her advice thought she was a witch. We didn't know if she was or not.

"Nine lives? You mean, like a cat's?" Lenny sat in the back of my mother's Dodge Dart, directly behind Miss Darling who sat in the passenger's side. Rarely did Lenny crack the obvious joke—his mind wasn't wired that way—but then we realized he wasn't kidding.

"Nine cycles. It's the cosmic order. Queenie! Git outa here, Queenie! Go on!" Miss Darling eyed the dogs, which were starting to move away. "Give me your right hand."

Lenny scooted forward, scrunching Julie and Greg into each other against the car door. He held his hand out and poked his head over the front seat.

She peered down at his palm as though into a deep well. "Your right hand gives me your future, the left your past." The middle finger of her speckled hand traced the lines of Lenny's palm. Her breathing wasn't exactly heavy but you could hear it, a low hum as though a chord strummed deep inside. "You're sensitive, especially to nature. You're like a coyote. You sniff the wind and rain without thought."

Greg threw his head back, pursing his lips as though ready to howl. Julie smothered a giggle into her wrist.

"But your hands are kind and very creative. They express who you are and, like everyone's, they tell me your destiny." Letting go of his hand, Miss Darling turned and studied Lenny over half-moon reading spectacles. They were black-framed with white tape wrapped at one corner to secure the earpiece and pop-bottle lenses that made her eyes jump out. "'Your path may be clouded, uncertain your goal / Move on, for the orbit is fixed for your soul. And though it may lead to the darkness at night / The torch of the Builder will give it new life.' What's your birth date?"

"September twenty-ninth."

"Year?"

"Fifty-three."

She raised her short arthritically swollen index finger and began figuring, as though it were a piece of chalk. Lenny stared at the imaginary chalkboard. Miss Darling's toothless mouth moved, whispering calculations. "One." Her hand dropped. "Go on, Queenie. Go on now."

"One?" Lenny glanced at Julie, Greg, and me.

The car was parked in what might have been a driveway behind Miss Darling's adobe hut if it weren't for a stand of kochia weeds already tall enough to brush the underside of the car when we pulled in. Through the sun-streaked windshield I could make out the tips of the dogs' tails and ears bounce as they moved to the dirt beneath Miss Darling's old Cadillac; it was the only shade around that didn't grow weeds. Three of the Caddy's tires were flat and the right front wheel, which once held the fourth, rested on a split of oily tree stump, the wheel's rusty edge cutting into it. The Caddy's windows were smoky white and rolled up, and the inside was packed to the roof with cardboard boxes.

"One what?"

Julie and Greg squirmed for elbowroom, the skin of their legs adhering like tape to the vinyl seat covers, but Lenny wouldn't budge.

"One cycle. You're a young spirit, you see—an infant soul. 'You are and you will be, know while you are / Your spirit has traveled both long and afar. It took on strange garbs for eons of years / And now in the soul of yourself it appears.'" Miss Darling cackled and readjusted her garments under one arm, the smell of raw chicken rising from her, chicken left out too long. "That's from my poem 'Child of Infinitude.' Did you know I was in *Who's Who of American Poets* in nineteen-fifty-five? This is just your first body to inhabit.

In your next life you'll be a woman. Good Queenie. Good dogs."

"I will?"

Julie coughed, muffling another laugh.

I frowned at her. "It goes every other life, Lenny. Right, Miss Darling?" My sister Dana had brought me to Miss Darling's the Friday before, when I first heard how everyone has nine lives before leaving this planet, alternating between male and female, how you could figure out the cycle you're in by adding the numbers of your birth date.

Miss Darling nodded. "September is the ninth month, nine plus twenty-nine is thirty-eight, plus fifty-three is ninety-one. Nine plus one is ten."

"I thought you said I was in my first—"

"One plus zero is one."

Lenny shook his head, sitting back in the seat.

Julie scooted over to give Greg more room. If Julie had it her way she would have kept Greg pinned against the upholstery for the rest of the day, night, and into the next morning. She pinched Lenny's cheeks. "I told ya you're just a baby."

Lenny was one of the oldest members of our graduating class but looked the youngest: five-foot-seven, slender, whiskerless, and a boyish face that the girls in our class found cute. Yet cute hadn't helped him find a girlfriend during our three years of high school and he was sensitive about it. From a distance his loose-limbed gait made him appear even younger. Walking down the hallway at school or down the street afterward, he gave the impression that he was off to one of the carnivals that stopped in Grand River every summer or to a party or anywhere but to class or that weird home of his. But his quirky artist's brain made up for his apparent lack of years. Besides, Lenny was wiry, could run the shorts off anyone in the valley, and was a pretty good one-hundred-and-twelve-pound wrestler.

"Actually, I'm in my tenth life. I'm already in a higher realm."

Greg snickered. "Actually, you multiply not add. One times zero is . . ." He rolled thumb and index finger into a zero, then pointed at Lenny.

I cleared my throat, glancing over my shoulder. "Miss Darling, we came over because our friend Greg Woods here—"

"Hi." Greg waved.

"—well, we're all graduating from high school next week and Greg wants to know if he should accept a scholarship to the—"

"Appointment."

"—an appointment to the Air Force Academy."

Miss Darling jerked her head around and studied Greg. "Air Force? So you can fight?"

Now it was Greg who scooted forward. Being a pragmatist, albeit a maniacal one, Greg had been against the idea of seeking Miss Darling's advice. That he came at all was an indication of what he was going through (not to mention that this was Magic Club, the only rule being that you had to attend every meeting—if you could even call them meetings).

"No, uh, I'll be in school for four years and by then Nixon'll have us out of—"

Miss Darling held up her hand, then motioned to Greg. "Come up here."

I climbed out the driver's side and Greg got out the back, slipping his sunglasses off and into his front shirt pocket. As we passed each other he stretched his mouth and eyes wide in a silent scream and wagged his head back and forth. With his long angular face, he looked like the guy in the Edvard Munch painting. The shapes he could twist his face into were a source of entertainment to us; in fact, everything he did was for amusement, from annoying teachers with his irreverence and then spiting them by getting straight A's, to risking his physical well-being for a laugh (like when he drunkenly skied off the Chalet Hotel into the swimming pool; we had to fish him out using a ski pole because as soon as the skis hit the water, his boots popped from them and took on the properties of an anchor).

Greg's face returned to its sarcastic gleam as he slid in behind the steering wheel.

Miss Darling took his left hand. "Greg Woods, was it?"

"Gosh, you're already one for one and we've barely started."

She looked at him then threw her head back and cackled wide-mouthed, revealing toothless gums. "He's a corker now, isn't he?"

"Two for two." Julie and I laughed.

If ever there was a corker, it was Greg Woods. You either loved or hated him: co-valedictorian, court jester, editor of both the school newspaper and yearbook, juvenile delinquent, president and sole surviving member of the Chinese Language Club (Julie was the only other charter member, but after a month and a half of learning nothing but "hello" and "good-bye" from Greg and "penis" on her own, she was unanimously voted out—two to zero; they both knew it wasn't Chinese she was interested in), boozer, number one player on the tennis team three years running, captain of the debate team, and as he liked to put it, all around *bon vivant*. And then, of course, there was Magic Club: his idea.

"What's your birth date?" Miss Darling brought his hands to her lap.

"December fifteenth, fifty-three."

"Ah, a fellow Sagittarian." She calculated under her breath. "An old soul, too. You're in your eighth cycle." She began kneading his hands between thumbs and index fingers.

"What're you doing?"

"For your headache." She turned his left hand over. "Self-induced, I believe."

Greg smiled. "Hmm. Guess that makes you three for—"

"Shhhh." She studied the palm, tracing the lines with her middle finger. Greg leaned back against the car door, right elbow resting atop the seat, head propped at an angle.

"This line that runs under your thumb around the Mount of Venus here is your life line. See how it sweeps along here? This means you have a great capacity for work, for physical endeavor."

Greg shrugged, huffed the fingernails of his free hand before shining them on his shirt. "Naturally."

Julie opened her mouth and stuck an index finger in, pretending to gag.

"But see how the life line tends to end up near the Mount of Moon here? This means that sometimes your energies are unstable and badly directed. Be mindful of this."

We covered our mouths and pointed at Greg, mocking him.

"Yes, you have a long head line, as well."

His eyebrows arched. "No doubt a reflection of other parts of my—"

Julie snorted before she could catch herself. She held up a hand, thumb and index finger indicating an inch.

"This is a sign of a good intellect. You have good concentration and you can be quite practical in many matters. See how your head line curves up at the end?"

"Then again, Greg, probably not a reflection of—"

I elbowed Julie to shut up.

"You sometimes lack empathy. You don't always take others into consideration. Let's see what your heart line says." Miss Darling's face drew closer as she traced under the faint calluses of his hand. "Your heart line is quite short compared to your head line and life line. This is somewhat unusual in a fire sign. See how straight it is and how it ends, pointing at Jupiter. You're more a pragmatist, a thinker, than an emotional type, aren't you?"

Greg shrugged. "I guess."

Julie laughed out loud. "You guess? Are you kidding?" Her lust for him was a well known fact. That they remained friends at all was less a testament to

Greg's charm than to Julie's persistence, although his ability to make light of her affection—as he did almost everything in his life—helped ease her frustration.

"See these lines?"

He bent forward and nodded.

"They tell me you've lived overseas."

Miss Darling looked up as he continued to stare at his hand. The three of us in back glanced at one another.

"Somewhere across the Pacific. You were very young. You probably don't remember."

Greg licked his lips, slightly nodded. His father had worked for the State Department in Taiwan, returning when Greg was six.

"Let's have a look at your future."

He pulled his left back as Miss Darling took the right. But instead of looking down, she closed her eyes, clasping his hand. "Someone has been sick on your mother's side."

"Yeah, my mother—she has a cold. She's probably on her side right now." Greg looked at Lenny and wagged his eyebrows, rolled his eyes, and flicked an imaginary cigar.

"No, this is serious." Her eyes remained closed. "Your mother has a brother. He's younger, right?"

Greg stared at her; his left hand moved from his head and he slowly gripped the steering wheel. "Yeah. My Uncle Phil."

Miss Darling nodded. "Something inside him isn't right."

She released her hand and pressed her own mid-section. She opened her eyes. "His stomach or something."

He bit his lower lip. "Colon. He has cancer."

Julie gawked at Lenny and me, mouth open. We knew his uncle had been sick for a long time, moving in and out of hospitals, but hadn't realized how sick.

"If you want to see him or say anything, do it now. He'll soon pass through to his next cycle. This uncle—Phil, you say?"

Greg nodded.

"He likes you very much, but he's worried." She took his hand again, brought it closer, flexing it at the wrist. "These lines tell me how long you'll be in this cycle. Each complete line represents thirty years."

He pulled his hand away. "Look, Miss Darling, this is very interesting—really—but we've got to get back. Henry said I could just ask you a couple of questions."

"She'll do that after she finishes reading your palm, Greg."

"Hey, I'd like that, Hank, I really would, but we have to get to class. We have that history final. Remember?"

Miss Darling threw her head back and cackled. "Oh, you're a Sag all right. As impatient as I. No matter. Now, what's the question? Should you go into the army?"

"Air Force. The United States Air Force Academy in Colorado Springs." He glanced at Julie and rolled his eyes.

"Give me back your hands." She clasped them in her lap and, closing her eyes, began kneading them again. The humor in Greg's face was gone now as he stared and waited. The car was suffocating in the afternoon heat. The leaves of the single cottonwood that loomed over Miss Darling's small home hung limp, and the only movement was from one of the dogs circling to reposition itself near the Cadillac.

Her eyes popped open. "Do you want to go or do your parents want you to?"

Greg's jaw flexed and then his mouth broke into a lopsided smile, which it did whenever he felt tested. "Is that your answer?"

She let go of him. "I can't answer. I can only tell you what I feel."

"Which is?"

She grinned. "Your parents want you to go, but you don't."

He looked down, shaking his head. "But *should* I go?"

Miss Darling's grin faded and she lifted a crooked index finger. "No. No one should go. It's wrong. The war is wrong!" She jabbed her glasses up her nose, the pall of raw chicken washing over us. She stared at Greg and then turned, scanning across our faces, eyes enlarged and jumping out at us through the lenses, before narrowing. "'From cycle to cycle through time and through space / Your life with your longings will ever keep pace. And all that you ask for and all you desire / Must come to your bidding as flame out of fire. You are your own devil, you are your own god / You fashion the steps that your footsteps have trod. No one can save you from error or sin / Until you harken to the spirit within.'"

She suddenly grinned. "That's from that same poem, *The Child of Infinitude*. Oh, it's a lovely poem. I'll let you read it sometime. Okay, that's all for today. Tell your friends. See you next time."

I jumped out the back seat and hustled around to the passenger's side. Julie got out also and we each took an arm, helping Miss Darling from her seat. She stood in the weeds, steadying herself against us, and grinned up at me. I smiled back, nodding. "Thanks, Miss Darling."

She continued to grin.

"Oh—" I jammed my hand into my jeans pocket and pulled out a wadded five-dollar bill. I looked at Julie, but she shrugged and shook her head. I poked my head into the car. "Hey, you guys, I need another five."

Greg had already gotten into the back seat with Lenny. Rarely did Lenny have money so out of habit he looked to Greg. Greg arched up and pulled his wallet out of his back pocket, unfolded it, and removed the bill. "Kind of an expensive poetry reading there, Hank. I thought Magic Club was supposed to be free." He handed me the five.

Miss Darling was struggling through the tall weeds with Julie. Her legs bowed wide, causing her to walk on the outside edges of her feet. Her upper body moved side to side from the hips, like a dwarf's.

"Would you believe, dear, that these legs use to dance?"

Julie smiled. "Really?"

"I was once a member of vaudeville with my uncle and twin sister, bless their souls. We performed in Denver at the Brown Palace for the vice-president of the United States and the governor."

"Wow."

I hurried over to support her other arm. The Pomeranians were up again, yapping and twirling around us in the weeds as we worked our way to the gate of a tall chain-link fence, which looked to be the most expensive thing she owned. It skirted the house—or what was left of it—not three feet from the adobe bricks, many of which were scorched. One entire room was burned out, and the charred smell wafted through the room's window and mingled with perfume from a Russian olive. Miss Darling braced herself against the gate, cheeks puffing with exertion.

"See how I have to live?" She fumbled in the sweater pocket. "This valley . . . has been nothing . . . but misery for me." She pulled out a silver ring of keys. "Since I moved here in fifty-seven—Queenie, stop it!—that Ute curse has clamped onto me. I've done everything in my power to break it, but I still haven't managed to. My last cycle on the planet and I'm going out like this. I believe they call it a cosmic joke." Miss Darling laughed, softly this time.

I glanced at Julie. "Curse?"

"Come back sometime and I'll tell you about it. Here, Queenie. Come on." She unlocked the padlock and the dogs scampered through the gate. Bracing against the fence, she struggled in. I handed her the money as she gave me the lock.

"Could you lock that for me? My fingers are all stoved up today."

I closed the gate and snapped the padlock as she moved the few steps to her door.

"Come back to see me. And bring your friends. Thank you. I'm fine, now. Good-bye."

"Bye. Thanks, Miss Darling." Julie and I started back through the weeds to the car.

"Wait. One more thing—"

We turned.

"—about your other friend." Cradling one of the dogs, she tilted her head forward to look at us over the lenses, through the hatch pattern of fence wire. "He must be very careful around cars. I sense extreme danger for him."

Julie and I looked at each other and nodded, then watched the door swing shut, Miss Darling and the Pomeranian she called Queenie disappearing behind it.

2

*I*f asked, Julie would call the summer after graduation purgatory. She's Catholic, although she does everything she can to disprove that fact. Greg would describe it using a French derivative—ennui—or would speak metaphorically—the anteroom—while suffering through his decision about whether to attend the Air Force Academy. Lenny, if he said anything, would call it just another weekend and then maybe sketch it. And me? Well, compared to my friends, I'm pretty ordinary. I'd probably just ask the question.

Early in the school year we read *Invisible Man*. It was about this black guy who couldn't be seen. Not in a literal or magical sense but figuratively, Mr. VanHorn called it. He lived in a basement underneath a building in a large city, probably New York. In a symbolic attempt to be visible, to have substance, the man lined his room with light bulbs. Black, Mr. VanHorn said, is an absence of light, of color, and in America black people don't think they can be seen or heard. He said *Invisible Man* is about race and anonymity and isolation. Lenny raised his hand and said maybe the guy really was invisible because in Grand River they sure are—at least he hadn't seen any black people. Mr. VanHorn smiled and said that most minorities feel the same as the black man, but that in Grand River the invisible man is brown. So that's when I raised my hand and asked if you could be white and invisible. Whether color and number had anything to do with it. But I already knew the answer and that it had nothing to do with magic, either, or even living in a basement—although that's where this guy I was thinking about happened to live—in a basement where, though white, he most definitely felt the absence of light.

"Hank, did Greg say anything to you?"

"About what?"

Julie glanced at me. We were sitting in her Volkswagen Bug at a traffic light on our way to pick up Lenny for school. "About yesterday. Magic Club."

"Not really. I think he wants to keep it going though."

"Hmm." She ran her fingers through sun-streaked brown hair—a habit she had when thinking, as though it helped untangle all the ideas in her head. "Does that surprise you?"

"What?"

"That he wants to keep meeting. I mean, all year he's been sounding like he can't wait to get out of here. And now after yesterday and what Miss Darling said and everything."

"I don't know."

Julie sighed, leaned across and, using her palm, popped open the glove box. "He's such a psycho. Pick something."

I began rummaging through the tapes. "Greg didn't show up for the history final yesterday."

She shook her head. "Great. The last week of class and he's decided to have one of his episodes. What a dick."

I chose a tape and slid it into the eight-track.

"Hank, I guess we're just going to have to keep a better eye on him."

I smirked. "Yeah, right—'we'."

"As much as I hate to, I'm going to start sleeping over there. You know, make sure he studies, tuck him in, check his vital signs during the night. Maybe do a little dream analysis. It's going to be a burden."

"Uh-huh. And what are you going to say to his mom every morning?"

She smiled brightly. "Pass the sausage?"

When we pulled up to Lenny's, his Jeep Wagoneer was parked in its usual spot across the street in the vacant lot with the hood propped open. His uncle had willed it to him when Lenny was only fifteen. Mrs. Bartelli was convinced that he'd done so just to spite her. It had shown up on their front lawn as though by an act of God, although Mrs. Bartelli was convinced it was Satan's handiwork; that is, until the mail arrived later that same day—her brother's Wagoneer had reached them before his funeral announcement. Why it was parked on the lawn instead of the street no one ever knew, but Lenny had recruited his older brother Vince and one of Vince's friends to help roll it off the grass and across the street to the vacant lot before their mother could reach it with the flat side of her garden shovel. And because of his mother, in the vacant lot was where Lenny was resigned to parking it, spending most of his time lying underneath or crouched under the hood or dashboard, tinkering with wires.

Julie swung into the Bartelli's driveway and honked. "She hates it when I honk."

"So why do you?"

The picture-window curtains parted and then abruptly closed.

She smiled. "She hates it when I do anything. As Rog would put it, I'm just allowing her the opportunity to more fully experience her emotions."

Julie's father, Roger McClellan, was a clinical psychologist who chronically dressed his language with the same bow-tied jargon he used to diagnose patients at the hospital psych ward. She worshipped him not as a daughter does a father but as a junior colleague worships a mentor, and her words proved it—just as peppering them with profanity proved her Catholicism.

The front door opened and Lenny sauntered out, wiping hands on a dishtowel. His mother, clad in a terry-cloth housecoat and wearing a million bobby pins, stood in the doorway. Pushing the screen door open, she yelled something, which we couldn't hear over Julie's stereo. Lenny ignored it and lifted his chin at us before crossing the street to let Louie out. The dog lumbered from the back seat, waving his tail, a tennis ball lodged in his mouth, and followed Lenny around to the tailgate. We waited as Lenny took a bag of Purina and poured some into the cast-iron skillet that doubled as a dog bowl. Louie watered the nearby elm, shook for good measure, then trotted obediently over to him. Lenny scratched the dog's ears then tied a long rope, which was looped around the Wagoneer's back bumper, to his collar. The tennis ball dropped, and with ears pinned back, Louie plopped down and watched Lenny shut the hood and walk back across the street to Julie's VW.

"Hey."

"Hey, Lenny. What's up?" I leaned forward so he could squeeze into the back.

He shrugged. "Mom's blood pressure."

Julie rolled the window down and waved as she backed down the driveway. "Bye-bye, Mrs. Bartelli! Great seeing you again!"

The front door slammed as Julie shifted into first and eased up along the vacant lot. "And good-bye to you, too, Louie-boy. Be a good dog and don't go poking any of Mrs. Capp's poodles while we're gone."

Louie perked his ears up at the sound of Julie's voice and his tail thumped.

The first time Lenny got his uncle's Wagoneer to run, the summer before our sophomore year, we had driven into the desert on a Sunday morning for a test drive while Mrs. Bartelli attended morning services at Pentecostal Holiness Church. As we came up over one of the many adobe hills north of town, just able to peer over the dashboard, we saw a black dog lying on its side under a lone piñon tree. In the morning slant of light, we could see the sunken shadows between its ribs. Its head lay flat in the dust and we thought the dog was dead, but Lenny pulled the Wagoneer over anyway. He walked over and knelt down, placing his hand on its shoulder. Lenny said it whimpered when he touched it, but I was standing right there and didn't hear a thing. He scooped the dog up—its head hung limp over his forearm and its tongue lolled out—and I cradled its hindquarters as we placed it on the back seat. And it was there, for the next few weeks, that Lenny nursed the dog back to life, in the Jeep he'd inherited from his late Uncle Louie.

I glanced back at Lenny, who was still rubbing his hands with the towel.

"Why'd you tie him up?"

Usually, when the Wagoneer was running, Lenny took him to school. The dog would hang out in the dirt parking lot, sleeping under the back bumper and waiting for Lenny to return from classes. Everybody knew Louie—Greg used to joke that Louie was more popular than Lenny—and would feed him treats and throw tennis balls across the lot into the football practice field for him.

Lenny shook his head, picked grease from his thumbnail. "Mom likes Louie 'bout as much as the Jeep."

"Hey, Bartelli—" Julie turned down the volume. "—that isn't gasoline I smell back there, is it?"

She glanced in the rear-view mirror and Lenny half-smiled, slipping his hands into the pockets of the baggy Army pants he always wore.

"It's the only thing that cuts the grease."

"But it makes you smell like a gas station."

Lenny looked down, slid a pencil and folded notebook paper from his pant pockets and began doodling.

"I'm sorry, Lenny." Julie glanced at me and shrugged. She ejected the eight-track. "Lenny, did Greg say anything to you about Magic Club?"

"Nope."

I looked at her. "What's he supposed to say?"

"I don't know. I just think this fortuneteller thing has traumatized him."

"You mean traumatized you."

Julie reddened but didn't say anything.

"Hey—" I reached into my gym bag and slid out my new, 1972 Grand River High School Yearbook. "—did you see our picture in the annual?"

"We're in the annual?" Julie jerked the steering wheel and screeched to a stop. A car honked and whipped around us.

I thumbed to the Clubs section. "Greg snuck it in."

Julie snatched the yearbook from me and scoured the page. "Where?"

Lenny leaned forward, squinting over her shoulder as she whispered under her breath, her finger sliding down one page then the other. ". . . Key Club, Ski Club, Speech Club, 4-H . . . where?"

I tilted the annual back. "I think it's on the next page."

She flipped one over. There, spread across the bottom, was a photograph of a bare hilltop with Rimrock National Park in the background, the red sandstone outlined against a brilliant orange and pink sunset.

I nodded. "It's the only color photo in the entire annual."

Lenny pulled the book toward himself, still squinting. "Look. That's shot from the top of the Third Sister."

He relinquished it to Julie and sat back, smiling and shaking his head. "Good old Greg, man."

Julie lifted the annual up to her face as though it were a menu at Quan's Chinese Restaurant. "'Magic Club. Left to right: Greg Woods, Julie McClellan, Henry Kessler, Jr., and Lenny Bartelli. Not pictured: Clifford Irving, William Calley, Jr., Charles Manson, and Jim Morrison.'"

She closed the book and handed it back. Glancing over her shoulder, she pulled out and continued toward school.

I stuck the annual back into my pack. "Magic Club. We're invisible. Isn't that great?"

She glanced at me as she pulled into the high school parking lot. "Yeah, Hank. Great." She ran fingers through her hair. "Immortalized forever."

It was a Yogi Berra comment, uncharacteristic of her, but no way was I going to point it out to her, not when it had anything to do with Greg Woods.

◇◇◇

Greg Woods sat cross-legged in the middle of Sherwood Park, his face tilted toward the sun and arms braced behind him. He wore prescription sunglasses, aviator style, and his curly blond hair hung loosely over the back of his collar. A spiral notebook lay next to him on the grass.

"Greg!"

It was my lunch hour on the next to last day of final exams, our final week of classes. I walked across the park toward him and cupped my mouth. "Hey, Greg!"

Finally reaching him, I tossed my books on the grass. "Geez, are you deaf or what?" I sat down but he didn't move, except for his lips.

"Hi, Henry."

I plucked a blade of grass and stuck it in my mouth. The sky was cloudless, which wasn't unusual for Grand River, sitting as it did in a wide valley where the Colorado and Gunnison Rivers meet. I could see the Bookcliffs, the low shelf of mountains running along the city on the north; Spruce Mesa, the largest flattop mountain in the world, looming to the east; Rimrock National Park standing in the distance to the southwest; and a few adobe hills of the high desert rolling in from Utah to the west. Grand River, the local Chamber of Commerce was fond of saying, is not only where two mighty rivers join but where mountains meet desert.

I leaned on one elbow, stretching my legs out. That morning I had taken the P.E. final, and I could feel my calves starting to tighten. "Did you hear about Lenny?"

Greg slightly shook his head.

"He almost smoked the school record in the mile this morning. Four minutes, thirty-seven seconds. In his sneakers."

Greg smiled, mouth closed, the sun gleaming off his glasses.

"You ready for that Chemistry test tomorrow?"

"I'm thinking my studying days are over, Hank."

I nodded as though I knew what he was talking about and looked across the expanse of grass at the single-story brick houses with the double-car garages and manicured lawns that surrounded Sherwood Park. Julie's home was one of them, sitting on the curve of Sherwood Drive before the street butted into Fifth.

"So how many finals do you have to go?"

He smiled again, slightly shaking his head. "I think I've taken my last one, buddy."

I brought my gaze back to him. Sunshine raised the veins in his tan forehead, faint shadows tracing from both temples up either side into his hairline.

"Well, not me. I've got a geography final in five minutes." I picked up my book and started back across the park toward school.

"Hey, Hank!"

I turned. Greg still sat, unmoving, in the same position.

"Yeah?" I walked back.

"Morrison really isn't dead, man."

"What?"

"Jim Morrison. He's still in Paris. Probably shacked up on the Left Bank with the L.A. woman. Writin' songs for his comeback tour."

His smile stretched wide now, straight white teeth bathed in sunshine. I nodded.

"Hank."

"Yeah." I looked down at him. From where I was standing I could see his eyes over the top of his dark glasses: they were open, staring straight into the noon-day sun.

"Tomorrow. Last day of high school, man." He pushed his glasses up the bridge of his nose. "The end."

◇◇◇

Lenny sat at the desk in front of me sketching, his left leg bouncing as though he were still running the mile. As usual, he was the first to finish the exam. If he didn't know the answer to a question, he would leave it blank and go immediately to the next one. After the first test of the year, Mr. VanHorn tried to talk him into taking a guess, to improve his chances for a better score, but Lenny said that if he did that, Mr. VanHorn wouldn't know which questions he really knew the answers to and which he didn't. Mr. VanHorn smiled and didn't mention it again. And it was from that point that Mr. VanHorn and Lenny began to form a friendship, and it was to this that Lenny was now paying homage.

"Stop." Mr. VanHorn clicked the stopwatch that hung from a leather shoelace around his neck. "Okay, pencils down. Make sure your names are printed legibly in the upper right-hand corner." He strolled down the aisles, trading insults as he collected papers. "Nice, Bartelli." He stopped at Lenny's desk.

"What?"

Mr. VanHorn took the stapled pages and flipped them over.

"It could be anybody, Mr. V."

"Uh-huh." Mr. VanHorn held the caricature up for the rest of the class, and there was an immediate whoop of recognition: a huge head with a single hair on top and a wild unkempt mane growing around a massive neck and cauliflower ears, a strong jaw, dimpled chin, and a sausage-fingered hand cradling a dog-eared copy of *Moby Dick*.

"Okay, okay. Enough applause for Leonardo here. You'll need five pieces of notebook paper for the essay section."

A groan rose up as everyone settled down and began rummaging for paper.

Mr. VanHorn wrote three questions on the blackboard, then spun around, holding the chalk aloft. "Questions?"

"What's verbatim?"

"Means word for word. I want to see examples of the author's writing. Anybody else? Kessler."

"You mean like, 'Let us go then, you and I, when the evening is spread out against the sky like a patient—'"

"That's right. As close to the exact quote as you can get."

The girl sitting across the aisle, Margaret Kohler, who ever since first grade wore a tight ponytail and the same cat glasses, rolled her eyes and made the same "khhh" sound she had been making for the last twelve years.

"Come on, quiet everybody. If there are no more questions, let's get to work."

Mr. VanHorn sat in the back as we labored over our answers. For all his girth, he was an agile man both of body and intellect. He had decided to become our assistant wrestling coach the year before—he'd wrestled heavyweight at the University of Arizona—but it was his intellect that kept the head wrestling coach, Lawrence Hicks, from asking him back for the following season. Coach Hicks said that VanHorn's persuading some to wrestle their natural body weight and not to cut pounds since they were still growing, caused his team to lose the conference championship for the first time in nine years.

When Coach Hicks came down with the flu one week before the biggest dual meet of the season, Mr. VanHorn had conducted practices by himself. Foregoing the usual regimen of stair laps, endless pushups and situps, wrestling in plastic suits to lose water weight, and the high-pressure challenge matches for varsity, which with Coach Hicks' prompting could be more brutal than any dual meet with another school, Mr. VanHorn had instigated a half-hour free-for-all, tickling not only included but encouraged. That was followed by a serious talk about internal wrestling, about fear being the only enemy of an athlete, and then an hour of what Mr. VanHorn called experimental wrestling, where the single stipulation was that you could only score by trying moves or holds you'd never used during a match. Coach Hicks was livid with the number of wrestlers who, at that critical dual meet, not only didn't make their usual weight class but came off the mat defeated and grinning about it because they'd tried some unorthodox move they'd never attempted before. Afterward, Mr. VanHorn had tried to explain the concept of fearlessness to Coach Hicks, not in the sense of being ferocious but in trying new things as the surest path to improvement, but that was as fruitless as Coach Hicks explaining to Mr. VanHorn why he wanted his wrestlers to cut weight.

The two men simply did not see eye to eye. The world from Coach Hicks' five-foot-four-inch perspective was a thing to be conquered, or at least twisted into a shape you could live with. When applied to his wrestlers, he called it "hammering boys into manhood." To Mr. VanHorn the world was something in which to be immersed, whether reading Shakespeare or throwing your fellow man into an enthusiastically sweaty headlock.

And headlock was what I was feeling as I struggled with the last sentence of my answer to *Heart of Darkness*, while everyone filed by to turn in the final exam.

"Okay, Kessler. Cough it up. Your buddy's out there waiting for you." The wooden chair screeched against tile as Mr. VanHorn unweighted. "Hey, Bartelli! Come back in here for a minute."

I tore at my hair, searching for that last sentence as Lenny re-entered from the hallway. "Yeah?"

"What are you up to this summer?"

"I dunno."

"Well, Molly's got a whole list of projects for me. So if you need work, let me know."

"Okay."

"You and Kessler going to wrestle in the Senior Classic?"

Lenny shrugged. "I haven't wrestled since the season ended."

"I know you're in shape for it."

"Will Cisco be there?"

"Cisco, Coca, Stryker, Guillen—all the studs."

"I don't even know what I weigh."

"The lowest college weight is one-eighteen. You don't weigh over that."

"So what if I draw Cisco?"

"Then we can have a nice wake afterward. Come on, Bartelli. I'll pay your fee. All you have to do is show up. How about you, Kessler? That is, unless you're still in here attending summer school."

I tapped the end of my pen on the desk, chewed my lower lip. "Just a sec, Mr. VanHorn." Gripping my pen, I scribbled something about "the horror of existence when you have a black heart like . . ."—and that was the funny thing I wrote, funny in the sense of strange, I mean—I wrote ". . . a black heart like Cisco's." What I really meant, of course, was "a black heart like Kurtz's." Mr. VanHorn would point that mistake out to me four months later, after the wake.

3

Somewhere between the illumination of the sun and Miss Darling's all-seeing eyes, Greg decided to take the final Chemistry exam. It was Friday afternoon, the last hour of high school, and as I drove across the parking lot through notebook paper, cigarette butts, and curled remnants of Black Cat firecrackers, that fact began to dawn on me. Without uttering a word—he hadn't said much to anyone since Wednesday at Miss Darling's—Greg got out of the car, walked across the grass, and entered the front of the building one last time.

"Well, there he goes: the Marquis de Sade of Grand River High." Julie sighed.

"At least he's taking the Chemistry final."

"Yeah, with his head as the test tube."

"What do you mean?"

"Come on, Hank. You think he was staring into the sun for his daily requirement of vitamin D?"

"I don't know."

Lenny tapped me on the shoulder from the back seat. "Try vitamin A."

"What are you talking about?"

"Acid."

"Greg? No way."

Julie glared. "Then what was he doing with his eyes open?"

I shrugged. "I don't know. Maybe he just opened them right then, when I looked down at him."

"Hank, his eyes look like the pimentos from a pair of stuffed olives." She shook her head. "Didn't you hear what Miss Darling said? He's in danger."

Lenny leaned forward and stuck his head between us. "Who is?"

"Greg."

"I didn't hear her say that."

Julie traced a long strand of hair behind her ear. "You were in the car with him, Lenny. She said he has to be careful around cars."

"Maybe we should tell him."

She shook her head. "No way. We can't say anything. It would only inspire him. Trust me."

I glanced at my watch. "I've got to get to class. I'm going to be late. Is my notebook back there?"

Lenny handed it to me as I got out.

"You guys going to the kegger tonight?"

"Yeah, but I'm going to take Louie for a little run first. Want to go?"

"Only if you go slow. My legs are still killing me from the mile yesterday. I don't know how you do it."

Lenny shrugged.

I gazed in at Julie, who stared out the passenger's side window away from me, palm cradling her chin.

"Could you lock the car before you go? My mom's kind of funny about that."

She nodded slowly without looking at me.

"See you guys later." I hurried across the parking lot toward the building where we'd spent much of the last three years of our lives. Reaching the entrance, I hesitated and looked up at the classroom windows, at row after row of staggered red brick running in straight lines of gray mortar and at the sign atop the school marquee with the locked screen over it: *Good Luck, Seniors!* Grabbing the metal handle, I glanced back across the lawn and dirt parking lot. Lenny and Julie still sat in the car, but Lenny had already moved from the back seat to the front.

◇◇◇

Normally, Greg would have commemorated the last day of high school with a speech, a prank, or an antic for which, over the previous three years, he'd become famous. The first day of our senior year, when everyone was still running around between classes trying to remember locker combinations and room numbers, someone had lured the janitor, Mr. Horton, across the street for an Arctic Circle Slurpy and at the same time chained all the outside and hallway doors together. When the next hour's bell rang, the school was suddenly dammed with its own students. At that incipient juncture of our senior year it never entered the outer reaches of the administration's collective mind that Greg Woods—athlete, straight-A student, yearbook editor—was the perpetrator of that first-day fiasco. As the year progressed, though, and Greg continued to have the uncanny ability to show up at the most opportune moments, suspicion about him rose. But who was helping him? He couldn't have lured Mr. Horton away and locked all the doors, too. Just as, later that fall, he couldn't have, by himself, scaled each light pole at City Park Stadium and unscrewed every light bulb before the Homecoming football game; it had been postponed to the next day. Nor could Greg Woods alone have rewritten the greetings atop the auditorium, some of which were profound—Beer is a brain food, Happy Hanukkah Rednecks, My Karma ran over your Dogma—and some political—Mao loves Dick, McGovern the McPeople, Spuck Firo Agnew.

It took the administration the first four months of 1972 to realize that, with each new message, the size of the alphabet soup was growing, which is when they finally decided to secure the sign with a locked screen. But they never did prove anything, even though Mr. Guerrie traced the purchases of the lettering to Mountain Office Supply and one Albert DeSalvo (Greg's alias). And, as if that weren't enough, every Monday morning after Guerrie delivered the morning announcements and turned the P.A. system over to various club officers, Greg would be the first to step solemnly up to the microphone, utter a greeting to Mr. Guerrie in Chinese—"*Guerrie Laoshi feichang xihuan chi chou-gou-shi.*"— announce the Magic Club's Sweetheart of the Month selection (although no one actually knew what the Magic Club did or even was, ourselves often included), and then denounce, in no uncertain terms, the dastardly deed of the mystery messenger. Ceremoniously and with hardly a glint of irony, Greg would step away from the microphone over to the red-faced Mr. Guerrie and pump his hand as though they were comrades in the long, arduous fight against delinquency.

And now, amidst the whoop of students running down hallways and across the school lawn and the honk of cars pulling out of the parking lot, Greg Woods was making his last unceremonious walk down the sidewalk away from Grand River High and his last examination.

"Greg! Wait up!"

His thongs flapped rhythmically as I hurried alongside him.

"So what do you think, Hank?"

"Boy, I don't know. I think I blew it."

"No, I mean what do you think about this."

"This?"

The sprinklers were stuttering across the grass and splashing sections of sidewalk. All but a few cars were gone from the parking lot as we walked to Greg's new Dodge Swinger.

He opened the door. "Now it begins, man. Now we break on through to the other side."

I nodded. "Yeah, but the other side of what?"

Greg smiled, gently slapped my shoulder and ducked into his new car. He inserted the key into the ignition and turned it; the engine immediately fired. He revved the motor then let off the gas.

"Great Magic Club the other day, Hank."

I looked down and stepped back as he shifted into reverse.

"As much as I hated going, I think I figured some stuff out."

"So what are you going to do?"

He gazed out the windshield. "Hard to say. I'm supposed to report to the Academy the first week of July. I really don't know what I'm going to do right now."

"Yeah, me neither. But Redd already has me lined up to talk to some backhoe operator. Can you believe it?"

He smiled, shaking his head. "Why does your mom hang out with that guy?"

I shrugged, studied the gravel between my feet.

"Hey, I'm picking up Julie around eight, so I'll swing by and get you guys right after."

"Does Julie know that?"

"What?"

"That you're picking her up."

"I don't know."

"She thinks you're mad at her."

"She always thinks I'm mad at her. Jules thinks too much, period." He slammed an eight-track into the console. "She thinks you have to love somebody to really get mad at them. Friend or lover, Hank, it just doesn't matter."

I nodded.

"I'll give her a call—Jesus, maybe I'm not picking her up. But I will be by to get you guys. Okay?"

"Okay."

"Later." He backed up, shifted into first, then pulled out, gravel ticking the underside of the car. I could hear the stereo turn up as he drove by the school, the music blaring and echoing off the brick building. I stood in the lot and watched him turn onto Fifth then accelerate down the street until he disappeared in his new 1972 graduation present, only Leon Russell's new song trailing after him: *Tight Rope.*

◇◇◇

The sun burned low over the red and tan sandstone cliffs of Rimrock National Park, throwing a canopy of shade over canyons, gullies, and ravines that creased the earth below. Farther to the east, light showered boulders that dotted the clay hillsides, and sprayed the piñon and juniper that grew high along the ridges. Lenny and I stood next to my mom's car, tying our laces and watching Louie sniff a hamburger wrapper and a crushed styrofoam coffee cup blown up underneath rabbit brush along Monument Road.

"How far we going?"

Lenny straightened and shrugged. Lacing fingers together and crossing his legs, he stretched overhead. "It's up to you. How's your legs?"

I rubbed my hamstrings. "Stiff."

Lenny bent forward, legs crossed and locked, and touched palms to the ground. Louie trotted over and licked his face.

"Louie, that's a good boy."

He wagged his tail and kept licking until Lenny straightened.

"Ready?"

I lifted one knee to my chest then the other. "I guess."

After hiding the keys inside the back bumper, I followed Lenny along the shoulder of Monument Road until we came to a barely discernable trail that cut through rabbit brush down to a dry rocky wash lined with tamarisk. Louie loped in front as we crossed the wash through the feathery pink blooms. We started up the steep hillside of the third of The Three Sisters. The trail first rose straight up among loose rock and scattered juniper, over tufts of Indian rice grass and cheat grass, until it broke right at a slab of granite, angling across the hill toward the saddle between the Second and Third Sisters. Lenny ran easily, feet shuffling up the hillside on his toes, dodging loose rocks, and his veiny calves bulging above saggy gym socks. I labored twenty steps behind as we reached a patch of sego lily that grew between the hills, a reprieve from the first half of the climb that someone had misnamed Tulip Bench.

"You okay?"

I sat on a rock, head down and forearms resting across my thighs. "Yeah . . . I just . . . hafta . . ." I spit. ". . . catch my breath. Where's Louie?"

Lenny stood hands on hips, one foot on a rock. He pointed across Tulip Bench to the Second Sister. I looked up just in time to see the white of a cottontail disappear into some brush. Louie loped after it.

"Think Louie'll ever catch one?"

"No. Wouldn't know what to do with it if he did. You ready?"

I stood, wiped my face with the T-shirt. Looking up at the last two-hundred-or-so feet of the Third Sister, which for Lenny was just a warm-up, I nodded. "I guess."

Lenny jogged beside me as we started up the hill. "Keep your feet low. It's kind of a shuffle. Watch." He sped up and moved in front. "See? You try it." Slowing, he let me pass. "Lower, Hank. That's it." He moved back in front, exaggerating the outward pumping of his arms. "See how my elbows lift me?" He bounded up the hill, Louie trotting behind now. He stopped at the top to watch my form.

Gasping for air, I finally reached him and buckled forward, head down around my sprawled knees.

"Come on, Hank. You can't breathe down there. Hands on your head." He helped me straighten.

I clasped hands atop my head. "Oh, man . . . that . . . hurt."

He nodded. "It gets easier."

"Yeah . . . when it's . . . over."

"Walk it off, Hank."

I staggered across the top of the Third Sister, gulping air, then spit and walked back.

He was sitting on the ground with his legs crossed. His dog stood panting next to him. "This is right where Greg took the yearbook picture." Lenny raised his thumb and sighted in the view. "He probably stood right over there so he could get the hilltop in the foreground."

"What do you think's bugging him, Lenny?"

He shrugged, swinging his thumb in different directions like a drawing compass. Louie licked his ear. "What do you mean?"

"I don't know. Julie thinks he's losing it?"

"Probably no more than anybody else. Did you check your draft number?" Lenny's thumb stopped on a point off in the distance toward Serpent's Trail, which snaked its way two miles up a slab of sandstone on the eastern face of Rimrock Canyon. Lenny often ran this trail, usually continuing to the top, from where he would run part or, sometimes, all the twenty-three miles of blacktop called Rimrock Drive, which skirted canyons and cliffs all the way to the farming community of Otto.

"No, I was born in fifty-four."

Lenny's hand dropped as he looked into the sun across the ridges, ravines, and clay hills toward Rimrock National Park. "Guess you lucked out then." He tossed a rock a few feet in front of him.

"Wasn't Greg born in fifty-three?"

Lenny nodded. "His number's way up there, two-hundred-and-something."

"I guess it doesn't matter anyway if he's going to the academy."

"Look. A redtail." He pointed at a circling hawk.

Louie lay down and began licking his front paw.

"What ya got there, buddy?" Lenny took the foot in hand and examined it as the dog rolled to his side.

"Julie thought the picture was stupid." I sat, watching Lenny gently poke between the pads. Louie lifted his head.

"There it is. Easy, boy." Lenny squinted into the furry depths of the dog's paw. "Julie was freakin' about Greg, not the photo. The photo captures our spirit."

"You're starting to sound like Miss Darling."

"Yeah?" Searching between Louie's pads, he quickly yanked out a cactus needle. The dog immediately stood and shook. Holding the sticker up, Lenny inspected it. "I liked her. I want to go back. That was a good one, huh, Lou?" He pitched the sticker to the side and gazed back across the hills, one hand shielding his eyes and the other resting across the dog's back. The sun peeked just over the cliff line of the canyon, catching the wispy edges of cloud streaked over the green and gold patchwork of farmland that stretched toward Utah.

"Why do you want to go back to see Miss Darling? I didn't think you liked her."

Lenny shrugged. "I don't know. She's so . . . out there."

"She's out there, all right." I stood. "I've got to get my mom's car back. It's gotta be almost eight. Redd's going to kill me. So, Lenny, what number are you?"

He looked into the deepening sunset. "One."

"No, not what Miss Darling said. I mean your draft number."

Lenny got up, using Louie's tail as if it were a rope helping him out of a deep hole. "So do I."

◇◇◇

Redd didn't kill me. He barely saw me. As usual, he was too involved with Mom's presence to notice anybody else's absence. Of course, not that he saw Mom, either. When we were studying *Middlemarch* in English class, Mr. VanHorn said sometimes you can't see something that's too close—literally or figuratively. Since Mom was, for the last six months, stuck to Redd's big florid face, I figured that held true for her, too. George Eliot called it a blot, around which you can only see the margins of the world. And while my sister and I were definitely feeling our way around the margins, Redd Morgan was just as definitely a blot. Unfortunately, it wasn't just margins he was feeling around.

I ran downstairs to my bedroom, changed from running shorts to jeans, and vaulted back upstairs. "Hey."

"Hi, Hank. 'Bout time you got home." Dana sat at the kitchen table chewing a shredded carrot and bean sprout sandwich—if sandwich is the right word for such a concoction. She nodded toward the hallway and rolled her eyes.

"Is that . . . is that you, Hank!?!"

"Yeah, Mom! It's me!" I plopped down across from Dana, shaking my head, and gazed at the goldfish bowl that sat on a barstool against the kitchen wall. It served as our barometer for what was going on in the bedroom. When things got too heated, the water jiggled. We called them passion fish—Stella and Frank—though they didn't like the turbulence any better than we did. "At it again, huh?"

"Always." Dana smiled through mayonnaise oozing at the corners of her mouth. "At least Stella and Frank aren't upset."

"How can you eat that stuff? 'Specially with that goin' on."

She picked up her plate, dropping a strand of bean sprout on my head on the way to the sink.

"Come on, don't." I fished in my hair as my sister rinsed the dish.

"I got a letter from Jeff today."

"How's he doin'?"

"Same old. Slogging through muck, carrying a pack and a gun, fighting mosquitoes and leeches and stuff."

I grimaced. "They don't call it a gun, Dana. It's a rifle."

"Then they do night re-, recon- . . . what'd he call it?" She unfolded her husband's letter from the back pocket of her bell-bottoms. "Let's see '. . . and we go on night reconnaissance. All before we eat this gruel they call breakfast.'"

"Maybe you should join up—just for the food."

She slipped the letter back into her pocket, toweled off the plate and placed it in the cupboard. "Where's the car keys?"

I pulled them from my jeans, jingled them overhead. "Don't tell me you're actually going out for a change."

"Jill wants me to see a movie."

"Can you drop me off at Lenny's? Greg's picking us up over there."

"Sure, but we have to go. It's already ten till."

"Lenny got his draft number today."

Finishing the last gulp of hot water—she had read in *Time* about Nixon's trip to China, that the Chinese drink hot water, that it's healthier for you—she looked at me over the rim of the glass then placed it on the counter. "What'd he get?"

I held up my index finger.

"Oh, my god . . . you're kidding."

"Nope."

"Jeff's wasn't even that low."

"Yeah, it's kind of hard to get lower than one." I opened the refrigerator and grabbed a drumstick. "See you, Mom!"

We hurried out the back door before our mother could even come up for air; Redd Morgan's face was probably stuck to her like goggles on a deep-sea diver—red freckled goggles without, we could only hope, a red snorkel.

As Lenny once put it, his mom was bent.

When he said it we were standing in the Bartelli driveway staring down at his brother's ten-speed. Vince had found it in an alley leaning upside-down against a trashcan. Its tires were rotted, the frame was rusted, and the handlebars were cracked. He had carried it home draped over his shoulder like a length of hose and spent days sanding and spray painting the frame, soaking the chain and components in gasoline, installing new handlebars and tires, tightening and replacing spokes, truing the wheels. Later, he attached toe clips and an odometer. And with every improvement Mrs. Bartelli screamed louder. Her behavior didn't outwardly affect Vince, but as we looked down at the mangled frame, at how both front and back wheels had caved in and curled up around the weight of a superior force, we knew this would. That's when Lenny said it, as though recognizing his mother in the twisted wreckage before us: "Mom's bent."

Flora Bartelli had lost her husband when the boys were toddlers. Conrad Bartelli, or Connie as he was known, was a seed salesman, covering western Colorado, eastern Utah, and southern Wyoming. Much of his territory was sandy and dry. The blacktop and gravel roads between co-ops, farms, and seed stores stretched before Connie like long strips of licorice and taffy. Clouds against the pale skies appeared to him as cotton candy and the adobe hills resembled chocolate ice cream scooped from the prairie and sprinkled with almond flakes, butterscotch chips, or brown sugar crystals. Connie recreated the landscape on the console of the company station wagon as he drove, then became one with it, eating everything. At every town or gas station, he would re-supply himself, loading boxes of groceries atop the sample bags of corn, barley, and alfalfa in the back.

Lenny couldn't remember his father, but Connie's growth as a seed salesman was displayed chronologically down the Bartelli hallway and around the corner to the bathroom, where the final photograph hung over the toilet. He was standing at the back of the station wagon, smiling as he struggled with a torn bag of seed over his raised left knee. Although it was January, he wore a short-sleeved shirt, and a clump of black hair lay matted across his forehead. The photograph was taken three days before his death, and the seed spilled across this same driveway where his eldest son's bicycle would be run over fourteen years later. Their father weighed three-hundred-and-sixty-two pounds in the picture. The autopsy report, which Mrs. Bartelli also framed and hung in the hallway, documented this fact and read "ruptured esophagus" as cause of death. Mr. Bartelli had hiccupped himself into oblivion in a motel room outside Rangely, Colorado. A package of pinwheels lay by his side; Uncle Louie, who had told Lenny and Vince everything they knew about their father, had guessed there must have been a tire dump nearby. "Pinwheels," Uncle Louie had repeated, shaking his head.

After her husband's death, Mrs. Bartelli received a hefty check from his life insurance policy, collected pension payments, and immersed herself in the Pentecostal Holiness Church, the poorest church in Grand River. She often took baked hams and roasts and cakes to needy families, made dozens of cookies for church functions, and spent an entire winter stitching a dove across a silk tapestry to be hung in the church vestibule. When church members fell ill, she visited them in their homes or the hospital, bearing remedies and heartfelt prayers. Once she'd even delivered an impromptu sermon when the pastor, Hector Lujan, had taken a wrong angle across the railroad tracks and skidded from his bicycle, cracking his tailbone. That was when Lenny was twelve; he refused to go back after that. He said he couldn't merge the woman standing before the congregation reciting scripture and speaking about the love of the Almighty with the one he and his brother had to contend with every day.

At home Mrs. Bartelli indulged herself in furniture and knickknacks. Their living room was jammed with coffee tables, candy dishes, glass lamps with pleated shades, painted vases, a black piano, and two long sofas—one gold, the other lime green. Plastic sheeting covered the entire collection as if all living in the room were on hold, wrapped in a gauzy time capsule. A clear hard-plastic walkway ran over the shag carpeting down the hallway and into each of the three bedrooms. Mrs. Bartelli's bedroom was white as wedding cake but every available surface—dresser, vanity, twin nightstands, bookshelves, and windowsills—was crawling with knickknacks like ants at a picnic. Ivory elephants, wooden donkeys and ducks, glass swans, thimbles, ceramic yodelers, angels, peacocks, horses, gingerbread houses, hourglasses. Lenny had joked that she collected them so she didn't have to dust; they caught lint as barbed wire catches tumbleweeds.

But her kitchen she kept clean. Stove, refrigerator, cabinets, counter, sink, curtains, tables, chairs, tile floor, even the telephone dripped with a bright pink as if the entire room were freshly dunked in Pepto-Bismol. Though the oven radiated with breads and cakes almost every day, it smelled of something vaguely industrial. Or maybe it was just this combination of color and temperature that conjured images to rise and then settle uncomfortably in the pit of the stomach. But it didn't matter; Mrs. Bartelli's food was for church.

"You in a trance?" I waved my hand in front of Lenny's eyes.

"Hey." He sat with Louie on the Wagoneer's tailgate, staring across the street at the house.

"Dana honked but you didn't even twitch."

He shrugged.

"She wanted to stop but she was late for the movie. I told her about your draft number."

"My mom's losing it, again."

I hopped up on the other side of Louie and we both stared at his house, the dog dropping the tennis ball and slowly licking my hand.

"So what's she doing this time?"

"Same old. Locking me in my room, accusing me of stuff."

"Like?"

"Drugs. Homosexuality."

I burst out laughing. Lenny looked at me, deadpan.

"Sorry, I just . . . I mean, homosexuality? That's a new one, isn't it?"

"No, not really."

The last time I had been at the Bartelli's we were in his room listening to *Live at Woodstock* when Lenny pointed to the shadow beneath the door. Holding one index finger to his lips, he had gotten up and turned the volume down. "So, Hank," he said, settling back into the beanbag chair, "how about all those chicks last night? Weren't they great?"

Smothering laughter into the back of my hand, I nodded. "Yeah, especially that real tall one."

"You mean the one with the whip and pet lizard?"

"Yeah." I doubled over, face reddening.

"I especially liked what she did with the blonde in the Dale Evans costume." He got up and stepped toward the door. "And the way she called Louie 'Bullet'. I don't think I've ever seen Louie so happy." He rolled his other hand, a director instructing the action to continue.

"Me, either." Tears welled in my eyes as I silently shook on the edge of the bed. "This room just wasn't big enough for all of 'em. Next time we'll do it at my house."

He flung open the door. Mrs. Bartelli stumbled a half step through the doorway. Recovering, she jumped backward, plastering herself against the hallway, eyes squeezed shut and mouth pursed. Her hair was in its usual torture, bound with bobby pins—to her this was a style, not a means to one—and she wore her usual weekday uniform: fuzzy slippers and a pink housecoat over a floral muumuu. Her chin strained upward and to the side as though hooked from above.

Lenny gazed at her. "Come on, Hank. Let's go find Louie before Mom gets back."

As we edged by her and crackled down the walkway through the plastic-covered living room and hot pink kitchen and out the back, our joke somehow ceased to be funny, as if laughter and humor flew out the house as soon as the door opened to the reality of Mrs. Bartelli standing there trying to blend into the wall, invisible in her own mind, unimaginable in my own. Once outside we acted as though nothing happened. We never mentioned it again.

"So where's Greg?"

Lenny shrugged. "Maybe we missed him."

"How long have you been out here?"

"A while."

I gazed up the street. "He's probably with Julie."

Lenny looked at his grease-splattered tennis shoes. Sliding off the tailgate, he made the usual kissing sound for his dog. "Come on, Lou." They walked around the edge of the vacant lot, Louie sniffing along the curb until he found that perfect spot to lift a leg.

"Hey, Lenny. Let's grab a ride with Dillard. He should be off by now. He'll be going up there."

"No, I'm going to just hang."

"Come on, Lenny. This is the last kegger of the year."

He walked back to the Wagoneer. "You go ahead. I've gotta get up early and get this Jeep running." He motioned for Louie and the big dog leaped into the back. Seeing that Lenny wasn't going to take him for a ride, he began circling over the tattered sleeping bag Lenny had thrown down for him. With a couple of twitches of his tail, he curled down and rested his muzzle across the tailgate.

"You gonna leave your back open?"

"It'll be okay. Louie's gotta get out when he needs to."

"Where's Vince?"

"I don't know. He's not around much anymore. With his girlfriend I guess."

I looked back across the street.

"She in there?"

Lenny nodded. "Yep. Probably watchin' us right now."

"Like Boo Radley."

"Yeah. Boo-dette."

"Sure you don't want to go?"

"Yeah, I'm sure. I'll catch you later." He walked across the street and up the driveway, removed the window screen, and crawled back into his bedroom, lifting the screen in place after himself.

4

*D*illard's Corvair shimmied up the winding washboard of Jacob's Ladder Road. Dust lingered in the headlights and, as we crested the last hill, flattened out over a field of cars and mingled with smoke from the bonfire.

"Oh, man! Look at this place!" Crouching forward, Dillard squinted through the dirty, cracked windshield for a place to park. Cars lined both sides of the road, spilling into the sagebrush and spreading out among the piñon and juniper. The Corvair slowed, its headlights dimming like a pair of weak flashlights, then dropped with a thud. Our heads hit the ceiling.

"Ouch! Geez, Dillard!"

"Sorry, man."

He jumped out to survey the damage. The car was stuck nose-first into a drainage bed, rear end in the air like a pig rooting for grub. In fact, because of its faded-pink exterior, shredded upholstery, and littered floorboard, we'd named it Porky. Any key you could get into the ignition would start it, and the passenger's seat was a peach crate with an Army-issue blanket folded over to guard against splinters.

"Guess we'll park here." He grinned his goofy Dillard grin, gapped teeth in an oversized mouth set into a freckled oblivious face framed with frizzy red hair. He got back in and turned off the engine. "Want a toke?" He fumbled in the glove box.

"I'm going to go find Greg and Julie."

"Come on, man. We're behind schedule. Let's get this thing crankin'."

"See ya, Dill. Thanks for the lift." Shouldering open the door, which was lodged in sand, I slipped out the passenger's side.

"You don't know what you're missin', man. Look." Holding up the baggy under the dome light, he grinned. "Paonia Purple." He slid a pipe from his shirt pocket, scooped it into the lid, and brought it out, covering the bowl with his thumb.

Lenny, Julie, and I had gone to school with Dillard since first grade. During elementary school and junior high, just saying hi would flush his already red face, and his being called on in class would deepen it further, wringing him inside out. But whatever it was that embarrassed him didn't like smoke; in tenth grade he'd discovered pot, his shyness at last exorcised.

Threading my way through cars toward the throng gathered around the bonfire, I looked back at the pitched Corvair, the bowl glowing inside against Dillard's intent face.

"Kessler! Come on, man! Let's get twisted! Kesslerrr!"

His strained, smoke-filled voice trailed after me but then was lost in Jimi Hendrix's *Purple Haze* blaring from a truck backed up near the fire. The speakers sat on either side of a toolbox across the bed of Joe Lister's pickup. Joe and Herbie "Crazy Legs" Murch were, as usual, the organizers of the party, which was dubbed "Senior Soak Fest '72." They had sold enough tickets at five dollars a pop for twenty-one kegs of beer, breaking the old record by three. Now, to make the record official, the senior class with help from sophomores and juniors had only to drink them.

"Henry! Over here." Julie stood in line with Margaret Kohler, each holding a plastic cup.

"Hi, Julie. Margaret."

Margaret glanced at me.

Julie wore blue jeans, a cashmere sweater, and jean jacket with a McGovern button pinned to the pocket. "Did you just get here?"

"Yeah. I got a ride with Dillard."

"Khhh." Margaret rolled her eyes.

"Where's Greg?"

Julie looked around. "Good question. He brought me but then disappeared."

"Typical Greg Woods move, wouldn't you say?" Margaret leaned forward. "I'll talk to you later, hon."

They pretended to peck each other's cheek.

"Okay, Marge. Great seeing you." Julie turned back to me, crossing one eye, a habit she picked up from Greg.

"What's she doing here?"

"Trying to make up for twelve years of being a hag. She's carrying that empty cup around as an icebreaker—her word. Can you believe it?" She took a drink of beer. "Did Lenny come?"

I shook my head.

"You're kidding."

"Nope. His mom's on a rampage."

"That bitch. Now what?"

"She tried locking him in his room again."

Julie sighed. "Great."

"Plus Greg didn't show up to get us."

"Was he supposed to?"

I shrugged. "Dillard was coming up, anyway."

"Greg didn't even mention picking you up. What a jerk." She held her cup out to be filled.

"Hey! Julie McClellan!" Herbie sat on the tailgate and drew back, wagging his eyebrows and scanning every five-feet-seven-inches of her. "You're lookin' mighty fine tonight. Mighty fine."

"Just fill the cup, Murch."

"And who do we have here? Sir Henry."

"Hi, Herb."

"A little grog, mate?" He held the spigot out.

"Naw, I was just talkin' to—"

"Come on, laddie. It'll cure what ails ya."

Julie hooked my arm in hers. "Knock off the crap, Murch. By the way, Herb, did you pick that shirt out yourself?"

"Next!" Herb peered down at his shirt as Julie led me through the loose knot of students that grew tighter the closer we got to the fire. Joe Lister stood at the center, feeding the flames from a pile of scrap lumber scavenged from one of his father's construction sites. A gust kicked up behind us, blowing smoke into people on the other side, turning them around.

"I brought all these McGovern pamphlets to hand out, but they're in Greg's trunk."

"I'll see if I can find him."

"Thanks, Hank, but maybe this isn't the right setting for it." She squeezed my arm. "Have you decided what you're going to do?"

"No, not really. Bet you're excited about Notre Dame, huh?"

"Yeah, I guess. Mother thinks it's very important that I'm in the first class of women there. Now I'm kinda wishing I'd stayed in state."

"Can't you transfer if you don't like it?"

"Yeah, but Daddy's a Notre Dame alumni and he's got butt-buddies in the psych department so I think I'm kind of stuck." Julie lifted her chin. "Look at that genius."

Joe Lister stood halfway in the fire stomping on the charred end of a post. Sparks shot up around him and flakes of ash lifted into the sky like aspiring stars before disappearing into the night.

"A couple more beers and old Joe'll show us how to poop smoke rings." Julie took a drink. "Want a sip?"

"No, thanks. I think I'll go see if I can find Greg. You going to be here?"

"Yeah, unless I find some stud-muffin I can drag around with me."

I worked my way through the crowd then walked the outskirts of the circle where scattered groups of students stood talking and drinking, but I didn't see Greg. I headed back through the cars and sagebrush toward Jacob's Ladder Road to see if I could spot his new Dodge.

"Keeesslerrr." Dillard was on his way to the bonfire. "Heeey, maaan. Ya missed ooout." He slapped my shoulder and shook my hand. We always joked that Dillard's words were a precise measurement for the amount of pot he had smoked; the longer they stretched, the more he'd puffed.

"This stuff's primo, Kess. Four fingers, few seeeeds, and the prettiest little buds you've ever seeeen." He kissed his fingers, a connoisseur.

"I'll see you later, Dill."

"Hey, man. Where you headed, amigo?"

"I'm trying to find Greg."

"Cisco and the boys are over there scammin' on his new car."

"Where?"

"Follow *moi*."

A black '55 Chevy pickup idled in the middle of Jacob's Ladder Road. The high machine-gun laugh of Peefee Maldonado, the truck's owner, echoed down Eagle's Wing Canyon and stopped us on a high shoulder across the way. Peefee stood in the headlights, looking at the lean figure of Cisco Salazar. Cisco was resting back against the shiny hood, arms folded and legs crossed, watching his gang of friends inspect Greg's car.

Peefee and Cisco were cousins but looked anything but. Julie said that Peefee, our Anglicized version of *Pefe*, was the lump of clay God left after sculpting Cisco. Short, round, and loud was Peefee. And that hyena cackle grated on everyone. His job, at least in mind, was to chauffeur Cisco around and make him smile—no one could make him laugh—and if he could accomplish that, he was happy. The problem was Peefee wasn't funny except to Peefee, and his rapid-fire staccato usually echoed alone. But he did have that truck; cherry his friends called it. And in it—in the chrome wheels, bumpers, and grillwork; the dual exhausts with glass-packed mufflers; in the all-leather interior and shag-carpeted steering wheel, dash, and floorboard—he found some semblance of manhood. Besides, he was Cisco Salazar's cousin, which according to Julie should have been enough.

"You think they're vandalizing it?"

Dillard shook his head. "No way, man. Not with Cisco there."

"I better find Greg."

"He's up there." Dillard pointed to Eagle's Wing Ridge.

"He is?"

"Yeah. He cruised by right after you left. Said he was goin' up there."

Dillard drifted off toward the bonfire, and I walked down the road away from Cisco, Peefee, and friends then crossed over to the trail that scaled Eagle's Wing Ridge. We had learned of this place from Lenny, who spent hours sitting on the sandstone slabs, studying the hawks, ravens, and swallows that glided on air currents above the canyon and along the cliff line. The top of the ridge was the turn-around for Lenny's usual six-mile run over a rocky trail to this point some eight-hundred vertical feet from the bottom. On his back he always carried a small orange pack and, when he reached the top, he would remove his watercolors or sketch pad and sit Buddha-like, lost in the landscapes he transposed to paper, lost soaring in the air with birds.

"Whew!" I rested my foot on the last rock before the top of the ridge, forearms crisscrossing my thigh.

Greg sat on Lenny's usual stoop, a sandstone pedestal shaped like a mushroom, his back to the canyon. "Look over there." He pointed to the southeast sweep of the Grand Valley, Orchard Mesa, where peach, apricot, and cherry orchards began and city lights thinned to just a sprinkle. "Florida."

Sitting down next to him, I followed his gaze across miles of rugged terrain, across two rivers and lighted railroad yards to the valley floor. Drumbeats from Lister's stereo bounced off the canyon walls.

"Ever been?"

I shook my head.

"My Uncle Phil used to live there. In Boca Raton. We'd go down in the summers and hang out on the beach with him."

"How's your uncle doing?"

"Look." Greg stood and pointed, his finger tracing an arc. "The Gulf of Mexico. And right there's Texas. Lenny come?"

"No. I had to catch a ride with Dill." I glanced at him as a reminder, but he didn't flinch. "His mom wouldn't let him."

He nodded slowly as though it were expected. "Parents do things. Always messing with you." Sitting down, he suddenly laughed. "Dillard?"

"Yeah." I shook my head.

He stood again, his gaze dropping back to the city lights, and stabbed his finger three times: "Washington—Oregon—California. Apples, grapes, and . . . what? California what, Henry?"

"Raisins?"

"California raisins. How about nuts? Or fruitcakes. That's it. California fruitcakes."

"Julie's looking for you."

"There's a news flash."

"She needs the McGovern pamphlets."

"Yeah?" He stooped so I could sight down his arm. "See that string of lights over there? The Canadian border. Let's see, the Great Lakes are there. New England. Then the Atlantic seaboard."

"I told her I'd try to find you."

"*Ni leile ma*?" He straightened up, dropping his arm. "Don't you ever get tired of being so nice?"

I got up and started down the ridge.

"Hank. Sorry, man. I didn't mean it."

"Yeah, you did."

"Hank, look." He was standing on the mushroom, pointing eastward. "The Big Apple."

I turned. "No it's not, Greg."

"Aha! The old 'the map is not the territory' argument, huh? Proceed, counselor."

"It's just Grand River, Greg."

"Not true, Kimosabe." He struck his fist against his heart and, holding it there, swept his other hand out. "To our people, it's the Sioux nation."

"You mean Ute."

He thumped his chest. "'This land is our land—'" He hopped on one foot, kicking the other out like a can-can dancer. "'—this land is my land. From California—'"

"Cisco and his buddies are looking at your car."

"Cisco is a champion, my friend. He can have my car. I bequeath it to him. 'From the redwood forests—'"

He suddenly froze on one leg, arms swimming backward. "Henry?" His vague outline wavered against the dark sky.

"Greg!" I sprinted back up the ridge and lunged in the darkness, landing on the edge of the sandstone. "Greg! Nooo!" I scrambled on my hands and knees onto the mushroom, peered over the edge. The music was between songs and I could hear voices from the bonfire scrape along the ledges and filter through trees down below. The canyon was black. "Nooo . . ." My voice echoed back to me. Collapsing to my stomach, I buried my face into my sleeve, the canyon walls whispering to me: "HHHaaank."

I raised up.

"HHHaaaaank."

I whipped my head around.

"Allekazam." I could see his white teeth in the darkness, arms stretched out like the savior's.

◇◇◇

"Don't." Julie gripped the dashboard. "Don't, Greg! You're scaring me." The Swinger fishtailed around a curve coming down Jacob's Ladder Road.

"Yeahhh!" Greg was leaning out the window, steering with one hand. The guardrails flashed silver in the headlights, and from the back seat I could see gravel kick up from the shoulder.

"Far ooout! Do it, maaan!"

"Shut up, Dillard." I braced my elbow against the armrest.

"Get in here!" Julie grabbed Greg's sleeve. "It's not funny."

Greg ducked back in, wind gushing into the back seat. "Look, Mom! No hands!" He ran both hands through his swept-back hair and adjusted his collar in the mirror. "Lookin' good—"

"Would you stop it!" Julie grabbed the steering wheel. "Just stop it!" She began to cry.

"Okay, Jules, come on. I'll be good." The car slowed as he wrapped his arm around her and pulled her close. "I was steering with my leg."

Dillard stuck his head between them. "Yeah, I do that sometimes, you knoooow, when I need both paws. I, like, put my leg under the—"

I pulled Dillard back. "We all know how to do it, Dill."

We were the last ones off the mountain, having first tried to pull Dillard's Corvair out of the drainage bed. After hooking the ends of a chain to both cars, the only things we accomplished were bending Dillard's bumper and scratching Greg's. As the engines revved madly, filling the air with burned oil, Julie kept shaking her head and shouting that something wasn't right, that sand should be flying. Finally, waving Greg off, she stuck her head into Dillard's car, yelled something at him and then walked back over to me, smiling. Magically, the wheels began spinning and throwing sand only to eventually bury themselves up to the axles. Dillard had had the car in neutral—with the emergency brake on.

Led Zeppelin played on the eight-track as Julie rested her head against Greg's shoulder, city lights twinkling through the windshield. By the time we got into town the streets were quiet, and most restaurants and gas stations closed.

"I've got the munchies."

I looked at Dill.

"I could eat a cooow, man."

"How 'bout a hen?" Greg swung the car into Kentucky Fried Chicken, Colonel Sanders standing guard at the entrance.

Julie ducked down and looked up at the tall sign. "Are they open?"

"Yeah, they close at one on weekends. We've got twenty minutes." Greg parked. "Hey, look. Our buddies are joining us."

Peefee Maldonado's truck rumbled up next to us, Cisco sitting shotgun. Before it stopped, their friends began springing from the truck bed as though a lid were lifted.

Greg stood, elbow resting atop the open door. "What's happening, Cisco?"

Cisco remained in the truck and, facing straight ahead, imperceptibly raised his chin. His cousin leaned over from the driver's side to look at Greg.

"Nice wheels, man."

"Why, thank you, Peefee. Thank you very much." Greg smiled.

"Wha's it got in it?"

Everyone was out of the back, crowding between the two vehicles.

"Well, as you can see—" Greg bent down holding his hand out. "—three of my closest friends."

Cisco turned and, glancing at Greg, faintly smiled.

Peefee jumped out and hurried around the front of the truck. "No, dude. I mean the engine, man. How big is the engine?"

"Well, let's just take a look, shall we?" Greg reached under the dash to pop the hood.

Peefee slid the hood pins, found the latch, and lifted. "Oh, man, a three-forty." Propping the hood open, he unscrewed the wing nut and removed the air filter. "Look at this, man. *Carburadur doble.*"

The gang huddled around the front end, jockeying for position. Most of them we knew from junior high. By high school their ranks had evaporated, steamed and frustrated by a Grand River school district that discouraged Spanish. But a few remained: John Gutierrez, the ninety-eight-pounder on the wrestling team and a straight-A student; Carl Lujan, the Reverend Lujan's son and an accomplished accordionist; Kenny Madrid, the toughest one in our class with the exception of Cisco and his own sister, Geraldine; Silver Renteria, a shy kid with a faded birthmark on his neck that splattered like bleach up the side of his face; and Jimmy Gonzales, a muralist who survived expulsion for, one night, painting an eagle clutching a snake on the U.S. Bank building downtown with *I am Joaquín* painted underneath it. The others dropped out or were forced to at different times over the years. Gabe Fuentas, whose favorite line was "Borrow me some money," was expelled in tenth grade for extortion. Manuel Garcia, who hated teachers, punched his way completely out of the system before the first week of high school ended. Frank Serrano dropped out in eighth to cook at *Los Reyes*, the family restaurant. And Dan Abeyta, who was chronically truant, ended up at the state reformatory in Buena Vista for pulling a jackknife from his boot on the last day of junior high and scratching a crude likeness of our shop teacher, Mr. Cox, across the blackboard.

My own first meaningful encounter with this group was in the boys' bathroom in seventh grade. When Lenny and I entered, lights blinked out and darkness was suddenly punctuated with knees, fists, and foreign epithets. While my pockets were being ripped inside out, someone hissed from below "It's Bartelli!" at which point the lights came back on to Lenny applying a head-lock to the owner of the voice splayed across the tile floor. The other three were on me. There were half apologies, vague gestures of smoothing our clothing, and much laughter about it being a joke. But I didn't get the joke—or my lunch money back—yet Lenny was laughing along with them, having lost nothing but pocket lint. Lenny's wrestling ability and Latin roots almost made him one of them. They liked him.

"Maybe I can learn something." Greg closed the door to join them.

Dillard snorted. "Yeah, right, maaan. Like how to bleed in Spanish."

Julie turned and looked at Cisco through the rolled-down car windows, waving her fingers. "Hi, Cisco."

Cisco smiled, nodding.

"Are you going to wrestle in college or anything?"

He raised his eyebrows and shrugged, then gazed down at his lap.

Dillard tapped Julie on the shoulder. "He's not goin' to college, maaan. He didn't even make it through high school."

I elbowed Dillard's ribs. "Yes, he did."

"No waaay."

"Yeah, Mr. VanHorn told me."

"You're kiddin'. Sheez, man, I've been workin' my butt off for that piece of paper and this cheese ball barely speaks English and he's got it in the bag. Just 'cause he's such a big jock."

Julie laughed. "Well, Dill, if you looked like Cisco Salazar, you too could wear a big jock."

"Screw you, Julie. I'm gettin' something to eat." He got out of the car but then ducked back down. "And remember, they don't call me Dill for nothin'." He laughed, proud of his comeback.

"I'll try to remember that, Gherkin."

"Huh?" Dill stared bleary-eyed into Julie's face, sensing he'd been bested but not certain why. He pushed off the car and staggered in a wide arc around the back of the truck and into Kentucky Fried.

"Come on, Hank. Let's join him before it closes." She leaned across the front seat. "Cisco, you want to get a bite with us?"

He shook his head, so we slipped out of the car and began walking around the group crowded over the engine.

Greg stood in the middle, listening to Peefee explain something. He glanced over at us. "I'll be there in a minute."

Peefee raised up, turning around. "Hey, come over here, man. I wan' to show you my big pistons." He fired off a salvo of laughter.

Julie smiled. "Thanks, Peepee, but I think I'll pass."

"It's *Pefe*!" He glared as we hurried past the Colonel and swung open the glass doors.

Someone grabbed my arm. "You're Bartelli's friend, huh?"

I nodded.

"Lenny's cool. Tell him Kenny Madrid says hey and Cisco's gonna kick his ass."

"Yeah, okay."

He let go.

Julie held the door for me. "What was that all about?"

"Oh, nothin'. That wrestling tournament next week."

By the time we ordered in a booth near the front window, Cisco and Peefee had roared off with the others down Gateway Avenue and Greg rejoined us.

"Thanks for almost getting me killed."

Julie smiled and shrugged. "My pleasure, Greg. You almost kill me, I almost kill you."

"Took me ten minutes to convince him that you really didn't use the vulgar diminutive of his fine Catholic name."

"Oh, yes. Saint Peefee. One of the original holy men."

"Seriously, Jules, he wasn't happy."

"With a name like that, who would be?"

Dillard gnawed a chicken wing and then dropped the remains on the flock of bones that had already landed on his napkin. "Who's Jerkin?"

Greg and Julie looked at each other across the table then burst out laughing.

The manager, a tall gaunt man with a sharp slice of Adam's apple and horn-rim glasses, walked around the counter. "Okay, kids. Time to close. Let's wrap it up."

Greg and Julie doubled over, red-faced and in tears.

Dillard stared at them, slowly chewing another wing. "What'd I say?"

"Come on, you heard me. I've got to start cleaning up. Let's go." The manager tossed a dishrag on the table.

Greg and Julie slumped in the booth, holding their sides.

I cleared my throat. "We're going. You're finished, right, Dill?"

Dillard was grinning at his friends and chewing at the same time. "Oh, I get it, man. Jerkin'. Like who's jerkin' off, right?"

Greg rolled off the seat and onto the tile floor. Julie was crying into a napkin.

Hands on hips, the manager nudged Greg with his foot. "Come on, young man. Get up. I've got work to do."

Julie slid out the booth, wiping her eyes, and helped Greg to his feet. "Dill, it's gherkin. It's a kind of pickle."

Dill continued to chew. "Oh."

Straightening up, Greg looked the manager in the eye then snapped to attention. "Aye-aye, Colonel." He glanced at his watch. "It's past one-hundred hours, sir. Shall I sound the alarm? Roust those chickens out of their coops?"

"Come on, smart guy. Hit the road before it hits you."

"Oooh. A comedian."

The man started toward Greg, but Julie stepped between them and guided Greg toward the entrance.

Walking backwards, Greg saluted over Julie's shoulder. "Carry on, Colonel."

Julie pushed him through the swinging glass door as Dill and I followed.

"Aaahhh! Man overboard! Throw me a line! Sound the alarm!"

The manager, shaking his head, locked the door behind us and pulled the blinds.

"Greg." Julie squared him in front of her. "Greg, be quiet. I've got some terrible news."

He stopped, lowering his hands. "What?"

"There are no colonels in the navy."

"No. Don't say that."

"Army, yes. Air force, yes. Marines, yes. Navy, no."

"No colonel? You mean to say the Colonel's a—" He paused for dramatic effect. "—fraud?" Glancing furtively around, he suddenly lunged for Colonel Sanders, covering the statue's ears. "He hears this, mates, and it'll kill him. There'll be a mutiny on the bounty . . . a mounting on the beauty. No one will be safe." He stared into the Colonel's bespectacled face. "Forgive us, Colonel." He kissed him full on his plastic lips.

Dillard winced. "Ohhh, maaan. Don't do that."

"You're next, ya big palooka."

Dill jumped behind me, holding me as a shield. "Don't kid around like that, maaan. You're freaking me out."

Greg wrapped an arm around the statue's ample waist, pointed his other fist straight ahead, and, lifting, tangoed Colonel Sanders onto the parking lot dance floor. Throwing his head back, he swept the white-haired gentleman across the pavement then wheeled, dipped, and led him along the building, around a dumpster, and over to his Dodge Swinger.

"Oh, no you don't." Julie hurried over to the car and grabbed the Colonel's feet as Greg was sliding him through the passenger's window. "Greg, they'll know it was us."

"It's a sinking ship, matey. Stay here and he's doomed." He wrestled the Colonel in farther.

"Come on, man. Hurry. We're gonna get busted." Dillard pushed past them into the back seat. The Colonel's head was lodged in the back corner, chubby torso resting across the front seat.

"Let's get out of here." I ducked under the plastic statue into the other side next to Dill. "Come on, Jules, before the guy looks out here. He won't know it's gone 'til tomorrow. Anybody could've taken it."

"Not anybody, Hank. Us."

"Yeah, man. It's the guy's own fault for spacin' it out and not puttin' it inside." Dillard closed the passenger's door.

Julie looked at Greg, who was standing at attention as though waiting the command of a superior officer. "Great. Just another little something to add to the list." She shook her head. "Kidnapping Colonel Sanders. What the hell's next?"

He threw his hands up, shrugged, and cocked his head, Marcel Marceau style. Laughing, she allowed him to escort her around to the driver's side and in next to the prone colonel.

The red and white Kentucky Fried Chicken sign blinked out as the car fishtailed out the parking lot onto Gateway Avenue, tires squealing and stiff white legs and black shoes jutting like two-by-fours from the passenger's window.

◇ ◇ ◇

Redd Morgan's pickup was still parked in front of our house. Its dual toolboxes and overhead rack—a headache rack, he called it—shone under the streetlight. Greg had dropped me at the corner so I could sneak quietly into the house without waking Mom and Dana. But it didn't matter. Mom was sitting in the rocker, smoking a cigarette.

"Hi, hon. Did ya have fun?"

The reading lamp highlighted her bleached hair and illuminated a ring of smoke floating then disappearing into the darkened living room.

"Yeah, it was okay. How was work?"

She inhaled deeply and stubbed the cigarette into the ashtray sitting on her lap. "I didn't go." She set the ashtray on the coffee table, then reached up and turned the lamp a notch brighter.

"Night off, huh? That's good."

She smiled, leaning back against the rocker and drawing the silk kimono tightly around her slender shoulders. Our father had given it to her after the war, before Dana and I were born. A history Redd didn't know.

"Redd doesn't like me workin' nights anymore. Especially on weekends."

"Dana's been telling you that for months."

"I know. Come sit."

I shut the door and turned the latch. "Dana asleep?"

"Mmm-hmm. She got in a couple of hours ago."

I sat on the edge of the couch.

"Honey, I'm real proud of you, graduating and all."

54

"Thanks, Mom."

"Wish Dana had. But I know how it is. Your father and I eloped, too, before they shipped him off to Korea."

She picked up the Virginia Slims from the coffee table, lit one, and placed them on her lap. She smoked as always, left forearm snug against her middle as though comforting a stomachache, hand cupping the other elbow, propping the right hand chin-level so the cigarette was never more than inches from her mouth.

"When you're young, love is so big you can hardly see over it." She stared at the ceiling, blew smoke at it.

I glanced around our living room, at the scattered newspaper and fashion magazines, the used Zenith Mom had picked up at the Rent-to-Own store, the plaid sofa with a painting by Arlene, our mother's best friend at the diner, hanging above it. Arlene had painted a mountain scene with teepees tucked into a valley and a river running by them. Lenny once pointed out that the teepees were half as tall as the mountains and the river ran as straight as an irrigation ditch, but we never mentioned the flaws to Mom. It had been her birthday present. At the end of the sofa sat Redd's black railroad boots, sweat-stained white socks stuffed into them.

"Mom?"

"Hmm?"

"Why's Redd's truck still out there?"

She continued staring at the ceiling, then her gaze dropped to her lap as she crumpled the cigarette. Raking fingernails through her hair, she looked at me and tried to smile. "He's tired, hon. He's just restin' before he drives home."

Standing, I faked a stretch and yawn. "Guess I better hit the sack. Night, Mom."

I started through the kitchen to go down to the basement.

"Henry?" Mom was still sitting in the rocker.

Light from the corner street lamp split the curtains, draping like ribbon across the fish bowl. I looked at Stella and Frank, suspended in their glass refracted world. "Yeah?"

"Henry, I . . . I'll see you in the morning. Okay?"

"Sure, Mom. Night."

"Good night, honey."

Then I was downstairs in my room, standing in the darkness, listening to her slippers shuffle down the hallway to her bedroom and Redd Morgan.

5

The morning light slanting across the valley from the rim of Spruce Mesa splashed against the trailer. Shielding my eyes, I could make out the antenna jutting from the prairie like a yucca stalk, and as I rounded the last curve of the rutted dirt driveway, the light shifted and I could see the wording: *Airstream*. Two barrels sat out front among the sagebrush and greasewood, and a third lay on its side with rusted bullet holes bored through it. His green pickup, as usual, was backed up alongside the trailer, inches from the door (to gain entrance he'd have to slide out the passenger's side and walk around to the back; a slight inconvenience for a measure of security, I guessed). A canvas tarp was cinched down over the truck bed.

I pulled behind a clump of sagebrush and stopped, squinting through the windshield. The curtains were closed. He was either asleep, which was doubtful—he never slept—or was already scouring Rabbit Valley for petrified dinosaur bones. Either way, I could check what I came to without his knowing.

I turned off the engine. As I got out, the canvas tarp popped with a sudden gust whipping across the desert off Rimrock National Park and I jumped. I almost got back into the car but, steeling myself, hurried up the dirt driveway instead and ducked behind the tailgate. Glancing around, I eased up, lifted the tarp, and peered underneath. Nothing.

Hunched over, I hurried to the cab. The passengers' side floorboard was covered with chunks of rock; smaller pieces scattered across the dash into the far corner of the defroster vent as though he had taken a curve too tightly. His scratched sunglasses, the black wrap-around kind favored by the blind, fit snugly onto the steering column over a faded family photograph taped to the horn. From the gearshift knob hung his sweat-stained Detroit Tigers baseball cap with a blue bandana draped over it. Topographical maps, gem and mineral magazines, and a blown-out section of radiator hose lay strewn across the seat, which was also littered with Tootsie Pop wrappers— red, purple, orange, and brown—as though a child's birthday party had been celebrated there. I shook my head. Sugar, I knew, he'd never give up.

Staring into the cab, lost in these artifacts of what his life must be, I reached around and slipped a hand under the other end of the tarp. The cool curve of metal brought my head back as I folded the canvas over. There were two tanks, green and shiny, lying on their sides. He must have laid them down after he arrived; they would have rolled around the bed otherwise. I laced my fingers together underneath one and lifted, felt the tape intact around the base of the nipple where the hose fits. Full.

Grinning like a kid at Christmas, I gazed at the trailer sitting there unprotected, smack in the middle of the high desert—in the center of his perfectly senseless universe—and then ran down the drive, jumped in the car, and raced over the gravel roads back to Grand River to tell my sister Dana that he'd done it again. Our father had pulled another one.

◇◇◇

"Well, hello, Henry. Please, come in."

"Thanks, Mrs. Woods."

She held the screen door as I squeezed into the entryway. "How have you been, Henry? All ready for graduation?"

"Yeah, I guess."

"That doesn't sound very convincing." Smiling, she leaned down the hallway on one bare foot, the other extended and pointing like a ballerina's. "Gregory! You have a visitor." She paused, listening for a reply or movement, then returned to both feet to study me. "And where have you decided on, Henry?"

"Excuse me?"

"Where have you decided to go? Which university?"

She wore tennis whites and her licorice-black hair was pinned up, a brightly striped sweatband wrapped neatly across her forehead. The scent of summer was about her, coconut oil mixed with the musk of sweat, the tropics—for a deeper, darker tan.

"Oh, I dunno. I guess I kinda haven't decided yet."

"Well, it's getting a bit late, isn't it? Have you thought about the local junior college? Gregory!" She looked down at her tan feet, listening. "Hmm. He's probably lost in some dream. You know how he is."

"Yeah."

"'*We are such stuff as dreams are made on—*'" She smiled. "Have you eaten? I was just fixing myself a sandwich. You can have one with me while we wait for our young prince to awaken from his slumber."

"Naw, that's okay, Mrs. Woods. I'm a little early. He told me to come by around one so we could go hit some balls."

She pirouetted and strode down the long hallway as though I hadn't spoken. I glanced toward Greg's room and then followed her into the kitchen. From the barstool I watched her make sandwiches, watched her move over the tile floor, her head sitting like a trophy on the pedestal of her neck, gliding from the refrigerator to the large chopping block that stood as an island in the middle of the spacious kitchen and then back to the refrigerator. A portable television sat on the counter, tuned to a symphony and competing with the theme song of *ABC Wide World of Sports* coming from the den.

"The agony of da feet." She laughed, licking *Grey Poupon* from her index finger.

"Huh?"

"Have you ever seen such pathetic feet, Henry?" She lifted her foot and placed it on the edge of the stool between my legs. "Look at that big toe. See how swollen the joints are? Go ahead, feel it."

I looked at it, the nail painted a bright red. "Yeah."

"Go ahead." She took my hand and guided my fingers over the joints. "Three stress fractures, a torn tendon, and now arthritis." Letting go of my hand, she brought the foot down and smiled. "And that's just one little piggy, Henry. Gregory did tell you I was a dancer, right?"

"Uh, yeah."

"I'm surprised he tells anybody anything about me." She turned back to our sandwiches. "Has he said anything to you about the academy?"

"Oh, you know, just—not really."

She handed me the plate and followed it with a handful of corn chips. "Isn't it marvelous, Henry? One of just three boys selected in the entire valley." She shook her head, gazing out the sliding glass door over the swimming pool and lawn chairs and across the tenth fairway of Grand River Country Club. "One of just three—" She glanced at my sandwich. "Eat up, Henry. If you're going to hit with Gregory, you're going to need all the energy you can get. I'll take this other one in to his father."

"Mrs. Woods, mind if I go knock on his door? It's already a little past one."

"So it is. No, go ahead. Just don't tell him I had anything to do with it. He's so grumpy when he gets up."

Grabbing the plate, I started up from the barstool.

"Henry, on second thought . . ." She placed her hand on the small of my back. ". . . take this in to him. I'll make his father another one. You're a dear."

"Thanks, Mrs. Woods."

"Don't forget the graduation party—Friday at six o'clock, after the ceremony. And bring your trunks."

"Okay." I carried the sandwiches through the dining room, past the den, and down the hallway to Greg's door.

"Greg?" I knocked lightly. "Hey, Greg."

"*Qing laile.*"

Balancing one plate on the other, I opened the door.

"I thought you were still zonked."

"No, I've been up for a while." He was sitting in his boxers on the couch that ran the entire length of one wall. The waterbed was unmade, sheets twisted as though wrung out and covers piled on the floor. "Sorry about that."

"What?"

"My old lady. I heard her haranguing you with her one Shake-the-spear quote—'We are such stuff that cream is made from; and our little life is pounding it before we sleep.' Makes her feel literary." He stretched, yawning and rubbing his forehead. "What a night, huh?"

"Yeah."

"Did you make it home all right?"

"Yeah. Mom was still up."

"Bummer."

"Nah, she was okay."

"Your mom's always been okay. Wish I could say the same for mine. Hey, take a look at this." He held up *The National Lampoon.* "The fight of the century. William Calley Jr. versus Charles Manson. What do you think? Manson in seven?"

"Where should I put this sandwich?"

"I don't care." He tossed the magazine to the side and stood, stretching. Jim Morrison loomed on a poster behind him above the sofa, arms out, pouty face slightly bent. "I know, give it to the Colonel. He's always good for a meal." Greg lifted his chin.

I turned. "Whoa." Colonel Sanders stood in the corner next to the waterbed, as amiable as ever.

"I've never had a roommate before, but I guess I better get used to it."

"Before it's all over, he'll probably be your cellmate."

He grabbed the Colonel by the shoulders and scooted him closer to the bed. "Bit on the white side, don't you think? But maybe I can eventually remedy that. A little political indoctrination never hurts." He took two scarves from the closet, selected one, and tossed the other back. "*Dongle ma?*" He wrapped the scarf, red with white snowflakes, around the statue's neck. "There. That'll keep him snug."

"He looks like Frosty the Snowman. You know they're going to bust us for this."

Greg smiled. "Presumed innocent, Hank—until proven guilty." He sat bobbing on the edge of the bed, water slurping against the backboard, and picked up a telephone book. "Which brings us to the next installment of our little drama."

"Who're you going to call?"

He flipped through the pages, tossed the book on the bed, and dialed. "Stick around, you'll see. That guy last night was a piece of—uh, yes, is the manager in, please? Thank you. Was a piece of work—Hello, is this the manager? Hi, sorry to bother you on what's probably your busiest time of day. Right? Uh-huh . . . well, good, good . . . I'm glad that pesky lunch crowd has left." Greg looked at me, rolled his eyes, and sloshed back against the headboard. "No, it's not that. I've got a great job, actually. But funny you should mention employment because standing right here next to me *is* one of your employees." Greg looked out the window and a smile began to form. "Well, more accurately, let's just say a former employee since he's no longer . . . No, I don't know Ed Shaw but I'm sure he was a fine fellow. But quite frankly—what's your name? Kevin—quite frankly, Kevin, I'm sure this employee is much more important to you than old Ed Shaw ever was. And chubbier." Greg looked at me and nodded, smiling. "I said 'and chubbier'—Kevin, why am I suddenly feeling like a contestant on *I've Got a Secret*—" He jabbed the phone out at arm's length and grimaced. I could hear the small tinny voice blasting from the ear piece. "Now, now, Kevin, let's not be rash . . . Come on, now, he's as fat and happy as he's ever . . . Kevin . . . Kevin, get a grip, man. We would never do anything to the Colonel . . . Kevy, come on, big guy. That kind of talk isn't gonna bring him back . . . Well, just settle down and I'll tell you . . . There you go, just take a deep breath . . . that's it. Now, here's what we want. One, a public statement from you that Colonel Sanders is a symbol of the oppressive, white elite used to enslave and brainwash the lower socio-economic . . ." He held the phone out, again. "Come on, Kevin . . . Kevin, if you don't ever want to see tubby here again just keep it up, pal." Greg swung his legs around and flopped back on the bed. "That Colonel Sanders is a symbol of the oppressive, white elite . . . used to enslave . . . and brainwash the lower classes.

Brainwash . . . the lower . . . classes. That'll do, Kev. I had more but I realize you're working with limited resources there at good old Kentucky Fried." Looking at me, he furrowed his brow, bucked his teeth, and crossed one eye. "Choose your medium, Kev—radio, television, newspaper. No, I'm not going to give you my address. That would be kind of silly of me, wouldn't it? Well, yes, I think so, too. Let's see, it's Saturday now . . . we'll give you one week and then—if you've met our demands—you'll get your head rooster back at a designated location." He nodded. "That's right. Kevin, it has been a pleasure. We'll call you back, let's say Tuesday night and you can tell us when and where your announcement will be. We thank you, Kevin, and look forward to your public confession. *Zai jian*." Greg hung up the phone and lay floating on the bed, staring at the ceiling and shaking his head. "That guy's a trip." He looked at me. "So what do you think, Hank?"

"With time off for good behavior, maybe no more than ten to twenty."

He smiled and sat up. "Nothin' like a little anarchy to make you really feel alive. You know what I mean?"

"Was that the same guy as last night?"

He nodded.

"So now what?"

He stood, slapping my shoulder. "Yes, now what? Now what? Well—" He wrapped his right hand over left thumb and brought the imaginary club head back, head down. "—we go hit some balls, what else."

"I thought you meant tennis. I brought my sister's racket."

"Sorry, Hank. You don't want to go to the club. Besides, I'm burned out on tennis and you have to be all decked out in white. Not even the Colonel is white enough for that place."

Slipping on a happy face T-shirt and sunglasses, he walked barefoot into the kitchen, grabbed a doughnut, and then went to the den. He slid the door back. "Where's Mom?"

"Gregor! How ya doin', buddy?"

Greg pointed facetiously at his father. "Where'd Mom go?"

Mr. Woods sat hunkered down in a leather easy chair with his feet crossed on the matching ottoman, holding a Coors and watching television. Looking over Greg's shoulder, I could see his father's sunburned head and the yellow clumps of dyed hair that fell across it.

"Got me. She brought me this sandwich and then she was out the door. Probably to the hospital to see your uncle. Hey, who do you have there?" He twisted his head around.

"Hi, Mr. Woods."

"Well, hello, Henry. Great to see ya." He took a large swallow of beer. "Greg, take a look at this. It's a preview of the Olympics. This swimming facility they built in Munich is fantastic." He held his beer toward the television screen. A gold watch was on his wrist and a heavy gold ring, as though three rings were melted into one, dressed his pinky finger. Even the hair on his tan arm was golden, and then there was the hue of the Coors can. King Midas in golf wear.

Greg began to slide the door back.

"Gregor—"

"Samsa."

Mr. Woods laughed and waved, still facing the halls of Munich. Then he tipped his head back, draining the can. "Have a grand time."

Greg slid the door closed.

"See ya, Mr. Woods."

"Have a good one, Henry."

I followed him through the dining room, kitchen, and outside through the sliding glass doors. "What's that you call him—Sam something?"

"Samsa. He thinks I'm saying *Samson*, like it's a compliment or something." He pulled over a couple of redwood lawn chairs and sat down, placing his doughnut on the armrest. "That's my old man, stuck on his back, suckin' brews." Squinting across the swimming pool at the tenth fairway, he took a bite of doughnut and wiped powdered sugar from his mouth. "Have a seat, Hank. I'll be back in a sec."

I sat down and looked at the kidney-shaped pool, the chlorinated water shimmering in cells of light and mantling against the pale blue tile, against shadows beneath the diving board. Four silver railings, two at each end, curled up out of the water and led to a red tile walkway. A low, neatly trimmed hedge separated the pool from the lawn, which was manicured like a putting surface. Across the fairway I could see people sitting in carts or walking with bags slung over their shoulders, smacking balls toward white flags fluttering against green. And in the distance stood the Bookcliffs and Mt. Garfield, washed pink under the high afternoon sun.

The Woods had moved to the valley from Taiwan when Greg was five. His paternal grandparents had been Baptist missionaries in southern China in the thirties, at the height of that country's civil war and concurrent invasion by the Japanese. Then, three days before Pearl Harbor 1941, they returned to the United States, living almost six years in southern California. Greg's father graduated from high school in Pasadena before following his parents to Taiwan in 1947, two years before the Communist takeover of mainland China and the vanquished Nationalists' exodus to the island. They settled in Kaohsiung on the southern coast, where they started a mission and Greg's father taught elementary school. After a year and a half of helping his parents, Mr. Woods went back to California to attend Pomona College, studying history and international law. There, over the book checkout counter at the school library, he met Mrs. Woods.

Greg's parents married just before his father's graduation and moved to Palo Alto where Mr. Woods attended Stanford Law School and Mrs. Woods got a job in the law library. In the middle of the first year at Palo Alto, she was invited to join the San Francisco Ballet Company. After heated debate about the financial burden such a change would entail—her salary would be half of what the university paid and her husband still had more than one year left of law school—she accepted the offer and began driving every weekday morning to San Francisco for rehearsal. Gradually, as the year's first production drew near, she returned home later and later until, on opening night, she didn't come back at all. Eventually, she would stay in the city all week. Mr. Woods grew increasingly agitated, shouting and cursing over the phone, until finally he threatened divorce. Then, Greg liked to joke, they had me; probably the last time they'd ever done it, he said. The year was 1953.

Upon graduating from law school, Mr. Woods landed a job with the State Department at the American consulate in Taipei because of his fluency in Mandarin Chinese. After five years interpreting, translating, and assisting the American consul general himself, Mr. Woods was abruptly let go under hazy circumstances. Although just a young boy and with no knowledge supporting it, Greg suspected an affair; by which parent, he didn't know. It was then the family traveled to Grand River.

Initially, they came to Colorado to visit Mrs. Woods' brother Phil and to rest, but when Mr. Woods fell—ass-backwards, Greg described it—into a position as legal counsel for the Atomic Energy Commission, they stayed. Quite a distance, his son ruefully pointed out, from being a missionary in China to a mercenary in Grand River, working for the military complex in the mining of yellow cake—uranium—for atomic bombs.

"Check these out."

Greg sat down, a pair of binoculars hanging from his neck. He pushed the sunglasses atop his head and, elbows resting on knees, squinted through the lenses at a foursome getting ready in the tee box, which was only about thirty yards from where we were sitting.

"*Blue Max.*" He handed me the binoculars.

"Wow, these are powerful."

"See the blue bull's eye on the ball?"

"Yeah."

"He's teeing up a *Blue Max*. If it's just black cursive with a red or black number underneath, it's probably a *Titleist*. A *Top-Flite* has all black capital letters. Got it?"

He took back the binoculars. There was the flash of metal and Greg's head raised as he followed the ball's flight. "Sliced it." He shook his head, lowering the glasses. "Come on."

I followed him to the far corner of the yard where there was a rough-cedar shed set into a cluster of lilac bushes. He opened the door—the scent of grass clippings, motor oil, pesticide products hitting us full in the face, mixing with perfume from the lilac—and rolled out the lawn mower. He reached in and brought out a plastic pail and a club, a one wood.

"Good ol' Percy." He kissed the club head. "And this—" He set the pail down. "—is the sacred bucket of lost youth."

"The what?"

"See? Here's a *Blue Max*." He picked out a golf ball and examined it, turning it at arm's length. "Each one represents some Arnold Palmer wannabe who couldn't find his ball for the hole in the ground."

"You stole them?"

He handed me the binoculars. "If you were a fan, Hank, you would read in the local sports section of an occasional—and sometimes not so occasional—hole-in-one on that wicked, heavily wooded dog-leg sixth. In fact, one day there were three—all before noon."

"You mean, you put their—"

"And defile the sacred grounds of Grand River Country Club?" He smiled, bending over and teeing up four balls in a row. "It's just the kiss of good luck, Hank, no matter what it does for their clubs. Take the binocs over to the pool and tell me what the next guy's hitting."

"What're you going to do?"

Gripping the driver in both hands, he wagged the head at the first ball in the row. "Give 'em a better lie. But first—" He leaned the one wood against the shed, bent over the mower, and flipped the choke. "Drivers, start your engines." Grabbing the rubber handle, he yanked the starter cord once, twice—adjusted the choke—and a third time before it coughed, belched gray smoke and then smoothed out to a steady roar that would drown out even the most mighty blast from the lucky wood of an aspiring Arnold Palmer.

◇◇◇

I lie on my back in the cool darkness of the basement, staring at the ceiling. The late-afternoon light filters through the fabric covering the small rectangular window, seeps around the edges. Holding my right hand up against the shadow across the ceiling tiles, I trace the outline of fingers and thumb with my eyes and say my name. "Henry." I do the same with my left, stretching them both upward, fingers splayed black against the gray. "Henry Kessler." The house is silent. No footfalls across the floor above me, no water hissing from faucets or television blaring. No Redd Morgan. Just me in the cool darkness of my bedroom.

My stomach gurgles. Air I can hear exhale through my nose. I hold my breath. *And where have you decided on, Henry*? My fingertips tingle, there's a vague pulsing at my temple and my chest grows tight. *It's getting a bit late, isn't it*? I close my eyes, tongue pressing the roof of my mouth, blood coursing through my head. Little stars orbit against my eyelids, one way then the other, luminescent threads catching like webs spun across sunlight. *We are such stuff as dreams are made on*— I open my eyes; the stars release into the room and turn different colors—orange and red, yellow and green. I let my breath out, loudly, and my hands, now clenched into fists, fall to my side. *The agony of da feet*. I place hands on my stomach, feel the rise and fall. *Have you ever seen such pathetic feet, Henry*? I turn to my side and draw my legs up, smell the sour scent of sleep across my pillow. I run one hand down her leg and over her knee. I bring it up inside her thigh, between her legs. *Go ahead, feel it*. I roll back facing the ceiling, my fingers tracing the growing length of me. *And that's just one little piggy, Henry*. I close my eyes but the stars are gone now and there's only darkness spinning toward nothing and the smell of coconut and sweat. *Go ahead*. And I do, but she forgets my name as I squeeze my eyes tight, her back arches, and I cease to exist. "Henry!" *And our little life*— "Henry Kessler." —*is rounded with a sleep*. And she knows not who I am. "But you can call me Hank." Nameless. "As in Henry." Invisible. "My name is Henry Kessler, Jr." As in nobody at all.

"Henry?"

I opened my eyes.

"Hey, Henry." My sister stood in the doorway. "What're you doing?"

"Nothing."

"Why were you saying your name?"

"What?"

"I heard you saying your name."

"No, I wasn't."

"Somebody was."

"What do you want?"

"Redd wants to talk to you."

"So?"

"So he's pissed, so hurry it up." She flipped on the light and disappeared from the doorway.

◇◇◇

Redd Morgan worked swing shift for the Rio Grande Railroad. A permanent pink band from his face shield dented his forehead, announcing his job of welder in braille. The torch he held to steel every day gave his ruddy complexion an even deeper glow, as though it was perpetually sunburned, and the skin on his chest and forearms was scarred. His hair, or what was left of it, stubbled his flat head like the charred remains of a forest fire and the beginnings of a mustache smudged his upper lip under a sharp bent nose. But the heat of his appearance was nothing compared to what smoldered underneath. Julie, ever the mistress of understatement, said he had an anger problem. Dana, every bit as perceptive but without the education, called him what we all thought, a flaming asshole.

"It's damn strange, is what it is." He re-crossed his legs for about the hundredth time as he drew on a cigarette.

"Honey, Redd's not blaming you or anything. He's just trying to figure this thing out." Glancing at Redd, Mom patted my shoulder.

We sat at the kitchen table, Redd at one end, me at the other. Dana and Mom both stood behind me, leaning against the counter drinking iced tea.

"But every time something happens he asks me the same things."

"And I'm gonna keep asking them, by God, until I get some answers." He mashed the butt and dropped it into the beer can, smoke streaming out his nostrils like steam from a bull's nose.

"Now, Redd, Henry's told you he doesn't know—"

He pointed a finger at Mom. "He hasn't told me squat, Sally. That's what I'm trying to tell you."

"But I don't know anything. I wasn't even around yesterday."

"That doesn't matter." He patted his shirt pockets, pulled out a pack, and fished in it with two fingers. "You think the skunk that stole 'em ate dinner with us, too?"

"Since when do we eat dinner together?" Dana shrugged then gazed into her glass as everyone stared at her. "Sorry."

"Redd, couldn't it be somebody at work, somebody you had a falling out with?"

"How many times do I have to tell you, Sally?" He glowered at the pack, wadded it in his fist. "None of this stuff happened 'til I started dating you." He held up one finger. "First, the Linberger cheese in my manifold. Took me a month to get the stink out of there. On a hot day I still smell it. Then that contest I thought I won. Felt like a damn fool going down to pick up my prize at that radio station. And in the middle of the night, no less."

Dana giggled but quickly stifled it into her hand. Redd glared, then held up his thumb for the third thing.

"Next, all that damn mail. I still get it. At work, too. Fashion magazines, catalogues, sweepstakes this, sweepstakes that, all that church crap. I belong to more churches than God himself and they're all after my money. I never got any of that garbage before. Then there's that rock." He crushed the beer can in one hand, working his tongue behind his bottom lip for remnants of chew. "Had to bring a backhoe all the way from the railroad yard. Made me the laughingstock of the whole place. And ever since that damn reporter's article, everybody calls me Meteor Morgan."

"Redd, that could've been a meteor. We can't know for sure."

He stood, pointing somewhere beyond the ceiling. "It's the same damn rock you can find any day of the week up there on Spruce Mesa. It wasn't no damn meteorite, Sally."

"Well, how did somebody get a boulder that size on your front lawn without anybody noticing?"

"You tell me." He sat seething, arms folded across his barrel chest. "And now this, damn it. Stealing my tanks. We're talking criminal behavior now." His eyes bored into me.

"What?"

"I know you know something."

"No I don't."

"Redd, that's enough." Mom put her arm around me. "Henry said he doesn't know anything and I believe him."

"I don't give a goddamn what you believe!" He stood. "You've been nothing but bad luck ever since I met you!" The volcano was erupting. "The day I laid eyes on you, I should've just kept on walking! You and that stupid diner and your stupid smart-ass kids! Always siding with them!" He stomped through the living room to the front door.

"Redd, don't be like this."

He wheeled around and pointed at Mom. "I'll be like anything I damn well please!"

The door slammed, and Mom flinched and closed her eyes.

"Least he didn't break anything for a change." Dana put an arm around her. "It's okay, Mom."

I felt like I should say something, anything to make her stop.

"He'll come back, Mom." Dana hugged her as she silently shook. "He always does." She looked at me and raised her eyebrows.

"Mom, I . . . maybe we can . . ."

She took a napkin from the kitchen table and wiped her eyes. "Henry—" She blew her nose into it. "Henry, you don't know anything, do you, honey?"

I hated it when Mom cried, hated it when Redd Morgan engulfed our lives.

"Henry?"

Hated that our father was gone, that memory no longer fit reality.

"Do you?"

But nothing could extinguish the memory. "No." Not even Redd Morgan. "No, Mom. I don't know anything." Not even the knowledge of what happened to Redd Morgan's two welding tanks.

6

*J*ulie stood barefoot in the McClellan backyard, a fishing rod in one hand. "Catching any?"

"Hi, Hank." She cast the fly out, brought it back before landing—the line whirring an S above her—then took it out again, nestling it into the middle of the grass. She wore faded blue jeans and a fishing vest over a gray T-shirt. Her long sun-streaked hair was wrapped and bobby pinned under a straw cowboy hat decorated with colorful homespun flies. "Just practicing. Soon as graduation's over, I'm outa here."

"Where you goin'?"

She shrugged, shooting line out again. "Doesn't matter. Anywhere I can get this number sixteen gold-ribbed hare's ear wet."

"What?"

She glanced at me and smiled. "Come here."

I walked over as she took in line, the reel clicking like cicadas in midsummer.

"Hold this in your right hand and the line in your left. That's it. Now take some out." She reached over and helped me pull arm lengths of lime-green line from the reel. "This is a number six floating double taper. If you get it caught up in some rocks or something and snap it off, you can turn it around and use the other end. That's why it's tapered at both ends."

"Oh."

"Okay now, draw up some line. Raise the tip. Elbow in. Now just bring her back between eleven and one o'clock and power the rod forward."

I took the tip back and then whipped it out, line looping over the pole, piling in front of me.

"Let the rod do the work, Hank. It's a fluid motion. Watch." She took it, twirled line off the tip, pulled in slack, then whisked the line one, two, three times above us, laying the fly out farther on the lawn. "This line's just a thirty-yarder with a couple feet of tippet, perfect for short casting in streams and rivers.

That's the kind of fishin' Rog and I like to do. Here, try again. Nice and smooth now."

I mimicked the motion of her arm, the line singing one, two, three times above me before sailing across the yard.

"Good, Hank! Bring her in and try it again."

I started reeling, the fly skittering across grass toward us.

"Keep the tip up and just pull it in with your left hand. You'll use the slack for your next cast."

"Getting a little lesson, huh, Henry?" Julie's father stood at the corner of the house, forearms crossed and resting over the back gate. A white smock was draped over one shoulder.

"Hi, Dr. McClellan."

"Hi, Daddy. Watch Henry cast. He just learned."

Fingering the line in my left hand, I raised the tip, brought it back, and flicked it forward, line looping and falling at my feet.

"Tricky business that fly fishing, Henry. I once lost five flies along the same stretch of water. And I'd tied every one of them just the night before." He chuckled, shaking his head. "Remember that, sweetie?"

Julie took the rod and held the tip low, jiggling the line free. "That's okay, Hank. All you need's a little water and you'll be an expert in no time." She reeled it in. "I don't remember you ever losing five flies, Daddy."

"Don't listen to her, Henry. I've lost my share, believe me. You're not a fisherman if you haven't. You want to stay and eat with us?"

Julie examined the hare's ear on the flat of her palm before hooking it into the cork handle and cranking the line taut. "We're going over to Mr. VanHorn's."

"Bet that'll be fun. Did you tell your mother?" He held the gate for us, Julie carrying the rod and pointing it under the eaves. "Honey, break it down. You're going to snap the tip off." Dr. McClellan took the rod and pulled it apart, leaving line sagging in the eyelets. He handed it back to Julie. "Well, did you?"

"Did I what?"

He stopped and looked at her. "I take it that's a no." He poked her in the side. Shaking his head and clapping me on the shoulder, he led us into the kitchen where Mrs. McClellan stood holding Bubby, Julie's year-old brother.

"There's the big guy." Dr. McClellan walked across the kitchen, pecked his wife on the cheek, and took Bubby. Holding the baby aloft, he jiggled him then brought him gurgling down over his shoulder.

Bubby was the latest of Julie's five younger brothers and a surprise. Mrs.

McClellan, who had served two terms on the school board, had decided not to run for a third because Bubby, she said, whined less than her fellow board members and *his* bottom she didn't mind powdering. The other four—Mark, Doug, Paul, and Darin—came in two-year increments starting fourteen years before. Though four and six years younger than Julie, Mark and Doug were already taller than she, taking after their lanky bespectacled father. Paul was a perfect blend of both parents, looking like neither, and Darin, like Julie, favored their mother: thick brownish blond hair, brilliant green eyes, and a slightly husky build with matching voice.

"Henry—" She walked over and hugged me. "It's good to see you."

"Thanks, Mrs. McClellan."

"Will you stay for dinner?"

Julie picked up the pole and started across the kitchen toward the hallway. "We're going out."

"Thanks anyway, Mrs. McClellan."

"Anytime, Henry. Well, I guess we'll see you Wednesday then. Julie, make your bed before you go. I don't want to have to tell you again."

I followed her into the bedroom.

"My mother drives me crazy." She leaned the rod in the corner, flipped the cowboy hat onto a chair stacked with folded laundry, then peeled her T-shirt overhead. She chose a Levi shirt from the closet, slipped it on, and turned around, tucking the tails inside her jeans.

"If I was Greg you wouldn't have done that."

"You're right. I would have taken my shirt *and* bra off."

Someone pounded the door.

"What!?!"

There were muffled giggles.

"Knock it off, Darin!" She selected a perfume from the army of bottles lining her dresser. "Anyway, you're nicer than Greg. If I needed another brother, god forbid, it'd probably be you—or Lenny."

"Thanks. I think." I watched her spray fragrance inside her wrists then rub it on her neck. "But you'd never take me home to meet Mom. Right?"

She smiled, removing bobby pins and shaking hair loose. "I think you've got it backwards, Hank. Isn't it the guy who takes the girl home? And, anyway, where do you think we are now?"

I sat on the bed as she brushed her hair. Her bedroom was an odd combination of feminine and masculine, frill and fish. To one side of a window curtained with pink lace hung a framed poster of trout, the common name printed under each one and the Latin in parentheses—Rainbow (*Salmo gairdneri*), Cutthroat (*Salmo clarki*), Brown (*Salmo trutta*), Gila (*Salmo gilae*), Apache (*Salmo apache*), Brook (*Salvelinus fontinalis*), Lake (*Salvelinus namaycush*). To the other side, next to a poster of Woodstock, was mounted a plaque of flies lined in rows across black velvet and meticulously labeled in her own hand—Muscrat Nymph, Green Drake, Blue Dun, Pheasant Tail Nymph, Yellow Stonefly, Brown Hackle Peacock, Elk Hair Caddis. Her father had taught her how to tie while she was still in grade school. In fifth grade she brought her collection for show-and-tell, which immediately made her a hit with the boys. She talked about flies as most girls talk about clothes, pointing out the colorful plumage of a Royal Coachman, the airy sheen of a Pale Morning Dun, or the striped orange and black body of the Rio Grande King. She fell in love with flies long before trying to hook a trout with one, and soon began tying her own flamboyant concoctions. Most looked like Las Vegas showgirls, bearing little resemblance to a hatch or insect, and few ever saw water. To Julie they were an art unto themselves. We used to sit around thinking up names for her latest addition to The Flypaper, as she called the transformed photo album. Greg's suggestions tended toward the literary—Zelda Fitzladybug, Gertrude Stonefly, E. E. Hummings, William Caddis, John Dun—while Julie's and mine were random—Yellow Humpty-Dumpty, Frog's Hair Fantastic, Prince Nimrod, Blue Steel Boogie. Lenny, as usual, just listened and then one day stopped us all, presenting her with a two-by-three-foot detailed ink and watercolor of a Pheasant Tail Nymph. The painting's perspective was from the top of the cast, the fisherman and line just shadowy suggestions in the lower left-hand corner. It hung above her bed between a McGovern placard and autographed poster of Paul Newman and Robert Redford as *Butch Cassidy and the Sundance Kid*. The rest of her bedroom was covered with freeze-dried corsages, family vacation pictures, a collage of black and white photos she had taken with her antique box camera, and a large plastic crucifix, hanging like a reminder above the dresser. Ski poles and a maroon pair of Rossi 203's, with the trademark rooster on the tips, leaned in one corner and in the opposite, a well-worn guitar she wouldn't play for anyone but herself.

"What're these?" I picked up one of the envelopes that were spread across the bedspread.

She looked at me in the mirror where she was bent over applying chapstick. "Fliers. The rest are on my desk. I've got to stuff all of them by next Monday. Want to help?"

I walked over and picked one up. George McGovern stood amiably to one side, *Come Home, America* printed in bold lettering across the top. Endorsements from different celebrities ran the length of the other side.

"Does he even have a chance?"

"He just won Rhode Island and Oregon. Tonight's California and three other states. He wins those and he's in. Of course he has a chance."

"But this is just the primary."

"It's the first step." She capped the chapstick and walked over to me. "Look, this is the first time in history eighteen-year-olds can vote. The first time." She shook the black and white chapstick canister at me. "And guess what?"

"What?"

"We're it." She opened her mouth, eyes wide. "The first ones! You think we're gonna waste it on Dick Nixon and Spiro Agnew? Remember when we helped Greg—Spuck Firo Agnew."

"Julie loves Dick Nixon! Julie loves Dick Nixon!"

She turned to the door. "And spuck Dick Nixon, too, you little brats!"

There was silence, then footsteps fell gravely down the hallway. "We're tellin' Mom!"

She looked back at me. "Great." Picking up her purse, she dropped the chapstick into it and began digging for keys. "Save myself seventeen years for Greg Woods, then get grounded for spuckin' Dick Nixon. What could be worse?" She sighed, shaking her head. "You know what, Hank?"

"What?"

"Virginity's a tough gig."

I nodded. She was telling me.

◇◇◇

The horizon of my hamstrings and crotch stretched across the ceiling like low mountains against white sky. The ragged edge of an old water stain crept from one corner, yellowish brown in the flickering fluorescent lights.

"Come on, Hank! Get up!"

I had grown weary of these exhortations over the course of the wrestling season. Junior varsity cheerleaders clapping and beseeching me to get up—Get up, Hank, get up! Get up, Hank, get up!—as though I had a say in the matter. The slow tearing in my groin and the digging of my chin into my own shallow chest while trying to breathe and alternately keep one shoulder blade and then the other from touching the floor, to keep the dispassionate zebra studying my predicament from blowing that whistle and slapping the mat with an exclamation point, ending my misery and the monotonous droning from the sidelines.

"Come on, Hank."

"I think he's got him, Julie." Mr. VanHorn's bearded face appeared above the horizon. "Okay, guys. Let's eat."

Lenny relaxed, letting go of one leg and unscissoring my other. He rolled on one shoulder and popped up, clasping my hand and pulling me up. "Nice job stayin' out of the guillotine but you were ripe for the grapevine."

"Yeah, like a mashed grape."

Mr. VanHorn laughed. "Ah, my prize students extending metaphors even in the heat of battle."

Julie giggled. "Bet that's not all they extended."

I glared, adjusting shorts, T-shirt, and certain external organs. "Do you ever think of anything else?"

"No, not really." She put her arm around my shoulders and escorted me from the wrestling mat in Mr. V's half basement and outside through the sliding glass doors. "No, I take that back. Sometimes I think about food."

The barbecue smoked with hickory and cooking meat. We walked up the grassy slope, into which Sam and Molly VanHorn's brick house was built. Peach and apricot trees stood in rows over the twelve-acre lot, and Molly's carefully pruned roses grew along the patio.

"Grab a plate and bun and help yourselves. There's pop in the cooler." Molly lifted the barbecue lid and, leaning back from the smoke, slid the spatula under the patties. "No, Louie. Go on." She gently put her knee against the dog's muzzle and nudged him away.

We could hear the hollow barks and yips from dogs kenneled inside the cinder-block clinic standing at the edge of the fruit trees. Louie sauntered over to the patio and plopped down in the shade of the house, salivating like the dog he forgot he was. Minnie, the VanHorn's miniature striped cat, sashayed over and nuzzled against Louie's chest.

"Hubba, hubba—" Mr. VanHorn kissed Molly on the back of the neck and wrapped his hairy arms around her pregnant middle.

"You big goof." She smiled, pushing him away and stacking burgers to the side with the spatula. "Go get me the platter. It's on the kitchen counter."

Mr. VanHorn looked at Lenny. "Leonardo, go get the platter. It's on the kitchen—"

"You go get it." Molly elbowed her husband's belly. "These kids are graduating. You can't boss them around anymore."

"All right, Molly!" Julie, Lenny, and I laughed, clapping and whistling.

"An insurgency hangs like a pall upon the fragrant air. My own Calpurnia conspiring with assassins to unseat me."

"Unseat yourself and go fetch the platter."

Mr. VanHorn chuckled, nuzzling his beard into his wife's ear. "Mol, you better stick to patching up the kingdom's canines and leave all executive dictates to your honorably hirsute hubby-bubby." He patted her stomach and strode into the house, shaking his fist at us.

Molly shook her head smiling and poking at the hissing meat as the back screen door slammed. "Is he like this in class, too?"

"Worse." Julie laughed. "No, I mean, he just expects so much. We had to memorize and quote almost everything."

"And every day he made us write." I glanced at Lenny. "Most of us, anyway."

"What?" Lenny looked up from the napkin he was sketching on.

"Bartelli, this is a barbecue. A picnic." Julie snatched the drawing. She looked down, smiled, then held it up. "Look, Molly." She handed it across the picnic table.

Mr. VanHorn returned with the platter and peered over his wife's shoulder as she gazed at the sketch. If you didn't know her, you would have thought Molly was blushing, but she always had that freckled sunshiny glow of someone who spends most of her time kneeling in a garden or cooking over an open fire. In fact, she did both but only when she could. Molly was a veterinarian, the best in the valley.

"Lenny, I like it. It's wonderful." She gazed over the napkin at him.

"But not too realistic. Look." Mr. VanHorn pointed. "He's got your belly at two months instead of six. I looked more pregnant in that crucifixion he drew of me on the back of the final exam."

"Yes, but quite an accurate portrayal I thought. Especially your legs." She slipped the napkin into the pocket of her sun dress. "Thank you, Lenny. Okay, everybody, chow's on."

Louie stood and shook, a string of saliva looping over his muzzle.

"Louie's ready, too." Lenny patted his dog's side. "Aren't you boy?"

His tail waved as he mouthed Mr. VanHorn's wrists, one and then the other. Finally, he jumped up, paw's thwacking against Mr. V's chest.

"You sloopy old bear."

Louie stretched his neck out, sniffed the end of his beard, licked it.

"I don't know what you have in mind, fella, but I don't think I like it." Mr. VanHorn let go, Louie's front paws ker-thumping back to earth.

"Must be my animal magnetism. Right, Mol?"

Molly glanced over her shoulder as she shook the burger off the spatula onto my bun. "Actually, dogs go by smell."

"Thanks a lot." Mr. VanHorn walked over and turned on the hose to rinse his hands.

Late afternoon melted into twilight, into liquid dusk as frogs and crickets began their evening chorus and mosquitoes started lighting. Louie nosed along the ditch bank to the far corner of the VanHorn property line, worked his way across the gravel parking lot, and sniffed eureka in the low evergreens outside the clinic where Molly's nervous clientele lifted or squatted before entering. The VanHorn's ancient black Labrador Huck rolled out from under his cloud of years to join the sniffing. His front elbows were rubbed furless from so much down time, and his muzzle was grizzled with white whiskers sprouting every which way.

We settled into lawn chairs around the glowing briquettes, the air moist and earthy from ditch water stuttering across lawn. Mr. VanHorn broke out his guitar and strummed while Molly and Julie joined in, singing. I sat opposite Lenny, pretending to gaze into the coals but studying him instead. He appeared so small and fragile scrunched down in the lawn chair, arms and legs crossed, staring unblinking into the heat. As usual, he was quiet—rarely did he say anything unless asked—but that night his silence was different, as though his placid calm was now rippled with a brewing storm across his eyes. Maybe it was the wrestling tournament Mr. VanHorn talked us into, the prospect of wrestling Cisco. Lenny didn't particularly like wrestling; he was just naturally good at it, like running or drawing. Or perhaps his draft number was troubling him—who wouldn't it?—but he had only mentioned it that once atop The Three Sisters. Or it could have been his wacko mom, again, or something simple, like replacing the Wagoneer's cracked distributor cap or deciding what to take on the next morning's run, watercolors or pencils. He had sets of both. Or maybe it was our graduating, of life being altered, mixed with Mr. VanHorn's melancholy guitar. As I studied him across the dying briquettes, *Blowin' in the Wind* swelling the evening air, his eyes moved back and forth from the red coals to Julie singing. Maybe nothing was bothering him. Maybe it was just me, reading too much into everything.

"Julie, your voice is lovely."

"Thanks, Molly. Thanks for everything."

We were standing in the driveway, Mr. VanHorn's arm draped around his wife. Julie and I climbed into the VW, as Lenny whistled for his dog.

"You kids be careful driving home, now." Mr. VanHorn shut Julie's door and leaned down. "We'll see you Wednesday at graduation."

"Thanks, Mr. V. It was fun." I looked at Lenny, who was coming up the driveway with Louie. "Let's go."

"I'll catch you tomorrow, Hank. At practice."

"I didn't think you were going."

He glanced at Mr. VanHorn and shrugged. "I wasn't."

Julie backed down the driveway, leaving the VanHorns waving in the headlights, standing with Lenny and his dog as we pulled away.

"How'd he get over here?"

Julie nodded up ahead at the Wagoneer pulled over next to the fence. "He's been over here all day helping Mr. V prune trees and burn weeds and stuff."

As we eased by it to turn off the VanHorns property onto the road, I looked back and squinted into the darkness. "What's all that stuff in his Jeep?"

"I don't know." She turned on the radio, snippets of music and conversation crackling in and out as the needle slid down the dial.

"So he finally got it running, huh?" I turned around and glanced at Julie, her face faintly aglow from the dash lights.

"Guess so. For a while, at least. Listen—"

"*With sixty-three percent of the vote in, Senator George McGovern has been projected winner of the California . . .*"

"He did it!" She slapped the steering wheel. "He's in, Hank. Didn't I tell you?" She smiled.

"Now what?"

"It's on to the convention in Miami."

"Great." I watched fence posts whiz by in the headlights as she drove toward town. "Did Lenny seem different to you?"

"Not really. Just the same loud, obnoxious guy."

"No, I'm serious."

"Well, there was one thing."

"What?"

I looked at Julie, her eyes shiny, watching me out the corner.

"It did seem to take him a little longer to pin you this time."

"You know, Julie, sometimes you can really be an ass."

"Well, Hank—" She looked at me wide-eyed, beaming. "—I didn't think you'd ever notice."

◇◇◇

Mom's boss, Punk Moreaux, purchased The Acropolis Cafe in 1952. He renamed it Sage Diner not only for the brush that surrounded Grand River but for the spice, although in his own cooking he used only three: salt, pepper, and horseradish. Punk painted the plaster walls sage, put down a matching linoleum floor, and covered the long counter, round stools, and six booths in a vinyl of the same hue. Two booths wore duct tape down the middle, and from years of cigarettes and burned orders, the pale ceiling had turned the color of Punk's split-pea soup. The regulars occasionally grumbled about the appearance, which only diminished the possibility that he would ever paint or repair the place again. Besides, Punk liked split-pea; "wicked" he would say after a test taste. In addition to the daily soup, Punk cooked three dishes: scrambled eggs with diced ham and horseradish for breakfast, cheeseburgers and fries with a quarter-size cup of horseradish on the side for lunch, and chicken-fried steak with mashed horseradish potatoes for supper. Any diversions from these were usually met with an insouciant shrug and a "Fresh out," muttered in the clipped tone peculiar to his home state of Maine. Food wasn't the reason most frequented Sage Diner; it was the coffee. Punk brewed a pot unlike anybody in Grand River. Customers tolerated the cooking—and Punk—just to be able to sip his brew.

"Punk, I need extra cheese on four." Mom reached across and clipped the check on the silver order-wheel hanging in the open window between the counter and grill in back. "How have you been, young lady?"

"Fine, Mrs. Kessler. Just trying to keep Henry out of trouble." Julie elbowed my ribs.

Arlene leaned against the counter, smoking and studying us. "Now there's a tall damn order." It was her night off but she couldn't seem to stay away. Her frizzy permed hair and short round figure gave her the presence of a scouring pad. Though abrasive, she was Mom's dearest friend and staunchest supporter. "You two probably gettin' ready to go screw now, aren't ya?"

I looked away, rolling my eyes.

Julie coughed, her cheeks flushing, a rarity. "No, actually, we already have. We're just here basking in the afterglow."

Mom laughed, slipping the pad into her apron and grabbing two plates Punk set on the sill. "Careful, Arlene." She carried them around the counter and over to one of two window booths that looked out onto Gateway Avenue.

Arlene drew on her cigarette, squinting. "The only afterglow I ever remember—" She flicked the ash. "—was from their taillights when they'd pull away."

Punk peered out around the order-wheel. "Fer chrissakes, Arlene. It's your night off. Get the hell out of here so we can get some work done." He yanked down the check, his prairie dog head disappearing back into its hole.

Arlene jutted her jaw, smoke languidly escaping like silk underwear from a dresser drawer. Punk and Arlene were in love, though neither would admit to it. He had hired her as soon as he opened, and except for a brief stint as a blackjack dealer in Vegas, she had been with him ever since. Though never married, they loved each other with the comfortable familiarity of middle age, steeped in food and chronic bickering.

"Butter on two!" Mom stopped to re-pin her hair. "My word, it's been like this since I got here."

"Take a breather, hon." Arlene took the coffeepot from her and began a round of refills. I could hear Punk scraping the grill with his spatula.

"So—" Mom sat down, picking up Arlene's cigarettes and tapping one out. "What're you two up to tonight?"

I shrugged. "Not much. Just thought we'd drop by and say hi."

"Thanks, honey. You excited about getting out of high school, Julie?"

"I'm excited about getting out of my house."

"Oh, you have a lovely family."

"With five unlovely brothers."

"You'll miss 'em. Just wait and see."

The front door dinged open.

"*Que pasa!*" Dillard strolled in wearing a smile the size of a waffle iron.

"Hey, Dill. What's up?"

"*Nada.* Hey, Juuules. Hi, Mrs. Kessler."

"Warren." Mom got up to clean off a table, leaving the cigarette burning in the ashtray. Dillard picked up the cigarette and took a drag.

"Hey!" Julie grabbed his forearm, plucked it from his fingers, and placed it back on the lip of the ashtray. "You jerk."

"Whaaat?" He grinned, looking around. "It's just sittin' there burnin' down. Why waste a good weeeed." He turned around. "Hey, there you are! I thought maybe you lost your way."

"No, just my mind." Greg walked in and straddled a stool next to Julie. "Have you seen Lenny?"

"Yeah. We had a barbecue at Mr. VanHorn's. Maybe he's still over there."

Greg nodded. "Hmm."

"Why?"

"Nothing. We just went by his old lady's. I think she's wiggin' again. All the lights are on and the curtains are wide open."

"Was she parading around naked or anything?"

"Yikes. Now there's a frightening image. I've gotta use the phone."

Julie watched him walk the length of the diner to the back.

Dillard sidled up, leaning in and wrapping his arms around us. "You two are the greatest, maaan."

I pulled back. "Geez, Dillard, you smell like a pot factory."

"Thanks, man."

"It wasn't supposed to be a—"

"Hey, guess what? I did it." He squeezed us.

Julie glanced up. "Yeah, you did it all right."

"No, I mean, I like reeeally did it."

"And we're, like, reeeally happy you did it but if you squeeze me once more I'm going to, like, do it all over this countertop." She rolled her shoulders, loosening his grip.

"I passed."

"What? A fur-ball?"

"Nooo, I passed my freakin' test, man. I'm graduating!" He raised a fist. "Yeeew!" He bear hugged us again.

"Way to go, Dill." I half slid off the stool.

"Let's party!" He looked around, customers glancing up from their cups. "'Member when we were cruisin' down from the woodsie the other night? Well, that was nothin'. Shoulda seen us tonight, maaan. Greg let the mother go."

Julie swiveled toward him, shrugging off his arm. "Let what go?"

"Easy does it." He held his hands up in surrender. "He just opened her up a little. We had to see what she'd do."

"And?"

"Topped out at one-twenty-seven." Dill closed his eyes, hands still up. "Shoulda seen it, man. It was beauuutiful."

I gawked at him. "A hundred-and-twenty-seven miles an hour?"

"What's a hundred-and-twenty-seven miles an hour?" Mom picked up the cigarette, inhaling some before crumpling it in the ashtray.

Julie stood. "Greg's new car. That's how fast they said it would go."

"My goodness. I didn't think they made cars like that. You kids want a booth? There's a window open."

"No thanks, Mrs. Kessler. We better go. Come on, Henry."

Greg returned from the back and grabbed Julie's hand. "Hey, what's the rush?" He pulled her toward the booth. "Don't you even want to know who I was talking to?"

"No." She glared at him, tongue working one cheek.

"Hello, Mrs. Kessler."

"Well, hi there, Greg." She gave him a hug. "I hear you have quite the fast car."

He shot a look at Dillard and shrugged. "It's okay, I guess."

We slid into a booth.

"You kids want menus?"

"Naw, that's okay, Mom."

"Speak for yourself, Kessler." Dillard grinned at Mom. "Yes, pleeease."

She handed him a menu and left.

Julie looked at Dill. "Gosh, *Warren*. How is it that you have such a big appetite for being such a little weenie?"

"Up yours, Julie."

"Whoa—such hostility." Greg ran both hands through his hair then stretched his left out along the seat behind Julie. "And on the eve of our undoing."

She turned to him. "What's that supposed to mean?"

"You still haven't even asked me about my phone call."

"So?"

"So, I just talked to Kevy."

"Who's Kevy?"

"The manager of Kentucky Fried Chicken."

I sat up. "You talked to him again? What'd he say?"

"Said they're going to do it."

"Do what?"

"What I told them. They're going to put us on the radio."

"You're kidding."

"Nope. Quarter 'til midnight tomorrow."

Julie sighed. "You'd think kidnapping Colonel Sanders is one of the defining moments of western civilization."

"Who got kidnapped?" Mom set down a basket of crackers and rolls.

"Nobody, Mom. Dill, you going to order?"

"I'll have the soup. Extra large."

Mom walked away, jotting on her pad.

Julie turned to Greg. "Quite the little terrorists, aren't we? Are they going to interview us, too, so we can slip in a few dirty Chinese words or maybe hum the Grand River High fight song one last time?"

I sat forward. "What are they going to do, Greg?"

He shrugged. "Denounce their piggish tendencies like I told them to."

Julie snorted. "Pigs, chickens—a veritable barnyard of activity."

"He said they'd exchange buckets of chicken and pop for the Colonel."

"Wow. This is a big deal." Julie rubbed her hands. "Ransoming the Colonel for one of his own roosters, I mean roasters."

Folding his arms, Greg gazed around the diner at the clientele. "Funny, Jules."

"I don't think we should accept any deals, though, until they give us at least one more look at their menu, Colonel or no Colonel."

"Can I get you anything else?" Mom set down Dillard's bowl of soup.

Dillard looked around the table. "Naaaw, this'll do."

Julie glanced at Mom then glared at Dill. "What do you say, Warren?"

"Not much." He shook salt and pepper at the soup. "What do you say, Julie Marie?"

"I think we're probably set, Mom."

"Okay, honey. Let me know if you need anything else."

I watched her carry the coffeepot to the next table, and then gazed outside at headlights traveling down Gateway Avenue, the main drag in Grand River. With school out, traffic had multiplied, teenagers from all over the valley cruising from First Street all the way east to Teller Arms, the turnaround point and first shopping center in Grand River.

"So, Greg—" Julie scooted farther into the corner, turning toward him. "—one-twenty-seven, huh?"

In the window's reflection I could see Greg look away, shaking his head. "Here we go again."

"Tell me you really didn't go one-hundred-and-twenty-seven miles an hour."

"I really didn't go one-hundred—"

"Truthfully."

"I truthfully didn't go—"

Dillard laughed.

"Shut up, Dillard." Julie jutted fingers into her hair and gazed at the ceiling, shaking her head. "Look. This isn't a joke. If you keep pulling this crap, you're going to . . . you're going to end up—"

Greg stared at her. "End up what?" He broke into a smile. "This is the ennnd—"

"Greg, really, this isn't . . ."

Dillard laughed, chiming in. "This is the ennnd—"

"Greg, listen. Miss Darling . . ."

"Sage, seer, soothsayer, and part-time used car dealer at Skeeter's Auto-rama."

"She said there's danger."

Greg gawked at Julie, mouth open, then panned slowly across to Dillard. "There's danger?" His eyes widened in terror, voice slow and ghoulish. "Danger at the edge of town." He panned back to Julie. "Our ancient lady—"

"Forget it." She scooted across the seat, pushing against him. "Let me out."

"Oh, come on, Jules. You're getting too serious on us." He stood as she elbowed by him.

"And you're getting too weird."

"Morrison would take that as a compliment." He nodded. "We'll never gaze into each other's eyes againnn—"

"Let's go, Hank."

I shrugged at Greg, slid out the booth, and followed her to the door. Looking across the diner, I could see Mom cradling an armload of dirty plates, wiping a table clean with her free hand. I waved but she didn't notice.

Julie opened the door, hesitated, then stepped back. "Oh. One more thing, Greg."

"What?"

"Jim Morrison wouldn't take it as a compliment. You know why?"

He shrugged, still smiling. "Why?"

"'Cause he's dead."

We walked outside onto Gateway Avenue, two long lines of cars idling at the intersection a half block away and people milling around Arctic Circle across the street, waiting for ice cream.

"I guess you told him." I could see the light change and hear engines rev as she stood staring at the sidewalk.

She nodded. "Yeah—" A stream of cars rushed by; one honked and she instinctively looked up, half raising an arm, but then caught herself, letting the hand drop back to her side. "—guess I told him."

7

*H*ey, Lenny!"

Waving and shielding my eyes from the morning light, I looked up at Lenny's Wagoneer silhouetted atop the Third Sister. It moved along the crest, lurched down the side to Tulip Bench, then dipped and disappeared behind the Second Sister. I could hear the Wagoneer drone unevenly as it labored over rocks and ruts around the hill before reappearing minutes later, forging the sandy creek bed, bouncing from a stand of tamarisk, and bucking to a stop at the trailhead.

"What're you doin'?"

He got out, followed by Louie with a tennis ball in his mouth, and slammed the door. "Testing her out."

"There's not even a road up there, is there? Hi, Louie boy. What's that in your Jeep?"

He glanced back and shrugged. "Stuff."

"How long you been out here?"

"All night."

"What?"

"I slept up there. You should've seen The Milky Way. It was . . . well . . . milky. Like stars were pouring out of it."

I stared at him. "First Greg and the sun, now you and the stars."

He shrugged. "The sun is a star, Hank."

"It just sounds weird, that's all. Comin' out here in the dark, by yourself."

"Louie was here. We came over after Mr. V's. Don't you ever go camping?"

"My Dad used to take me. When I was little."

"Sleeping out's the best. Ready?" He slipped the orange pack over his shoulders and started through the tamarisk.

I followed. "Where we going?"

"Eagle's Wing. But first we gotta cool Louie off. Drop, Louie—drop." He reached into the dog's slobbering mouth, extracted the ball, and tossed it into the Wagoneer.

"Oh, man. We're gonna run all the way to the canal then up Eagle's Wing? How far's that?"

"I don't know. We'll go slow."

"But we still have practice this afternoon."

"It'll be good for you, Hank. It'll get the soreness out and give you a base. You'll have something to build on."

"Who says I want to build?"

"You wouldn't be out here if you didn't like it."

"Yeah, right."

But I did like it. Despite myself. Running had always been something Coach Hicks made us do at wrestling practice or in P.E. But running trails with Lenny was different, as though it wasn't even the same motion. Shuffling through sagebrush, dodging rocks and cactus, climbing hills, skirting sandstone ledges, moving over the high desert with my best friend, wearing nothing but shoes, socks, and shorts. Its simple beauty made startling by the summer landscape: Indian paintbrush, pink and yellow prickly pear blossoms, sego lily, orange globe mallow, and needle-and-thread grass waving in the breeze like palomino tails. And the sky, Lenny's domain. Then to arrive and watch him capture birds, horned toads, or collared lizards with a sketch or watercolor. He always dated his work and made notes on the back where he ran, what the subject was, and with whom. Of course, the "with whom" was a new notation because it had been nobody but Louie until now, until I started running with them that summer after high school.

"Ever feel like nobody sees you?"

Lenny shrugged. He was perched cross-legged on the sandstone mushroom Greg had pretended to fall from, pencil in hand, a sketchpad across his lap.

"Like when you're walking down the hall at school or downtown on a Saturday and nobody notices you. Their eyes go right through or past you like you're not even there." I picked up a rock, felt its weight.

"I don't know." Lenny watched a pair of swallows dipping and cutting through air currents along the ridge with their sickle-shaped wings. A steady breeze swirled around us, riffling the pages of the sketchbook and parting Louie's drying fur as he lay panting under a juniper.

"Yeah, it's like you're there but you're really not. Like you're just air or something. Like you look at them but it doesn't matter 'cause they don't look back." I tossed the rock over the cliff, listened to it hit the side then click through tree branches before thumping the ground. Louie lumbered up and moseyed to the edge, sniffing the air.

"How do you know they're not looking?"

I picked up another one. "I just do. They don't meet my eyes."

Lenny looked up from his drawing. "Hold it up."

"What?"

"That rock. Hold it above your head. See, I'm looking at it."

"So?"

"How do you know it's not looking back?"

"What?" I laughed. "'Cause it's a rock, Lenny."

"It is a rock. But how do you know it can't see me?"

"'Cause it's a rock. It doesn't have eyes."

"Maybe. Or maybe it just sees differently, eyes or no eyes, and it really is looking at me." He gazed at the sky. The swallows had reappeared, performing their aerial acrobatics. "What I see is different from what you see, is different from what the rocks and swallows see." He continued drawing.

I looked at the rock, imagined two eyes, a nose, and mouth. Imagined long hair with eyelashes gazing back at me. "Fish the depths of all mankind/and you, my friend, will never find/the love of a rock."

Lenny looked up.

I laughed self-consciously and shrugged. "Pretty stupid, huh?" I tossed the rock over the edge, long hair and everything. "I wrote it for English class."

Ripping the drawing from the tablet, he held it above his head: two dark swallows darting through sky over a ragged rock ledge with pear cactus and junipers and wisps of clouds beyond. He let go, the page taking flight over the edge.

"Hey—" I peered over with Louie, watched the white page seesaw through air, catch on a piñon branch below, then float to the canyon floor. The wind had suddenly stopped. "Why'd you do that?" I turned and looked at him. "It was good."

He was already standing, zipping the pack closed. "So was yours." He slid his arms through the orange straps. "Pretty stupid, huh?"

Louie's ears flattened, mouth grinning and tail thumping the ground as though slapping a knee, as though understanding something I still couldn't.

◇◇◇

Riverside was the poorest yet defiantly proudest neighborhood in Grand

River. Whitewashed clapboard homes and trimmed lawns hunkered down over a twelve-block pocket between the buttressed banks of the Colorado River to the south and the railroad tracks to the north. An auto-salvage yard stretched along the riverbank and abutted it from the southeast, and an expansion bridge, which carried traffic over the tracks to the suburbs and Rimrock National Park, loomed to the north. Below the bridge sat Riverside Grade School, a fierce building of few windows and much mud. Encircling it was a sweeping expanse of dirt littered with broken glass, Russian thistle, and a scattered pile of creosote timbers, which served as playground equipment. From the street above, the school looked like a pueblo or miniature prison, and within its walls walked the toughest kids in the Grand Valley, the toughest of these being Cisco Salazar.

Cisco was the second of eight children born to Ernesto and Felicia Salazar. At high school wrestling matches the entire family lined the bottom row of bleachers: Cisco's older brother Rudy in front, wheelchair bound, hands curled with fingers and thumbs unevenly extended from cerebral palsy; six younger sisters, twins Frida and Fiona, one year younger than Cisco and drop-dead beautiful, and in descending order of age and beauty, Nancy, Sharon, Juanita, and Carmella to either side of proud parents. Cousins, aunts, and uncles sat at least three rows deep behind them, always arriving earlier than anyone else in the packed gymnasiums. Mr. Salazar—who drew workmen's compensation for a back injury suffered while in the employ of the county road crew—sat sternly at these events, arms crossed, surveying the mat over his ample belly as though he himself were responsible for its unfurling. His jet hair was slicked straight back like his son's and each of his swollen biceps bore a cross tattooed over a strand of thorns. At his side sat Mrs. Salazar, every bit as imposing if not a little rounder, nodding and smiling majestically at passersby with the same chiseled features and dazzling teeth she had passed to her children. Her long hair was piled on top, crowning her with an elegance befitting the mother of the best wrestler ever to grace the mats of Grand River High.

When the wrestling team ran from the locker room, smallest to largest with Cisco leading the charge, and circled the mat for calisthenics before taking their places in foldout chairs to one side, everyone but Mr. and Mrs. Salazar and their crippled son would rise roaring to their feet. As the ninety-eight pounders wrestled their match, Cisco skipped rope, smiling and lifting his chin at the people who had jammed the gymnasium to watch him. After his name was called for the one-hundred-and-five-pound bout, he would walk to the side, give his mother a kiss, his father a handshake, and Rudy a hug, then sprint to the middle of the mat to meet his next unfortunate opponent. One-hundred-and-two times across three years he had done this, resulting in one-hundred-and-two victories, which included eighty-three pins, four injury defaults, and three state championships. And his family hadn't missed one.

Cisco was unbeatable everywhere but at home, where Mr. Salazar won, finding his mark with ringing regularity. But these battles became less frequent as Cisco matured and began lashing back, if only in self-defense. Mr. Salazar sensed his son's strength and hit him infrequently and then only unawares. Finally, at the end of his senior year, father and son were at a standoff, both wary not only of each other but of the future. Now what? Like prince and king, their reign courtside had come to a close with Cisco's graduation. Only one tournament remained for Cisco to show off his prowess: The College Coaches' Senior Classic, where he would have to move up to one-hundred-and-eighteen pounds, the lowest weight in college wrestling. This would be his ultimate test. If victorious here, over bigger and stronger opponents, he might be offered a scholarship to a junior college despite his weight and marginal grades. The reign could be salvaged, his father appeased. But his opponents were formidable: Clay Meeks, the one-hundred-and-nineteen-pound state champion from North Fork, who had also gone undefeated his senior year; Dane Kirkland, the one-hundred-and-twelve-pound state runner-up from Otto, to whom Lenny had lost two close matches during the regular season but lost badly to at districts; Ted Kohls, another twelve-pounder from Oakridge, with whom Lenny had split, each winning two; and Lenny, Cisco's practice partner, who knew his moves better than anyone though he had never beaten him in practice nor wrestled him in a sanctioned match. Cisco, for the first time in his career, though not in life, was an underdog.

Like other young Chicanos in the Grand Valley, Cisco's choices were limited. There were jobs on farms and in orchards, but Mexicans from across the border drove wages down so far as to make those almost pointless. Construction was a possibility, but the only positions available were either back-wrenchingly difficult—at the end of a shovel or wheel barrel—or temporary—with no benefits or future. The City or County would occasionally hire a token Mexican-American, but Mr. Salazar's workmen's comp case had been a bitterly fought one, making Cisco's chances at employment nil even if he wanted to follow his father's path, which he didn't. Moving over the mountains to Denver, where Corky Gonzales was stirring things up in a less pacific manner than César Chávez in California, was unappealing; he had never been out of the Grand Valley and wasn't political anyway. Then there was Vietnam, where many of his older cousins and friends ended up, most shipped overseas immediately after basic training and a few already returned strung-out on drugs or in a box. No, to Cisco it was clear: wrestling was his one hope, the only thing he loved to do, the only thing that gave him respect. And the College Coaches' Senior Classic was his for the taking, Clay Meeks notwithstanding.

Coach Hicks had confirmed that Meeks was moving down just to wrestle Cisco. A natural one-hundred-and-thirty-eight pounder, Meeks was notorious for the amount of weight he could put on and then drop. It was rumored that the summer before his senior year he had ballooned to one-fifty, only to lose thirty by Christmas to be able to wrestle one-nineteen at state. Cisco, by contrast, had only to cut one or two to make his weight class and could have even dropped to ninety-eight where the competition would have been laughably thin. But Cisco was tall for his weight and had the frame to put on more. Naturally lean, he was a finely tuned athlete, using leverage, speed, and cunning as his weapons. His legs were as lethal as his arms and he used them as instruments of torture, wrapping and squeezing opponents into submission. It was said that Cisco didn't pin people as much as he just made them want to quit. He could squeeze tears out of the toughest kids. And Meeks was tough. Cisco had to be ready.

As soon as final exams were over, Coach Hicks began holding morning and afternoon practices for graduating senior wrestlers interested in participating in the tournament and, as in Cisco's case, drawing college attention. And all were interested except one: Cisco's practice partner. Lenny wanted only to draw.

"Scoot, Bartelli! Scoot those hips! Scoot, scoot, scoot, scoot!" Coach Hicks chewed the rubber end of the whistle jammed to the corner of his mouth like a cigar butt. Veins snaked up his thick neck, across his forehead, and into a black flattop. "Move, Bartelli! Move!"

Cisco crowded Lenny's left leg, which had been scissoring Cisco's in a cross-body ride. Reaching around behind him, he grabbed Lenny's far hip, pulling him under like a rip tide. At the last second before going under, Lenny went with the current, shifting his weight to roll through. But Cisco hooked his far arm with his own, blocking momentum and pinning him to his back. The whistle shrilled through the stale wrestling room air.

"How many times, Bartelli!?! How many damn times do I have to tell you!?! You have to scoot those hips to maintain that cross-body! You go the other way—a good wrestler is gonna catch you every time. Maybe you can get away with that crap with Kessler or somebody. But not with a quality wrestler at the college level. You understand what I'm saying?"

Cisco helped his practice partner up and patted him on the seat.

"Don't do that, Cisco."

Cisco looked up as Coach Hicks ran his hand over the flattop, head down and swaying side to side.

"It just encourages him, son. You're telling him it's okay when it's not." He tried to smile. "It's not helping you either. You think Meeks is gonna pull a bone-headed move like that?"

Cisco shrugged.

"How's Bartelli ever gonna wrestle in college if he keeps pullin' this unorthodox crap? Vintage VanHorn, that's what I call it." Coach Hicks turned and faced the rest of us seniors paired off across the mat. "College wrestling is a different ballgame, gentlemen. You think overtime's tough? Try three three-minute periods and then overtime. With the top high school wrestlers across the country every damn time you step onto the mat. Then tell me how mean you think you are." He glared at Lenny. "And I don't care if you can run a mile in *three* minutes and thirty seven seconds." He blew his whistle. "Okay, takedowns. Let's go. Let me see some—"

"I don't care either."

Coach Hicks froze. His eyes snapped back to Lenny's. "What'd you say?"

Cisco clasped Lenny's neck to tie him up for a takedown, but Lenny peeled his fingers away. Cisco reached up again, trying to distract him.

"Hold on, Cisco." Coach Hicks walked over. "Did I hear you correctly, Bartelli? Did you say you don't care?"

Lenny shrugged. "It doesn't matter."

"It doesn't matter? It doesn't matter!?!"

"It doesn't matter how long it takes to run a mile. I just like to run."

Coach Hicks stood hands on hips, bowlegs flexing. "Okay, Mr. Bartelli." He nodded exaggeratedly like a horse at the bit. "You like to run?" He turned to the rest of us. "Hear that, people? Bartelli here likes to run. Course we knew that, didn't we?" He blew his whistle. "Okay, everybody! Let's move it!"

A moan rose up as we got off the mat and followed the coach's stocky shadow from the wrestling room down the dark empty hallway to the gymnasium, our wrestling shoes squeaking against the newly waxed floor. I had been practicing with Steve Pacheco, our varsity one-hundred-and-twenty-six pounder, who I could never beat even though I was at one-thirty-two—a second-string one-thirty-two.

"Okay, gentlemen, give me twenty!"

"Twenty!" Donald Stankey slumped against the wall. Coach Hicks, hurting for a heavyweight, had recruited him from the basketball team his sophomore year. He could see in the white-knuckled way Stankey clutched a basketball—unable to pass, dribble, or even release—that there was a desperate energy in that hulking awkward frame, a potential wrestler. And he was almost right; Stank was just one victory away from winning ten matches his senior year after two winless seasons of getting pancaked by beefy behemoths up to sixty pounds heavier.

"You can thank Bartelli on your way, Stankey! Now let's go! Move out!"

We jogged across the gym and started up the bleachers, Lenny, as usual, leading the way. From where I was at the back I could see Cisco slap him on the shoulder as if to say don't worry about it. There was a mutual respect between them, but Cisco also knew that Lenny was the only one close to his size who could practice with him, who could give him a good workout. And if he wanted to beat Meeks, he needed all the practice he could get. Twenty laps wouldn't hurt either.

"Nineteen!" Coach Meeks stood mid-court on the out-of-bounds line, holding a lap counter. "Come on, girls! Pick it up! One more time! Let's go!"

Legs leaden from the morning run, I finished the last lap with fingers laced atop my sweaty head, a sharp stitch in my side. Lenny had already run more than twenty, having lapped everyone at least twice.

"Okay, okay. Hit the showers, gentlemen. See you back here Monday. Only one week to go."

Exhausted, we trudged across the basketball court toward the locker room exit, hands on hips, T-shirts soaked to a darker gray.

"Bartelli!"

We hesitated at the door.

"Not you, Bartelli. Since you like running so much, you're gonna give me twenty more."

Cisco stepped back from the doorway.

"Go shower, Cisco. This doesn't concern you, son."

Lenny looked at Cisco and slightly smiled before walking back across the gymnasium.

Coach Hicks clapped. "Come on, Bartelli. Get a move on, mister. Maybe this'll finally cure you of that Sam VanHorn influence."

We watched him jog the length of the gym, then vault up the bleachers two steps at a time before coming back across the top.

"Hit it, gentlemen. He doesn't need an audience."

We turned to leave but Cisco blocked our way.

Stankey gawked at him. "Oh, come on. I can't even walk—"

Cisco's eyes cut him off as everyone turned and started back across court to the bleachers. The whistle shrieked through the gymnasium.

"Hey!" Coach Hicks stood hands on hips, legs wide. "I said hit the showers, people. Now get back in there."

Cisco shook his head.

Coach Hicks blew his whistle. "Now!"

We turned to leave but Cisco stood his ground, then jogged over to meet Lenny who was again coming across the top, head back and arms out.

"Cisco—" Coach Hicks hurried over to cut him off. "—listen to me, son. You can't afford to lose any more weight." He put his hands on Cisco's shoulders as we watched Lenny bound down the stands, arms flapping to the side. Coach Hicks glanced over his shoulder. "Quit screwin' around, Bartelli!" He turned back to Cisco. "Listen to me—"

Cisco tried to follow Lenny, who sprinted across the gym behind Coach Hicks, but the coach wouldn't let go.

"Okay, Bartelli. That's enough for today."

Lenny bounded up the steps.

"This Meeks kid is big for one-eighteen, son. You've got to put on weight, not lose it."

Standing in the middle of the basketball court, we watched as Lenny ran across the top then back down, arms still flapping.

"Bartelli! I said that's enough." He removed one hand from Cisco's shoulder and reached for Lenny as he ran by. "Didn't I tell you people to hit the showers! Now get in there!"

We shuffled toward the locker room, heads turned to watch Lenny run yet another lap.

Coach Hicks let go of Cisco, tracking Lenny across the top. "You, too, Cisco. Practice is over." Patting Cisco on the shoulder but not taking his eyes from Lenny, he turned around, shifting his weight from one foot to the other. "See you tomorrow at graduation, son." He slipped the whistle inside his T-shirt and crouched, hands braced on knees like a linebacker.

We stopped. Cisco stepped back as though from a curb and oncoming traffic. Arms stretched wide and head thrown back, Lenny flew down the bleachers. I moved too, instinctively drawn forward like a pedestrian to a car wreck.

Coach Hicks' feet stuttered and his meaty hands flexed from his knees as

Lenny sailed toward him across the varnished floor, gliding headlong like one of the redtails he loved to sketch. And that's when I noticed—Lenny's eyes were closed.

I raised my hand, my voice catching in my throat. "Lennn—!"

Coach Hicks sprang—a human projectile fueled by frustration, aiming at a singular target, a free spirit he had been unable to harness in three years of coaching. Arms out and head down, our coach's compact body shot to its full length. Then the dull thud. A single grunt reverberated through the stale air.

We stood dumbstruck as our coach lay prone across three rows of bleachers—legs sprawled, arms akimbo, head cocked awkwardly to one side—while the object of his aggression, Lenny, faded with the dying echo through the gymnasium doorway—untouched, running, and free.

8

I somehow knew even before rounding the corner and seeing the truck parked in front, before opening the back door to my sister sitting there crossed-legged, eyes closed in a fog of patchouli oil. She postured like a Tibetan yogi—thumbs and middle fingers forming circles on either knee—though I knew for a fact she'd never been within a thousand miles of one and the only yogi she had ever seen was the bear. She wore bell-bottoms, a tank top, and leather choker with a tangle of orange coral against her throat. A feather was braided into a strand of her shoulder-length hair and a matching feather earring dangled from the other side.

Across the kitchen swayed Stella and Frank, water sloshing inside their glass universe from the thump-squeak thump-squeak of headboard against plywood veneer paneling. Maybe for them it was no different from floating within the rhythm of oceans, foamy waves slapping beachheads from gods thrashing about. But we already knew who was doing the thrashing, sending hurricanes across their bowl. Yet Stella and Frank seemed to be holding up pretty well, at least better than Dana and I. Redd Morgan was back and we could feel his vibrations to the bone.

"Hey."

Dana opened her eyes and smiled sleepily. "Hi."

"Sounds like stormy weather."

"Mmm." She uncrossed her legs and yawned.

I stooped down to ogle Stella and Frank. "Were you sleeping or meditating?"

"Not sleeping. Who could sleep through that. What time is it?"

"Five." I tapped the bowl. "Hello." Frank wiggled sideways, disappearing into the refracted curve of glass. I grabbed the fish-food and shook flakes across the surface, watched them absorb moisture and fall like snowflakes in Mom's crystal winter scene. But Stella and Frank seemed uninterested; hard to have appetite during natural disasters, even for fish. "When'd the storm hit?"

"Which one?"

"How 'bout the first one."

"Probably long before I got home."

I scooted the bowl's pedestal—a barstool salvaged from the alley behind Sage Diner—away from the wall. "Do they know we're here?"

"I don't think they know *they're* here."

"Sure didn't take 'em long to make up."

"Just all day."

"You know what I mean."

Away from the wall now Stella and Frank were recovering, hoovering food along the bottom. Arlene had given us the fish as a replacement gift after Dad moved out—not for Dad but for the twin canaries he'd taken with him. Like the goldfish, the birds had been barometers for natural disaster. In Dad's case, carbon monoxide and methane, a gas more flammable than Redd Morgan.

While other miners used safety lamps and meth meters—or sniffers, as they called them—for detecting dangerous gases, Dad relied on the canaries. He would take them to work, lunch box in one hand and wire cage in the other, and hang them from a protruding rock or jamb the cage's hook into a crack just as his father and grandfather had done in the coal mines of Wales. Others teased him about the birds, chiding him for using such a primitive method of detection. But for Dad, Beamer and Chip were more than method; they were living reminders of daylight in the pitch-black recesses of mines.

As he worked as foreman—accompanying mining inspectors and orchestrating everyone from the continuous-miner operators to the roof bolters—he would carry or safekeep the canaries nearby so he could hear their fluttering wings, their pecking and preening beaks. Occasionally, if he stared at the cage long enough, bathing the birds with light from his battery-operated headlamp, Chip would sing. Above ground Beamer was the singer, starting as soon as Dad surfaced at the end of his shift and continuing through supper until he covered them at bedtime. But it was Chip, the brilliantly yellow one, that on occasion would trill the vibrato of the jungle, of his ancestral past, in the black dank of the coal mine.

"Let's get out before the wall caves in, which sounds like anytime."

"Where we going?"

"I don't know. Does it matter?"

But we did know where and it did matter. Dana drove, sagebrush and sandstone blurring past and clouds appearing on the horizon. We headed west between the base of Rimrock and the banks of the Colorado, finally turning off gravel onto a sandy jeep road and winding around rocky ledges up a bluff to our usual spot overlooking the sweep of high desert known as Rabbit Valley.

"Look. The truck's right where it was."

"Why not just back it into the living room?" Dana shook her head.

We got out and sat on the hood. Over Rimrock Park, thunderheads were gathering, lightning illuminating their dark underbellies and lighting up canyons.

"When he first moved out, I couldn't imagine why he wanted to live out here. Now I think it's just about the most beautiful place I've ever seen." Dana drew her knees up, hugging them. "How does that happen?"

"I don't know. Lenny says it depends on who's doing the looking."

A warm wind washed over us. Dana closed her eyes and inhaled, taking in the moist desert scent of approaching rain. Down below in the middle of Rabbit Valley our father's short-wave antenna wobbled and the tarp over his truck bed rippled.

"That's where he put Redd's tanks. Under that tarp."

"It's so hard to believe."

"I saw them."

"I know, but it just doesn't sound like him. Calling the radio station, that rock, and now stealing. How can somebody change so much?"

"He does it because he still loves Mom, Dana. And Dr. McClellan said part of it could be chemical."

"How do you know?"

"Julie told me. She heard him on the telephone with Mom after the accident. He said that trauma can change things with your personality and stuff."

"Like we didn't already know that." Dana rested her chin over her knees, staring at the trailer far below. "I meant how do you know he still loves Mom?"

"I just do, that's how." I glared. "Why else would he be pulling this stuff? He wants Redd gone as much as we do. Probably more."

She turned away and gazed across the valley at the misty sheets of rain now falling in the canyons, streaking the sandstone, making it glisten. "Maybe so. But it just doesn't seem like him."

And it didn't. Our father had been a quiet man who, when away from the mines, wore creased pants, starched white shirts buttoned to the top with T-shirts underneath, and suspenders. He slapped Old Spice on his hollow cheeks, parted his short hair high on one side, and rolled mints or lemon drops in his mouth that clicked against molars when he spoke. His fingernails were always manicured and clean of grit and when he stepped from the bathroom and a shower, bits of toilet paper were often stuck to his sharp jaw line or under his chin. He had about him a kind of scrubbed dignity. Only his eyes gave away his profession, rimmed with coal dust like mascara.

He and Mom rarely socialized, and I knew of only one time that fellow miners visited our home. There were two and they arrived as officers of the local UMWA to ask for support in an upcoming election. One rotated a hat between his knees, and I knew by the way they sat on the edge of their seats that they respected him. He listened politely, never offering them a drink or an opportunity for small talk. When they finished their spiel, he thanked them and showed them to the door just as Mom appeared from the kitchen with cookies and tall glasses of iced tea on a platter. As she stood awkwardly behind him, he told them he would think over what they had said. The men nodded affably, over-thanking Mom for she didn't know what, and left. Later was the first time Dana and I had heard harsh words between them. But not the last.

It was mid-afternoon on a Friday, payday, when the phone rang. Dana was home early from school and said she was alarmed by how Mom clutched the receiver then limply let it drop into its cradle without saying anything more than hello. There had been an accident. By the time I got home nobody was there. Not even a note. Around ten-fifteen our neighbor Mr. Shimizu arrived, rapping his knuckles against the back screen like a bird pecking a knothole. He said he heard it on the news and was sorry and would do anything he could to help. When I asked what he was talking about, he told me. Dana pulled up into the driveway—she had just gotten her license—and the headlights hit Mr. Shimizu full on the face. I had the crazy impulse to laugh because I was reminded of a joke Dad told about Japanese during the war not having to squint when the bombs fell. It was the only joke he knew. I felt giddy as Dana rushed into the house. I followed her into our parents' bedroom where she pulled out all the dresser drawers like people do in movies when they're trying to find something important or valuable. Stuffing clothes into a paper sack, she raced back to the car. With me sitting dumbly next to her, she squealed the tires in reverse out the driveway—Mr. Shimizu standing in the same spot at our screen door—and drove the twenty minutes back to the mine. A week later, when Dad was safe and out of harm's way and we thought everything was almost normal, we laughed about what she had packed in the paper sack: a pajama top, three pairs of socks, two unmatching shoes—both rights—and a pair of Mom's burnt-orange slacks.

It had taken two days to reach Dad and the three other men. Two days buried to his waist in shale and coal. Beamer and Chip survived, too, their cage saved by the lee of a nearby piece of heavy machinery. But the three other miners weren't as lucky.

When his cracked ribs finally knit, pinned hip healed, and it was time for him to return to work, Dad didn't budge. He lay on the couch in the darkened living room and stared at the television, doing nothing but grow whiskers. Shortly after is when the arguing started, quietly at first with Mom's hoarse beseeching whisper going unanswered as Dana and I sat listening from the kitchen table. Her voice seemed to grow louder with each passing day until, weeks later, there were full-blown screaming and crying and accusations about things unrelated to injury or work or lying around all day. Dad barely defended himself, which made Mom yell louder. Something deeper than bone had been crushed inside him, something inconsolable, and it eventually crushed Mom, too. Then they stopped talking altogether.

Three-and-a-half months later our father loaded up his truck. He hung his pressed pants and shirts from the hook behind the seat, placed Beamer and Chip's covered cage on the seat next to him, started the truck and drove away. We didn't hear anything for almost eight months. A change-of-address notice from the post office finally told us where he lived, and Dana and I had been visiting him ever since. Or, as Mr. VanHorn would have put it, figuratively visiting him.

"He's just out here to collect his thoughts, that's all. He's just sortin' things out for a while before he makes his move."

"Henry, it's been over a year and a half."

"No way."

"It was one year last November."

"It was?" But I knew it was; it was the same month Dana dropped out her senior year, eloped with Jeff Bruner, and began waiting for reappearances—Dad from inside his *Airstream* and Jeff from Vietnam.

"I have my own theory about him." Rolling her head sideways, she looked at me. "I think he moved out here because it's so wide open."

"So wide open?"

"This is the farthest he could get from a hole without leaving his dinosaurs."

I gawked at her. "Yeahhh—" I looked back at the trailer. The storm was rolling across the desert toward us, lashing sagebrush and kicking up dirt devils. "That's the smartest thing you've ever said."

She smiled. "Second smartest. We're gonna get soaked."

And we did.

9

*T*here you have it, ladies and gentlemen. Colonel Harlan Sanders kidnapped from Kentucky Fried Chicken. So come on in, fill out an entry blank, and tell us when you think the Colonel'll be safely returned and win a whole free month's worth of finger-lickin' good chicken. And remember, through the weekend, three pieces of chicken cooked in the Colonel's own special recipe, coleslaw, roll, and a nice cold drink, all for just two ninety-nine. And a special thanks to the manager of Kentucky Fried, Mr. Kevin Larston. Thanks for being with us, Kevin."

"Uh, thank you, Robert."

"And best of luck rescuing the Colonel from those sinister forces out there. Heh-heh-heh."

"Heh-heh. Thank you."

Greg reached over and clicked the stereo radio off. "Heh, heh. Thank you." He bucked his teeth and crossed his eyes. "No, thank you. No—heh, heh, heh— thank you. No, please—heh, heh—thank you."

I looked at Julie and shrugged. "So what happened to the interview?"

Julie laughed. "I think Kevy's a little shrewder than we thought. Huh, Greg?"

He got up from the bed, walked over to the Colonel, grabbed the ends of the scarf, and began tugging.

"Hey, it's not his fault."

He stopped, unwrapped the scarf, and snatched the stocking cap off the statue's head. "You're right, Hank. It's not his fault." He unhooked the hanger from the closet door and pulled off the dry cleaner's plastic. "He's just a symbol, a figurehead if you will, for old white elitist men who get their jollies slaughtering chickens to prey on the starving masses."

"Here! Here! Death to the capitalist pigs!" Julie glanced at me then smirked. "You sound like a Marxist."

"I am." He drew up the gown and slipped it over the Colonel's head. Smoothing it out, he grabbed the mortarboard. "Say the magic word and a chicken drops down."

"So are you going to call him back or what?"

He wagged his eyebrows. "Bet your life." Placing the cap on the Colonel's head, he cocked it slightly to one side. "After all, we've got to make this contest as interesting as possible for the listening public." He draped the tassel across the cap.

"If I only had a braaain—" Julie got up from the couch.

Greg turned around, smiling. "And what would the Colonel say if he had a brain, Jules?"

"What makes you think I was referring to the Colonel?" She grabbed her purse.

"Ohhh, *Ni zi wo*. You slay me."

"And *Ni ye zi wo*. You slay me, too."

"Whoa! She does know more Mandarin than just the filthy word for male genitalia!"

"Dickhead's kind of a universal, isn't it? I'd recognize it in any language." She walked to the door. "I've got to go get ready. See you young Bolsheviks at the revolution."

Greg watched her leave then stared at me. "What the hell did I do this time?"

I shrugged.

He shook his head and turned to the Colonel, chuckling. "You gotta love her."

"I've got to get ready, too, Greg. It's almost one."

He took the tassel in his hand. "May I present to you—the very honorable, the very white, the very plastic yet somehow personable—a close friend of mine—Colonel Major General You-buy-it-we'll-fry-it . . . Harrrlannn . . . Sannnderrrs!" He flipped the tassel across to the other side. "Congratulations, Major Colonel General, you're now the proud owner of a state-certified one-of-a-kind shimmering gray glob of brain. Unless, of course, we decide to recall it, an option we may exercise anytime at our own discretion." Greg saluted. "Carry on, soldier."

"Are you gonna call them back?"

"Soon, my friend, soon. But first, first—" He fell to one knee, hand against forehead. "I can't take it anymore, I just can't—Lord knows I've tried, but—" Standing, he slid a long arm around the Colonel's waist, thrust out his hand, and threw back his head.

"Oh, no." I flopped back on the couch. "Not again."

He pointed his foot. "Music, Maestro!"

◇◇◇

There was a price to pay for being the first eighteen-year-olds in history to gain the right to vote. A price exacted at the hands of school administrators, who thought it important that we dive straightway into the waters of adulthood and immediately immerse ourselves in the tricky currents of public policy. With the upcoming election, there were serious issues to ponder and now the class of 1972 was a voting block, solidly seated one last time in the sweltering school gymnasium, girls in yellow satin caps and gowns, boys in maroon.

The keynote speaker, proudly introduced by vice-principal Guerrie, was Dr. Francis Aruba, the state superintendent of schools, who that morning had driven the two-hundred-and-fifty miles over the mountains from Denver to steer us, our families, and friends on which direction to turn concerning twelve amendments to the state constitution. For an hour and a half the doctor harangued us on the virtues of a public consumer counsel (Number 10), the pitfalls of compulsory partial no-fault insurance (Number 11), and the merit of replacing property taxes with school financing (Number 12). With each summarized amendment, coughs grew louder, fidgeting multiplied, and fluttering programs quickened as more hot air filled the gymnasium. After one last pitch for why the Winter Olympics should be held in Colorado, Dr. Aruba mercifully sat down to a standing ovation from the dais, led by Mr. Guerrie who beamed as though this were the most inspirational send-off imaginable.

Next, before the handing out of academic awards and diplomas, it was the class co-valedictorians' turn. Margaret Kohler rose from the chair next to me and approached the podium with Greg Woods, who appeared by virtue of the first letter of his last name from the back. Margaret, in an uncharacteristically quavering voice, recited two pages of achievements—a kind of handwritten highlight film—starting with a second place finish in the state spelling bee in fourth grade, winding through a maze of science fair and 4-H victories, and ending with this "unbelievable honor of class valedictorian" (she omitted the "co-"). Smoothing pages against the lectern, she then spoke from her heart, telling us we could do anything "we set our minds to" and thanking us for being "such a wonderful class to have led." This last statement drew a smattering of laughter not only for its content—which was funny enough—but also because Greg, stepping forward for his own turn at the podium, deftly graced the back of her head with a pair of rabbit ears. When Margaret, sensing his "typically immature high jinks" (as she would later characterize them), whipped around to glare at him, he quickly turned the rabbit into a peace sign, thrusting the two fingers out to his classmates. Margaret, wanting to remove herself as far from him as possible, returned to her seat, where I coughed out a "khhh" and rolled my eyes, something I'd been waiting to do for twelve years.

Greg, both peace signs now extended overhead, pivoted left and right, alternating between his best Richard Nixon and Ed Sullivan impressions. After the laughter subsided, he thanked Dr. Aruba for his inspiring words that "we'll surely carry with us the rest of our days." The superintendent smiled tightly and re-crossed his legs, no doubt weighing in his mind the possibility of irony and being made the butt of something. Greg removed a folded paper from inside his robe and began thanking every teacher he'd ever known—school nurses, janitors, and cafeteria workers included—until good-natured heckling stopped him about fifth grade. Intoning us to settle down, he observed that "decorum dictates that I be serious for one heartfelt moment." He then proceeded to thank that one special person in his academic life, that one educator who had made a profound difference, the one he considered his mentor, model, and, above all, friend—Vice Principal Clarence Guerrie. As we roared our approval and the audience unwittingly applauded, Greg turned and clasped Mr. Guerrie's hand one last time, pulled him to his feet, and raised his arm with his own as though they were victorious running mates at a political convention. Red-faced as ever, Mr. Guerrie sank back down into his chair and tried an uncomfortable smile at Dr. Aruba, who by now had fully caught on to the tenor of the proceedings.

Greg returned to the podium and removed his mortarboard, taking from its band a roll of rice paper tied with ribbon. Unfurling it with the flourish of a town crier, he remarked that he could only hope that his words would carry "a fraction of the resonance and inspiration" that Margaret's and Dr. Aruba's had. He began to read. The Grand River High School class of 1972 exploded with pent-up glee as he delivered a two-minute speech, the meaning of which we could only imagine. Finally, as his familiar singsong gibberish and the resulting pandemonium died down, Greg Woods—co-valedictorian—announced that the written English translation of the speech would be available later in the day at his house and that everyone was invited. He ended his career with two words— Morrison lives!—whereupon he returned to his seat, having regaled the audience (we read later) with something beginning like this:

"*Wode Tongzhi: Jintian wo feichang gaoxin yinwei women yiqi keyi likai jige shiqi. Shiernian women tingyiting jige pangtou, jige hulihudu. Xianzai women keyi gaosu tamen zaijian he chi womende qide pigu. . . ."*

("My comrades: Today I'm extremely happy because we together can finally leave this shit hole. For twelve years we listened to these fatheads, these incoherent people. Now we can finally tell them to kiss our collective asses good-bye. . . .")

The rest of the ceremony was marked by Julie winning one of four scholarships from Grand River Elks Lodge 575 for academic and civic excellence, Greg formally and publicly accepting his appointment to the Air Force Academy, Cisco receiving a standing ovation from a small army of relatives seated along the bottom of the bleachers, Dillard being so stoned that he took the diploma with his right hand and shook Mr. Guerrie's thumb-to-thumb with his left, Lenny missing the ceremony altogether (the only class member to do so), and me whispering "Junior" as I accepted my diploma from Mr. Guerrie who had forgotten the last part of my name (it was also omitted from my diploma).

Afterward, everyone gathered on the high school front lawn for pictures. Dr. McClellan clicked the three of us arm-in-arm, as did Dana using her Kodak Instamatic, while Mom stood nervously behind, smoking and dabbing her eyes with a tissue.

She walked over and hugged me. "We're so proud of you, honey."

"Thanks, Mom."

"Way to go, squirt." Dana kissed me on the cheek. "Hey, Greg. Nice speech. I was very touched."

He nodded, tapping finger against temple.

"Emotionally touched, smart-ass." She hugged him.

"Dana, don't talk that way." Mom hooked her arm through Greg's and gave it a squeeze. She had known him as long as I had, since Greg and I were five and she taught our Sunday school class. Over the years it was Mom who had picked him up for school activities and driven him home afterwards. "Do you really speak Chinese, Greg, or have you been fooling us all these years?"

He put his arm around her and smiled. "Both."

Dana snapped their picture. "Can you cook Chinese, too?"

"With the right spices, but I prefer Pakistanis. They're meatier."

"What?" Dana shook her head. "You *are* whacked."

"So I keep hearing."

"Anyway, the reason I ask, I'm a vegetarian now—"

"At least this week she is."

Dana punched me. "—and I'm thinking about taking a cooking class over at the college."

"Come over sometime. Mother's a killer with that sort of thing. She can show you."

"Where is your mom, anyway?"

"Tennis tournament." Greg smiled. "Mixed doubles, I believe. Semi's. Very important stuff." He craned his neck. "Hey, Jules. Take a look at that."

Under the marquee, Vice Principal Guerrie, Dr. Aruba, and school board members were lining up for group pictures taken by a photographer from the *Grand River Sentinel*.

"Daddy, give me that. I need this for posterity." Julie grabbed the camera and hurried over, two of her little brothers trailing behind.

Greg laughed. "Such a sentimentalist. Mrs. McClellan, aren't you going to join the photo op?"

"No, thanks, Greg. I'm afraid my tenure has almost run its course. I'm just going to low-key it for now and count the days to November." She switched Bubby from one arm to the other and held out her hand. "Congratulations. That was quite the entertaining speech. At least, I think it was. And congratulations to you, Henry Kessler, Jr."

"Thanks, Mrs. McClellan."

"Way to go, guys." Dr. McClellan shook our hands. "My goodness, Julie's really enamored of that group. How many pictures is she going to take?"

Julie was backing up on the lawn with a growing number of photographers, adjusting the lens at the beaming group under the marquee.

"What now, Kessler?"

I turned around to Sam and Molly VanHorn. "Hi, Mr. V. Hey, thanks for the A."

"Don't thank me. You earned it." He clapped me on the back. "What're you going to do now? Hold up gas stations?"

"Probably."

"Where's Bartelli?"

"I don't know. He didn't show up."

"So I noticed."

"Did you hear what happened yesterday at practice?"

He nodded. "Right from the horse's patooty. Hicks called last night just to tell me he kicked Lenny off the team."

"What team? We graduated."

"Precisely what I said. The guy's a nut." He shook his head. "Well, if you see Lenny, tell him I have his diploma." He tapped it against his palm. "Guerrie didn't want to give it to me, so I had to break his arm."

I grinned.

"Hey, Woods." Mr. VanHorn walked over to Greg. "What the hell are we going to talk about around here now that you're finally out of our hair?"

Greg shrugged and looked at the grass. "Education?"

Mr. VanHorn grabbed the back of his neck, squeezed him then let go. "You haven't seen Lenny, have you?"

"No. He's probably under his Jeep somewhere."

"Hmm." Mr. V shook his head, looking around, hands on hips. "What in the name of Nyx is going on over there?"

We looked over at the large semi-circle of people with cameras glued to their faces.

Greg leaned into Mr. VanHorn, pointing. "Wonder what their asking price is?"

"What?" Shielding his eyes with the diploma, Mr. VanHorn looked up.

Greg grabbed my arm. "Hank, I've got to go home and help get ready for the party."

"That'd be a first."

"See you around five. 'Bye, Mrs. Kessler."

He jogged across the grass toward the parking lot just as Mr. V's baritone belly-laugh broke across the lawn after him. Mr. VanHorn pointed. Shading our eyes, we turned and followed his gaze above the smiling dignitaries.

Mr. VanHorn looked over his shoulder and watched Greg pull from the lot and accelerate down seventh in his graduation present. "What do you do with a guy like that?" He shook his head before turning back to join the laughter. We must have been the last group to notice the final message atop the Grand River High School marquee, the last group except the one posing happily and obliviously underneath:

FOR SALE
PRICE NEGOT.

◇◇◇

"Wonder who unlocked her cage?"

I shrugged as Julie shifted the VW into neutral and popped Joni Mitchell from the tape deck.

Mrs. Bartelli didn't look up, clad in bobby pins and housecoat, pointing the garden hose at her flower box under the front window. A mist of spray carried by the breeze glistened across a swatch of grass, casting a rainbow behind her.

"Is that Vince?" I looked back as the car coasted to the curb a few houses down the block. I got out and with eyes trained on Mrs. Bartelli, edged along the sidewalk then up the driveway. Under the carport, kneeling and poking through boxes, was Lenny's brother. His girlfriend leaned against the house watching him.

"Hi, Vince."

He glanced up. "Hey, what's up, man?" He picked out a sock and threw it onto a pile of clothes to the side. Behind him in front of the storage doors spanned a Ping-Pong table, splayed under the weight of Mrs. Bartelli's domestic wars: an upturned ironing board with legs scissored open, a sewing machine inside a rain-crinkled cardboard box, a cracked and faded kiddie pool piled with metal fence posts, milk baskets full of extension cords and garden tools, and a sheet of plywood with an outline of the United States drawn in Magic Marker and six-penny finish nails driven in for state capitals. Kite string was strung between the cities with mileage printed underneath, and a seatless unicycle hung overhead, like the moon, from its silver rim.

"Have you seen Lenny?"

He shook his head, shoving the box away and pulling a grocery sack over. "Sheila, look at this." He took a T-shirt and held it up.

"So?"

"We got it at the Grand Canyon last year. Remember?"

"No, we didn't."

"Yeah, we did. Look." He held it higher.

Sheila, arms folded in front, studied her toes, wiggled them. Vince tossed the shirt on the pile and picked up another box.

I coughed. "Lenny wasn't at graduation."

Balancing the box across his thigh, he began rummaging through its contents. I looked back for Julie who had slipped out of the car and was hurrying up the driveway, glancing over her shoulder.

"Hi, Vincent."

He looked up. "I thought it was you. Who else calls me that?"

"Where's your brother?"

"What is this, an interrogation?"

"Lenny didn't show up—"

"—for graduation. So I hear." He straightened up and threw a shirt at Sheila, hitting her across the face.

"Don't!"

"See if it fits."

Lips pouty, she gazed at us from under low, black bangs and began fingering the red flannel. Vince walked out from the carport wiping his hands on the seat of patched bellbottoms and flicking his stringy hair to one side. In the sunlight, you could see faint acne scars across his cheeks and the fledgling hairs of a mustache. Only his eyes resembled Lenny's, dark and sleepy yet somehow intense. "Look, man. Lenny's been outa here a couple of days. I just came over to check things out."

Julie glanced at me. "What do you mean?"

He looked down, wiping his mouth with the back of one forearm. "The old lady did the same thing to me."

"What?"

"Kicked me out. Changed the locks and everything. But at least with me she waited 'til after graduation."

Julie and I stared at each other. She ran both hands through her hair. "Wait a minute. You mean he's—"

"Gone, man. Split. In this fun family that's the deal. Out of school, out of luck."

I looked at the boxes under the carport. "So this is all his?"

"Most of it."

Julie glowered. "Unless you get to it first. Right?"

"Hey, least if he wants anything he knows where to come. My stuff went straight to the alley and the city garbage collectors. There's a guy that's still wearing my coat—three years later. Besides, lots of this stuff used to be mine anyway."

Sheila had slipped the shirt over her halter-top and was tying it into a knot across her bare midriff. "What do ya think, Goob?"

"Far-out. Lookin' good, baby." Vince turned back to the carport and began pushing boxes around the oil-stained concrete. "Help me with this stuff, will ya?"

"Tuh." Sheila gawked at him.

"Come on, Sheila. Quit being a psycho. I'll take you to Arctic Circle later."

"So where is he?" I looked at Sheila then back to Vince, who began stuffing clothes from the pile into a plastic bag.

"Beats me, man. Hey, Sheila, look. You need a brush?"

"Come on, Hank. Let's leave these vultures to their—"

"'For the Lord abhors the bloody and deceitful man!'" At the corner of the house stood Mrs. Bartelli, her garden hose hissing like a serpent; the nozzle was turned off but leaking from all the pressure.

"Hi, Mrs. Bartelli." I stepped forward. "We're just looking for Lenny. You know where he is?"

"Ezekiel sixteen, thirty-five!" She raised her eyebrows and squinted as though this should mean something to us. "'Wherefore, O harlot, hear the word of the Lord!'"

I looked back at Julie who stood frozen as Mrs. Bartelli yanked at the hose, stretching it around the house. Stepping by her, I began backing down the driveway.

Julie licked her lips. "Hi, Mrs. Bartelli. We were just trying to find Lenny because we were worried, you know, 'cause he wasn't at graduation so—"

Bobby-pinned head fixed straight ahead, she struggled up the driveway with the hose as though leaning into a strong wind.

"—so we, you know, thought he might be, um, maybe he was still here doing something . . ."

Hands raised in front, Julie backed up as Mrs. Bartelli staggered forward. The hose was now looped over one shoulder, sopping the sleeve of her housecoat.

"Anyway, tell him to call us, okay? I mean if you . . . you know . . . see him or anything."

The hose abruptly reached full length, pulling Mrs. Bartelli upright. "'Our righteous acts are like filthy rags—'" Cheeks puffing in and out, she raised the hose in front of her. "'—we all shrivel up like a leaf.'"

Julie moved to the side, eyelashes fluttering and hands shielding her face.

"Isaiah sixty-four, six!"

"Come on, Mom—" Vince dropped the box just as his mother twisted the nozzle, water blasting from the hose in a straight line, parting the red flannel target still standing against the house. "Mom! No!"

Julie and I ran down the street and jumped into the Volkswagen.

"She's insane!" I looked back as Julie, giggling wildly, fumbled with the keys. Vince was getting it now, too, he and his girlfriend crossing their arms hopelessly in front of their faces, hosed down the driveway and into the street like a couple of fallen, if not exactly shriveled leaves.

10

*G*raduation day had been empty with what Lenny would call negative space. He said in art, whether painting or sculpture, the space an object fills is only one of two forms, the other being the inverse shape around it. If we were all cutouts, like gingerbread men, the contours of leftover dough would represent negative space. In English class Mr. VanHorn said "we're just a shape to fill a lack," quoting *As I Lay Dying*. I guess this lack is what Lenny was trying to describe, the shape of emptiness. All I know is, whatever it was—or wasn't—graduation brimmed with it.

Take Dad. He was a cutout in the gymnasium bleachers. I could almost see him sitting between Mom and Dana or appearing in the same doorway Lenny disappeared through at wrestling practice, standing there as my name was announced, as I walked up to the podium to receive my diploma. "Junior" I had whispered to Mr. Guerrie, half-irritated. But the vice-principal didn't know what I was talking about, or even my name for that matter. He probably thought I was part of another Greg Woods prank, that I was actually a junior posing as a senior.

But I had grown up a Jr. Dad jigsawed the letters out of a scrap of one-by-six pine, sanded the edges smooth, and mounted them on the wall behind my crib the day I was brought home from the hospital. Mom painted the *J* in red enamel, the *r* in blue, and the period black. When I moved at five to the unfinished concrete bedroom downstairs, the letters followed me, re-glued to the outside of the door. My family called me Jr. all through grade school, junior high, and into my sophomore year. The day after Dad moved out, Mom called me Henry for the first time, though I wasn't sure if it was a slip or if she really meant to. That's when I knew Dad wasn't coming back. I pried the letters off with a screwdriver, but sunlight and dust left the image stamped there like a photograph's negative.

For years I was embarrassed by my abbreviation and would allow only family members to call me by it. If friends were over, I would ignore it and not answer if I could. I didn't want to be a Jr. It sounded too much like Sonny or Sonny-boy or Buddy. It was subordinate, less than, a subtraction if not an outright negation. At the very least a replica of the bigger, better model. I wanted to be somebody else. Jake or Cal or Gil, like the trail boss on *Rawhide*. Gil Fever. Even Rowdy or Wishbone was better than Jr. But then, along with my father, the abbreviation disappeared. It was as though he had taken it with him. I had become Henry through subtraction, without even understanding the equation. I was Henry because I wasn't anything else. Even Dana stopped calling me Jr. but couldn't bring herself to call me by our father's name. So like my classmates she resorted to Hank. Then, oddly, I began to like the whole of my name, even to long for it. I would spend entire afternoons practicing my signature in elaborate script with sweeping H's, high-kicking K's, and looping Jr's that flipped back on themselves. Sometimes I made the period a circle or a heavy dot that looked as though it might suck the preceding letters in after it like those places in space that Julie's father talked about—black holes. Places squeezed to infinite density. Places where stars go to die and not even light can escape. Henry Kessler Jr—period. But now it didn't matter; the original Henry Kessler wasn't there anyway.

And neither was Lenny. He was a cutout in the first row with the A's and B's, his chair so conspicuously empty that Mr. Guerrie, not missing a beat, didn't even announce his name. I relished the thought of Mr. VanHorn throwing his meaty forearm around Guerrie's throat, wresting Lenny's diploma from him. Or squeezing him until he coughed it up, like a cat expelling a hairball. Lenny wasn't atop The Three Sisters, either, or at the Black Bridge where he liked to hang out and draw or jump into that quiet section of river above the junction. Nor was he filling space at Sam and Molly VanHorn's or at Sherwood Park. Julie and I checked. In fact, Julie bravely drove by Mrs. Bartelli's a second time just to make sure he hadn't returned. The driveway had almost dried and the vacant lot was just that—vacant. Not even Louie's dog skillet was there, serving notice in a negative space sort of way that Lenny really was gone. Julie couldn't resist honking as we drove by, cupping and jostling her breasts, gleefully shouting "How dost thine wrinkled harlot look, Goob!?! Ezekiel sixteen! Verse thirty-five!" As usual, she looked great.

We heard from Dillard that Greg's party was a rager (his word) with almost every class member there but the three you would most expect—Lenny, Julie, and me. Even Greg himself disappeared barely an hour into the evening. After holding court in his bedroom (the Colonel standing incognito at the door dressed in mortarboard, sunglasses, blackened-in goatee, and one of Greg's many silk, hand-painted Hawaiian shirts), he left abruptly with his mother for St.

Matthew's Hospital. Uncle Phil had been downgraded and placed on a ventilator, confirming what we suspected all along. Greg's uncle was dying. Greg hadn't acknowledged he was even in town. But the three of us already sensed it, even before Miss Darling said anything. His father stayed at the party though and, according to Dill, was the perfect chaperon. He hunkered down in his leather chair, beer and television serving to drown out the din blasting from every room of the house, spilling from the swimming pool and the fringe of the tenth fairway in back, and echoing from the circular driveway and cul-de-sac in front. Dill said cars stretched around the corner and the party didn't thin until three kegs later, around one in the morning. A rager.

As for Julie and me, we meant to go to Greg's but ended up at her house instead, where Mrs. McClellan served peach cobbler and homemade ice cream and Dr. McClellan presented her with two gifts: a telescope and an eight-foot, bamboo fly rod that had belonged to her grandfather. The telescope brought tears but the fly rod broke her in two. Little brother Darin didn't understand the emotion and kept asking his mother why big sister didn't like her presents. By the time all brothers trickled off to bed, it was almost eleven and she and Rog had hatched early-morning plans for Pheasant Tail Nymph and *Salmo gairdneri*, kicking off a summer's worth of fishing—for trout with her father, for votes with McGovern. She offered to drop me by Greg's or take me home, but it was only about a mile to either place so I decided to walk, though I wasn't sure in which direction.

Grand River High was a block away, its dark windows and tepeed trees lending it a haunted quality. White toilet paper draped the evergreen branches like gossamer as I walked up the sidewalk to the auditorium steps. The sign atop the marquee was blank now and the wire cover in place, although slightly bent; Greg had needed a crowbar to remove it. I circled around to the back, looking in windows but not seeing much, then cupped my hands to the glass of the band room door. Light from the parking lot lamppost shone through an open window on the far side of the room, falling across orchestra chairs and sheet music. Julie had been second-chair flutist to Margaret Kohler (who insisted on being called a "flautist", prompting Greg to respond "flatus" since, he said, Margaret herself was the perfect personification of a wind instrument), so I sometimes hung out there to listen to her practice. I rounded the corner and, glancing around, pushed the window open, hopped up stomach-to-sill, and wiggled inside. As my feet followed my hands to the cool tile floor, one of them struck a music stand, sending it crashing against the heat register. Stumbling around and over chairs and stands to the far door, I finally pushed out into the hallway.

A muted glow splashed the waxed floor, washed the silver locker handles in a tarnished shine. Padlocks had been removed, so I opened a locker to the lingering scent of leather-bound textbooks, notebook paper, pencil shavings, eraser crumbs. A half-peeled sticker of Mr. Natural plastered the inside of the door, the toe of his oversized shoe and a wisp of beard kicking up over the locker vent. *Truckin'* remained, but *Keep on* was torn away like a label from a beer bottle. Julie said if you could peel a Coors label without it tearing, you were a virgin. Of course, this she said while shamelessly shredding away, as though torn labels alone might relieve her from the burden of virginity. I, on the other hand, peeled without fail and, digging my thumbnail under a corner, tore the rest of Mr. Natural away.

Clicking the door shut, the sound disappearing as sharply as a BB down a drainage pipe, I stood in the empty hallway. Now what? What would Greg do? What outlandish farewell could I leave, stamping my existence in the school with an exclamation—or at least a period?

"Whooo!"

My voice echoed down the hallway and around a corner so I followed it, glancing in classrooms, running my hand down the smooth metal lockers, the varnished brick walls. Using the handrails, I vaulted upstairs to the second floor and entered Mr. VanHorn's room. A papier-mâché model of a medieval castle sat on the desk and his squeaky roller chair remained next to the sill in back. The window overlooked the dirt parking lot, the tennis courts and track, and in the distance, the baseball and football practice fields. I could almost see Mr. V standing there, resting his size fifteen wingtip on the chair, elbows crossed on one knee, reciting his favorite passages from Faulkner or Steinbeck while gazing down at cars and P.E. students or tracing the row of poplars that lined the alleyway behind the school.

"'. . . no battle is ever won . . . not even fought. . . . The field only reveals to man his own folly and despair, and victory is an illusion of philosophers and fools.'"

Removing my shoe from the chair and turning from the window, I gazed across the desktops at the freshly washed blackboard striped with street light filtering through the Venetian blinds, the metal cabinet where Mr. VanHorn stored teaching props and school supplies, a map of Europe during the Renaissance, and the cork bulletin board tacked with pictures of his favorite writers: Faulkner, Steinbeck, McCullers, O'Neill, O'Connor. I walked up the aisle to the front and stood at the podium. "Good evening, fellow students. It is indeed my pleasure to share with you my thoughts on this important writer and his work." I turned to the blackboard. "Miss Kohler, would you please fetch me some chalk." Unable to find any, I wet my index finger and moved it across the slate.

Standing back, staring through the twilight of the empty classroom, I couldn't quite make it out against the clean surface, couldn't quite discern whether what I wrote was there or not. Bending down and squinting, I realized it had evaporated, if my name had been there at all. Appropriate, I thought, leaving high school as I lived it. Then I heard the crash.

I rushed from the classroom down the hallway, hesitating at the top of the stairs. Voices, scuffs, and laughter reverberated from the first floor. I crept down and peeked around the corner—nothing—then jogged along the lockers toward the band room. At each hallway intersection, at each open doorway, I slowed, glancing left and right through the darkened high school. Why had I ever come back here? What had possessed me, after twelve years struggling to escape, to break back in? Like a ghost fleeing to make the shadow of me tangible, I only wanted out. Then I froze, my mind crystallizing with fear that, yes, there are others: five silhouetted heads bobbing shoulder-to-shoulder down the hallway. I held my breath, shrinking against the wall, against the sudden longing to be invisible. Can shadows—ghosts—see each other? I closed my eyes, listened to shoes click against tile, grow fainter, then a door open. I waited, straining to hear more. Silence, then a whistle shrilled, startling me, followed by shouts and grunts echoing through the halls. Blood singing in my ears, I turned and saw a blade of light fall across the floor at the end of the corridor. Steeling myself, I tiptoed toward it, the sounds growing more familiar, the smells stronger, until finally I was there.

I peered through the cracked doorway. Yes, I was right. There were five, made tangible under the harsh familiar lights: Peefee Maldonado perched regally on a chair, whistle in hand; Kenny Madrid, Manuel Garcia, and Silver Renteria in T-shirts, dark pants, and white socks—their black shoes piled to the side—and Cisco Salazar, fully uniformed, fully visible, grappling one after another across the pungent wrestling-room mat.

◇◇◇

"Here he is!" Mom got up from Redd Morgan's lap, hopped and giggled as he pinched her. "We've been waitin' for you!" Setting a can down and balancing her cigarette across it, she turned and faced the kitchen table, raising her arms like a conductor. "One . . . two . . . three. Haaappy birrrth—"

Arlene waved both hands as everyone laughed. "No, no!" She squinted through the smoke leaking out her mouth and took a quick swig of beer. "Forrr—"

"—heee's a jolly good fellow! For he's a jolly good fellow! For he's a jolly good fellooow . . . and nobody can denyyy!"

"Hurrah!" Mom turned and clapped, facing me.

"Nobody can deny! For nobody can deny! For he's a jolly good fel-lowww—"

"—and here's a spit in your eye!" Redd Morgan raised his can—more laughter—then chugged it, slamming it to the table and wiping his mouth on his sleeve.

Dana walked in from the living room. "Congratulations, Hank." She handed me an oversized manila envelope made lumpy with something. "It's not much but I thought you'd like it."

Mom stood wavering in the middle of the kitchen, studying me. Her hands were still now but remained together at her lips as though in prayer. I pinched the metal clip and worked a finger under the seal.

Dana kissed my cheek and whispered. "This party really was 'sposed to be for you."

"Thanks." Opening the envelope I stepped under the kitchen light. Cans and glasses lined the counter and a package of potato chips lay among them, ripped wide with crumbs trailing out. I pulled out a piece of wood—black walnut polished smooth on one side—and turned it over.

Mom reached out and lifted my chin with the tips of her fingers. "My little Henry." Her bleary eyes welled.

"Not little anymore, by god." Redd Morgan popped a Coors and loudly sucked foam from the top.

She hugged me. "I'm so proud of you, honey-bunny." I could smell the musty mix of perfume, smoke, hairspray, beer.

"Honey-bunny?!?" Redd Morgan snorted. "Rummy-dummy's more like it."

"Shut up, Redd." Arlene stood. "Henry here's only one of a couple in this room who ain't rummys. And guess what, you ain't the other one." She rubbed my back and patted me. "Okay, Momma, that's enough. It's my turn. You're gonna give the boy a rash. And I'm sure there are others he'd rather get one of those from. Right, handsome?" Arlene relieved me of Mom's hug and gave me one of her own. "Whatcha got there?"

I looked down at the wood. "Pictures." Dana had singed edges of family photographs into different shapes before gluing and varnishing them into a collage. "Thanks, Dana."

"Oh, ain't that nice." Arlene ran her fingers over the smooth surface then handed it back. "Very nice. Okay, everybody, let's have some of that cake."

"You mean s'more of it." Redd cackled.

"Punk, why don't you do the honors."

Sitting in the corner with one leg scissored over the other, Punk took the spatula, lifted the plastic cover, and sliced into a half-eaten chocolate cake with butterscotch frosting and RATULATIONS NRY!!! in red script across it.

Mom plopped in a chair, snatching her cigarette and can. "'Member Leland Hewitt, honey? Redd's friend? Well, Leland and a couple fellas from the railroad dropped by but they couldn't stay. I hope you don't mind, we gave them some of your cake." She smiled, taking a pull from the can. "To be polite."

"You mean they took some—" Redd belched. "—to be not polite."

Arlene held the saucers as Punk slid pieces off the spatula. She handed them around. "Saucers for saucers."

Redd reached for Mom but she pulled away. He pushed the saucer back at Arlene, pouting. "Don't want none."

Arlene shook her head. "Did li'l Redd git hims feelers hurt?"

Punk rubbed his burred head and coughed. "So what's next, fer chrissakes? College? Work? What?" He squinted at me, wringing a napkin around his fingers. Punk didn't drink—never did, never would, he liked to say.

I shrugged holding the cake, an acolyte with a candle but no light. "Guess I'm not sure."

Redd grunted. "I am. Already got you lined out with Earl McFadden. Best backhoe man in the county." His spirits seemed to lift. "First thing tomorrow, buster. Shovel city."

"That's nice of Redd, honey, but don't you have school tomorrow?" Mom reached a hand toward me as though to touch my cheek but, failing that, let it drop, hitting the edge of my saucer. Cake splatted the linoleum, frosting first. Her gaze panned from my face to the floor, the spilled cake registering in her bloodshot eyes. "Ohhh—"

Arlene knelt with Dana to pick it up. "Slice him another one, Punk. It's startin' to feel like Sage Diner in here."

Dana straightened, cupping the cake in a napkin. She shrugged and tried a smile. "Can't have your cake and—"

I smiled back. "Can't cry over spilled—"

But Mom could. And was, face in hands, shoulders quaking.

"It's okay, Mom." I placed a hand on her back. "You didn't mean to."

"Yeah, she did." Redd staggered up. "She pulls crap like that all the damn time."

Arlene came over and put both arms around her. "Redd, if you had half a brain, you'd be twice the prick you already are."

"Look who's talkin'! Mrs. Alfred Einstein!" Redd guffawed.

"It's Albert, you big stupid—"

"Stop!"

Everyone blanched, even Mom—even Redd Morgan—gawking at Dana as she moved backward across the kitchen.

"Please—" She reached the top of the stairs, bumping into the wall, still holding the frosting-smeared napkin. "Please—just stop."

We stared as she turned at the top of the stairs then slipped out the back, the screen door barely creaking and bumping behind her.

"What the hell's wrong with her?" Redd Morgan sat back down.

"Her?" I looked around the table at their bleary faces. "What's wrong with *her*?" Then went outside to look for my sister.

11

*H*is arms looked the size of my legs, his legs my chest. As I adjusted my headgear and Coach Hicks sent me toward the center of the mat with typically sage advice—"Go git 'em!"—and a swat on the seat, I realized he was also a head shorter. A normal-size head, anyway; his was of the flat variety, a tray sitting atop a marble table. I'd had good luck with opponents like this, kids twice as strong—and mean—but completely bereft of coaching or training. From wrestling Lenny all those years I had learned that leverage beats strength, angles negate brute aggression, and hips are the fulcrum from which most effective moves begin. And all this I needed in order to chip away at the rough slab of rock extending his hand. I shook it, my own crushed suddenly to bone meal.

Coach Hicks had called the night before with the bad news: I had to win a qualifying match to enter the tournament. My weight class, one-thirty-four, was one of five that had too many in it. Since I was seeded last, sixteenth, I had to defend my position in the bracket, he said. Not that it would matter; if I won, my next match would be against the number one seed, Marcus Acker, a state runner-up from Otto whose only two losses were DQs for biting. But this was a question of honor. Like Stankey, I had won almost as many as I lost my senior year—although they were junior varsity matches—and now I had a chance to win one more. Secretly, of course, I would rather have been powdered in sugar and pegged naked across an anthill than wrestle Acker, but that's how I felt before every match.

I hated wrestling. Why I did it was as much a mystery to me as the origin of the universe was to Julie and her father. I spent hours imagining ways to get out of it without losing dignity. Sticking a finger between the metal plates of the weight-lifting machine, sucking cinnamon oil to elevate body temperature, jumping barefoot off our roof onto the cement driveway, putting a contract out on myself by insulting Peefee Maldonado and the boys—anything. Anything to be permanently removed from the spongy surface of a wrestling mat, which was exactly where I found myself—reduced to a stain the second the referee blew his whistle.

Marble-head shot across at me as though from a sling. I had heard he was a football player who, because of his stature, wanted to make the transition to wrestling. And now I was his tackling dummy, ears squeezed between biceps and forearm, all sound lost in the clamp of flesh. Arching from my toes and twisting against him, I rotated one shoulder blade off the mat. Across the horizon of the floor, through the headgear's ear piece screwed sideways over my eyes and nose, I could see Mr. Vanhorn standing in denim overalls and rubber boots—he had been irrigating his orchard that morning—hands on hips, furiously chewing gum. A smattering of spectators dotted the bleachers behind him. As I scooted in a circle, head turning in the middle like an axle, my legs a couple of bent spokes, I spotted the entire family of Marble-heads: the father's mouth cupped and working, the mother smiling wide-eyed, and their two daughters and youngest son popping from the bleachers behind them like marbles on a trampoline. I could sense their son's breathing and just when I thought he could squeeze no harder, he did. As I circled around to keep from being pinned, his cheering family disappearing from my field of vision, I caught a glimpse of the official scoreboard—fifteen seconds to go—and there underneath, Lenny. Our eyes locked. Like a mime, he pushed against air then rolled shoulders and hips the other way. Following his lead, I pushed as hard as I could, quickly pivoted the opposite direction, and was suddenly on top, turning Marble-head's headlock into my own reverse half-nelson as the buzzer sounded ending the first period.

Five to two—no back points but at least I was on the scoreboard and, surprisingly, on top for the second period. Marble-head had chosen bottom.

"Get up! Shake it off, Kessler! Let's go, mister!" Coach Hicks took each of his wrestler's matches personally, as though he himself were under siege. If he saw Lenny on the other side of the mat he didn't show it, bent forward on the foldout chair, his face its usual red. Mr. VanHorn was clapping near the officials' table, looking across the gym at the scoreboard. I wondered why he wasn't with Lenny.

The whistle chirped and I was aboard a bucking bronco. He shot every direction but down. Finally, realizing he also had the strategy of a bronco—that is, none—I wrapped a figure four around his waist and cinched it tight, waiting for him to tire, which he did a minute into the second period. The remainder I spent grinding my elbow and forearm into the back of his neck and head, trying to pry him while his father's booming voice beseeched him to get up. Turning Julie's VW over would have been easier.

When the buzzer sounded and he dragged himself up for the last period, I knew he was in trouble. Every muscle of his weight-lifter's body bulged with veins. If you offered him a hundred bucks to comb his hair he couldn't do it, that is, if he'd had any.

"Kessler!" Coach Hicks flicked his thumbs up, knowing I had to escape then take him down to knot the score and send it into overtime. The whistle sounded and I hopped up, only to be hoisted and slammed to the mat. He was still stronger than three of me and, though exhausted, seemed impossible to get away from. Again I stood and again found the mat with a heavy thwack. Up I struggled a third time and, freeing my arms, began running with his arms clamped around my chest. I tried a switch, twisting to the side, but was bulldozed out of the circle. I ran back to the center, hoping a show of energy might deplete him further. He staggered back, wrapped an arm around my waist, gripped my elbow and, at the sound of the whistle, slammed the air out of me with the tightest deep-waist ride I'd ever felt.

"Up, Kessler! Get up, mister!" Coach Hicks was off his chair on all fours, looking up at the clock. "Forty-five seconds! Let's go!"

I willed myself up, head straining skyward, barely able to breathe from the pressure around my middle. I wobbled to my feet and began running again, trying to peel his fingers from my stomach. Around the mat we went, Marble-head hanging on, his father's voice drowning out all others in the gymnasium. Just as I was about to wiggle loose, he shoved me out of bounds.

I looked up at the clock—nineteen seconds—then at Lenny. He mouthed a single word—"Kip"—rolled one shoulder, his head cocked to the side. I dropped to hands and knees, eyeing the ref. Marble-head collapsed into position and leaned his full weight across me. With the whistle he clenched, driving his shoulder into my back in anticipation of another standup. But this time I went with the pressure, curling head and shoulder inside, rolling out the back and kicking my legs out and over. The momentum threw him face-first and, as I kicked out, flipped him to his back and into another reverse half. The buzzer sounded. The referee raised two fingers, brought them down and raised two more—a reversal and predicament—six to five.

Turning to his knees, forehead and elbows resting against the mat, he extended one hand. I shook it and the referee raised my arm. As I walked off the mat Coach Hicks handed me the warm-up jacket, unsnapped my chinstrap and slid the headgear off. "Too bad you didn't wrestle like this sooner, Kessler." He popped me on the rear.

Mr. VanHorn clapped and whistled, a one-man cheering section, and raised his fist, smiling. Marble-head's father was on the mat now, bent over his son, whispering to him.

I scanned the gym for Lenny. Fumbling with the jacket, my fingers barely able to move and forearms throbbing with the pounding at my temples, I stumbled to the drinking fountain. My mouth felt stuffed with cotton. I spit.

"Way to go, Kessler." Mr. V stood behind me and slapped me on the back. I coughed, water oozing from my nose. Out on the mat Marble-head's father was lifting his son, hugging and half-dragging him to the sidelines.

"Where'd Lenny go?"

"Who?" Mr. V studied me as I straightened and wiped my mouth.

"Lenny."

He rubbed the back of his neck, glancing around. The next match had begun and Marble-head's mom, sisters, and brother were clustered around him. "Well, I don't know. Where'd you see him?"

"Right up there under the—" I looked at the clock, high on the far wall. "He was showing me what to—"

"Come on, Kessler. Grab a shower, mister! Let's go!"

Mr. V turned around. "Hi, Lawrence."

"Get a move on!" Coach Hicks ducked into the locker room.

Mr. VanHorn shook his head. "Good old Lawrence. He never turns it off, does he?" He grinned. "So you're in."

"Yeah, for about twenty-five seconds. I've got Acker first round."

"Maybe you'll get lucky and he'll bite you."

"Thanks for the encouragement."

"You'll be okay." He tousled my hair. "If you wrestle the way you did today, you might surprise some people."

"If Lenny shows up."

"Well, he better. I paid his entry fee." He clapped me on the shoulder. "I gotta get back to my trees. Molly'll have my hide. You see Lenny, tell him to call me. Okay?" He started toward the exit then turned around. "Hey, Kessler."

"Yeah."

"You all right?"

I nodded.

"You sure?"

"Yeah."

"You did a good job out there, son. See you tomorrow."

Out on the mat the action had stopped and the referee was wiping up splotches of blood with a towel. The few spectators sat quietly as both wrestlers lay on their backs getting instructions from their coaches. You could hear them gulp air while one was getting his nostril packed with cotton.

Across the gym trudged my opponent, his sisters and brother leading the way. His father's arm was draped around him and his mother clung to his side. As they reached the doorway one of them must have said something funny because the whole family suddenly laughed, the sound echoing through the gym then ringing hollow as they moved into the lobby.

I turned to go into the locker room to shower and see Coach Hicks. He was going to tell me the time for weigh-in and my next day's match with Acker. But the locker room was the last place I wanted to be. I had won. It just wasn't feeling that way.

◇◇◇

Late-morning shadows receded from the canyons of Rimrock National Park, creeping up walls, narrowing down gullies and ravines before disappearing altogether under the flat glare of noon. Across the sweep of stubbled sagebrush and cactus and desert grasses that is Rabbit Valley, Dad's trailer glinted like a shard of washed glass against the sand.

From the hood of Mom's car parked atop the bluff, still in my tights and wrestling shoes, I watched a thread of smoke rise and tail off into the pale sky. Maybe he was cooking lunch and would soon emerge from the *Airstream* and go tramping off into the arroyos or along the rocky cliffs above the river to look for gizzard stones or his beloved dinosaur bones. But I knew better. His movements had become erratic lately; we hadn't seen him outside for weeks. The only signs he was there at all were this smoke, the lights and shadows through the thin curtains at night and, most recently, the tricks he played on Redd Morgan, which were maybe reason enough to stay inside. If he couldn't make it to graduation or a wrestling match, I reasoned, why now would he risk going out for something extinct?

Dad was seven the first time he was captured by dinosaurs. His father had taken him into the States Mine on the south slope of Spruce Mesa, leading him by the hand some two-hundred feet below ground where they stopped. His father took the lantern and held it overhead against the sandstone to illuminate the imprints of a three-toed Xosaurus. The miners had blasted out a five-foot seam the day before, leaving the perfect stone negatives of the tracks hanging from the mine ceiling. They spanned thirty-four inches in length, with a stride of more than fifteen feet. The footprints had filled with sand, his father told him, preserving them across sixty-million years through the same heat and pressure that turned decomposed vegetation to coal. The miners were little more than amused by the tracks—after all, they had coal to get out—but Dad's imagination was forever lit with what monsters could have left such a mark.

Ten years later, in 1937, after Dad dropped out of school to follow his father underground, a famous Dr. Brown of the American Museum of Natural History showed up at the States. He hired Dad and eight other miners to work three shifts for three weeks drilling rock, re-timbering the roof, and building a special mine car to bring the dinosaur prints a thousand feet to the entrance. Dad was so excited about the excavation that he would often work two of the three shifts and, on the last day, all three. The block of sandstone they chiseled from the mine roof, then lowered with ropes onto the car, measured seventeen by five feet and weighed several hundred pounds. Before Dr. Brown left with the prints on a train to New York City, where they were to be placed on display as the world's largest footprints, he took Dad out to dinner to reward him for his hard work, patiently answering all questions about dinosaurs and paleontology and the art of excavation.

The following weeks the other miners grew weary of Dad's chatter about dinosaurs and began chiding him, calling him Doc, so he bottled his enthusiasm until, years later, it broke with his ribs and he moved from the darkness of mines and our living room to the light of Rabbit Valley and his trailer—or as Dana had put it, as far from a hole as he could get without leaving his dinosaurs. But as I slid off the hood and into Mom's car for the drive back home, it seemed the trailer had become just another hole, the dinosaurs, like Dana and me, another memory.

◇◇◇

Mrs. Woods lay face down on the inflatable mattress, toes and fingertips skimming the pool and the string ties of her bikini top floating to either side. Her long black hair was pinned high on the back of her head, but fine wisps were matted wet against the nape of her neck. Along her spine moisture glistened, puddling at the swale of her tan back.

I stepped from the corner of the house onto the patio as a gust kicked up, rippling across the surface, slowly turning the mattress and exposing the pale curve of one breast. The blue water sparkled like cellophane around her.

"Can I help you?"

I whipped around face-to-face with Mr. Woods, standing behind the sliding-glass door screen.

"Uh, no—I mean, I was just—"

"Walter, who is it?" Mrs. Woods paddled with one hand to the side and slid sunglasses down from her forehead.

"Hi, Mrs. Woods."

"Oh, it's Henry. I'm mad at you." She slipped off the mattress, elbows out as she pinned the bikini top under each arm. "Come help me with this."

I looked at Mr. Woods.

"Sorry, Henry. I didn't recognize you." He smiled, motioning with his glass, ice cubes tinkling. "Be my guest."

"Oh, uh—" I hurried over and squatted down as Mrs. Woods turned around, waist-deep in water.

"You didn't come to the party. Did you?"

I grabbed the strings and cinched them across her back.

"Ouch!"

"Sorry."

"It isn't a straightjacket, Henry."

Her husband laughed. "In fact, it isn't a swimsuit, either."

"Don't start with me, Walter." Mrs. Woods lifted herself from the pool and ran a finger under the elastic along one hip. "Thank-you, Henry. You didn't answer me." She unpinned her hair and shook it out.

"Well, I—Julie and I, we—"

"Oh, never mind. It doesn't matter. Greg and I were barely here an hour ourselves." She turned and kissed me on the lips. "Happy graduation."

I felt my cheeks flush. "Thanks, Mrs. Woods."

"Isn't he polite, Walter? He's such a doll."

"Is Greg around?"

"There's a good question. Walt, where's Gregory?" She looked toward the house. "Walter?" She picked up a beach towel and wrapped it around her waist. "I swear, it's like talking to a post. Would you like something to drink?"

"No, thanks. I should be—"

Barefoot and dripping, she tiptoed across the patio and slid back the screen. "Come on, Henry. Since you didn't come to the party, we need to celebrate."

I followed her inside. Mr. Woods stood at the bar mixing a drink.

"Walter, make us something festive, would you?"

"How 'bout a *piñata*?"

"You mean *piña colada*? That would be good."

"No, I mean *piñata*." Mr. Woods swung an imaginary bat, then picked up his drink and carried it down the hallway toward the den.

Mrs. Woods watched him, hands on hips, then snatched a glass and clinked a couple of ice cubes into it. "What will it be, Henry?"

"That's okay, Mrs. Woods. I don't drink, anyway."

"You don't?" She studied me. "I mean, of course you don't, but this is a special occasion. How about a Virgin Mary then?"

"It's like a Virgin Julie, Hank." Greg stood in the doorway. "But not as bitter."

"Hey. Your mom was just—"

"Corrupting the youth of America?" He grabbed an apple from the counter, tossed it in the air, and sprawled across the barstool in boxers and an unbuttoned dress shirt.

"Gregory, where have you been? I've been worried sick." She touched her fingers to his hair, but he jerked back as though from a left jab.

"At the hospital, Mother. All day." He bit into the apple and chewed noisily, staring at her.

"I was there. I didn't see you."

"That's because I was actually in his room, not reading magazines or drinking coffee in the cafeteria."

Mrs. Woods picked up another glass and tried a smile. "Greg, I was just asking Henry what he would like to drink. Let's have a party since none of us really made it to the other one. Okay? I'll make some snacks." She walked into the pantry and we could hear her rustling packages.

"So what's up, Hank?" He took another bite before tossing the apple into the sink. "Come on, let's go outside."

I followed him around the pool to a cast-iron table with an umbrella and chairs. Out on the course a foursome in two separate carts motored by, bantering back and forth as they rolled down the fairway.

"I haven't seen you since graduation." He reached into his shirt pocket.

"I know. Hey, I won my match."

"Way to go, Hank." He pumped my hand. "So where does that put you?"

"Well, actually, just in the tournament. It was a qualifier."

He pulled out a book of matches and a small metal pipe. "A win's a win, right?"

"You should've seen him, Greg. He was a gorilla. He had arms like this." I made a circle with my hands, eyeing the pipe as he tore off a match.

"And you beat him? Far-out." He struck the match and it fired with a hiss as he brought it to the bowl.

"I thought he had me, you know, but right at the end—" I watched his cheeks indent and eyebrows knit. "—I rolled through and put him on his back."

Greg nodded, holding his breath, forehead wrinkled. He offered me the pipe.

I shook my head and looked across the pool at the screen door.

"So now what?" He exhaled, his strained voice returning to normal. "Who do you have next?" He stirred the bowl with the spent match head.

The screen door slid back, Mrs. Woods' head appearing. "There you two are. I'll be right out."

"What?"

"I said who do you have next."

Mrs. Woods reappeared, carrying a platter with glasses and napkins. "Henry, would you give me a hand?"

Glancing at Greg, I jumped up and hurried around the pool to the patio.

"Thanks, hon. Take this over. I'll be right back."

I carried the platter to the table. Greg sat still, his chest puffed out and lips pursed.

"Your mom's coming right back out, Greg." I set the platter down.

He nodded, his upper body rocking before bursting forth with a billow of smoke. The screen slid open and Mrs. Woods, wearing a sheer white cover-up over her bikini, carried a cutting board of cheeses, cold cuts, miniature breads, and brown mustard. She set it down. "Smells like they're still burning ditch banks, doesn't it?"

Greg nodded. "Yep. Still burnin' weed."

"Summer is upon us. Didn't this year just fly by?" She picked up a slice of rye, placed some Swiss across it. "Help yourself, Henry. These are all leftovers that I'll just have to throw away if somebody doesn't eat them."

Taking some cheese and starting for the bread, I stopped, glancing up at Greg. He winked: the metal pipe sat bowl-up in the middle of the table. I looked at him again and grimaced, motioning with my head.

"Just think, Gregory, in less than a month you'll be in Colorado Springs marching in uniform as a cadet." She took a drink, gazing over the golf course.

"Yes, Mother—just think." He took a bite of bread. "Hey, Henry, would you pass me the bowl please?"

My eyes widened as I glared at him across the table.

"Here, Gregory, just use this." She handed him a napkin.

I eased my hand along the tabletop and slowly closed my fingers over the pipe.

"Henry, you're not eating."

"Thanks, Mrs. Woods, but I'm not too hungry." I slipped the pipe into my jeans pocket.

"You boys stay here. I want to show you something." She walked back into the house.

"What're you doing? Are you crazy? She almost saw it."

"Easy, Hank." He straightened up, smiling.

"What's with you?"

"Hey, listen, man. If you don't think she knows I smoke, it's you that's crazy."

I gawked at him.

"She knows whether she wants to or not. She'll just never admit it, to me or anybody else. Including herself. Why do you think she's so anxious for me to go to the academy? Among about a hundred other reasons." He shrugged, holding out his hand.

I took the pipe from my jeans and handed it across the table.

Greg slipped it into his shirt pocket. "Hey, listen. I talked to Kevy again. Saturday night. That's when we make the switch—the Colonel for his chicken."

"Where?"

He turned and pointed across the fairway. "Tenth green. At midnight."

"What? It's practically in your backyard!"

He held up a hand. "That's the beauty of it. They'll never suspect us. Besides, with all this publicity, they don't care anyway." He smiled. "The radio station's going to be there."

"You're kidding."

"Nope. Live coverage. They're milking it for all it's worth."

Mrs. Woods walked back and bent over the table, carefully placing a frame against the umbrella rod. "I had it mounted."

Greg turned away looking up at the sky. "*Ni meiyou tounao.*"

"Gregory." She set down her drink. "You know the rule. No Chinese around guests unless—"

"—they speak it too." He stood. "Come on, Hank."

"What's it say?" I leaned in and squinted at the bold script across the top.

"The United States Air Force Academy."

"It's my acceptance letter, Hank. Says I'm now an instrument of the U.S. government." He saluted and began marching in place. "An instrument of destruction—two, three, four—"

"You'll be an officer, Gregory." She took the frame and held it up. "You make it sound so . . . sterile."

"Company, advance! Hep—hep—hep—" He marched around the pool, hand to brow.

"Gregory—don't forget your letter." She held it aloft.

"Hep—hep—" He stepped over the diving board and under the patio awning.

"I had it framed for you!"

He stopped, sliding back the screen. "Company, at ease."

"Gregory?"

The screen slid closed behind him as he disappeared into the house; Mrs. Woods glanced down at me. "Greg never has been much for ceremony." She lowered the letter and set it flat on the table, lightly tracing the frame's edge with her fingertips, then smiled. "Has he, Henry?"

12

*A*cker didn't bite me. He didn't need to, ending my wrestling career with something called a corkscrew forty-five seconds into the second period. He was mad it took so long and gave my head an indignant shove as he stood to have his arm raised. Walking off the mat, I felt like a vanquished warrior retreating from battle, grateful that all limbs were attached and that the long war, though lost, was finally over. As for Lenny, he continued to march for one more day, pinning a kid from Uncompahgre in the afternoon session, then at night with Mr. VanHorn's baritone prompting, beating Caruso from Pinecrest by three points to put himself into the Saturday afternoon semifinals against second-seeded Kirkland from Otto. Cisco won his first two matches also, each by more than ten points, and had to face top-seeded Meeks, who pinned both opponents within the first thirty seconds.

The rest of our seniors didn't fare as well, placing just three in the semifinals, making Coach Hicks livid. He scheduled a punishment practice, as he called them, for the Monday following the tournament and posted the notice on the locker room bulletin board before realizing no one would show; school was over and someone (whom we later found out to be Stankey) communicated this fact by outlining his fist and extended middle finger across the notice in black Magic Marker.

His pique was further pricked by Lenny not only winning but doing so at the behest of Sam VanHorn. Though Coach Hicks' ribs and shins were still bruised and sore, it was his ego that suffered. How could a flaky, undisciplined kid, coached by an equally goofball English teacher, make it all the way to the semi's? All this, of course, made memory of his missed tackle all the more painful while his hulking, hairy nemesis was the happiest guy in the gym, which caused him additional misery. There seemed no end to it.

After watching Stankey get pancaked one last time, I walked home to find that Redd Morgan wasn't happy either. Another prank had befallen him. Seems a masseuse, heavy on makeup and fishnet stockings, had shown up at Sage Diner while he was drinking coffee, waiting for Mom to get off work. She was loud, demanding payment for "services remembered" three weeks before. If it weren't for Punk's generosity—he comped her two breakfast specials with all the coffee and horseradish she could stomach—and Arlene's consoling voice, she might still be there, Mom said. Redd was beside himself with rage and kept insisting that Arlene seemed far too familiar with the hussy, effectively making her his latest candidate for resident prankster, if not harlot. Sensing the volcano was about to blow in my direction and stifling the urge to burst out in glee over my father's growing ingenuity, I waited for Redd to go to the bathroom before asking Mom permission to use the car.

"Okay, honey. But don't be too late." She picked up her purse and began rummaging through it. "Remember your job interview tomorrow. Redd rescheduled it for you. He was pretty upset you missed it this morning."

"Mom, I had to wrestle. Remember?"

"Well, Redd put himself out for you, that's all I know, so the least you can do is show up." She pulled the key ring out and began flipping through it.

"Redd's not putting himself out, Mom. He's only doing it because he knows I'll hate it."

"That's not true, honey." She found the key and began working it around the ring. "Redd's doing the best he can." She tugged at the key.

The toilet flushed and he walked back down the hall and into the kitchen, tucking shirttails into starched Levi's. He stopped and gazed at me just long enough to rotate a toothpick from one corner of his mouth to the other, then continued over to the refrigerator. He opened the door; the light illuminated his craggy face as he bent down to peer inside.

"Redd, tell Henry about this job you got him."

"Mom, I gotta get—"

"Oh, yeah—" He turned around shutting the door. "—the job I got him." He stepped toward me smiling, head down tapping the beer can; then from nowhere a hand appeared, slapping the side of my head.

I crumpled sideways, the kitchen table screeching across the linoleum.

"Redd!" Mom rushed over and threw her arms around me as I straightened up trying to rub the ringing from my ear.

He pointed at me. "Pull that again, buddy-boy, and next time the hand won't be open."

Twisting from Mom's grip, tears welling in my eyes, I stumbled across the kitchen to the back door.

"Henry!"

I looked back at my mother, whose fingers spread like pickets across her face.

"Henry—" One hand slid down into the pocket of her waitress' dress, then came out opening palm-up like a flower to the sun—the car key. I turned away and plunged out the back door, down the street, and into the night not caring if I ever saw her or Redd Morgan or anyone again.

◇◇◇

"Where?" I lay on my back at the end of the runway next to Julie.

"See that bright star right there?" She pointed.

"Yeah."

"That's Spica. Now just go east—across two, up one, and back two."

"Okay."

"Then from the same point, from Spica again, there's another leg that forms kind of a wide Y. See it?"

"Oh, yeah. So that's you, huh?"

"Yep, that's me—Virgo—the virgin, legs wide, waiting an eternity." She sighed. "See the constellation Ursa Major there below it."

"The Big Dipper."

"Yes, that's the biggest part of it. It means Great Bear and the Little Dipper is in Ursa Minor, Little Bear. Want the whole story?"

"Sure."

"Well, Callisto was the beautiful daughter of King somebody or other of Arcadia. Jupiter, king of all gods, had a thing for her, which made Juno, his wife, jealous. So Juno turned her into a bear. Later, Callisto's son, Arcas, was out hunting one day when he came across this bear—"

"His mother."

"Right, but he didn't know it was his mother. And just as he was ready to shoot her, Jupiter jumped in and changed Arcas into a bear, too."

"And there they are."

"And there they are. After Jupiter changed them into bears, he swung them by their tails into the sky, which is why their tails are so long."

"Hmm." I looked over at her, the side of her face illuminated by the runway lights. "How do you know so much?"

She rolled to her side, head propped in one hand. "I'm a chick." She smiled. "Rog taught me about stars. When I was a little girl, we'd sleep outside in the summer and stare at the sky for hours and he'd tell me stories. But the long tail thing I just learned. And you'll never guess who told me."

"Greg?"

"Pfff, are you kidding? Greg may get straight A's, Hank, but if it's not from a book, forget it."

"Who then?"

"Lenny."

I looked over at her and she nodded. "He's still sleeping up on that hill in his Jeep. I went up there last night after Daddy and I got back from fishing. We built a fire and he told me all kinds of stuff. I couldn't believe it."

"I can."

"I think it's because of Miss Darling."

"When did he see Miss Darling?"

"That's where he's been hanging out, Hank." She sat up. "Listen. Hear it?"

I sat up and searched the black sky for blinking lights. "There it is." I pointed west above the horizon.

We lay back as the roar grew and watched the flaps and landing gear deploy. We covered our ears as a shrill thunder descended. Blinking red, white, and green lights loomed over us, opposing vortices whipping our clothes and hair before blasting overhead. Then the 727's wheels skidded and squealed against the asphalt some thirty yards beyond, sparks shooting to either side.

Julie clutched my hand as we raised up and the plane roared down the runway. She pulled hair from her face and traced it around one ear. "Kelly Simms told me she and Brad Ferris come out here and do it just as the plane lands like that. She said there's nothing like it. The noise, the lights, the vibration of the ground when it hits the runway."

I looked at Julie, both of us propped on an elbow next to each other, the plane's lights fading down the runway.

"What do you think, Hank?"

I swallowed and blinked, her face blurring as it drew closer. "I don't know—"

Looking over my shoulder at the taxiing plane, she licked her lips then gently brushed her fingertips over the red welt on my temple, studying it. "I can't believe he did that to you."

"It's okay—"

"No, it's not." Her lashes fluttered, fingers moving through my hair. "It's not okay, Hank."

"I'm all right."

"You always say that." She pressed into me, one leg hooked over mine.

"But I—" I rolled over, stars sprinkled in her hair and the taste of strawberry chapstick on her mouth.

"Julie, what're we—"

She straddled me, her warm breath against my cheek, hands working between us, undoing shirt buttons. Then she pulled her shirttails out and, with her hair, there formed a tent around us.

"Julie—"

Sliding hands underneath, I could feel the faint ridges of her spine, the smooth twin triangles of shoulder blades coming together like fledgling wings. I tugged and fumbled at the clasp—tried pulling, pushing, sliding. She arched above me—knees still to either side, head back and elbows out as though she *had* sprouted wings—and undid the bra. Bending down she braced herself, hair and bra dangling over me.

I pulled her down until her breasts were heavy and firm and warm against my face. Her legs stretched as she lay atop me, feet clasping my ankles, pelvis pressing my stomach. She cradled my head. I kissed between her breasts, tasted her skin as she began rocking into me. I opened my eyes; hair swayed around me like curtains in a summer breeze. I could smell perfume deepen with the warmth of her body. I kissed one nipple, breasts now brushing rhythmically across my face, eyes, forehead. Head down, she nodded as she worked against me, jeans grinding jeans. She quickened, her movements gaining strength. Her throaty breath in concert with the thrusting.

"Oh . . . oh . . ." She panted, breasts smothering me, her head lifting now toward the stars. "Oh . . . oh . . . oh . . ."

I tried to match her movements, felt the sting of my zipper. She quickened, her movements stronger now. I arched and held it, unable to keep up.

"Oooh . . . oh, god . . . oh, god . . . oh, Greg . . . oh, Greg! Oh, Greee—" She heaved, head throwing side-to-side, eyes stitched, thighs squeezing, body tense and quivering. Then a slow elongated release as she groaned, relaxed, and then a few shivering aftershocks before finally going limp, collapsing atop me.

I could still see stars through her hair, the black quilted sky all around, and smelled the musky sour of sweat and saliva and perfume against her neck. Her cheek rested against mine, her breath gradually slowing. An airplane droned somewhere.

Sighing, she kissed my ear, my neck, and rolled a half turn off. "Henry?" She raised up to look at me. "Henry, I—"

But I closed my eyes then and lay perfectly still—as though suddenly asleep or suddenly gone or suddenly just somebody else.

◇◇◇

Miss Darling mesmerized Lenny. Her body, crippled and bent with arthritis, was earth-bound, a broken crab scuttling across sand. But her spirit, like lightning, arced freely across the sky, illuminating the heavens and flashing in Lenny's eyes.

Unknown to Julie, Greg, and me, he had been visiting her regularly since Magic Club first went to have Greg's palms read. Directed to park his Wagoneer on the canal bank behind a tall cottonwood so as not to deter customers from pulling in, he would walk around the charred hovel to the locked gate where the yap of the Pomeranians eventually brought her outside. Then through a haze of cobwebs, dust, barks, and her many words, Lenny worked: pulling kochia weeds, pruning branches, hauling water and wood, fixing a latch here, a broken tool there, and lugging oil-drenched boxes of newspaper and sooty items salvaged years earlier from the fire. He labored a few hours every day as she sat supervising on a nearby stump or over-turned bucket.

Between the short staccato of her orders—"Put that there." "Move this over here." "Pull that." "Leave this." "Burn those."—Miss Darling showered him with an earthy wisdom culled from the experience of many lives. Acne can best be treated with an infant's urine. If a baby is unavailable, one's own urine, which is also healthy to drink, will do if it's collected midstream rather than beginning or end. Sunburned eyes, like Greg's, should be treated with a poultice of grated apples placed on closed eyelids. Crushed juniper berries cast over the heated rocks of a sweat lodge drive away evil spirits or bad magic and stimulate menstruation. Sliced onions or peeled garlic cloves bound to the bottoms of feet will break a fever, as will bloodletting. An open wound heals faster if a dog licks it or maggots are allowed to feed on the dead flesh. And clay dulls the appetite, firms up stool, and can be eaten for bellyaches and in times of famine, especially *ampo* from the island of Java, which has the texture of fine chocolate.

But mainly she regaled him with things less worldly. Cosmic truths, she called them: astral travel, reincarnation, spells, curses, and dimensions ad infinitum. Inhaling *prana*, psychic energy, releases the soul from the shackles of the body, she said. Preceded by bodily vibrations, the spirit escapes from the top of the head or drops downward through the physical floor or furniture. After separation, a silver filament as fine as spider's thread connects body to spirit as the traveler moves through time and space to points inconceivable to the uninitiated mind. Miss Darling had scoured the bottoms of oceans, zoomed over the highest peaks, sat invisibly with friends in need, cavorted with other spirits in cosmic dance, volleyed down corridors of entire cities existing in dimensions apart from yet parallel to our own. To know consciousness can exist without the body is to know eternity; to experience it is to know God. And Miss Darling knew God, in all His earthly garb. Buddha, Jesus, Confucius, Mohammed—all physical symbols for the eternal energy, all bridges to the multitudinous dimensions of existence. And she could quote them all, while knowing that, by their very physicality, they had been flawed human beings—as we all are, she said. But now, untethered from imperfect bodies, they are pure energy and light. Perfection, just as she would be when her pain-riddled body took its last breath—a breath she longed for.

"Does she pay you?"

Lenny reached over and placed a couple pinõn boughs across the fire. "Not with money."

"With what then?" I stared at him through smoke smoldering from the pinõn, sap popping. An army canteen was wedged between his thighs and a stem of wheat grass hung from his mouth. At his feet lay Louie, his muzzle resting against Lenny's tennis shoe.

He shrugged. "She said she's going to teach me how to astral travel and dream share and stuff."

"What's dream share?"

"It's having the same dream at the same time with somebody."

"Oh." I sat on Lenny's extra sleeping bag, holding my head in my hands. "Life's weird, huh, Lenny? I mean Greg's smoking pot and dancing the Tango with Colonel Sanders, you're flying around having dreams with a fortuneteller, and Julie's . . . well . . . Julie . . ."

"What?"

"Well, she kissed me."

Lenny sat across the fire on his Coleman cooler, studying me.

"You know how we sometimes go out to the airport to watch planes take off and land? Well, last night we went out there and we're lookin' at the stars and stuff and she's telling me about Kelly Simms and Brad Ferris, how they go out there, you know, to do it. And next thing I know we're rolling around on the ground."

Lenny sat motionless, flames flickering in his eyes. Then he stood slowly, staring above me through the quivering heat, through the flakes of ash curling up like fireflies into the night sky. "Hear 'em?"

"What?"

He raised his arm and pointed into the darkness. "Coyotes."

Louie was standing, too, ears perked to attention.

"We've heard them every night so far. Haven't we, boy?"

Louie let out a low growl, and Lenny patted the dog's side. "They yip early in the mornings, too. Last night Louie howled back at them." He sat back down.

"So what do you think?"

"I think it's just their way of welcoming us."

"No, I mean about Julie."

Lenny gazed up at the half moon and shook his head. "They get a bad rap, Hank. Ranchers shootin' and poisoning them all the time. Somebody needs to do something. They're just animals, man." He continued looking skyward, shaking his head, then finally brought his eyes down and picked up the cooler. He started across the Third Sister toward the Wagoneer backed up against a sandstone ledge, Louie padding after him.

"Hey, Lenny."

They continued to the Wagoneer and Lenny opened the back end. "Come on, boy, get in. Time for a little dream sharin', right Louie?" He laughed. "Tomorrow's the last day I ever have to wrestle again, Hank. Be sure the fire's out before you turn in, okay?"

I heard him rustling into his sleeping bag, whispering to Louie, and then nothing but the coyotes yipping and fire popping until those too fell silent, until all I heard was the breeze washing across The Three Sisters.

13

"Hank! It's for you!"

I got out of bed, trudged upstairs, took the phone from Dana. "Hello."

"*Hi.*"

"Oh, hi."

The kitchen table was cleared, and Dana was drying and placing dishes in the cupboard.

"*Hank, I . . . I just wanted to—*"

"It's okay."

"*No, it's not. It's not okay. Are you all right?*"

I ran a finger around the rim of the fish bowl. "Yeah, I'm fine."

"*I don't know what to say . . . I just—*"

"It's okay. Really." Dipping my finger in the water, I slid it over the glass. Stella and Frank, feeling movement, swam up and lipped the surface. A cigarette butt floated into view from the curved glass, tobacco bits separating from soaked paper. "Oh, geez."

"*What?*"

"Nothin'. I just . . . never mind." I pinched the butt with my thumb and middle finger, lifted it from the bowl and, cradling the receiver between chin and shoulder, held it dripping over my other hand.

"*Hank, I just want you to know that I think you're the greatest—*"

"No, stop."

"*No, really, I want to—*"

"Please. It's fine."

"*Are you sure?*"

"Yeah, I'm sure."

"*Well—*" Julie breathed into the receiver. "*Okay.*"

"Okay." Stella and Frank were mouthing the tobacco bits. I dropped the butt onto my palm and grabbed the fish food shaker and salted the water with shrimp flakes.

"Well, I guess I'll—"

"I better go."

"I'll see you later then, okay?"

"Yeah, sure."

"'Bye, Hank."

I hung up holding the cigarette butt and watching Stella and Frank gobble shrimp, wondering if fish could get cancer.

Dana looked up from the sink where she was drying her hands. "Who was that?"

"Somebody threw a cigarette into Stella and Frank's bowl."

"What?"

"Look." I held out my hand.

"Sick." Dana wrinkled her nose. "Probably Redd. Who else would be so creative?" She brought a paper sack and held it open. "They broke up, again."

"They did?" I emptied my hand, brushed it off.

"Mom said for good this time."

I looked at Dana, deciding not to say anything about getting hit.

"So who was it?"

"Huh?"

"On the phone."

"Oh, nobody." I bent down to check the fish, to make sure they weren't turning from gold to green.

"Didn't sound like nobody. Was it Julie?"

I straightened, half shaking my head.

"It didn't sound like her. She okay?"

"I guess." I walked back across the kitchen.

"So it was Julie?'

"Yeah." I started down the stairs. "What's her face—Julie."

◇◇◇

Father, Son, and Holy Ghost. Three Blind Mice. Body, soul, and spirit. We Three Kings. Birth, life, death. The Three Stooges. Miss Darling said cosmic forces, both good and bad, trigger things in what appear to be threes but are actually fours. She said three dimensionality is an illusion, that there's a fourth, which doesn't appear in the world of the senses, lying beyond human perception, beyond reason and scientific proof. Three represents conflict, four unity; from the third comes the one as the fourth. Four triangles she pointed out, eyes narrowing, comprise a pyramid.

I wasn't sure what she was talking about, what number or shape had to do with anything. All I knew was that by the end of that Saturday night two significant things had happened; what I didn't know yet was that the third would take the rest of the summer—then from it, the fourth.

Cameron Pippin III was a force, too. A political one, and Julie fell under his spell almost immediately. That Saturday morning found her downtown stuffing envelopes at the Mesa County Democratic Headquarters—a converted stationery shop. Band-Aids covered paper cuts on three fingers and her hair was loosely pinned up as though she'd just rolled out of bed. McGovern placards and the mugs of local and state candidates plastered the storefront window as Greg peered in. He was pointing, laughing at her habit of sliding the tip of her tongue back and forth across her bottom lip when intently doing something. Without glancing up or even breaking rhythm, she flipped him the bird between sealing an envelope and reaching for another.

"I wouldn't think that's a very good strategy for winning votes, Jules."

"You're just jealous, Woods, that it's not you I'm lick—" She glanced at me as I followed Greg inside, then gazed down into another envelope.

"All that glue's made your tongue stick." Greg sat next to her, picked up a brochure, and stretched a leg across the table corner, leaning back. "Too bad it hasn't stopped that twitchy middle finger of yours."

"Hi, Hank."

"Hi."

Greg unfolded the pamphlet. "*Come Home, America*. I didn't know we were away." He scanned the column. "What's up with the Band-Aids?"

Holding her hand out as though checking fingernail polish, which she never wore, Julie shrugged. "Just a sanitary measure. A girl can't be too careful."

"Right. 'She takes a lickin', but keeps on lickin.'" He tossed the brochure on the pile in the middle of the table. "Looks like grounds for a workman's comp suit to me. You should talk to my old man. He'll get you lined out."

"I don't think paper cuts qualify."

Greg glanced around the room at the posters. "Where is everybody? There's gotta be at least a couple more Democrats in this valley. Or are you the only one they can trust with such an important job?"

"Are you just innately bored, Greg, or is there something you actually want?"

"Testy, testy. Yours must be the longest period in the history of man—I mean woman."

"Testes, testes. You just need a couple."

"Ohhh—she stops. She shoots. She—" He stood, raising hands overhead. "She scores!"

A guy half a head taller than Greg stepped through the doorway and dropped a briefcase on the table. "Hi, Julie."

She scrambled up, smoothing strands of hair from her face. "Hi."

He peered through wire-rimmed glasses, his head a shoulder-length mass of curly black hair. "See you're hard at it—as usual." He opened the briefcase.

"I just—I wanted to finish these up before—um—Cameron, these are my friends Greg Woods and Henry Kessler. Greg, Henry—Cameron Pippin the III."

"Call me Cam. A pleasure." We shook then he offered his hand to Greg.

"Sorry." Greg held up his as though he were a surgeon awaiting gloves after scrubbing. "Impetigo. Both hands." He lifted one foot. "But my feet are clean."

He smiled. "You guys here to help or are you just passing through?"

"We're here to help Julie pass through." Greg lowered his hands and foot. "You know, to the other side."

"Ah, a Doors fan."

Julie snorted. "Are you kidding? The original knob."

"Yeah, and I just keep on jambin'." Greg glanced at me, wagged his eyebrows.

Cameron nodded, still smiling. "Apparently to the point of becoming unhinged."

Julie abruptly giggled but then cut it off as Greg snatched another brochure, his face crimson.

"Julie, I'm going to get somebody else to finish these. You're far too talented for us to waste your efforts on mailers. In fact, next weekend's the State Democratic Convention in Denver and I'd like you to go. It's the first time we have proportional representation and, based on caucuses, McGovern should have the bulk of our thirty-six delegates to Miami." He took a scrap of paper and scribbled. "Can you go?"

Julie rubbed hands against her pant legs. "Yes, I'd love to."

"Great." He handed her the paper. "We'll leave Friday morning and be back Sunday. I'll meet you right here at, say, seven a.m. Is that too early?"

"No."

"Good. See you Friday then. Nice meeting you gentlemen." He closed the briefcase and carried it to the door. "Oh, and no more envelopes. Go enjoy the weekend."

Julie gazed at the now empty doorway, a stunned smile across her face.

Greg folded the brochure and stuck it in his hip pocket. "Don't worry, hot-shot. We will."

◇ ◇ ◇

Lenny was shaking hands with Kirkland from Otto as we took our seats. Except for a few scattered spaces toward the back, the gymnasium was packed for the Saturday afternoon semifinals.

"Damn!" I slapped my leg. "We missed it!"

"Yeah, but look." Julie pointed at the scoreboard: seven to six. "He won!"

The referee raised Lenny's arm. Mr. VanHorn lumbered onto the mat, bear hugging him and then carrying him off as people politely applauded. Behind the scorer's table sat college coaches and scouts, clipboards in hand.

"All right, Lenny!" I whistled. "Way to go!"

Greg rolled a program to his mouth. "Bar-tel-liii!"

Lenny looked up.

"Yourrr mom-maaa!"

"Good, Greg." Julie shook her head as we waved. "I'm sure that's just what he wanted to hear."

A cowboy three rows down, wearing a Stetson and red satin rodeo jacket, turned and looked at us. Across the gym, front and center, sat Mr. and Mrs. Salazar with chair-bound Rudy and their string of daughters to either side. Assorted aunts, uncles, and cousins clustered behind them and three rows up perched Peefee and the boys. The rest of the crowd was a patchwork of color. We sat on the opposite side among red-clad fans from North Fork; Greg relished sitting among enemy ants, as he liked to call opposing fans, stirring them up with the end of his sharp tongue.

"Git alonnng—li'l doggies." Greg smiled.

The cowboy glared over his shoulder and the woman sitting next to him in matching jacket and boots turned around too.

Julie nudged Greg with her elbow. "Can we just watch the match, please?"

Patting her knee, he gazed across the mat where Coach Hicks stood behind Cisco massaging his neck, talking into one ear. "Cisco's turn."

Julie sighed. "God, he's beautiful."

"Yeah, but look what he has to contend with." Greg pointed to the opposite side at Clay Meeks, who was taking off his warm-up jacket. "Wouldn't want to kick sand in that guy's face, huh, Hank?" Meeks' biceps looked like oranges resting inside his arms.

The crowd began to murmur; this was the match most had come for.

Definitely the one the college coaches wanted to see. Between them, Cisco and Meeks had a high school record of two-hundred-and-one wins, two losses (both Meeks'), and six state championships.

As the two wrestlers approached the center, there were scattered shouts of encouragement until the whole place erupted, standing and cheering as they shook hands. By the time the referee blew the whistle, only Mr. and Mrs. Salazar, Rudy, and the college coaches remained seated.

Meeks immediately went to work, slapping Cisco on the cheek and shooting in for a double-leg dive. Arching his back, he hoisted Cisco skyward then brought him down to the mat. But like a cat falling from a roof Cisco twisted sideways, landing on all fours. Reaching back, he whizzered Meeks' arm and leveraged him out of bounds.

The crowd was already in a frenzy. Even Julie was screaming, fingers jutted into her thick hair.

Coach Hicks leaned back in his chair and, out of habit, glanced up at the clock. Only when Cisco wrestled was he calm; with everyone else our coach was a ranting lunatic.

The referee blew his whistle and Meeks shot in. This time Cisco countered high, both arms under Meeks'. But the North Fork wrestler straightened and bulled forward, bear hugging Cisco and throwing him to the side. Cisco twisted and countered, landing them side-by-side like twin coffee tables joined in the middle of the mat. After several seconds of tugging and pushing, the referee signaled a stalemate, fists pressed to his chest.

Again the whistle chirped and Meeks adjusted his headgear, which was all Cisco needed. Sweeping in from the side, he caught the inside of Meeks' right heel with his long arms and elevated it over his shoulder. Meeks hopped on one foot, pushing against Cisco's face, but Cisco, a couple inches taller than his stocky opponent, lifted higher before deftly kicking Meeks' foot from under him. Meeks fell heavily onto his back and quickly squirmed to his stomach, spreading his limbs so as not to be turned. But this was where Cisco was best. Letting him push to hands and knees, he slapped a figure-four around his opponent's middle and squeezed him back to the mat. Meeks appeared confused, looking at his coach as Cisco applied pressure to one shoulder, prying it back into a chicken wing. Torquing the arm with both his, Cisco released the figure-four and worked his way forward. He hooked one leg behind the neck then pried until he could scissor the other one, moving his figure-four from Meeks' waist to his head. Meeks was now gazing straight up from between Cisco's legs into the lights, a position he had never found himself, one arm pinned behind his back, veins popping across his forehead. The referee studied his shoulder blades, three fingers extended for a near-fall. The buzzer sounded, barely audible in the din of the gymnasium—five to zero.

"He's a wimp, Cisco! A pantywaist!"

The cowboy turned and glowered.

"Greg—" Julie tugged on his sleeve. "Greg, you're going to get us killed."

"A freakin' little girl!" He glanced down at the cowboy. "Spank her, Cisco! Spank that cowgirl!"

Julie elbowed him, a fake smile frozen across her face. "Greeeg—"

"Yeee-haaa!"

Cisco chose top and Meeks, gulping air and slapping his own cheeks as though trying to awake from a nightmare, knelt into position. Not only had Meeks not been beaten that season, he had never trailed and only rarely been scored upon. The whistle sounded, Meeks exploding to his feet, tearing at Cisco's hands. But Cisco didn't resist, casually pushing him away and allowing him one point for the escape. Meeks looked incensed that Cisco would give him anything and immediately rushed in, feigning a double-leg then throwing a headlock. Cisco went with the momentum and rolled through as Lenny had so often done to me. Meeks again found himself on his back and, in an incredible show of strength, bridged straight up as though no one were atop him and pivoted around. Cisco responded by standing and pushing Meeks away a second time. Receiving points for a second takedown and a predicament, Cisco now led nine to two. The period ended with Cisco arm-dragging Meeks and just missing yet another takedown and two points.

"Spankin' her!" Greg hopped on one foot then the other. "Spankin' that cowgirl!"

While Meeks bounced up and down trying to shake off the unimaginable and Cisco crouched down for the last period, Lenny wended his way up the bleachers through the stunned North Fork fans to join us.

Julie hugged and kissed him. "Way to go, Bartelli!"

"My hero!" Greg kissed the other cheek.

"Good job, Lenny!" I pumped his hand. "Seven to six."

"Yeah." Lenny looked down and grinned.

"Can you believe this?" I pointed to the mat.

He raised his eyes and nodded. "Yeah, I can believe it. That's Cisco Salazar out there, man."

The whistle blew and Cisco attempted to stand but Meeks' superior strength drove him to the mat. Cisco sat out, turned in, sat out again, then stood before switching out of bounds.

"Man, he's fast." Greg shook his head. "But you have to be, right, Lenny?" He turned to Julie. "You have to be fast when you wrestle with—" He raised his hands. "Cowgirls!"

The guy turned around again, glowering.

Greg smiled. "Yippy-yi-ki-ay."

The cowboy's eyes bulged as he pushed from his seat, but the woman latched onto an arm and leaned into him, whispering something.

"All hat, no cattle!" Greg winced, turning toward Julie. "Ouch! What was that for?"

She stared straight ahead, gritting her teeth.

As they returned to the center, Meeks appeared finished, mouth hanging wide, hands resting on hips, his head cocked back for air.

Lenny cupped his mouth. "You got him, Cisco! He's all yours!"

Again Cisco sat out, then stood and switched, reaching back for a leg. Meeks crowded into him so he quickly winged an elbow and rolled. But this time Meeks guessed right, jumping across and catching Cisco with a half-nelson.

"Nooo!" Julie's hands were back in her hair, elbows pressing against mine as we leaned into each other, trying to somehow help Cisco fend off the hold.

North Fork fans were on their feet now, stomping and clapping around us. The muscles in Meeks' back worked and twitched as he applied pressure. Cisco tried peeling the fingers from the back of his neck, but Meeks was too strong, sinking his forearm deeper under Cisco's shoulder and behind his head. Finally in familiar territory, Meeks confidently looked up at the clock and then, driving his legs, rolled Cisco onto his back.

Across the gymnasium people stood open-mouthed, glancing at the scoreboard. Peefee was out of his seat, standing at the edge of the mat, begging Cisco to get up. Behind him sat Mr. and Mrs. Salazar, he as stoic as ever with arms folded across his chest and she pressing a tissue to her mouth, the other hand buried in her daughter's lap.

Eight seconds to go and the two wrestlers seemed locked in time, Meeks bearing down and Cisco arching up, negating each other as though stuck between past and future, in a struggle for the present. Then, abruptly, it was over. The buzzer sounded as the referee slapped the mat.

People around us jumped up and down, and the cowboy turned around grinning and shaking a fist.

"No way! No way!" Lenny and I stood on the bleachers, straining to see over the crowd.

"Poor, Cisco." Julie squinted through a strand of hair that had fallen over her eyes, hands clenched to her mouth.

Screwing his face into a mass of wrinkles and chewing an imaginary toothpick, Greg wrapped his arm around her. "Don't worry, li'l darlin'. I'm gonna go kick that yeller-belly's boney, horse-thievin' butt." He gave her a squeeze before excusing himself across the row toward the aisle.

"Greg!"

Out on the mat Meeks and Cisco stood together—hands on knees, heads down, backs heaving for oxygen—while their coaches and referee huddled at the official scorer's table. Coach Hicks was stabbing a finger at the clock, barking across the table, veins standing in his neck. The North Fork coach, a dignified man in short-sleeve dress shirt and black tie, calmly shook his head. Along the Grand River side of the mat stood Peefee and the boys, some fifteen strong, feet wide, jaws and chests jutting out, ready for battle. The referee started toward the wrestlers, hesitated, then turned back to make one last point to the scorer's table.

"Okay, here we go." Clutching Julie's and Lenny's arm on either side of me, I caught a glimpse of Greg below, filing through the crowd toward the cowboy.

The referee returned to the middle of the mat, asked the wrestlers to shake, then raised Cisco's arm as I saw the white hat plucked from the cowboy's head, then bob like a buoy against a sea of heads down the bleachers to the gymnasium floor.

"Yes! Yes! Yes!" Julie and I jumped up and down, hugging each other—then Lenny—before hurrying down the aisle.

North Fork fans booed and shouted around us, pawing the air and throwing wadded programs. Cisco was being swarmed at the edge of the mat by his friends as Meeks walked dejectedly off, his coach draping the warm-up jacket across his muscular back and patting him on the seat.

I hustled down the aisle after Julie and Lenny. "Look!" I pointed across the gymnasium. Greg, one hand pressed atop the hat, hotfooted along the edge of the crowd before dodging into the lobby, the cowboy on his heels. The cowboy's bare head was bleached white as a mushroom as if it'd never seen sunlight.

"He just never stops, does he?" Julie shook her head. "If it's not pot or acid, it's adrenaline." She scanned back across the gymnasium. "Look, there's Cisco."

The next match had begun, and Cisco was three rows up, engulfed in relatives. Only his father was unmoved, everyone else hugging, kissing, and clapping Cisco on the back. Julie and I walked over to take our turn. Lenny was already standing on the bottom bleacher, stretching his hand out. Cisco reached toward him, but Coach Hicks was there and he grabbed Lenny's jacket sleeve and pulled him off the bleacher.

"Beat it, Bartelli. You can shake after the finals, after he pins your little—"

"Hey, you're not harassing my wrestler, are you, Lawrence?" Mr. V walked up and placed a hand on Lenny's shoulder, guiding him away from Coach Hicks toward the locker room.

"Your wrestler?" He watched them walk away. "Yeah, VanHorn, we'll see what kind of wrestler *your* wrestler is!" And he turned away, glancing up at the scoreboard clock.

◇◇◇

Dana stood on the street corner talking with Mr. Shimizu. She had befriended him after the mining accident and would occasionally walk down the sidewalk to chat through the wrought-iron bars of his red brick wall. Sometimes he opened the gate to show off his bonsai shrubs, an exotic pine, or the flowering lily pads, which floated like clouds across the shallow pools that dotted his yard. I went with her that first trip to the corner, to thank him for his concern about Dad. As we followed his thonged feet across the spongy fern and moss-covered rock, through the scent of potting soil and sounds of water gurgling from a miniature waterfall, I was shocked to discover he spoke like we did, without any trace of an accent; I hadn't noticed this the night of the accident. But, as Dana put it, it wasn't how Mr. Shimizu spoke but what.

She had commented on what a beautiful house he had. Like the wall, it was laid in red brick with ivy growing halfway up the north side and wrought-iron railing running along the steps and around the patio in back. He stopped, thanking her with a slight bow, and replied in precise clipped English, as though he memorized it: "The reality of the building does not consist in the roof and walls, but within the space to be lived in." Dana was impressed. "Wow, is that one of those, what do you call them, Chinese proverbs?" He shrugged and continued leading us around the yard. "Beats me. I just read it in *Readers' Digest*."

When we returned home, I went into the living room where Dad was still recuperating on the couch. I told him about Mr. Shimizu, about the way he talked—or didn't talk—and about all the different shaped bushes and trees and things he had growing over there. The curtains were drawn and his eyes reflected the changing images from the television. Without moving his head, he glanced up at me. "Go get your sister."

We stood in the darkened living room like soldiers before the fallen general as our father, still staring at the TV, ordered us to stay away from Mr. Shimizu and never go over there again. When Dana asked why, he repeated himself in a voice that meant the discussion was over. I never walked to the corner again, but for Dana our father's words were like neon pointing the way. For a couple of weeks she went every day, whether Mr. Shimizu was there or not, gazing through the wrought-iron bars at the cool shady spaces within.

It was only a month later that Dad packed up his canaries and was gone.

◇◇◇

The year Mr. Shimizu moved to the corner of our street, when I was nine, my father gave me a sweatshirt. Across the chest in rubbery dark-blue lettering was written KILROY WAS HERE. He told me Kilroy was a famous soldier in World War II. No one knew his other name, first or last; he was just Kilroy. For weeks, maybe months, I wore that sweatshirt, imagining myself to be a spy, a secret agent, a demolitionist, a war hero. Kilroy. Even the name seemed to hold cryptic meaning. No coincidence the first syllable, I thought; the second probably slang or a code name for the enemy, like Kraut or Jap or other words I heard my father say over highballs he sometimes drank with Mr. Penn, another World War II veteran who lived down the street. Dirty bastard Japs. Dad rarely swore—or drank—but this he would say to Mr. Penn. I sat on the top step in the darkened stairway, only the yellow light from the kitchen falling high on the wall, and listened to their words with rapt astonishment—mortar, artillery, concussion, thirty millimeter, torpedo. Back in the safety of bed I would whisper these words into my blankets as though sacred verse from a sacred order. Before school, Mom made me take the sweatshirt off and put on clean T-shirts or turtlenecks or shirts with collars. Once outside and on my way I would take the sweatshirt from my coat or gym bag and pull it back on, over the clean clothes. Ketchup and grease spots covered the front because Mom refused to wash it after a while, but these became bloodstains, shrapnel burns, and battle scars. Then a kid named Lyle Hansen, a short round boy with a flattop and a lisp, walked up to me on the playground and told me Kilroy was nobody. I laughed disdainfully and said what do you mean nobody; he was a hero. He repeated it—Kilroy was nobody, just a name—so I said it, dirty bastard Jap, and slugged him in the ear, making him cry. Though I felt bad, it was the patriotic thing to do and somehow made me a part of my father's war. I walked home then, past Mr. Shimizu's with the sweatshirt stuffed inside my coat and sat in the living room with it on my lap before we ate supper. Dad was reading the *Grand River Sentinel* and, in turn, peering over it at the evening news on television. Walter Cronkite was talking and then it switched to footage of Vietnam. The reporter held the microphone in one hand, mashed a camouflage hat atop his head with the other, and shouted into the camera. A helicopter whirled overhead, flattening grass and whipping trees and foliage about. The helicopter landed, making the reporter crouch and yell louder. Pairs of medics carrying stretchers ran toward it. One stumbled and the injured soldier, his head bandaged in gauze, slid awkwardly to one side. The medic was flopping an arm and a leg back onto the stretcher when Walter Cronkite appeared again and began talking about a guy named Dow Jones in New York. My father continued to read the newspaper. I sat on the couch, the sweatshirt still on my lap, and thought about Mr. Shimizu and what I had done to Lyle Hansen and what Lyle had said about Kilroy. Kilroy was nobody. Just a name. I pulled the sweatshirt from my coat, traced the letters with my fingertips—K-I-L-R-O-Y— then walked downstairs and threw it underneath my bed where, like phantom socks, it would eventually disappear.

◇◇◇

Seeing me cross the street, Dana waved good-bye to Mr. Shimizu and hurried down the block, bird-dogging me into the house. "Guess what."

"What?"

"Guess."

"I don't want to guess."

She flicked my ear.

"Don't! Where's Mom?"

I walked down the hall into Dana's bedroom, which was in its usual whirlwind disarray, clothing tossed everywhere and every square inch covered with such a mishmash that no single item was distinguishable from the next. Two things, however, I did recognize: Mom plopped cross-legged in the middle of the sagging bed and a half-open vinyl suitcase sitting lopsidedly to the side atop more clothes. Her eyes were shut.

I stared. "What're you doing?"

Dana flew by me, giggling, and flung herself across the room, across Mom's lap, knocking them both against the headboard, shrieking like geese on the way to water. "Dreamin', Hank! She's dreaming!"

"Dana! Stop it!" Mom laughed and squirmed as Dana dug her fingers under Mom's arms.

"Caught you, didn't we!?! You're 'sposed to be meditating, Mom, not napping!"

The suitcase tipped and slid clunking to the floor.

"That's enough, honey. Let me up—Dana!"

They sat on the edge of the bed—half laughing, half fussing with hair—then looked up as though just remembering I was there.

"You're both moving to the State Home."

"What?"

"You said guess what."

"Cute, Hank. Nooo—" Dana grinned at Mom and clasped her hand in both hers. "But I am moving—at least for a week or so."

I glanced around the room.

Mom smiled. "Dana's going to Hawaii, honey."

"What?"

Dana popped up and started doing a hula dance, waving arms and hands to one side then the other, her voice warbling like an untuned ukulele.

"She's meeting Jeff in Honolulu. It's called R&R—rest and relaxation."

"How's she gonna pay for—"

"The tickets came today in the mail. From the Army. She's leaving Monday morning."

"Wow. And Jeff's flying there from Vietnam?"

"Yep." Dana grabbed me and tried to get me to dance. "And guess what else?"

"What?"

She looked at Mom. "Should I tell him or should you?"

"I quit smoking, honey."

"You did?"

She drew her knees up under her chin, hugging them. "My second day."

"That's great, Mom."

"Well, I figure I got rid of one bad habit, might as well get rid of a few more."

Dana stopped dancing and picked up the suitcase, hefting it back onto the bed. "I don't know which one was worse." She began folding clothes, repacking them.

Mom looked searchingly at me, chin resting on knees, then reached her hand out. "I think I do."

I clasped it and gazed back, recognizing suddenly in our mother's tired eyes what the other habit was, and fearing that both, when left alone, might smolder.

14

*L*enny drank the rarefied air of birds. When he wasn't studying or painting them, he was racing over the desert landscape, over cactus and rice grass and yucca, with the same freedom redtails and swallows wheeled in the sky above. His running was liquid, elbows and knees flashing with sunlight, his head floating smooth and calm as a leaf down the river. As for me, what had seemed in the early part of that summer to be drudgery or, at most, a painful release, was gradually evolving into something else, lending me a glimpse into that quiet corner of Lenny's mind where no one resided but birds. At least no one else I knew spent one, two, three hours every day running up and down sandstone ledges, adobe hills, or endless arroyos that furrowed the landscape like deep wrinkles across the weathered face of the Grand Valley. But Lenny did. And over that one long summer, I had accompanied him, with Louie dawdling dutifully behind.

Louie. While I gradually grew stronger, more able to bring in oxygen and convert it to energy up steep inclines, Louie lagged. Though not old, he was a large dog made not for speed or distance but for power, probably a descendant of northern rescue dogs. The heat depleted him and Lenny knew it. As the summer wore on and temperatures rose, dousing him in the canal didn't suffice, so we resorted to leaving him to pant underneath the Wagoneer or a bushy juniper that cast ample shade even at noon. Louie seemed to understand, thumping his great tail as we trotted off into the sage and noontime heat. When we returned, Lenny whistled him to roam as he wished, as Lenny set up his portable easel, his brushes and paints. If it was still too hot, he would simply pad off to the nearest urinous scent to lift a leg then curl up in the same spot we had left him. But more likely than not he would follow his nose wherever it led him, often to return wreaking of the foulest death, perfuming himself to be—in his canine mind— even more charming than he already was.

Theirs was a symbiotic relationship. What Lenny provided in food, shelter, and fond scratches around scruff and ears, Louie returned tenfold by way of tomfoolery, affection, and constant companionship. Louie loomed large in Lenny's world, and the rest of us respected it.

What also loomed, but as a storm not sanctuary, was wrestling. After one more match he would be free of it; like me, free of the thing he disliked most. Unfortunately, that final match was against Cisco Salazar—pound for pound, the best ever to emerge from the pungent wrestling room of Grand River High. Yet most knew that Lenny could wrestle with him; after all, he had done so three months of every winter since seventh grade. Though not quite as quick, strong, or wily, Lenny was good and knew Cisco's moves better than anyone. And with Mr. V in his corner, rather than the vitriolic Coach Hicks, Lenny might cut loose and wrestle like never before, maybe even giving Cisco the match of a lifetime. Clay Meeks certainly hadn't, despite the fact that, in the end, one split second was all that had separated them. But because of that second, Cisco had something to prove.

Embarrassed he'd almost been pinned, he had to look especially sharp in the finals to redeem himself not only in the eyes of college coaches but also in his father's. Mr. Salazar was convinced that Cisco had lost. To make his point he refused to attend that final match, as though he'd been waiting all those years not for a perfect record but for this, his son's only defeat.

On our way to Greg's, Julie swung by Mr. V's to wish Lenny luck and to tell him about Magic Club later that night. He no longer was required to make weight, so Molly had cooked his favorite meal, spaghetti and meatballs, and they were right in the middle of it when we arrived. The VanHorns didn't know he had been kicked out of his house and was living atop a hill in his Jeep, and Lenny wanted to keep it that way. He liked staying up there, and the fewer people who knew about it, the better. Besides, Sam and Molly might have disapproved of his living arrangement and may have felt compelled to invite him to stay with them. Molly was due in three months, and Lenny decided that he himself was the last thing they needed to worry about.

As we left, Louie and Huck were having their own wrestling match on the front lawn. It was a one-sided affair with Louie barking, dodging in and out, and racing around as the ancient Huck stood stoically still, eyes half-closed in almost religious tolerance of the younger dog. When Louie saw Julie emerge from the house he stopped roughhousing—to Huck's relief—and greeted her with the ear-pinned fawning of a repentant suitor, tail twitching to the side, his belly exposed for a rub.

At the Woods, Greg and Dillard stood in the circular driveway laughing and examining the side of Greg's graduation present. The car was filthy with mud-streaked sides, a bug-splattered windshield, and beer cans and fast-food wrappers strewn across the back and on the floorboard in front. It had become a newer version of Dillard's Corvair.

"Shining her up, huh, Greg?"

He turned to Julie and smiled. "Hey, what's going on?"

I pointed to the side of the car. "What happened?"

"Oh, just a little accident, Hank. Opened my door into a cowboy boot."

Dillard chortled.

Julie bent down and ran her fingers over the sharp dent in the middle of the door. She glanced disgustedly at her hand before wiping it on the seat of her jeans.

Greg smiled. "You should see the other guy."

"Yeah, you should see the other guy!" Dill grinned. "Woods, you knock me out, maaan."

"We should be so lucky." Julie gazed down the street then back at Greg. "So did you give him his hat back?"

"Not exactly."

"Not exactly?"

"No, but I did give it away. It now rests on the ample pate of one Harlan Sanders. The old boy's actually flush with excitement. It matches his white suit. He's thinking it might even inspire a new ad campaign."

Dillard snorted. "Hey, Woods, I love it when you talk like that, man, like you're really savvy or somethin'."

Julie laughed. "Well put, Dill. The operable word being 'like'."

"Julie, you're weird, maaan." Dillard's head swayed side to side, gazing at the toe of his scuffed-leather shoes sticking out from under frayed bell-bottoms. "What is it with you? You just don't make any sense 'bout half the time, you know what I mean?"

Julie nodded. "Dill, you're absolutely right. I don't know what gets into me. It's like I'm never quite in my right mind."

He stared at her, mouth open. "Really?"

"Yes, really. It's a real problem. Any suggestions?"

His unblinking eyes panned to Greg then back to Julie, brows knitting. "Pot."

"Pot." She stared at him. "Thanks, Dill. That's just . . . perfect."

He nodded, backing up then hurrying across the street to his Corvair.

She turned to Greg now rustling in the back seat. "You know that cowboy's going to be looking for you tonight."

"And look as he may, he's not going to find me." He straightened, pulling out a grocery sack.

"You mean you're not going?" I grabbed his arm. "But it's Lenny's last match, Greg."

He wadded the top of the sack and held it up. "And it's also Magic Club, Hank." He patted the bottom. "The Colonel must be briefed. And debriefed. Assuming, of course, he wears briefs."

Julie shrugged. "So be brief."

He wagged his finger at her, lowering the sack into one arm. "I would, Jules, but I'm growing nostalgic."

"About Magic Club? We can still meet again before you leave."

"No, I mean about the Colonel. We've really bonded."

"Oh, and now Lenny's just another schmuck, I guess."

"No, but you've got to admit, he's probably going to get killed out there tonight."

"So since he's not going to win, you don't want to watch. Is that it?"

"Listen, we'll have a big party afterwards. We'll eat buckets of chicken. Drink pop or whatever the hell they're giving us."

"Great."

"Come on, Julie. I've got to make sure we pull this thing off."

"What's to pull off? We give them Colonel Sanders, they give us chicken. We're not exactly talking about the conference at Yalta here."

He shut the car door. "Tell Lenny good luck and I'll talk to him afterwards. He can tell me all about it. Remember, we're supposed to be on the tenth green at midnight so come over as soon as you can." He carried the sack across the drive to the Woods' front entrance. "Dill! You comin'?"

Dillard waved for Greg to wait as he hurried back across the street, sidling up to Julie. "For you."

She took the joint and held it up, examining it.

He grinned, nodding. "That'll get you goin'." He started across the driveway.

"Hey, Dill."

He turned around, pleased. "Yeah?"

She tossed it, hitting his chest. He fumbled with it as though it would break and then, gaining control, looked up, a question across his face.

Julie smiled, batted her eyelashes. "Eat me."

We climbed into the VW. It was time to leave, to go watch Lenny wrestle Cisco.

◇◇◇

Julie and I took seats a couple of rows behind Peefee and the boys, who encircled Cisco's relatives like personal bodyguards. Peefee smirked at Julie, lifting his chin, while Kenny Madrid looked at me, whipping a finger across his throat. I could only hope that the gesture meant Lenny would lose.

Molly moved down to join us, patting Julie's leg. "Exciting, huh?"

"Hi, Molly. How's Lenny?"

"He and Sam decided he would just go out there and try to enjoy it, being his last match and all. I really don't think he's planning on wrestling in college."

I leaned around Julie. "He's not."

"I didn't think so. How about you, Henry? Are you going to wrestle anymore?"

"Maybe with my sister."

Molly laughed.

"I don't know, Hank." Julie elbowed me. "Dana's pretty wiry."

All twenty wrestlers, wearing a spectrum of color, emerged from the locker room in two rows and lined either side of the maroon and white mat for introductions and *The National Anthem.* Lenny and Cisco were the only two who, after shaking hands, hugged before retreating to warm up. Coach Hicks struck his usual pose behind Cisco, massaging his neck and whispering instructions. Cisco was his only wrestler to reach the finals. On the other side stood Mr. V, chewing gum while watching Lenny skip rope.

"*One-hundred-and-eighteen-pound final, Bartelli from Grand River and Salazar from Grand River, please report.*"

There was a smattering of applause as Lenny and Cisco trotted to the scorer's table to receive their red and green anklets for identification. They both wore the orange and black of Grand River High but Lenny's was an old uniform, his practice togs.

"Hey, Kess." Stankey slid in next to me with two of our other wrestlers, Lloyd Webber and Ben Fritzland. Stankey had worked harder than anyone at wrestling but was still barely mediocre. Yet that same ethic applied to studies had won him a scholarship to Stanford, and the thick horn-rims sliding down his acned face were testament to it. Because he was our heavyweight, Stank would be the last to wrestle, spending that great block of time in a textbook. When it was finally his turn, he would splay the book face down on his chair, slip the glasses off and then over the book's spine and, squinting, walk to the middle of the mat with hands extended as though feeling his way through a cave. We joked that at least he could find consolation in never knowing what the kid looked like who pinned him. Coach Hicks couldn't even get him to warm up first. But it didn't matter; Stank wrestled in braille. "I can't believe Hicks talked me into this thing. I thought I'd seen my last hairy armpit in February."

"Me, too, Stank."

"So you think Cisco'll stick him?"

I shrugged. "I don't know, but I know he's going to try."

Coach Hicks and Mr. VanHorn took their opposing seats as Cisco walked over and hugged his mom and Rudy before joining Lenny in the middle of the mat.

"Go git 'em, Lenny!"

Peefee turned around and glared at Julie, shaking his head then laughing. She leaned into me. "Keep it up, Peepee."

Unlike during the match between Cisco and Meeks, the crowd was milling around, some just arriving. Lenny was the lowest seed still wrestling, a dark horse who wasn't supposed to make it past the second round. That he was wrestling Cisco made it the least-anticipated match of the evening; that it was the first meant more people were still filing in.

At the whistle Lenny immediately shot in for his legs but Cisco spread, then shucked him to the side and tried to step around. Failing that, Cisco backed away and returned to the middle, waiting for him, hands on knees. They tied up, Lenny reaching for an ankle and Cisco yanking him forward and again trying to spin behind, one way then the other. Lenny blocked so Cisco released then abruptly swept in for a single leg, hoisting it and tripping the other one. Lenny fell forward, but caught himself before touching a knee. He reached for a headlock, which Cisco easily countered but out of bounds.

Stank nudged me. "Lenny's lookin' pretty good."

"So far."

Mr. V was up clapping, chomping gum while Coach Hicks sprawled exaggeratedly in his chair, a picture of unconcern. Peefee and the boys were casually looking around, too, checking people out as they filed in.

Lenny feigned a double leg then tried something I'd never seen him do in a match, an arm-drag. Yanking one arm with both his, he sat to one hip and pivoted behind Cisco for a takedown.

"All right, Lenny!" Julie, Molly, and I stood and cheered.

Cisco smiled slightly at his friend's move but couldn't afford to be too amused with college coaches watching. He immediately stood and was almost away when Lenny drove him out of the circle. Two to nothing, Lenny.

"Lenny! Lenny!" Mr. V quickly gestured with his hands, making a circle then clamping an elbow to his body.

They hustled back to the center and at the whistle Cisco quickly switched. Lenny re-switched but was caught sitting underneath and just as the buzzer sounded, Cisco stepped across for the reversal, knotting the score at two.

Peefee and the boys glanced back, nudging each other and snickering.

For the second period, Lenny chose top and immediately tied Cisco up with a figure-four around the waist. Coach Hicks stood, knowing top was Lenny's strongest position, his legs his strongest attribute. Cisco rolled, hooking one knee and trying to slip out the back, but Lenny clamped harder, now around Cisco's chest. Coach Hicks glanced at the clock—one minute and twenty seconds—and began rubbing his hands. Again Cisco rolled through but Lenny remained on top, pushing Cisco's head and prying an arm.

"Stalemate! Stalemate!" Coach Hick's face flushed, his voice booming across the gymnasium. "Stalemate, ref! Come on! Stalemate!"

The referee blew his whistle and pressed fists to his chest, signaling a stalemate, then pointed at Coach Hicks and raised another fist for a warning.

"What!?! What!?!" Coach Hicks stomped over to the scorer's table where he was joined by the referee and Mr. VanHorn. Mr. V placed a hand on the shorter man's shoulder but the coach shrugged it off, screaming across the table. The referee blew his whistle and pointed to each side, ordering the coaches to sit and the match to resume.

"Coach Hicks is such a poodle." Julie shook her head.

Molly smiled. "He is excitable, isn't he?"

"Hey!" Stankey leaned over, craning his neck and scowling at Julie. "That's my coach you're talking about out there!"

Forty-six seconds showed on the scoreboard as the whistle chirped and Cisco shot his legs out. Lenny followed and again slipped on the figure-four. But this time Cisco was ready, one arm wedged between his body and Lenny's leg. Cisco rolled, feverishly prying on Lenny's ankle as he slid his torso out the back, his head finally popping out for a reversal. Frustrated he was ahead by only two, Cisco reached between Lenny's legs with one arm and around his neck with the other, hooking his fingers and rocking him back into a reverse cradle. Lenny propped one shoulder blade using an elbow while tearing at Cisco's hands and kicking his free leg in the air, which Cisco scissored just before the buzzer. The referee extended three fingers, giving Cisco a seven to two lead headed into the final period.

"Come on, Cisco! Stick him, mister!" Coach Hicks scowled. "I want a pin! Let's go!"

Peefee and the boys began stomping against the wooden bleachers, the reverberation rolling like thunder until the entire Grand River side of the gym joined in a deafening stampede. Most spectators had arrived and settled now, and were drawn through the din to the mat.

Mr. V continued to clap and chew gum, egging Lenny on, but everything was now consumed by thrashing feet.

Lenny knelt for the last period and Cisco got into position. The referee raised an arm and with a flick of his hand, blew the whistle. Lenny kipped—the same move I had used against Marble-head—rolling on the inside shoulder and kicking his legs up and over. Anticipating a standup, Cisco had driven his own shoulder into him with an aggressive deep-waist ride, making Lenny's move that much more effective. Their joint momentum catapulted Lenny over the top, flipping Cisco onto his back.

The clamor of feet gave way to a screaming frenzy as Cisco fought the reverse half-nelson. Friends and family, except Rudy, were all standing now, stunned at what they were seeing: Cisco Salazar, for the second match in a row, fighting off a pin.

With his left hand Lenny cupped Cisco's chin, pulling his head to the side; with the other he pried the far arm, keeping it immobilized; and with his chin he dug into Cisco's near shoulder—a textbook pinning combination that Coach Hicks had taught every year he'd been at Grand River High.

The referee studied one shoulder blade then leaped over the wrestlers to study the other. In opposite corners of the mat, Mr. VanHorn and Coach Hicks struck the same pose, both off their chairs on all fours, both too shocked to even yell.

Cisco arched and bridged, flopping one way then the other, working his arm, trying to loosen it from Lenny's grip. Throwing his legs and twisting his hips, he inched toward the periphery of the circle. Lenny tried to pull him back, but with one final bridge, Cisco scooted out of bounds.

Lenny got up and, looking at the clock, walked back to the center. Cisco rolled to his knees, head down, trying to collect himself. The referee placed a hand on his back and pointed to the middle. Cisco stood, bounced up and down, rolling his neck and shaking his arms. Fifty seconds remained to prove himself a champion—to college coaches, to his father, to himself. He jogged to the middle of the mat and dropped down into position. Lenny leaned over him and the whistle sounded.

Cisco Salazar stood and broke Lenny's grip for a one point lead: eight to seven. He moved in, tying up then jamming Lenny's elbow skyward, ducking under the arm, arching and bringing Lenny down for another two points. He immediately let go and, glancing up at the scoreboard, shot in for a fireman's carry, lifting Lenny and bringing him down for another takedown. Again he released and, trapping one arm under his, hit Lenny under the far arm with his forearm—a move we called a Kelly—sending them to the mat and Lenny onto his back.

Ten seconds left but Cisco wasn't through. Receiving two more for a predicament, he let Lenny roll to his stomach and get to his feet. Cisco had one more move, one more opportunity. Hugging Lenny from behind, hands locked around the waist, he arched, lifting Lenny off the mat. Arching farther, chin to ceiling, he fell backward like a timber onto the top of his head—before which he was supposed to twist and throw Lenny to his back—but from where, instead, he didn't move, Lenny's full weight falling on him as the buzzer sounded, ending the match.

The scoreboard showed sixteen to nine as Lenny got up and walked to the middle to shake hands. But his opponent remained on his back at mat's edge, his head cocked slightly to one side. The gymnasium fell silent as though noise were smoke and wind had galed through. The referee, Mr. V, and Coach Hicks all converged and knelt as Lenny unsnapped his headgear and, turning, chest heaving, gazed across with everyone else, at the frozen figure of his friend, Cisco Salazar.

◇ ◇ ◇

The waiting room was full. Women sat two to a chair, children on laps, while men clustered in knots speaking in hushed tones, leaning against walls or squatting on their haunches. Rudy was parked as a sentry inside the door, his chin tucked sideways and bathed in saliva; his hands bent and skewed, fingers waving like antennae measuring the air.

"Come on." Julie led us down the hallway to the emergency room lounge near admissions.

I could see our reflection move across the large plate glass that separated us from the darkness outside. Stankey and I sat on the sofa and Lenny slumped into an orange chair. His hair under the gray hooded sweatshirt was still damp from showering, and he'd changed into army pants and dirty sneakers.

Nurses' shoes squeaked against freshly waxed tile, and a tray rolled past, rubber out-of-round wheels jittering with our nerves down the fluorescent corridor.

Julie gnawed a cuticle. "What time is it?"

Stank glanced at his watch. "Ten."

"What's taking so long?" She waved. "Excuse me."

A man in a green gown carrying a clipboard stopped and looked at her.

"Um, we're waiting to hear about somebody in the emergency room. His name's Cisco Salazar."

He studied us. "Are you relatives?"

"No, they're all in the waiting room. We're friends."

"Sorry." He continued down the hallway.

"Can't you at least find out if he's okay?"

He hesitated, glancing over his shoulder. "See what I can do."

Julie watched him disappear around a corner. "Friendly."

Stankey grimaced, shaking his head. "Maybe he should see what he can do about that stethoscope stuck up his butt."

I heard the familiar click of taps against tile and, turning, saw Peefee round the corner with Silver Renteria, Frank Serrano, and Kenny Madrid. They would have passed us, so purposefully were they walking, had it not been for Julie standing there. I sank lower into the couch as he stopped and raised his chin.

Julie walked over. "Have you heard anything?"

Peefee glared. "Wha's it to you, man?"

"Come on, Peefee. He's our friend, too."

"Yeah, man—surrre." He looked past her at Lenny, raised an index finger, and sighted down his arm, then resumed clicking down the hallway.

Stankey sighed. "Charmed, I'm sure."

Resting his head back against the chair, Lenny gazed at the ceiling. He'd said little since we left the gym for St. Anthony's, only that he didn't know what happened. Mr. V said the move Cisco tried was called a soufflé. It was advanced, used in freestyle not high school wrestling. Had it worked, Cisco probably would have been penalized; had Lenny been hurt, he would have been disqualified. As it was, neither one had occurred.

It had taken almost half an hour for the rescue squad to stabilize and move Cisco onto the stretcher and into the ambulance backed up on the sidewalk outside. Molly assisted a physician from the stands in keeping him quiet and checking vital signs before they arrived, and while they worked, she sat with her arm around Lenny on the bottom bleacher. Mr. V and Coach Hicks followed the ambulance to the hospital and we hadn't seen them since. We heard later that the tournament resumed but that many spectators had lost their appetite for it and had gone home.

Julie paced, combing fingers through her hair. "I can't stand it. I'm going down there."

I shook my head. "They won't let you in."

"Well, maybe the Salazars know something."

"Yeah, like they're going to tell us."

"What is this, Henry—an us and them thing? I could give a rat's hiney what Peefee and his—"

"There's Molly." I pointed down the hallway.

Stankey and I stood as Julie hurried over to her. They hugged.

"They've moved him to intensive care."

"Is he going to be okay?"

"They won't know anything for a while."

"But is he going to—"

"Sweetie, the best thing you can do is go home and get some sleep. All of you. It's getting late." Molly noticed Lenny still slouched in the chair. "I'll call you tomorrow as soon as I know something. Lenny, are you going to be all right?"

He stood and nodded.

"Listen, Cisco's in incredible physical condition. If anyone can recover, it's him."

Julie blanched. "But recover from what?"

Molly hooked an arm and led us toward the exit. "Don't worry. I'll call you first thing in the morning. We should know more by then."

"What took you?" Greg opened the door and led us down the hallway to his bedroom. "I was about ready to call the station and postpone. They've been publicizing this thing all day. Where's Lenny?"

His room was dark except for a small light from the TV that illuminated Dillard's grinning, intent face.

"Hey, man, check this out." Dill was sprawled on the sofa against the far wall, pointing to the screen. "*War of the Colossal Beast*, man. This general dude keeps gettin' bigger and bigger 'cause of radiation from this, like, nuclear blast.

That was in the first one, *The Amazing Colossal Man*. Now he's on like a rampage, maaan. Look at him, he's headed toward—"

"Dill, shut the hell up." Greg pressed palms against his head, massaging his temples. "So where is he?"

Julie sat on the edge of the waterbed. "You won't believe it."

"Believe what?" He lowered his hands. "Come on, Jules. We have to get rolling, here. It's almost eleven-thirty." He turned to me. "Don't tell me he won."

"Not exactly. I mean, no, he didn't win but Cisco got hurt."

"So he did win. A DQ. All right!" He pumped his fist. "Hey, a win's a win, Hank. You take it, man. A DQ's just another way of saying I beat your ass."

"Greg." Julie shook her head. "You don't understand. Cisco really is—"

"Ohhhh, maaan!" Across the room Dillard leaned toward the screen. "He's really gettin' it now! Look, he's tangled up in all this electrical wire and stuff."

"Dillard, watch the movie quietly or shut the damn thing off." Greg reached over and clicked on a lamp. "So Lenny is or isn't coming?"

"Isn't." Julie stood, sheets rippling across the waterbed. "And neither are we. Come on, Hank, let's get out of here."

"Hey, wait a minute—" He grabbed her arm. "Hold on, Jules. What're you doing? This is Magic Club."

"No, this is stupid."

He put an arm around her. "Come on, it's probably our last one. I just want everybody here, that's all. Like it's always been. Look." He pointed at Colonel Sanders standing in the corner, a black hood over his head.

I walked over and felt it. "What's this?"

"My old lady's satin pillowcase." He smiled. "He's a hostage, right? A kidnap victim. We can't have him leading the police back to the scene of the crime."

Julie stared at him. "You are losing it."

"Wowww! All rrright!" Dillard's face drew inches from the television, which was making a crackling and buzzing sound.

"Okay. That's it." Greg strode over and popped it off.

"Hey! Come on, Woods! The colossal man was just gettin' juiced! Electrocuted, maaan!" Watching Greg turn away, he reached out and flipped it back on, turning it low. "I'll be quiet. Hey, you better get going, man. You're late."

"Yeah, we are late." Greg rushed over to his closet and grabbed a paper sack. "Here." He tossed us something.

Julie gawked. "You're kidding?" She fingered the dark blue knitting. "Ski masks?"

"No, I'm not kidding. You want them to see us? Dill, you have the recorder?"

He nodded, eyes still stuck to the screen.

"Remember. Start recording about a quarter 'til. Dillard?"

"Okay, okay."

Greg bear-hugged the Colonel and lifted him. "Come on, big guy. Time for our last tango."

The air was cool. I could hear the chit-chit-chit of sprinkler heads stuttering across the tenth fairway as we circled the Woods' swimming pool and hopped across the gurgling ditch onto the golf course. The wet grass glowed with a milky sheen under a half moon, and we had to zigzag to keep from being hit by the wide sweeps of water.

Greg stopped, setting the Colonel down. "Whew! Feels like the old boy's been dipping too much into his own stock. What time is it, Jules?"

"No lungs, huh, Woods? It's straight up."

"Hank, help me with this. You grab his legs."

"Boy, this ski mask is making my face and head itch."

"You don't have to wear it until we get there, Hank. We already know who you are. It's them I'm worried about."

Julie giggled as I pulled the mask off. Hers she had folded on top of her head like a stocking cap.

We continued down the fairway toward the tenth green, Greg and I carrying the Colonel underarm as if he were a ladder. Houses skirted the fairway on one side, a row of cottonwoods lined the other, and the clubhouse perched on a knoll beyond.

"There they are." Greg pointed toward the green. A KRIV van was backed up on the grass and a cluster of people gathered nearby. "Okay, pull your masks down."

As we approached, the disc jockey's voice crackled from a speaker strung over to the parking lot and echoed across the adjoining tennis courts.

"Carl, we're getting too much feedback. Turn the volume down. Look! There they are!"

We stopped at the edge of a sand trap above the green and laid the Colonel down.

". . . four, three, two—"

"Welcome back to Grand River Country Club where, as most of you know, we're meeting on the tenth green with the kidnappers of our beloved Colonel

Harlan Sanders. And standing with me is the manager of Kentucky Fried Chicken, Mr. Kevin Larston."

"Hi, Robert."

"Kevin, please explain to those of our listening audience who may have been, I don't know, ice-fishing on the North Pole the last couple weeks—explain the contest and what's been involved."

"Well, uh, as you know, Colonel Sanders was stolen—"

"Kidnapped."

"—kidnapped about two weeks ago from our Gateway Avenue store."

"That's right. Spirited away under the cloak of darkness, I understand."

"Right out from under our noses."

"And that's, I believe, when it started, right, Kevin? Now tell us about the contest."

"Well, over the last couple of weeks, customers or anybody else could come in and fill out an entry-blank and write down when they thought the Colonel would be returned."

"Or rescued, as it were. And during this time I understand you've had quite a sale going on over there."

"Yes, during these last two weeks we've had a tremendous response. Customers can get three pieces of chicken cooked in the Colonel's own special recipe, coleslaw, roll, and a nice cold drink, all for just two ninety-nine."

"Well, what a bargain, Kevin. I know I've sure taken advantage of it. Now, is this special going to be continuing?"

"Well, because of the tremendous response and as a thank-you to our customers, we've decided to run it one more week in celebration of the Colonel's return."

"A kind of reunion sale."

"Yes, I guess it is."

"So now that brings us to the tenth hole of the Grand River Country Club golf course. What on earth are we doing here—heh, heh, heh. Can you tell us, Kevin, all that's been going on over these last couple of weeks?"

"Uh, yes, we've been in constant contact with the kidnapper, negotiating a, uh—"

"Ransom."

"Yes, ransom—and we finally agreed to meet today at midnight for the, uh, exchange."

"And what is the amount of the ransom because, as you know, Kevin, we've just been joined by those—it looks like three—extremely shady-looking characters. They're standing right across the tenth-hole green from us. What's in it for them?"

"Well, we're paying them four buckets of chicken, mashed potatoes and gravy, a half-gallon of the Colonel's own special slaw, and a case of cola."

"Quite a hefty ransom, I must say. But before we meet these desperados, I think you have someone else to introduce. Right, Kevin?"

"Yes, I do. Standing here with us is the winner of the Return the Colonel Contest, Mr. Warren Dillard."

"And he just got here, too. Congratulations. We weren't sure you were going to make it, Warren."

"Thanks, man—"

"Just speak into the mike."

"Right. My friends call me Dill."

"So, Dill—as in the pickle, right?—heh, heh. Tell me what your guess was and how you came up with it."

"Oh, I don't know. I just like, you know, guessed. I didn't have no, like, inside information or nothing. I just, you know—people are always telling me I'm kind of psychic or something, you know what I mean?"

"Warren the Psychic Pickle—sounds like a pilot for a new sitcom—heh, heh, heh. And Kevin, what was Warren's guess?"

"Well, it looks like he hit it right on the mark. Saturday the eleventh at midnight."

"My, he is psychic. And what has he won?"

"A free month's worth of finger-lickin' good chicken. I would like to present him with this certificate, which enables him to come by the restaurant at anytime within the next thirty days for free meals."

"What a great prize, Kevin. And congratulations to you, Warren Pickle."

"It's Dillard, man. My friends call me—"

"And now the moment we've all been waiting these two weeks for. But first, we're going to take a short break and then we'll be back with the kidnappers and the return of Colonel Harlan Sanders. Stay tuned." The disk jockey lowered the mike and waved us over.

"No, not yet." Greg held his arms out. "Dillard, that double-crossin'—"

"What?" I peered at Greg from the dark holes of the mask and hooked a finger, stretching the nose over. "You mean you didn't know he was going to do this?"

"Hell, no." Greg bent down and lifted the Colonel, standing him up on the edge of the green. "Hey! You come over here!"

The disk jockey dropped both arms in exasperation. "Let's go, kids! Forty-five seconds and we're going to be back on the air!"

"Come on, Greg." Julie tugged his arm. "It doesn't matter. Let's get this thing over with."

"It does matter." He glanced around, the white design on his dark mask glowing in the moonlight.

Julie started across the green.

"Okay, okay—wait." He fumbled in his jeans' pocket before bear-hugging the Colonel and walking him across the green. I followed, pulling at the mask and scratching through the knitting.

"That's great! Look, Kevin, they've got masks and the Colonel's wearing a hood!"

The manager's stare bored into us, so I turned my head, his face disappearing into the fabric.

The disk jockey stepped toward us. "What a great prank, kids. Now what are your names?"

Greg held up his arms and crossed them. The Colonel tipped, and Julie and I grabbed and righted him.

"Oh, yeah—heh, heh, heh. No names to protect the, uh, guilty in this case, right?"

"Twenty seconds!"

"Okay, Carl. Listen up now, kids—just relax and we'll play this thing up like a real kidnapping situation."

Greg nodded. "It is real."

"All right, good. Here we go."

"Four, three, two—"

"Welcome back to a very tense situation, ladies and gentlemen. Before me this very moment are three crazed kidnappers with none other than Colonel Harlan Sanders, who stands bound and hooded before us. Do you have anything to say, Colonel?" He held the mike to the hood. Through the mask I could see Dill grinning like a chimp as the manager continued to glare. Behind them stood a young woman holding a cord, and next to the van another guy, a technician.

"Ladies and gentlemen, the Colonel seems a bit dazed and confused, which is certainly understandable after enduring these difficult weeks in captivity. Now, let's see if we can't get a word with the kidnappers. Why have you three committed this heinous crime?" He held the mike out to Greg. I could see the disk jockey roll his hand to try to get Greg to speak. "No comment, huh? How about you, Miss? Here's what appears to be a female perpetrator, ladies and gentlemen. The Sadie Mae Glutz of the gang. Miss, what drove you to kidnap Colonel Sanders?" He reached the mike out.

Julie coughed and cleared her throat through the mask, glancing at me then Greg. "Well, I guess I just can't get enough of that big white meat."

Greg's head whipped toward Julie, and I could see the whites of his eyes gleam through the eyeholes.

"Not that I don't love dark meat, mind you."

I heard Dill snorting in the background. Greg nudged Julie over, wrapping an arm back around the Colonel.

"Oookay then—ahem. The joys of live radio, ladies and gentlemen. Maybe we should skip over the idle chitchat and get right to it—heh, heh. Yes, they're obviously seasoned veterans in the cruel business of crime. Let's bring Kevin Larston back in here. Kevin, before we pay the ransom and make the exchange, do you have anything you want to say to these heartless thugs?"

"Yes, I do." He pushed his glasses up his nose and jabbed a finger straight at Greg. "Crime—never—pays." He glared.

"Heh, heh, heh. Well, Kevin, apparently it does in this case, right? Because what do we have for these three blackhearts?"

The girl stepped back and picked up three large white sacks and dropped them on the green, and the manager followed, hefting a case of pop and setting it in front of us.

"Mr. Kevin Larston, the manager of Kentucky Fried Chicken, has just made the drop, ladies and gentlemen. He has just handed over the ransom and it is now the kidnappers who must return the favor. Any final words?"

He held the microphone out as Greg scooted the Colonel forward and slipped one hand under the hood. I heard a click and could see what I thought to be a flashlight glow through the satin.

"The kidnappers are removing the hood . . ."

Greg lifted the pillowcase and I saw the silver swatch of duct tape in the glow behind the Colonel's ear then I heard a hiss.

"Oh, my, ladies and gentlemen—the Colonel has now become a—heh, heh, heh—he's now a she! What the—"

"Death to the capitalist pigs!"

In a single hissing flash, I saw the Colonel's garishly painted face, the widening eyes of the disk jockey and his assistant, and the mortified expression of the manager as Greg yanked Julie and me backwards—half falling, half running—and then a deafening explosion of white showering over the ninth-hole green of the Grand River Country Club golf course.

16

Mom and I took Dana to the airport on the same day Redd Morgan began mowing. Dana wore a dress, something she hadn't done since her sophomore year of high school, and its hem was even higher than Mom's waitress uniform, barely reaching the tan line around her upper thigh. She said Jeff would be pleased; I said along with every other serviceman on the island. As usual, Mom cried as though she would be gone a year instead of a week, and Dana crammed three Samsonites with enough to stay ten. I lugged them up to the counter, while Dana carried her airline tickets and a red leather address book given to her by Mr. Shimizu. It held names of relatives she could call if she and Jeff needed any assistance or direction around Honolulu. Mr. Shimizu's family was in everything from food sculpture to foot massage, furniture re-upholstery to window dressing. And if she ran out of money, a second cousin could lend her enough to get back, he said, but only if she was desperate because his interest rates were locked in for bailing out the incarcerated.

When Mom and I returned home, Redd already had the lawn mower unloaded from his truck bed and fired up on the driveway. He was bent over, face flushed, adjusting the choke as we sat there in the car waiting. Mom gazed over the steering wheel chewing her bottom lip and Redd didn't even look up, the front bumper just feet from his head. She hadn't seen him since the night he smacked me, telling Dana to say she wasn't home whenever he called. Now he was taking his sweet time, letting Mom soak up the magnanimous act he was about to perform. Never before had he as much as picked up a dirty glass in our household except to maybe refill it or drain it down that stubbled sinkhole of his. Finally, straightening and revving the mower for effect, he blasted off the driveway and across the lawn like a man consumed, which of course he was.

Greg, too, was consumed but with the burn from a different fuse. After we ran stumbling across the tenth fairway and into his house—Julie sobbing, Greg laughing maniacally, and me vibrating like a gong—Mr. and Mrs. Woods abruptly returned from a Saturday night out. You could tell they had been drinking and arguing, and they were oblivious to anything else, not even commenting when Julie bolted from the house with another round of emotion and tore squealing from their driveway in her Volkswagen. As for me, I sat numbly on Greg's couch watching TV with the sound turned off and Jim Morrison and The Doors blasting from the stereo while his parents' tongues rose and lashed above the din. Manic as ever, Greg danced wildly by himself, singing the lyrics and, between songs, recounting the mayhem we had wreaked out on the golf course. He couldn't get over the manager and DJ's expressions at seeing the Colonel's transformation just before head and torso blew skyward. A coup de grâce, he kept saying, the perfect swan song for Magic Club; if only Lenny could have been there it would've been perfect. But Lenny wasn't there, and as the ringing in my ears began to subside I wished like anything that I hadn't been either.

That Monday, after Redd emptied the last catcher-full and drove away with his mower, I went outside to get the Grand River Sentinel. Loose clumps of grass lay here and there, and a skid of green ran the length of the driveway then double-backed to the curb where Redd had loaded the mower back into his truck. He had dumped the clippings in the alleyway, and I knew that the city garbage collectors wouldn't pick them up unless they were bagged. Now the pile smelled of summer; soon it would reek with flies. But I was amazed Redd had caught the grass, much less cut it in the first place.

I sat on the front step and unrolled the paper: *U.S. air strikes pound North Viet coast, Nixon returns from Moscow summit, Munich braces for '72 Olympics, Bomb threat empties McGovern's plane.* On the last page of the sports' section, under an article about the U.S. Olympic track team, was a rundown of The College Coaches' Senior Classic stating that, among others, Cisco Salazar defeated Lenny Bartelli sixteen to nine for the one-hundred-and-eighteen-pound championship. It didn't mention an injury, though, and I hadn't talked to Julie, the VanHorns, or anyone else since that Saturday night, choosing instead to stay in the cool of the basement and read. But I couldn't quit thinking about Cisco, couldn't stop imagining one family having two children in wheelchairs.

As I got up and folded the paper to go inside, a small heading on the bottom-right corner of the front page caught my eye. Taking a breath, I unfolded it: "Four injured in explosion. In an act of reckless endangerment, three people ignited an as-yet unidentified explosive, injuring four and blowing up the mascot of Kentucky Fried Chicken." I held my head and slumped back down. The DJ's assistant was treated for two cuts on her face, the DJ for hearing loss and headaches, and, oddly, the technician, who was several feet back, for shock, probably from witnessing the others hit the ground in a hail of plastic. The investigating officer was quoted as saying "we have a pretty good description of the three suspects" and I immediately thought of Dill and wondered if he was hurt and whether he really had known what Greg had planned. I finally decided he was probably fine and hadn't known anything. But how did the police get a description? Then I remembered the night at Kentucky Fried and convinced myself that the manager recognized Dill and more than likely pieced it together himself.

Feeling weak, I ripped the article out, stuffed it into my pocket, and trudged back inside to find Mom rifling through the kitchen drawers, the phone pinched under her chin.

"He just went outside. I'll go—oh, you did. Well, thank you, Gregory." She slid the drawer closed and opened another. "I'm flattered, but there's no reason to—" Stooping and grabbing the phone, she peered inward. "Well, that's nice of you." She reached in and felt around then straightened, shaking her head. "I will, Greg. Don't worry. We're fine. You better come by and see us before you leave. When do you have to be there?" She opened the cupboard and, standing on tiptoes and craning her neck, slid boxes around like pieces on a chessboard. "That soon? Oh, my. I'm sure you have a thousand things to do." She hesitated, staring into the cupboard, one hand atop her head. "You will? That'll be lovely, Greg. I'm looking forward to it. You, too. Okay, thanks for calling. Bye, Greg." She hung up and opened another drawer, rummaging through it.

I stepped into the kitchen. "What're you looking for, Mom?"

She stopped—one hand in the drawer, the other clutching a lighter—and looked up. "Oh, I'm just—" Sliding it closed, she took a deep breath and forced a smile. "That was Greg."

"What'd he want?"

"I'm not sure. Guess he was just wondering how we're doing."

"What'd you tell him?"

She placed the lighter on the counter and tapped fingers to her lips as though distracted, as though she had forgotten something. "Fine, honey." She walked to the back door. "I told him we're doing just fine." Then she went outside into the backyard, and I watched through the kitchen window as she began retracing Redd's mower tracks in our lawn like an ascetic fingering the lines of a mandala. Yeah, fine. We were doing just fine.

◊◊◊

Over the next week I didn't see much of anyone, staying home or going to Sage Diner where I began bussing tables to help Mom out. Without Dana or Redd around, she had increased her hours and started working almost as much as Arlene, who seemed never to leave the place. Punk barely acknowledged my work, but by Friday he was asking if I had cleared off a table or wiped down the counter or vinyl booths. Still I was surprised when he slipped two twenties into my jacket and Mom and Arlene chipped in with a couple fistfuls of change. I'd never considered working at Sage Diner; it had just happened, like the rain.

Temperatures in Grand River had already reached into the upper-nineties that middle part of June, not a cloud floating across pale skies. Then it poured for three days, swelling the Colorado and Gunnison Rivers and crumbling the banks near Riverside Park. The front page of the paper showed residents packing sandbags to stem the high water, and there in the background stood Peefee and Kenny Madrid loading wheel barrels. As soon as the storm passed, I drove splashing along the river to Rabbit Valley, pulling over finally and slogging the last mile for fear of Mom's Dodge sliding off the road. Standing at the turnoff, I stared across the prairie at my father's *Airstream*, puddles shining under the breaking sky like silver coins tossed around it, and then rushed back to Sage in time for lunch hour.

Julie called just before taking off for Denver and the State Democratic Convention with Cameron Pippin III. She had an argument with her mother about going but eventually prevailed by recruiting her father's support and inviting Margaret Kohler along. I smiled at the thought of Cameron's expression when Margaret climbed into the car, too, and then his blank stare all the way over the mountains as she demonstrated to him her vast understanding of American politics—from a Republican point of view. Julie was in a lather about the likelihood of McGovern winning most of Colorado's delegates to the national convention in Miami and chattered on about the possibility of going there to see his nomination herself. Neither of us mentioned the previous Saturday night on the golf course, but she did say that they upgraded Cisco's condition from critical to serious and that maybe we could visit him soon. Still no one had fully explained to me what exactly was wrong with him, only that he remained immobilized somewhere inside St. Anthony's.

I hadn't heard from Greg since his call to Mom, but Mrs. Woods phoned to invite me to the going away party. He was supposed to report to the Air Force Academy Monday July third so the party was to be the day before. She said she was going to surprise him with two upperclassmen cadets who had been instrumental in recruiting him. One was from Pinecrest, the other from

Otto, and they were going to drive all the way to Grand River just to attend the party before escorting him back. I tried to imagine Greg in obsidian shoes and a starched, sharply creased Air Force uniform, his ringlets of blond hair shorn to stubbled side walls, his slouchy golfer's shoulders slung back with puffed chest and bowed neck. I suddenly had an image of Dudley Do-Right of the Mounties spouting "I'll save you, Nell!" But instead of Nell lashed to the tracks it would be Julie. Her affection all those years was definitely cracking, though, and with the shattering of Colonel Sanders may have completely broken. Ironically, I thought, Julie's indifference—she had even stopped worrying about his driving—might be Greg's only punishment.

Lenny had disappeared again. When I saw Peefee and Kenny Madrid's picture in the paper, I thought how the rain was a good distraction for them, but then I started worrying about what they would do if they caught Lenny. I worried, too, where he and Louie were staying if his Wagoneer couldn't climb The Three Sisters in all that mud. Checking the most likely places—including Mrs. Bartelli's, which as usual looked deserted with all curtains pulled and not a light on anywhere—I finally decided there was only one place he could be.

I drove east out of town past peach and cherry orchards, past Trail's End Motel, Bookcliff Mortuary, The Palace of Fruits. Finally finding the right county road, I pulled Mom's car over on the gravel shoulder and began walking along the canal. The water ran fast and red from the storm's runoff, and the far bank was scorched black from a farmer burning weeds, the damp char smell wafting across the sweet scent of canal water and the half-burned cattails jutting like tempered spears from the ground. Lenny's Wagoneer was parked under a cottonwood a good distance from the house—if you could call it a house—and I remembered what he said about not scaring away Miss Darling's customers, which it probably would have, covered in dried mud as it was, with only the wiper-streaked windshield showing through and big old Louie snoozing under the back bumper.

I walked down the embankment through the kochia weeds to the gate, the Pomeranians barking like crazy, and knocked. The air felt thick as steam, as if the weeds were wilting from all the rain. I knocked again, louder, the dogs twirling and yipping hysterically. Then, turning to leave, I spotted them. They were standing over an open fire. Miss Darling fanning the flames with a sagebrush branch. Lenny squatting, tearing newspaper, balling it before feeding the fire. I blinked. Shook my head. Looked again. But there they were, beyond my imagination, beyond the dilapidated Cadillac in front of a tent-like structure the shape of an igloo. The sun beating down on them, the smoke rising between them. Them—naked.

Wanting to leave, but wanting more for them not to be there —like *this*—I coughed, a feeble throat-clearing cough and then as my mind began to clear with the sky above, coughed again, this time the rumbling cough of thunder, as though Zeus himself were hawking one up. Lenny looked up as Miss Darling continued to fan. He waved, waved as though he spotted me at a picnic. I couldn't lift an arm, couldn't utter a word. He motioned me over. Glancing around, half hoping this was a hallucination but knowing it wasn't, I walked over nonchalantly as though nothing was wrong.

"Hi, Hank."

I nodded.

"What's up?"

I shrugged, glancing at Miss Darling then quickly away. She had yet to look up so focused was she on the fire.

Lenny wadded more paper, tossed it in the middle of some rocks.

"That's enough." Placing a hand on the small of her back, she half-straightened. "Almost ready." She threw the branch to the side and gazed up. "Look!" She pointed a gnarled finger skyward. "Our friend the redtail." A hawk circled. Lowering her head, she peered at me over her thick glasses, the only article she wore. "You led him here—"

Not knowing if this was a question or statement, I looked at her eyes, her wild wisps of gray hair, her leathery skin lying in folds like the underside of some ancient mammal. Then I remembered what Greg had called her, the ancient lady. I turned to Lenny for an answer, as though he might have one, my best friend who had clearly plunged stark raving into the deep.

"It's a sweat lodge, Hank." He nodded toward the tent. "We're takin' a sweat."

"Strip so we can get started." Miss Darling pointed to a pitchfork. "The stones are ready."

I glanced at the canal road to see if anyone was happening by, rubbed palms against my pant legs.

Lenny walked over to a splintered handle jutting from a clump of earth turned up among the weeds. "It's okay, Hank. We'll go in as soon as you're ready. No one will see ya."

Miss Darling hobbled over to the entrance, a canvas flap held with a pink hair clip. She turned. "Don't then. But if a redtail circles and you don't enter, it's bad luck." She squinted, studying me. "Suit yourself, but you'll have to leave. The Great Spirit doesn't take kindly to lollygaggers." Cackling, she bent arthritically down to one knee, then the other, her cheeks puffing in and out with exertion, the two halves of her creased where she should be, but her back bent cruelly to one side. "*Mitakuye oyasin.*" She kissed the ground then struggled on all fours through the opening.

I looked at Lenny; he at me, grinning. "Well?"

"What'd she say?"

"It's Lakota, Hank. It means 'all my relations.'" He drove the rusty pitchfork under a lava rock, ashes lifting and swirling over the coals.

"What are you doing, Lenny?"

He pushed the handle down, prying up the rock. "My job's to move the fire." He lifted.

"No, I mean what're you *doing* doing—here?"

"It's a sweat, Hank. You know, an Indian deal."

"Yeah, but—"

"Quit yakkin' out there and bring those stones!"

Lenny carried the rock to the entrance, crouched and ducked inside before emerging with the pitchfork. I stood back and watched him repeat this six more times. "You comin'?" Grabbing the handle of a bucket, he knelt to enter.

I glanced around. "I don't know, Lenny. I—"

"Spotted Spider says spirits from the four directions have come!"

I turned toward Miss Darling's voice coming from the lodge and licked my lips. "Spotted Spider?"

Lenny shrugged then poked his head in, lifting the bucket and swinging it inside.

"Lenny, can I, um, keep my underwear on?"

He turned, smiling, then kissed the ground—"*Mitakuye oyasin*"—before disappearing inside.

I pulled off my shirt, kicked shoes to the side, and slid off my cutoffs. "I'm comin'." I knelt and hooked a thumb under the elastic waistband when something wet and smooth nudged my backside. "Ahhh!" I whipped around to a smiling black snout. "Geez, Louie!" Tail waving, he licked my leg. I pulled my underwear snugly *up*, crawled through as Louie cautiously stretched forward sniffing the air behind me.

Light from the small opening fell over Miss Darling's bare shoulder and across the fire pit in the middle of an earthen ring. In the shadows on the opposite side of the entrance knelt Lenny. "This way, Hank."

I crawled around the circle to the far side of the pit and sat beside him, cross-legged like I imagined an Indian would.

"Everything moves clockwise—remember that." Miss Darling stripped a handful of sage leaves from a branch and clenched them in her fist. "No asking for money in here, you understand? No wishing ill will on nobody, either. I got my own ways of doing that if I need to. What you want to do is give thanks and ask for reasonable things. Things of a positive nature. Spirits know when you're up to no good. Just be respectful and humble and the spirits'll bless you and watch over you. Got it?" She threw the sage over the rocks and stripped off another handful from the branch and held them out. "Okay. Go get the rest."

Lenny crawled out of the tent and there was the sandy clang of metal against rock as he transferred the rest of the hot stones one-by-one into the lodge. When he finished and knelt at the entrance to re-enter, his skin glistened in the low sunlight slanting behind him and the hot stones glowing before. "*Mitakuye oyasin.*" He kissed the ground.

Miss Darling nodded. "Come in and close it off."

Reaching outside, Lenny yanked the flap down then tied it off so not a drop of light leaked through. As Dad used to say, it was blacker than the inside of a cow. And hot. I could hear Miss Darling's hand cup water from the bucket and splash it over the pit. The stones hissed and the steam hit me flush on the face, burning along my arms and over my shoulders.

"*Wankan-tanka*, as you can see, two human beings are with us today. Spotted Spider tells me they wish to speak to you, oh Great Spirit." She cast the sage over the pile of rocks and they crackled in the heat. "Last night I was walking in a forest of pine trees and spruce and aspen groves and there, lying on a rock, was a bird with its wing broken. I went to it and asked how it had come to this rock unable to fly or move or sing its morning song. The bird told me that Lightning had struck it, plucking it from the sky and the rock was waiting there to catch it but that it broke its wing instead. I picked it up from the stone and kissed it on the beak and it took flight from my hands and disappeared into the highest branch of a majestic pine. The rock asked me why I had kissed the bird, freeing it from its bed of stone. I didn't know what to say, then it started to rain. Then Thunder came and with it Lightning, and the rock was wet and cold again without the blanket of feathers that was now perched high in the tree. 'I am cold again,' said the rock. 'The bird was a blanket upon my flat back. Why did you set it free?' Still I didn't know what to say, but the Thunder Beings spoke for me in their loud rumbling voices and told the rock that my destiny was to kiss the bird that broke its wing and free it to fly to the other side to be with them in the spirit world. The rock understood then and I could hear the bird sing high in the tree and even though I could no longer see it, I knew that it was there."

The lodge fell silent, not even the coals hissing or the sage crackling. Bathed in sweat, I could feel droplets sprout from me and trickle down my sides and chest and the back of my legs. The air was so hot that the tiny hairs inside my nostrils felt singed.

"Thank you, Grandfather. Thank you, Grandmother—*Unci*—thank you for the Great Mystery, for the moon and stars, for Spotted Spider and for Little Horse who now prances around the fire. Thank you for the spirit of Black Elk who sits with us to observe and fart and guide us on our journey. And thank you for the redtail who circles and helps us heal. Thank you Great Spirit, *Wankan-tanka*, thank you for your many gifts. *Hi-ya, hi-ya, hi-ya, hi-ya, hi-yo, hi-yo, hi-yo, hi-yo—*"

As Miss Darling prayed and sang I could hear Lenny quietly join in, his voice but a whisper, lilting and lowing with the sacred cadence of prayer and song.

"Let the air in, little brother."

Lenny untied the flap and folded it back. Through the opening I could see the sky blaze over Rimrock, and a faint rush of air soothed my burning skin. We sat silently for several seconds, then Lenny tied the flap down and blackness again embraced us with heat.

"*O'ha—*"

I jumped. The voice I heard wasn't hers—though a whisper, it was distinctly male.

"I am Eagle Horse. I come from the east." She flicked more water and it hissed over the coals. "I welcome the Thunder Beings and Blue Lightning who bring rain from the west to fortify Mother Earth." There was the thrush of sagebrush as the leaves were stripped, redolent as in the desert after rainfall. "I see Crazy Face from the north who brings snow to purify and blanket *Maka* in winter dress. And here's Walks Among the Clouds from the south, the direction all our brothers and sisters travel when we leave this life. *O'ha*—welcome, all of you." She threw the leaves and I could hear them shrivel and curl. "Little brother, it is time to speak. Tell, *Wankan-tanka* your troubles."

I could hear Lenny rustling, repositioning himself and then my friend—

my best friend who rarely said anything to anybody—began to talk into the still black heat of the sweat lodge.

"Thank you, Grandmother Moon and Father Sky and Mother Earth. I want to thank my friend Hank for—for first bringing me here to Miss Darling. And thank you, Miss Darling, for opening my eyes."

Silence filled the darkness again, and just as I began to say something—anything to break the hot black nothingness both enveloping me and welling up inside—Lenny continued.

"I want to ask the Great Spirit to please look after my mom. She's, well, you know—to keep her healthy and from not being so mad. And also my brother Vince. Please protect him from bad things. But most of all, Great Spirit"— Lenny's voice broke and I could hear him clear his throat and take a deep breath. "—for my friend Cisco. Please make him okay again. Amen. I mean, uh—what do I say?"

"*Ha-ho.*"

"*Ha-ho.*"

"*Wankan-tanka*, little brother is going on a journey. Keep him safe, purify him, answer his prayers as you see fit, Grandfather. *Hi-ya, hi-ya, hi-ya, hi-ya, hi-yo, hi-yo, hi-yo, hi-yo . . .*" Eagle Horse's chanting and singing filled the lodge but soon ended. "Redtail, go with my little brother and watch over him through his journey. Guide him to the place beyond the stars. *Ha-ho.*" Miss Darling let out a loud sigh and the lodge again fell silent. "Time for *Chunupa Wakan*, the Sacred Pipe."

Lenny pinned back the flap, walked to a dirt mound between the lodge and fire pit, and returned carrying a long pipe in both hands. Kneeling, he extended it through the entrance to Miss Darling.

"White Buffalo Woman has given the People *Chunupa Wakan* to help purify us and pray. No one speaks falsely after smoking of the Sacred Pipe. Thank you for this gift, White Buffalo Woman." She reached out with a wooden match and struck it against a lava rock; it fired and crackled as she brought it to the pipe. Her cheeks hollowed as she drew, the bowl glowing with the sweet scent of tobacco. Head back, she exhaled a billow of white smoke. Lenny too took from the pipe then crawled around the fire ring and handed it to me. I ran my fingers down its wooden length; it was long and smooth with a feather tied to it and a heavy bloodstone bowl.

"It's not good to let the pipe go out."

Miss Darling held out another match.

Bringing it to my mouth, I sucked; the bowl glowed then smoldered as the smoke burned down my throat into my lungs. I coughed, eyes watering, and handed the pipe back to Miss Darling.

"Purification can pain the soul." She chuckled softly then drew from the pipe one last time before thumping the bowl against her palm and laying it down in front of her. Taking the bucket, she poured the remaining water over the glowing stones, set the bucket aside, and crawled out. "*Mitakuye oyasin*."

And that was the last thing I remembered until Miss Darling appeared above us wearing a burlap shift and a straw hat with its brim pinned in front with a giant sunflower, her favorite Pomeranian, Queenie, cradled in her arms.

◇ ◇ ◇

"Get dressed now. I'm expecting customers any minute. What'll they think if they find a couple of nude young boys lounging on my property." Miss Darling cackled, Queenie excitedly licking her face.

We lay on the ground in the cool bracing air and stared up into a deepening blue sky, a splash of stars mantling across the Milky Way. Crickets chirped in the weeds, and frogs croaked in the distance along ditch banks and across irrigated fields. I shivered.

"Come on, let's go." She toed our ribs. "See you tomorrow—we've got the shed to clean out. Remember?"

"Okay, Miss Darling." Lenny stood. "See you tomorrow."

I coughed, my throat scratchy and sore, and wondered how and when it had turned so dark.

We hurried into our clothes, hopping along trying to slip sneakers on as she shooed us toward the canal. We hurried through the weeds up to the road where Louie stood waiting for us, stretching and yawning, waving his tail. Buttoning shirts and tying laces, we looked down the embankment and watched Miss Darling hobble across her property through the tall weeds to the gate. Queenie leapt from her arms and scampered to join the others yipping and baring teeth through the wire-mesh fence.

"What happened down there, Lenny?"

He shrugged, as though all in a day's work.

"Is your throat sore?"

"A little, but you get use to it."

"Use to what?"

"The heat and smoke."

"I don't even remember getting out of the tent."

"It's a lodge, Hank. And we crawled out." Lenny grinned as we stood looking at each other. Finally, we both shrugged then walked in opposite directions along the canal bank under the stars to our separate cars. It wasn't until I was back home and in bed that I realized I hadn't even asked him what I had set out to— where he had been sleeping in all that rain and whether he would like to stay in Dana's room until she got back.

17

om and Arlene sat at the counter like Siamese twins joined at hip and ear. It was midmorning at Sage Diner and we were experiencing a freak of nature—not a customer anywhere.

Without looking up, Arlene extended her cigarette. Mom slid an ashtray over, and her friend flicked the ash before balancing the butt on the edge. She turned the postcard over and brought it almost to her nose, squinting. Arlene's eyes were as dim as a newborn hamster's, but vanity and denial ensured that liner, mascara, and shadow would be the only things ever to encircle them.

"'Hawaii is beee-utiful! White beaches, warm water, and cool breezes. And tomorrow we're even gonna go outside (tee-hee-hee). Lots of love, Dana and Jeff.'" Arlene flipped the card back over: Dana and Jeff posed as chubby hula girls with pineapple breasts, grass skirts, and brilliant leis. Their round faces poked crazily from painted cardboard cutouts, grinning like addled pumpkins. "Little shits. You got it when, sugar?"

"Monday—" Mom's elbow slid the width of the counter and her head slumped into its crook. "—the day she was 'sposed to be back. We haven't heard a peep since, have we, honey?"

I shook my head.

Arlene dropped the postcard on the counter, plucked the cigarette from the tray, and inhaled mightily. "Hmm. You know what I think?"

"What?" Mom straightened.

"AWOL—bet you a dollar to a doughnut."

Mom stared at her wide-eyed. "Jeff wouldn't do that."

Arlene blew smoke over her shoulder. "Hard to say. My cousin Louise's boy, Freddy—he did. Course, they just slapped his hand. Got his pay docked or some damn thing, like they even make much. He was only gone a couple days though. Guess he could've got court-marshaled but what could be worse, a locked room or that god-awful war? So they just sent him back."

Punk strolled from the back carrying a glass of water, a white towel draped around his neck. "We having a strike out here or one of them damn hippie sit-ins or love-ins or whatever the hell they call 'em?"

Mom and Arlene ignored him so he slid into a booth. Taking off his cooking hat, a paper canoe-shaped thing with Holsum Bread printed along both sides, he stretched his grease-splattered slip-ons into the aisle, took a drink, then gazed up at me.

I wiped my hands on the seat of my pants, glancing around for something to do. I had already mopped the floor, washed and dried all the dishes, wiped off the counter and booths—even the salt and pepper shakers—scrubbed the sink and toilet in both bathrooms, and hosed off and squeegeed the front window pane.

Punk threw the towel at me, motioning with his head. "Sit."

I stepped over his white sockless ankles and sat down.

"See this?" He pointed to the faded red and blue inside his veiny forearm, an anchor with a rope around it and the words *Semper Fi* beneath. "Got it from a big Italian guy in San Francisco the night we shipped off for Korea. Thought *Semper Fi* was his name." He snorted. "Navy insignia with the Marine's motto. I wasn't even eighteen yet. Dumb. Real dumb. But the service was the best thing that ever happened to me. Wasn't like it is now. All these demonstrations and flag burning and carrying on. It's a disgrace. It's like the whole country's gone berserk. Use to be serving your country was something to be proud of. Now it's like a damn prison sentence." He took the hat and ran the back of his fingers over the crease. "Don't know what we're doing over there but if they called me today, I'd go."

"And I'd help ya pack." Arlene elbowed Mom and she smiled.

Punk shook his head, brushing at his hat. "I'd go in a New York minute."

"And I'd pack ya in a New York minute."

Punk looked up, perturbed. "And I'd go in a New York minute."

"And I'd pack—"

"All right!" He stood, snatching the hat and securing it back over his undersized head. "Always have to get the last damn word."

"Oh, Punkie. Come here." Arlene swiveled around and caught him by the arm, turning him. She cupped his chin in both hands, pecked his nose. "I'd never let you go, you know that. Who'd get me coffee and waffles every morning?"

"You'd find somebody." His small dark eyes flitted around the diner, chin still in Arlene's hands. "Where the hell is everybody? This ain't no holiday, is it? Why don't you two get out of here, fer chrissakes. I can't afford to pay you for sitting around jabbering all morning. Come back at eleven or so. And don't worry about that damn girl of yours. She's all right."

Mom kissed his cheek, hugged Arlene, and pulled me toward the door. "See you in a while."

When we rounded the corner onto our street a car was sitting in front and for a second Mom and I had the same thought—Dana was back—but then we spotted Greg sitting on the step.

"Your new car needs a bath, Gregory."

He smiled and got up, stretching his elbows back.

She hugged him, patted his side. "And *you* need a haircut." She held a lock out. "Look at that." It hung below his shoulder. "What's the Air Force going to say about this?"

"Nothing. They'll just whack it off. Are you coming to my going-away party?" He glanced at me, and I couldn't tell if he wanted us to or not.

Mom let go of his hair. "When is it?"

"Sunday afternoon. At two."

"I should be off by then. I'd love to. Come in. I'll make us something to drink."

We followed Mom into the house, and I could feel Greg watching me.

"How about you, Hank?"

"What?"

"You're coming, right?"

I shrugged. "Might have to work."

"Of course he is. You're off Sunday afternoons, honey. Punk said you just have to work breakfast."

We sat at the kitchen table while Mom made Lipton iced tea. I stared at Stella and Frank swimming around their bowl, mouthing the glass. I got up and sprinkled flakes at them.

"How often do you feed them, Hank?"

"I don't know."

They rose, lipping the surface.

Greg came over and stooped down next to me. "My Uncle Phil used to tell me cowboys down in Arizona would throw goldfish in the stock tanks and they'd grow to fit the tank. The bigger the stock tank, the bigger the goldfish would get." He leaned closer. "Kind of like living in Grand River, huh, Hank?" He tapped the bowl, our noses almost touching it. "See, these are just little guys."

"Okay, boys. Here's your tea. I'm going to take a quick shower." She set our glasses on the table then disappeared down the hallway.

"I love your mom, man."

I took a sip and gazed out the window into the back yard. The grass was deep green from all the rain, and Mom's tulips were blooming red and yellow against the fence along the alley. One of the neighborhood cats, a tabby, padded across the sidewalk, hesitated before springing onto the gate. I watched it patter the length of the fence then slink down into the Sandler's yard next door. "Why'd you do it?"

"Come on, man—it was great! I didn't know anybody was going to get hurt."

"But they did. It was in the paper."

He got up and walked across the kitchen to the sink. "They probably just exaggerated. Like when they reported all those holes-in-one." He grunted, shaking his head and running fingers through his hair. "We were as close as they were, man. Why didn't we get hurt?"

"We were on the ground, Greg. You pulled us down. Remember?"

"Hank, it was just a couple of firecrackers. It wasn't like we used dynamite or anything."

"You, Greg—*you* used."

"Okay, okay—I used. What difference does it make? It's done." He dropped his hands and walked back to the table, sat down. "It was a great prank, you've got to admit."

"Julie's had it, Greg."

"Julie's emotional. She'll come around."

I set my glass down. "Guess it doesn't matter anyway."

"What doesn't?"

I shrugged. "You're leaving. It just doesn't matter anymore."

Greg stared at me and for the first time since knowing him, since we were little kids in Sunday school together, he had no rejoinder, no humor flickering in those eyes.

"What are you two arguing about?" Mom walked in wearing her terry cloth bathrobe and a towel around her head.

"Nothing, Mom. We're just talking."

"We're talking about goldfish, Mrs. Kessler. How they only get as big as the bowl they live in." He glared at me.

Mom removed the towel and shook out her hair. "Sounds too deep for me." Holding her head sideways, she began brushing out tangles. "Oh, no—" She stiffened.

Greg and I got up and followed her into the living room to the front picture window. Redd's truck was idling in the driveway. Mom hurried over and pulled the curtains.

Greg walked across and parted them with one hand. "Isn't that what's his butt?"

"Yeah, what's his butt." Mom grimaced. "Come on. Let's just finish our tea."

Greg continued peering as Mom and I went back into the kitchen.

"He's checking out my car." He craned his head. "Now it looks like he's unloading a lawnmower or something."

"We know, Greg. That's what he does. He mows our lawn."

He came back and sat down, looking at me. "He what?"

"Mows our lawn."

"Why?"

Mom held her head, elbows resting on the table. "Good question."

The lady wore a dress with a floral print and high-heel shoes. She tiptoed to the car, hands out like a tight-rope walker's, then opened the door and took something from the back seat—a piece of hose. She returned to the *Airstream* the same way, through mud.

"Look." I pointed. "His truck's moved."

Greg nodded, staring out the window, arms resting over the steering wheel. He had driven me to Rabbit Valley in his new car, splashing through puddles over the gravel road along the river as though traveling the new four-lane I-70 that had just been completed through the Grand Valley. He parked behind a stand of sagebrush at Dad's property turnoff.

"He's had it backed against the front door the last couple of months. Wait—" I held my hand up. "Listen."

I opened the passenger's door and stood on one leg, my head above the car. "Hear it?" The familiar song of one of Dad's canaries—Beamer—trilled from the trailer. I ducked back in, excitedly pointing down the dirt drive. "Did you hear it, Greg? Could you hear my dad's canary?"

Greg gazed at me, a slight smile forming.

"See, Beamer's the one that sings above ground. You know, when it's light. Chip, the other one, he'll only sing underground when Dad takes them down into the mine. Isn't that something? Chip only sings if it's dark." I strained to see movement through the trailer window. "I wonder who she is? Maybe she's some delivery person or something. She's gotta be. Dad wouldn't be, like, dating anybody would he? There she is again."

The lady re-emerged and walked to the driver's side.

"Look, Greg. She's getting back in the car. She's backing up." I slid down in the seat, peering over the dash. "Let's get out of here."

Greg didn't budge as we watched the car back carefully down the long rutted drive, bouncing from side to side until it was on the gravel road in front of us. Its windshield flashed sunlight as she slowly turned then pulled forward alongside us. She was a pretty woman with lipstick as red as Arlene's, a matching red scarf, and short stylishly cut hair. She gazed over, then accelerated, continuing down the gravel road toward town.

"Shoot, she saw me. Did you see that? She looked right at me."

I sat back up as Greg slipped the key into the ignition.

"What was she doing clear out here?" I shook my head. "I mean it's so far. Did you see what she took from her back seat? It looked like a piece of hose or something. Maybe Dad has some kind of water leak and she's a delivery girl for a hardware store or something. You know what I mean? Or—I know—she's helping him. She's helping Dad with Redd Morgan!"

Greg looked straight out the window like a kid whose eyes are stuck on something he doesn't see, his mind fixed on something far away. Finally, he shrugged, shifting the car into gear and revving the engine, before popping the clutch and spraying gravel and rainwater all the way down the county road back to Grand River.

18

*A*t the front window of Kentucky Fried Chicken sat a couple with their infant daughter, tending to her more than they were to the cartons of food open in front of them. Another customer, a gray-haired man, stooped at the counter digging for change, but the rest of the seating area was empty. Taking a breath and wiping palms across my pant legs, I marched inside and took my place behind him.

"May I help you?"

"Uh, yeah."

A girl baring braces with rubber bands and curly red hair pulled back with a pair of pink barrettes held a pencil and pad. I vaguely remembered her from one of my classes but couldn't place her name and hoped she couldn't mine either.

"Let's see, uh . . . I'll have a, um—"

The man took his sack from a second clerk and sat down. I could hear kitchenware clanging in back, and hissing, sputtering vats of chicken and fries descending into grease. Letters on the menu board shifted side to side, up and down before settling into words: coleslaw, rolls, three-piece meal, mashed potatoes and gravy, thighs.

"—chicken. I mean part of a chicken. You know, a, uh, drumstick."

The girl gawked at me as if I were even slower than I already felt. "That's it? One drumstick?"

"Yeah, I guess. I mean, how many do you get?"

"Anything to drink?" She gazed at the order pad, no doubt deciding that eye contact might encourage me, might jeopardize her job or subject her to some kind of health violation.

"Sure, that'd be good."

"Sooo—"

"So what?"

She rolled her eyes. "Coke, Sprite, Dr.—"

"Oh, Coke's fine. Yeah, Coke. Coke's good."

Holding her head sideways, she rang up the order. "One-twenty-three."

I swallowed. "The manager around?"

"Yes, he's in back. Do you want me to get him?"

"No. I mean—no. I just, you know, I wanted to know if he was here so I could, um, say hi." I handed her a five.

"I'll go get him." She made change, held it out for me.

"No, that's okay. Really, I can't stay. Full day, you know, I'm working and everything." I glanced down at my wrist as though I owned a watch, owned a real job for that matter. "Fact, I'm running late." I backed toward the entrance.

As if on cue the manager appeared from the back.

"Mr. Larston, this guy wants to talk to you." She pointed without looking at me.

"Hi, there. May I help you?" He flashed those horsey teeth, those black horn-rims secured with the same athletic strap he wore the first night I laid eyes on him. In fact he looked exactly the same, no missing appendages or ear parts, no facial cuts or singed eyebrows.

"Uh, yeah, hi. I, uh, just wanted to tell you, um, I really love your chicken and I think it's the best, uh, chicken around."

"Well, thank you. Thank you very much. I appreciate it." He continued smiling, no sudden telltale tic or glint of recognition. His employee stood behind him, lips pursed.

"Okay, well—" I backed out the door. "—bye then." I bolted.

"Hey! Wait a minute!"

Peripherally through the window I could see him hurry around the counter toward the door. Heart pounding, I beelined across the parking lot. Gateway Avenue was loud with traffic as I jumped into Mom's car and fumbled with the keys. Then a sudden calm descended, the kind before a storm, the kind a condemned man must feel just before the switch is pulled, guilt melting into relief as the swift hand of justice falls surely, lethally.

"Hey! You!"

I looked up just as he finished his sprint across the lot and flung open the door, my calm escaping with the gust of air.

"I didn't do . . . it wasn't my—"

He reached toward me. "Have a nice day!"

I stared at the white paper sack, the soft drink, took my change from his sweaty palm. The car door slammed. Lifting my eyes I watched his arm-swinging, job-well-done stride carry him back to the same entrance where the Colonel once stood. He turned, a final wave, then the same horsey smile gleaming under the Kentucky Fried sign before disappearing inside.

◇◇◇

Rumors surrounding Cisco Salazar's condition somersaulted across the Grand Valley like tumbleweeds, gaining momentum with each revolution. Carl Lujan said that Cisco's injury had actually happened months before in a back yard skirmish with a half-drunken Mr. Salazar, that the move he performed on Lenny just completed whatever was already damaged by his father. Margaret Kohler's mother, who was head librarian at County Library and as much an authority on everything as her daughter, had it from reliable sources that Cisco's spinal cord was completely severed, making him a quadriplegic hooked up to a breathing machine. When he heard this, Stankey responded poppycock and said Cisco's spinal cord was bruised which, depending on swelling, made his outcome uncertain. Molly VanHorn said she had spoken to Cisco's primary physician and that the doctor told her Cisco's second and third vertebrae were fractured and that the condition of his spinal cord was tenuous, bringing us full-circle to where rumors often begin: we didn't know any more than we had the night he was injured.

Then there was Peefee Maldonado. He told anyone who would listen—and most who wouldn't—that Cisco wasn't hurt at all, that he was already home in the company of his mother and beautiful sisters, spending time playing checkers with his father. None of it, of course, rang true—especially the checkers—and Julie observed that Peefee was in denial. Now that Cisco was lying injured in St. Anthony's Hospital, Peefee was lost and had to protect himself from the truth, she said. Which also explained his obsession with Lenny. In Peefee's mind, Lenny had purposefully hurt Cisco and now had to pay. That Lenny was no more responsible than he himself sitting in the stands as a spectator, didn't matter; Peefee needed something tangible to lash out at. The paradox in Peefee's mind—Cisco wasn't hurt; Lenny hurt Cisco—co-existed Janus-faced, opposite one another but both part of the same construct to protect Peefee himself.

After Julie finished her hypothesis I stared at her dumbstruck, unable to form even a half-intelligent sentence. "Where do you get this stuff?" Did she just echo everything she heard from her father or was she our generation's Sigmund Freud—Sigfried—in cowboy hat and waders? She was barely eighteen, for crying out loud.

"I don't know." She shrugged, swiping at mosquitoes buzzing her ears. "It's just logical, that's all." Turning her head, she bit off the end of my leader before picking it from the tip of her tongue. "Peefee's about as complicated as Louie. And nearly as faithful." She removed a silver fly box from her fishing vest. "What did I do with that Green Drake?"

I gazed down river at Dr. McClellan. One hand braced on a boulder and the other holding his fly rod aloft, he was working his way around to slower water. Louie was plopped haunches-deep near the bank behind him, water and drool streaming from his jowls as he bit at bubbles floating past. Dr. McClellan had driven Julie, Lenny, and me to Spruce Mesa that morning, loading Louie in the back of his station wagon with our tackle.

"Hey, Jules! Aren't you 'sposed to keep the fly in the water?" Lenny grinned from a flat rock underneath a spruce tree. Wood chips flew from between his legs.

"Funny, Bartelli." Julie swatted her neck, turning. "Least we're not bait fishermen." With the end of one fingernail she resumed nudging flies around the box, their feathery wings clinging like cotton balls to each other.

Lenny, not owning a pole or any fishing gear for that matter, had cut a willow and tied line with a sinker and hook to it that he had untangled from a log. From underneath rocks, he had caught night crawlers that he plunked in a pool just feet from where Dr. McClellan parked and by the time we met back at the car for lunch, he had already landed three. I, on the other hand, hadn't had a strike, spending most of my time snagging an assortment of flies on tall grass or low hanging branches. Julie and her father had each caught and released five trout, although Lenny didn't believe it since they brought back no evidence of them. Why, he wondered, would anyone spend time and energy catching fish only to let them go? It was like working all week then not picking up your paycheck. Dr. McClellan smiled and tried to explain that the meaning for him was in the ritual—tying the flies, oiling your reel, checking knots and gear, packing a lunch, getting up early to make coffee for the drive, then standing in an ice-cold river or stream with the wind creaking in the pines and spruce, the flutter of aspen leaves and the gurgling, roaring waters swirling around as you zing that perfect imitation across the surface. Lenny listened respectfully and nodded. "But don't you think letting them go insults them?" To this Dr. McClellan had no answer, and the rest of the day he seemed more reserved than usual, puffing his pipe and studying the waters.

Julie snapped the fly box shut and snatched off her hat. "Ah, here we go." From the brim she removed an olive-green fly and began tying it to my line. "Whew, I thought I was out. Just try not to lose this one, Hank. I only have a few left with this green and brown hackle."

"I didn't *try* to lose any of them." I glanced back under the trees at Lenny brushing off his pants. "Maybe I should use worms like Lenny."

"Over my dead body." She handed me back the line. "Fly fishing is an art form, Hank. It's like the difference between an exquisite lasagna and macaroni and cheese."

Lenny stepped between us, handing Julie a wooden fish, complete with dorsal fins and gills. "What's not to like in macaroni and cheese?"

◇◇◇

I whirled the line out one, two, three times and let it settle in a riffle along the far bank. Louie had followed me, plopping down on a patch of grass at the water's edge. "Just me and you, Louie boy." I retrieved the fly, the line forming an S above me, and placed it right back where it was. "That's more like it." I pulled line from my reel, letting it pile suspended around me as the fly floated along the bank. "If Jules could only see me now, Louie. Course, you'll probably pull one out with your teeth before I ever catch one."

The dog cocked his head. Again I drew the fly overhead—one, two, three— before laying it toward the bank just a few more feet upstream. Louie yawned with approval.

The fly flew back and forth across the Saturday afternoon sky until it inevitably found another scrub-oak hanging over the far bank. I gave a short jerk and the Green Drake miraculously flitted from the foliage and plinked into the water. "Whew, that was a close one, Louie." I cranked in the excess line curling around me and began reeling and wading farther upstream when I felt a snag. "Oh, great. Not another—" The reel sang, my pole jerking as I stumbled forward over a rock and plunged elbow-deep into the icy water. Scrambling to my feet, I held the pole aloft and pinched the line off against its shaft.

Louie was barking somewhere behind me as the fish broke water, a silvery flash in the shallows over rocks on the other side. I waded a few feet out and worked the fish toward me into deeper, slower water. I backed up, trying to reel evenly, not too fast, trying to remember everything Julie had taught me. "Okay, okay—here we go." Stepping backward onto the bank, I clutched the line with one hand and grabbed the handle of the net, which was slung around my neck and shoulder, with the other. But the netting caught on a spool sticking from my creel. I could hear the fish rip the surface so I let go of the net and continued reeling, squinting to see through the glare. Forgetting everything I had learned, I reeled as hard as I could then hoisted it wriggling from the water onto the rocky bank.

Louie barked and yipped, bouncing around the flopping fish and biting at it. "No, Louie!" I squatted, holding my rod up and pressing the fish down with my other palm. Louie sniffed. "Good boy. Easyyy—" I grasped it by its gills and lifted. Its eyes bulged, mouth flexing as I pinched the fly and worked the hook from behind its bottom row of teeth. Louie licked blood oozing from its mouth. "No, Louie. Back, boy. Back."

Laying the rod down, I cradled the sand-caked fish in my hand, looked at its semi-translucent fins, at the deep-green, almost black head and back, the freckled silvery-red scales that dirt hadn't found, its white belly, those eyes, that foundering mouth. I squatted, feeling its life force pulse in my hand, then submersed and gently jostled it before letting it slither from my fingers and disappear to wherever fish go to recuperate from such insult. "Adiõs, Mr. Fish. Say good-bye, Louie."

I washed my hands and picked up my pole to go tell Julie and Lenny and Dr. McClellan that I had caught a fish—a trout, a beautiful rainbow—and that I'd even let it go. But my hook was snagged again, the line wrapped around a rock. So holding the tip of the rod up I grasped the line, unwrapped it and—searching around me for the fly—traced the leader along the ground while taking up slack with my hand, then followed it up the bank, up one furry leg into one furry panting mouth.

◇◇◇

"Daddy, slow down. You're driving like Greg."

Dr. McClellan acted like he didn't hear, his station wagon kicking up rocks coming off Spruce Mesa and, after we hit blacktop, squealing around long sweeping curves through pasture and ranch land then, farther down, around tighter corners in the canyon along the river before rolling out into the Grand Valley, into the leafy expanse of peach and cherry and apple orchards. Lenny and I sat in the back on either side of Louie, taking turns holding the short length of fishing line sticking out the front of his foaming mouth. In a panic, I had cut the line with my pocketknife, only to discover that Louie kept swallowing it and gagging before coughing it back up. Dr. McClellan instructed us to grasp the line gently so as not to repeat the cycle. Louie had enough problems as it was, my fly lodged firmly in his throat.

By the time we reached the clinic the sky was almost black. Yellow light streamed from the VanHorn's kitchen window, and I could see the tops of four heads bowed around the table studying cards.

Molly answered our knock, took one look at Lenny's and my stricken faces—each of us were stooped with an arm around Louie's neck—and knelt down to examine him. His tail swished.

"Hi, big guy. What do we have here, boys?"

Dr. McClellan, standing behind us with his arm around Julie, cleared his throat. "Seems the dog swallowed a hook."

"What kind?" She grabbed Louie by the scruff and lifted his snout, pointing his nose toward the porch light.

"A Green Drake."

"A what?" She eased his jaws open and peered inside. "It's not a treble hook, I hope."

"No, it's a fly. A number sixteen, I believe. About so big." Dr. McClellan held out thumb and index finger to show Molly the size but she didn't look up.

"We better get him to the clinic. I'll meet you over there in two minutes."

Molly went back into the house, so we walked across the driveway and along the orchard to the cinder-block building. No one spoke as we stood listening to crickets and watching Louie sniff evergreens before lifting a salute to Huck, letting him know—hook or no hook—his was the last to pass this way.

Molly came out, keys jingling in the darkness and Mr. VanHorn and Huck crunching gravel behind her.

"Hear you caught a big one, Henry." Mr. V held the door as we shuffled in under the flickering fluorescent lights of the waiting room and then crowded into one of three small examination rooms.

"Okay, I'm going to need a little elbow room here. Why doesn't everybody wait outside. Except you, Lenny, and, um, Henry."

"Honey, I can help." Mr. V pushed his glasses up.

"You're bedside manner leaves a little to be desired, Sam." Molly held a hypodermic to the light and flicked it. "There is one thing you can do, though. Come here, Louie."

"Name it."

Lifting the skin behind Louie's head, she inserted the needle. "Help me get this guy up on the table." She withdrew and set the needle on the counter.

Mr. VanHorn edged around Lenny and me, squatted, and cradled Louie's chest and butt. He straightened as though lifting a child instead of a one-hundred-and-twenty pound dog and set him on the stainless-steel table.

"Easy, boy." Molly wrapped an arm around his neck as Louie scrambled on the slick surface, legs splaying. Lenny and I grabbed hold, too.

"Thanks, Sam."

"I'll be right out here if you need me." Mr. V winked, patted Lenny and me on the shoulder and left the room.

Molly whispered in Louie's ear, stroking his head until the big dog relaxed to his belly then rolled unconscious to his side. She took a spring-like contraption and inserted it top-canine to bottom, propping his mouth open. "This is called a mouth gag. It'll help us find the culprit." She slipped a penlight and tongue depressor from her smock and, stooping down, stuck them into Louie's mouth. "Hmm."

"What do you see?" Lenny peered over her shoulder while I held my breath, sweat beading across my nose and forehead.

"Well, it looks like we got lucky. I think it's lodged in his soft palate." She turned, opened a drawer, and removed scissors, forceps, and needle-nose pliers. "Hold this light for me and, Henry, you hold his head up."

Lenny pointed the light into Louie's mouth as Molly first reached in with the scissors and clipped off the line, tossing it to the floor, then went in with the pliers.

"Can you pull it out?"

"No, not yet. First I've got to force it on through so I can cut the barb off. I'll try backing it out." The backs of her forearms danced as she worked inside Louie's mouth. "There, I think I got it." She withdrew the pliers and dropped a snippet of metal onto Lenny's palm. "Hmm, looks like the barb was already blunted. Now the fun part." Setting the pliers down, she picked up the forceps. "Lift the light a little higher. Right there." Again she went into Louie's mouth, eyebrows bunched in concentration.

Louie wheezed and gurgled as she worked, and his head felt a ton as I steadied it on the table. Lenny licked his lips, the penlight jiggling in his hand.

"Hold it still, Lenny."

"Is he chokin'?"

"No, he's okay. He doesn't feel a thing. Here we go." Molly pried, her weight on one foot, then slowly extracted the fishhook. She held it to the light, studying it. "What'd Julie's Dad call it?"

"A Green Drake."

She handed Lenny the hook, set down the forceps, then removed the mouth gag, easing Louie's head to the side. "We'll let him sleep here for a bit then Sam can put him in a kennel for the night."

"Will he be okay?" I stroked the dog's head.

"He'll be fine, Hank. I'll give him a shot to ward off any infection. He might have a sore throat for a while as the puncture heals. Sometimes the scar tissue bothers them as they age but other than that I don't think he'll have any problems. We'll see how he feels in the morning."

Relieved, we walked back to the house and sat around the living room sipping sodas and listening to Mr. VanHorn regale us with tales of Molly's practice. One concerned a driller's dog, a rottweiler-shepherd mix that clacked across the examination room as though it wore a chain collar, which it didn't. Instead, X-rays revealed it had swallowed four grease-laden ball bearings that "chattered like little round hobbits in the bowels of its being" whenever it walked. And then there was the poodle that had eaten enough leaven dough to have risen "like a loaf of French bread." Molly had stuck it in their bathtub overnight to monitor and administer enemas but it was still fermenting hours later from every orifice of "its pitiful little expanding body." To the roll of Molly's eyes, Mr. VanHorn said that their house "smelled for days like Santy's Bakery downtown and that it hadn't been that aromatic since Molly's mother visited three Thanksgivings before." And finally there was the tale of the lovesick chow.

A lady brought a male and female to the clinic from twenty miles down valley because she was breeding them and the female had yet to become pregnant. After examining them, Molly discovered that the male's penis was too short to gain entry. After consulting with the concerned owner—who had big plans to sell the litter before Christmas—Molly decided to manually extract the male's sperm and inject it into the female. The procedure went acceptably well and the lady drove the chows the twenty miles back home. But the next morning Molly and Sam were awakened by the baleful howl of the male below their bedroom window, madly panting between wails from its night-long journey and, in Mr. VanHorn's words, "hopelessly smitten by my wife's expert handiwork the day before."

By the end of this last story, Dr. McClellan's eyeglasses lay on his lap and he was wiping his eyes with a handkerchief.

"Come on, Daddy." Julie tugged his arm. "It's getting late. Mom's going to have a cow."

Dr. McClellan staggered up, shaking his head and stuffing away the handkerchief. "I knew I should've gone into a different profession."

Molly smiled and shook his hand. "It was a pleasure meeting you."

"The pleasure was all mine, believe me. And thank you for seeing the dog so late. We were pretty traumatized, especially Henry and Lenny."

"It was no problem. I just hope Sam's overactive imagination didn't give you the wrong impression of me."

"Not at all. His stories were delightful."

Mr. VanHorn smiled. "Just 'putting the face of a joke upon the body of a truth.'" He wrapped an arm around Molly and squeezed.

Dr. McClellan chuckled as he shook the larger man's hand. "Come on, kids. Your folks are going to think I kidnapped you."

Julie and I walked outside to the car, but Lenny hesitated, lingering at the front door still talking to the VanHorns.

I got in the back seat and gazed out the window. "I think he wants to stay here with Louie."

"Yeah, but I bet he doesn't."

"How come?"

"Look." Julie pointed as Lenny finally turned and walked down the steps toward us. "Bet they offered, but told him he has to call his mom first."

Lenny climbed in, and Dr. McClellan backed the station wagon out the driveway and eased it along the ditch until we were off the VanHorns' property, humming down the county road toward town. Through the open windows we could hear the distant pop and crackle of fireworks, and I thought of Greg blowing up the Colonel and leaving for the Air Force Academy and how, in some peculiar way, those two events seemed kindred. I looked at Lenny, his face flashing with the streetlights and headlights passing in the darkness, and wondered if he too would be going. If he passed his physical, he would probably go into the army, to boot camp then on to Vietnam like Jeff. And that too seemed to fit because Lenny was already in training, living out of his Wagoneer, cooking outside, running miles every day across rugged terrain.

19

Knickknacks. Or as Vincent Bartelli put it: "Knick-knack paddy-whack, give a dog a bone." We were standing in Lenny's room—Vince, his girlfriend Sheila, Lenny, and I—when Vince said it, pointing. And he was right. They were everywhere, little ceramic shapes spilling across Lenny's bedroom—or what had been his bedroom—like marching African ants cutting a swath through jungle.

The top shelf where Lenny had kept his stereo and collection of record albums was now aswarm with a miniature Noah's Ark, complete with ramp and pairs of every animal known to man—or at least known to Mrs. Bartelli. The procession ran the length and breadth of the bottom three shelves, too, before continuing across a walnut coffee table and along both windowsills. On the opposite wall, where Lenny once plastered the unlikely duo of Janis Joplin and marathoner Frank Shorter on either side of his hand-drawn map of the United States, hung three large whatnot shelves chock-full with more of the same. Bigger pieces, some ankle-high and all polished to a high gloss, encircled us on the carpet along the baseboard. Pink pigs. White horses with golden manes. A unicorn. Two bullfrogs. Donkeys. A pair of swans. A coiled rattler. Mice. Geckos. Piggyback dragonflies. Elephants. Giraffes, one with long eyelashes. Siamese cats. Collies. Even a rat, teeth bared at something clutched under its whiskered chin. And from a chain near one window, two brilliantly plumed macaws perched on a swing inside a silver cage.

"Where does she get this stuff?" I had come over to pick Lenny up for Greg's farewell party. His Wagoneer was on the fritz again, parked in the vacant lot across the street. With Mrs. Bartelli gone to visit her sister, he and his brother had arrived there at the same time carrying the same idea. Together they jimmied the bathroom window and squeezed Sheila through to unlock the door so they could make themselves at home—or as much as they could around and between that frozen menagerie, those thousand pairs of enamel eyes.

"Beats me." Vince shook his head, grasping Sheila's hand. "Be sure you don't touch nothin'. Me and Sheila have dibs on Mom's bed."

"What? You're sleeping in Mom's bed?"

Vince turned to glare at Lenny, who looked up from toeing the indentation of carpet where his own bed had rested. "*On* Mom's bed. The floor's too hard, man, and the plastic on the couch makes me sweat." He shrugged, flicking stringy hair. "Don't worry, little brother. We covered it. And, besides, we brought our sleepin' bags."

"She'll kill you."

"No she won't. We're careful. She won't even know."

"She'll know."

Sheila shifted a hip and placed her finger under Lenny's chin. "And what's there to know—" She smiled from beneath jet-black bangs. "—little brother?"

"Let's go, Sheila." Vince pulled her through the doorway but she resisted, yanking her arm free.

"Don't!"

"Come on, Sheila. Quit being a psycho, will ya? This is Lenny's room. Or, at least, was."

She stood, arms folded across her halter top, pouting. She suddenly giggled. "I like Lenny's room."

"Okay, fine." Throwing his arms, Vince stomped into the living room.

"Goob!"

"What!?!"

"Ain't you going to hold my hand?"

The doorbell rang so she ran out to join him to see who it was.

I looked at Lenny. "Whew. As Stankey would put it, old Sheila's 'bout two tacos short of a combination plate. Did you see her look at you?"

"Yeah. Pretty scary, huh?" He held up his hand. "Listen—"

Vince was talking and we could hear a muffled voice outside through the screen. Finally, the front door closed.

"Hey, Vince. Who was it?"

He walked back over the plastic walkway into Lenny's room. "Don't know. They didn't say."

"They?"

"Yeah. There were about six or seven of them. They piled out of a black pickup. I told 'em you weren't here but they saw your Jeep." He grinned, his girlfriend peering over one shoulder, huddled to his back nibbling a cuticle. "Problems, little brother?"

◇◇◇

Mrs. Woods was in her glory, flitting from guest to guest as though she were a prima ballerina and they mere extras in the most important production of her life. She wore short gold culottes and a vest that matched her tan, which is all she had on underneath save a black brassiere and the fragrant sheen of an exotic lotion. Even her sparkly gold flats looked, at first glance, like ballet slippers, but her hair she wore long and repeatedly raked through it with perfectly manicured, red nails.

The Woods' guests outnumbered Greg's ten to one, lining the streets with their cars—plush imports and chrome-laden sedans—or streaming from the clubhouse over the tenth fairway in their summer dresses and pressed khakis and open-necked golf shirts. They gathered under the patio around a long table of hors d'oeuvres, balancing plastic plates and champagne glasses. Tables for four with linen tablecloths and floral center pieces encircled the pool, and a white banner with Air Force blue stencil—GOOD LUCK, GREGORY!—was strung the length of the patio along the eaves. Lenny and I sat with punch and cookies at the farthest table beyond the diving board, watching them arrive.

"Look." I pointed at the two cadets, who were as obvious with their scalped heads as they would have been wearing uniforms, which they weren't. Ramrod straight they stood, each holding a glass and engaging adults as if one of them. And compared to us, though only a year or two older, they were. Lenny and I, on the other hand, were as comfortable as a pair of pinched feet at a tap-dance competition.

"Cocky."

"Huh?"

I lifted my chin in their direction. "That's what my dad would say. Look at them strutting around like a couple of roosters."

Lenny shrugged. "I don't know. They're just standing there."

"Yeah, but look how they're standing."

"On their feet?"

"No, I mean so tall and straight like they . . . like they just had their physicals—and liked it."

He grinned. "I'm not sure that would make them stand straight, Hank. Look, there's Greg."

We waved but he turned instead, shaking hands and engaging the cadets. He was as tall as they and dressed as well if not better in a pressed button-down shirt, tan slacks, and brown-on-white SKs. His hair was slicked straight back into a ponytail and neatly tucked into his collar, giving the illusion of a shorter cut. Though wavy, it hugged his head under the weight of Brylcream or butchwax or some kind of Vaseline. One of the cadets spoke and the three of them suddenly laughed, Greg placing a hand on the tallest one's shoulder. A middle-aged man, garishly dressed in white shoes, kelly-green pants and red golf shirt, joined them, their tight circle opening for him and he, in turn, pumping their hands.

"Hey, there's Stank."

Again we waved but Stankey already had us in his sights, squeezing in and around tables and chairs and party guests until finally reaching us.

"Hey, bird-brains."

"What's up, Stank."

"Nothin' much. Just makin' important contacts with all the pillars of the local commune. Have you seen Cisco?"

"What?"

"Guess he's out of the hospital."

I sat up. "How do you know?"

"I saw him with his mom and sisters at a stoplight over by Arctic Circle. He had a halo on."

"A what?"

"You know, one of those metal contraptions they screw to your head to keep your brains in."

"Whoa—" I glanced at Lenny, who was chewing his bottom lip.

"Where's Woods?" Stankey looked around.

I lifted my chin. "Over there with the jar-heads."

Stankey frowned. "Nice 'do." He reached over and grabbed a cookie off my plate, crammed it into his mouth. "Has anybody else shown up?"

"Yeah, Wiseman and Green are inside gorging themselves on shrimp and oysters. Watch, they'll both be liberating them into the pool pretty soon. Just in time for dessert. Oh, great—there's Margaret Kohler."

"What's she doing here?"

Stankey shrugged. "I guess Mrs. Woods only invited the top one percent of the class." He gazed at Lenny and me. "That is, with two notable exceptions." He slapped my leg. "It's refreshing though to have a couple of token peasants at the Queen's ball."

"Funny, Stankey. Uh-oh, here she comes."

Stankey quickly sat as the three of us pretended to be scanning the golf course or studying something interesting in the pool.

"Hi."

"Oh, hi, Margaret. How's it going?"

"Okay. Have you seen Julie?"

I shook my head. "No, I don't think she's coming."

She suddenly smiled. "Don't tell me she wasn't invited?"

"No, she was invited. I just think she had something more important going on."

"Oh, right." The smile melted into a smirk. "Like there's something more important to her than Greg Woods going off to the academy." She gazed around the party. "Well, if you see her, tell her I'm looking for her."

"Sure, Margaret. I sure will."

She remained, glancing at Stankey and scouring the area for a better spot to land. "Well, I certainly don't see many of our classmates. Do you?"

I shook my head. "Nope. I guess just us smart ones were invited."

She studied me, a lopsided smile crossing her lips. "Yes. I guess so." She took a sip of punch. "So when do you leave for Stanford, Donald?"

"What's that?" Stankey looked up, shielding the sun with one hand. "Oh—Margaret Kohler. When did you get here?"

She turned away, fidgeted with the ribbon on her white blouse. "You know, I didn't apply to Stanford myself, being on the west coast and all. Mother wanted something with more of an eastern influence for me."

Stankey continued to gaze up at her. "Of course." He nodded toward Mr. Woods who just emerged from the sliding glass doors to join Greg and friends. "And speaking of influences from the yeast."

With his arm draped around his son's shoulder, Mr. Woods tilted his head back and drained a Coors then, crushing the can, tossed it on the lawn. Greg walked over and picked it up, which his father found amusing, guffawing and slapping the man in green pants on the back.

Margaret propped a hand on one hip. "I can't believe he just did that."

Stankey sniggered. "Woods is really putting his best foot forward, isn't he? Picking up after the old man—now there's a role reversal."

Shaking her head, Margaret set the glass down and marched off around the pool, skirting the crowd as though a deadly virus resided there.

Stankey sighed. "Margaret needs to get laid."

I nodded. "And you're just the guy to do it."

"Not even with your . . . hey, where'd Woods go?"

The two cadets were standing by themselves now, eyeing Mr. Woods who had seated himself at a nearby table, a fresh can of beer in hand.

"Uh-oh." Stankey nodded. "Trouble."

Mrs. Woods threaded her way through guests, exchanging pleasantries and greeting everyone with a smile and hug until she reached her husband. Bending to his ear, her expression changed but then quickly returned as she straightened and helped him to his feet. Hand-in-hand, they walked back through the crowd before disappearing into the house, the beer left foaming on the table.

"Busted. If only she used the same discipline on her son. Hey, Kessler, go grab that brewski, will ya?"

"Yeah, right, Stankey."

"Come on. Where's your *huevõs*?"

"Scrambled." I jumped to my feet. "Hey, Mom! Over here!"

My mother, in the full skirt and blouse she once wore square-dancing with Dad, hurried around the crowd toward us. She clutched a colorfully beaded purse that matched her beaded shoes. "Hi, you two." She hugged Lenny and me and sat down.

"Mom, this is Donald Stankey. He's on the wrestling team with us."

"Was." He held out his hand. "Nice to meet you, Mrs. Kessler." He gazed from Mom to me then back, pushing his horn rims up. "Hank's obviously adopted, right?"

Mom laughed, cheeks warming to the shade of her lipstick. "Hank takes after his father, Donald. Sorry I'm late, honey. We had a steady flow right up to one-thirty, quarter 'til."

"Where do you work, Mrs. Kessler?"

"Over at Sage Diner."

"Hmm, I've never been in there. Is it good?"

"Ohhh—"

Mom and I looked at each other then laughed.

"It's got great coffee." She unsnapped her purse. "Honey, look. It was in yesterday's mail."

I took the card. Three doves against blue sky. I flipped it over: "'Dear Mom and Hank, Little change in plans. Don't worry. I'll explain later. See you in a few days. May God bless. Lots of love, Dana.'" I looked up. "May God bless?"

She shrugged, taking it back and slipping it into her purse. "Least she's okay."

"But where is she?"

"Dallas."

"Dallas?"

"I don't know, honey. That's where it's postmarked."

"Is Jeff with her?"

"Honey, I don't know any more than you do. That's all there was."

I sat back, thinking about my sister. First she flies all the way to Hawaii and now pops up in Dallas, Texas, of all places. This from a girl who rarely went anywhere. I wondered what Dad would make of this, wondered if she would've left if he were still living with us. Then it dawned on me; she would have gone sooner.

"Hey, Mom." I touched her hands clasped atop the purse. "She'll be back."

She quickly nodded, snapping the purse closed then looking away toward the ever-growing party. "There's Greg."

He was smiling, slowly making his way through guests who were parting to make room. I saw someone dragging a pair of chairs then shoving a table aside before realizing Greg was pushing something, too, a wheelchair with a man aboard. A plaid blanket was draped over the man's lap and, as he was wheeled around the edge of the pool toward us, I could see shadows darken his cheek and temple and deepen the space between his buttoned collar and reed-thin neck.

"Mrs. Kessler, hi. I'm so glad you could make it."

"I told you, Gregory, I wouldn't miss it for the world." She hugged him. "Now, who's this?"

"This is Phillip Granger. Uncle Phil, Mrs. Kessler—Hank's mom."

"You can call me Sally. Mr. Granger, it's a pleasure to meet you. You must be very proud of your nephew. I know we are."

His hands were bony and white, and the skin at his temple appeared translucent, a bluish pulse visible just under the surface, under the curve of skull splotchy with wisps of black hair. I had met Greg's uncle once before but had no recollection of the emaciated figure now before me.

"You remember Hank?"

I shook his hand and, though he didn't speak, I was startled to feel the cold strength of his grip, as if he was desperate to hold on to something.

"And this is Lenny Bartelli, Uncle Phil. You know, the artist friend I told you about."

Lenny reddened as they shook hands. Uncle Phil clasped Lenny's hand in both his and smiled, his eyes coming into focus for the first time.

"Lenny, long time no hear." Greg took hold of his uncle's wrists and eased him back in the chair, releasing Lenny from his grip. He squeezed Lenny's shoulder and bent down. "I hear you've been doing a little Harold and Maude gig."

"What?" Lenny looked at me.

"You know, with that fortuneteller lady." Greg straightened, punching Lenny's arm. "Fear not, dear friend, the Lizard King knows all." He smiled, turning back to Mom. "Can I get you anything, Mrs. Kessler?"

"I'm fine, Greg. This is all so lovely." She gazed around the Woods' back yard, at the decorations, the manicured lawn and shrubbery, the great expanse of fairway, the Bookcliffs and Spruce Mesa standing in the distance. "You must love living here."

He shrugged. "It's okay."

"Actually, he detests it." Mrs. Woods came up behind him half-smiling, a half-full champagne glass resting in her palm. "Gregory, it's time to get Phillip back to the hospital."

"It hasn't even been an hour yet, Mother."

"Come on, dear. I'm not going to argue with you. Connie Richards said she would run him back for us. There are people who have come a good distance to see you and wish you well. It's time to circulate." She took one handle of the wheelchair but Greg continued to hold the other. She hesitated, looked at Mom. "Hello. I'm Valerie Woods. I don't believe we've met."

Greg rolled his eyes then glared. "Yes, you have, Mother. This is Mrs. Kessler. Hank's mom."

"Oh, of course. The Sunday school teacher." She extended her hand.

Blushing, Mom smiled and took her hand. "I'm afraid that's been quite a few years ago."

"So it has, Mrs. Kessler. And what, after all these years, have you been doing with yourself?"

"Oh, not much really. I've been waitressing mostly."

"Oh—" She looked at me. "Well, we certainly do love your little Henry here. Don't we, dear?"

Greg gazed across the tenth fairway.

"At least I do." She giggled into her glass, took a sip. "Anybody need anything? Mrs. Kessler, may I get you some champagne? Gregory, go get—"

"No, I'm fine. Really. I can't stay very long."

"Oh, what a pity. Well, it certainly was a pleasure." Tossing her hair over one shoulder, she reached out to take her son's arm. "Gregory, come on. People are waiting for us."

He fixed her with an icy smile. "Yes, Mother." Relinquishing the wheelchair, he followed as she rolled it around the diving board, his uncle's head cocked to one side. "Thanks for coming, Mrs. Kessler. I'll come by to see you before I leave."

Mrs. Woods stopped. "Darling, you're leaving tomorrow. You won't have time to see anyone. You still have to pack and . . . here, wait a minute." She put her hand to Greg's head. "Your hair looks absolutely dreadful. Oh, there's the Prestons. Bob! Lorraine!"

We watched them—mother, son, invalid uncle—move into the crowd, absorbed like raindrops into a widening pool.

"Well, honey—" Mom stood.

"Mom, you just got here."

"I'm tired, sweetheart. And I saw Greg, that's all I really came for."

"At least have something to eat."

"I'll pick something up on the way home. Bye, Lenny. Nice meeting you, Donald."

We stood as my mother walked away from the crowd across the closely cropped grass and disappeared behind the hedge at the corner of the house.

Stankey slapped me on the shoulder and shook his head. "Don't sweat it, Kess. Greg's mom's always been that way. Catch you bird-brains later."

As we watched Stankey walk toward the house, Lenny tapped me on the shoulder.

"What?"

"Did you hear him? Cisco's out."

I nodded. "Yeah, I heard." I turned to him, his eyes wide with a look I didn't know. "That's good, right?"

He nodded but his eyes, they didn't blink. "Hank, did he say a halo?"

◇◇◇

Sprinklers across the tenth fairway hissed and clicked on at twilight, chilling the air with ditch water and driving most guests inside. Those remaining moved a short time later in fear of being splashed by Stankey, Wiseman, and Green who, bloated on seafood, began performing cannonballs off the diving board.

But few left the party. The kitchen, dining room, and sunken living room swelled with laughter, with clinking glass and loud conversation about lowering handicaps, Nixon's virtues versus McGovern's, the Olympics, *The Godfather*. Chopin's *Nocturnes* played from the massive oak stereo just inside the entryway, and from where Lenny and I were sitting on the sleek chrome couch we could hear the television in the den and see the back of Mr. Woods' sunburned head resting against his leather easy chair. A clump of yellow hair stuck up as though a gust had caught it.

"I feel sorry for him."

"Who?" I looked at Lenny. He had on a wrinkled white shirt salvaged from one of the grocery sacks in back of his Wagoneer and a pair of shiny black pants he hadn't worn since going to church with his mother a couple of years before. "Mr. Woods?"

"Yeah."

"He's rich."

"I still feel sorry for him."

I thought about this. Lenny, a kid kicked out of the house by his own mom, a kid living atop a hill in the back of a dilapidated Jeep more often broken down than not, felt sorry for the wealthy attorney father of the smartest member of our graduating class. Lenny, whose own dad had died, felt sorry for our friend's father, a guy who spent most of his time playing golf or drinking and watching television in the den. Samsa, his son had called him. And Greg was right—Samson, Mr. Woods wasn't.

"Yeah. Guess I do, too."

Lenny arched, pulling at his pant legs. They hiked an inch above his saggy gym socks and mud-stained sneakers, revealing both shins. "I mean, Greg's leaving tomorrow and all these people are here and his dad's in there watching TV. By himself."

"Not anymore."

Mrs. Woods glided down the hallway studying her hair in the long mirror before stopping at the den. She leaned in on one foot, her hand against the door, then slid it closed having said who knows what to her husband. Turning, she spotted us watching and smiled. We waved.

"Uh-oh. Now what?" I pointed to my chest. "Me?"

She nodded. I got up and walked toward myself in the long mirror: a skinny kid in corduroys moving across the living room among adults, a shadow among trees. Following her down the hallway into the kitchen, I checked my profile, smoothed my hair.

"Henry, would you give me a hand? This lid won't budge." She handed me a jar of maraschino cherries and began placing crystal goblets of vanilla ice cream onto a large round platter.

I gripped the lid and tried turning it. Nothing. Bending down pressing the jar into my thigh, I tried again.

"Did you get it, Henry?"

"Uh, yeah—it'll just be a second." I held it between my knees, twisted until red in the face, shaking.

"Here, let's run some water over it." She turned on the hot and held the jar under the faucet. "There we go." She handed it back.

Again I strained.

"Sometimes if you can push down with your palm like this." Setting the jar on the counter, she pressed down, elbow in the air. "It's really not a question of strength, Henry." She winked, handing me the open jar. "Just experience." She caressed my cheek with the back of her hand. "Most things in life are experience, Henry. You'll see. One per bowl, please."

I picked cherries out by their stems, carefully placed them atop each scoop.

"Let's see, how many is that?" She quickly counted under her breath. ". . . eighteen, nineteen—and this one makes twenty. That'll do for the first round."

"What?"

"I'll have the rest ready by the time you come back."

"You mean you want me to—"

"Put your hand up like this. Now the trick is to keep it balanced from the center. Don't serve off just one side or it will tip and make a mess. Okay?" She picked up the platter and held it in front of me. "Well?" She stared. "If you don't want to help, Henry, fine. I'll—"

"No, no, I just—"

"Bend your knees then. Get your hand underneath. That's it. Do you have it?"

I straightened, head tilted sideways. "I think so."

"If you need to, hold the edge with your other hand. Good."

"Where do I go?"

"Just start in the living room and be sure you hurry back when you're out so I can load you back up." She leaned into me, patted my bottom; from this new angle, her tan breasts were stacked one atop the other like a chocolate double-decker. "Be careful down the stairs, Henry. Here, I'll help get you started."

Shouldering the platter, I followed her lean calf muscles back through the kitchen, along the hallway, and down two steps into the living room.

"Dessert!"

"Valerie, it looks lovely! Give me one for Fred, too." "Oh, I really shouldn't.

But they look so scrumptious! Thank-you." "Yes, I'll take one. Thank-you very much." "Over here, Val. Great—thanks. . . ."

From underneath the oversized platter I could see only torsos, legs, a glass coffee table, plush gold shag carpeting, then finally two pair of obsidian black shoes, SKs, and kelly-green pants.

"Who's under there?" Greg's face appeared. "Hank! What the—you look like a mushroom." He relieved me of the platter.

"Thanks." I straightened, rubbing my neck and shoulder. "I was starting to feel like one."

"You know what they say about mushrooms, don't you?" The man in green pants puffed a cigar, round ruddy face squinting through smoke rings. "They're like Mexicans—keep 'em in the dark, feed 'em horse shit, and they stay happy."

The cadets laughed loudly as they took the remaining two desserts. Tucking the platter underarm, Greg scanned the room. "Where the hell'd she go?"

"Greg, it's okay."

"No, it isn't Hank. You're a guest. Not the bloody—"

"It's okay. I volunteered."

He studied me. "Well, you're unvolunteering." He bounded up the steps and down the hallway with the platter.

"Hi. I'm Henry Kessler."

The tallest cadet elbowed his buddy. "Henry Kesslinger?" He took a bite of ice cream. "So how do you know Greg, Henry Kesslinger?"

"Kessler. We graduated together. We're classmates."

"Is that right? Hmm. So tell me, Henry, who's the putz over there on the couch? The guy in the high-waters and freshly pressed shirt."

"Oh, that's Lenny. We all hang out together."

"Really? You, Lenny, and . . ."

"Yeah, and Greg. Julie, too, but she couldn't come."

He glanced at his watch. "Well, Paulson, I'd say it's time we roll."

The tall one nodded, scraping the last bit of ice cream with his spoon. "Past time." He handed me the goblet. "Carry on, Kissinger. Give our best to the Commander."

"What?"

"Remind Woods that we'll be here in the morning at oh-nine-hundred hours to pick him up."

"Yeah, sure."

Gazing over me, they moved off into the crowd toward the front door, shaking hands and nodding affably at the other guests. But as they reached the entryway, Mrs. Woods and Greg intercepted them and appeared to be insisting they stay. More people gathered as if the cadets were magnets and they metal filings. Finally, when it seemed the entire party had collected in the entryway, the front door opened and everybody poured outside.

Lenny and I stood at the front window in the now empty living room and watched Greg and his mother escort the cadets to their car. Through the glass, the moon shone three-quarters and with the Tiki torch lights that lit the circular drive and the city lampposts that illuminated the cul-de-sac, the air seemed magnetized with light particles, the people charged with it.

Everyone milled about or chatted in small clusters, reluctant to go until the guests-of-honor left. Just as the cadets ducked into their car and turned on the headlights, a second pair of lights appeared down the street. Unnoticed, it slowly passed the lineup of parked cars, made one pass around the cul-de-sac, then flashed across the front of the Woods' house before blinking out in the driveway.

People stood back as the two officers got out of the squad car and started up the sidewalk. I saw Mrs. Woods' hands drop to her sides then rise up to touch her son. As Greg stepped toward the policemen, he reached back with one hand to loose his hair from its ponytail.

The cadets popped back out and I could see Mrs. Woods say something to them, her face still wearing a smile. From the other side of the window Lenny and I were dumbstruck as though it were television we watched with the sound turned off. That is, until Mrs. Woods hit the volume running, screaming through the front door and into the den as if her hair were on fire.

"Walll-ter! Walll-ter! They've got Gregory, Walter! The police! They've got him handcuffed and are putting him in the back of their car! Handcuffed, Walter! Do you hear me!?! They have our son handcuffed in a police car!"

Faces outside remained blank, but a few leaned together to whisper after Greg's head was pushed down and the rest of him—shoulder, leg, foot—followed into the backseat. They shut the door just as Mrs. Woods reappeared, pulling a barefoot and wobbly Mr. Woods by the shirttail. The side of his face was red, imprinted with the paisley design of the den sofa.

The officer on the driver's side held his hand out to stop Mrs. Woods who accosted him, screaming. Her husband remained on the walk, arms crossed in an attempt to look lawyerly, to stop wavering. The officers got in their car and eased it out of the driveway with Mrs. Woods running alongside, pressing her palms against the back-door window and then, being restrained by friends, collapsing to the gravel. Mr. Woods, hair sticking straight up, remained wobbling like a top that has exhausted all but its final few revolutions before toppling, which he did, glancing off a Tiki torchlight then falling backward into his perfectly trimmed hedge.

And it was this—falling—that would be the last thing the Woods ever did together. For months afterward it would be argued and discussed across the fairways and greens of Grand River Country Club, in the pro shop and lounge and restaurant and card rooms, around the pool, on the tennis courts, and in the parking lot, the when and if and how of it—the when and if and how the Woods family ever really stopped falling.

◇◇◇

"So that's Mars—" Lenny stood on tiptoes, face pressed to the eyepiece. "It looks like a big marble."

"No, Mars is in Scorpio, Lenny. It's already gone behind the horizon." Dr. McClellan took the pipe from his mouth and pointed it toward the southern sky. "You're looking straight into the center of our galaxy. At Jupiter. It's in Sagittarius."

Lenny lifted his head. "Isn't Greg a Sagittarius?"

I shrugged. "Yeah, I think so."

Dr. McClellan chuckled. "That's astrology, boys. This is astronomy—a little different animal."

"But isn't astrology based on the stars?"

"Yes, I suppose it is, Lenny."

Lenny again positioned his eye to the telescope. "What's that big red area?"

"What you're seeing is an atmospheric disturbance on Jupiter's surface. Probably a massive dust storm. We call it the Great Red Spot."

"It's huge."

"Three times the diameter of Earth. Moves around, too. Quite a phenomenon, isn't it?" Dr. McClellan tapped the pipe against the heel of his hand. "See those smaller white and dark spots?"

"Umm—yeah, I think so. I can see the dark one."

"Well, that's the shadow of one of Jupiter's twelve moons. The white spot is Io, if I'm not mistaken." He blew through the pipe then slipped it into his shirt pocket. "Jupiter's mistress. He turned her into a white cow to disguise her from his jealous wife."

"Juno."

"That's right, Hank. Man's been staring at the stars, trying to make sense of them since time immemorial."

"My turn." I tugged Lenny's arm.

He stepped aside, mouth open.

I looked into the eyepiece like I knew what I was doing, much less seeing. "What kind of telescope is this, Dr. McClellan?"

"A six-inch Newtonian. I ground the mirror myself."

Lenny was right. Jupiter looked like a marble, a yellow-orange shooter. "So that little black spot's a shadow, huh?"

"Like that song, Hank." Lenny cleared his throat. "'I'm something, something by a moon shadow—mooon shaaa-dowww, moon shadow.'"

I looked up. "You better stick to painting."

He grinned, eyes shiny as the stars. I'd never seen him so happy as he was that moment, standing there beneath the heavens alongside gangly Dr. McClellan on the redwood observation deck in Julie's back yard. We had come to tell her about what happened to Greg, but she wasn't home. Now we were galaxies away from Grand River, lost in space with her father.

"Let me show you something else." Dr. McClellan swung the telescope around and pointed it straight up, leaning into it. "Let's see—" He took his eye away, looked up, then repositioned it. "Yes, there it is. Take a look."

Lenny went first. "What is it?"

"That one's Deneb, the brightest star in Cygnus or the Swan." He bent down to me and pointed. "Vega is to the right there in Lyra or the Vulture—see it? And there to the south is Altair in Aquila, the Eagle. They comprise the Summer Triangle. Every navigator worth his salt knows those three, boys. They're also known as the Three Birds although the Vulture is probably more commonly known as the Lyre."

I squinted. "How do you get three birds out of that?"

"You just connect the dots. See the Swan's long neck and wings? Daneb is sort of in the middle toward the tail."

I shook my head. "I can't see it." I blinked then strained again into the spray of stars until finally deciding there were so many that you could imagine anything you wanted.

"The Milky Way's really blazing tonight, boys."

"I can see it." Lenny moved from the telescope, gazing up and nodding. "The Swan and Eagle are flying right at each other."

"Excellent, Lenny. You can see that, huh?"

Lenny's mouth hung wide as he looked skyward. "Yeah, and the Vulture's perched, waiting to see what happens."

"Hmm." Dr. McClellan scratched his head. "I never thought of it that way. Actually, the Swan was placed there for Cygnus, who was the best friend of Phaethon, the mortal son of Helios. Seems that Helios was so delighted to see his son for the first time that he told him he could have anything he wished. Phaethon immediately said he wanted to drive the sun chariot, so Helios relinquished the reins. Soon thereafter, the fiery steeds realized it wasn't the mighty Helios driving them so they bolted, wheeling through the celestial heavens, endangering everyone who resided there. At last, Jupiter stepped in and cast a thunderbolt, smoting Phaethon from the chariot and into the celestial river, the Milky Way. Cygnus was stricken with grief over his friend's death and all he could think to do is dive again and again into the great river to collect his friend's bones for proper burial. So moved were the Gods by Cygnus' devotion that Jupiter himself changed his name to Cygnus and turned him into a Swan so he could forever dive into the Milky Way for his best friend Phaethon. That's where we get the expression 'swan song.'"

"Phaethon sounds like Greg. That's something he'd do. But instead of a sun chariot his swan song would be in his Swinger."

Lenny brought his eyes down and leveled them at me. He wasn't mad or anything, but the spell the heavens cast was now broken with mention of Greg's name, reminding us why we were there. "Yeah. We better get goin', Hank."

"You guys come over anytime. Astronomy is the poetry of the sciences."

"Hey, that's good." I gazed up at the three-quarter moon as we walked down the steps and across the yard, Mr. V's voice resonating in my head: *Let us go then, you and I, when the evening is spread out against the sky . . .*

"How's that dog of yours, Lenny?"

"I get him back tomorrow."

"But he's okay then, right?"

"Yeah, Molly just wanted to keep him a day or so to be sure."

"Thank God. I tried to call you but I kept getting your sister, I presume."

"No, I don't have a . . . oh, her. That's my brother's girlfriend."

"I see."

But Dr. McClellan didn't see. No one did. The fathomless universe with all its stars and galaxies and black holes and mysterious dust storms and mythologies made more sense than the Bartelli household with its knicknacks, visqueen walkways and furniture, dripping pink kitchen, and its satellite sons,

Lenny and Vincent, erratically orbiting the heavy gravity of their solar mom. But space itself could never duplicate the likes of another Mrs. Bartelli. I reached for the doorknob but Dr. McClellan beat me to it, opening the door and flicking on the porch light.

"Like I said, boys, you're always—"

"Daddy!" Julie turned, her profile highlighted through the screen door against a mass of black curls and wire-rim glasses, her back wrapped in the arms of Cameron Pippin III.

"Oh . . . well, um . . . sorry, honey—" Dr. McClellan switched the light off, eased the door closed and it clicked like a gunshot going off as we stared blankly at each other not knowing what to do or say or even whether we should breathe or not. Finally, Dr. McClellan took his hand from the knob and cleared his throat. "You boys want some tea or something?"

I looked at Lenny but Lenny stood as still as a constellation, as straight as an upturned telescope, and it was then that I noticed his eyes; they were as tightly shut as they'd been wide open just minutes before. The difference, I now know, between gazing up at heaven and glimpsing into hell.

20

That summer had evolved into one of excess—Greg smoking pot, Julie lusting after Cameron Pippin III, and Lenny and me running. By August we were going daily, usually in the mornings before the sun rose too high, before work began at Sage Diner. If Mom had the early shift and needed the car, Lenny would pick me up at sunrise then drive to the desert so we could run the adobe hills that rolled like the wrinkled gray backs of elephants along the northern side of the valley. Sometimes we ran on wild horse trails up the pink shale of the Bookcliffs. If the mornings were already too hot, we would drive east through peach and cherry orchards to the base of Spruce Mesa where we would jog up among sagebrush and pinõn until we hit the aspens and cooler air. But mostly we ran the usual trails, the ones from his campsite on the Third Sister: Eagle's Wing, Widow Maker, West Bench, Gunny Loop, Liberty Cap. Each run had its own personality, its own signature. Liberty Cap, for example, was within Rimrock National Park and was only a couple miles up but brutally steep. West Bench was up also—all Lenny's runs were—but it was gradual, flattening out and allowing us periodic breathers before the next climb. Runs over the adobes could stretch out to twelve or fifteen miles or even farther on weekends, depending on how much time or wind we had left. Some days, when I wasn't too tired, I would run again after dark, usually just around the neighborhood in an attempt to close the gap between us. I had a sneaking suspicion that he was doing the same, but without the same motivation; Lenny, as he had told Coach Hicks, just loved to run, putting sixty to eighty miles underfoot each week. But his most inspired runs weren't those of a particular distance or even at a particular location but, rather, from a particular person.

Not, of course, that Pecfee Maldonado could run. He had tried once, grabbing Lenny by the collar in front of 7-Eleven and yelling for his friends. When Lenny slipped his grasp, he gave chase about forty yards down the sidewalk along Gateway Avenue, only to return pale as an Anglo, drenched and gasping as if freshly pulled from the canal. From then on, he would sic Kenny Madrid or Frank

Serrano or maybe Silver Renteria after Lenny—and they could run, but only for a couple hundred yards. They knew their best chance was within the first fifty and after that would get no closer than shouting distance. And even these runs, though races for life and limb, Lenny seemed to relish.

As for Greg, he relished smoke. Pot. Hash. Thai stick. Even opium if he could lay his hands on it. And now with Dill out of the picture—Greg said he was convinced that that's who had turned him in to the police—he mostly smoked by himself, driving around the Grand Valley in his graduation present or holed up in his bedroom in boxers and T-shirt, with slitted red eyes and his stereo blaring: Jethro Tull, Led Zeppelin, Neil Young, The Who, Leon Russell, James Gang, and, of course, the ubiquitous Doors. But he read, too, biographies of Keats and Blake and Lincoln, novels by Hesse and Camus, and the nihilistic plays of Sartre. He had me read a few—*Steppenwolf* and *Demian*, *The Stranger*, and *No Exit*. They seemed weird and tangential yet rich and substantive, turning my head in directions I never knew existed.

Though his father managed to get him out of jail the same night he was arrested, he was unable—try as he did—to get him readmitted into the Air Force Academy. Shortly thereafter, although his draft number was relatively high, Greg too received his notice and was scheduled to be bussed to Denver for a physical at the same time Lenny was. Someone had placed him on the fast track, but Greg seemed unconcerned, mumbling something about the conscientious objector status his old man was working on or a student deferment, or maybe traveling west with Stankey to Stanford. After all, Mr. Woods was a Stanford law alum and Greg certainly had the grades to get in. If not, he would hang out and audit classes or practice his Chinese until he was accepted. Besides, the bay area was a happening place and one could easily disappear into Haight Ashbury if need be. This talk was all within the haze of blue smoke and metaphysical psycho-babble that hung as prominently in his bedroom as the psychedelic posters and pictures of Jim Morrison. I never did ask what he was going to do about the six months of probation he'd received for blowing up the Colonel.

Julie, it seemed, had finally gotten Greg out of her system, replacing one infatuation with another. Cameron Pippin III was six years older than she and light years ahead in experience. If she wasn't raving about their trip to the Democratic National Convention in Miami, she was helping him recruit volunteers at Democratic Headquarters downtown. She was even talking about forsaking Notre Dame for CU, applying to a program that would allow her to skip fall semester and still earn political science credits for her campaign efforts.

Her mother, she said, would go bananas (having already lost it over her going to Miami), but Julie just needed a sponsor and Cameron would be only too happy since it was probably his idea in the first place. I cracked that maybe her credits should be for anatomy instead of political science, but she ignored me and continued to prattle on about McGovern and all the possibilities life held. Where, I wondered, had Sigfried our fisherwoman gone?

My life held possibility, too. Like how much tip money I was going to receive on any given day. Arlene's generosity seemed to wane as I moved from novelty to fixture at Sage Diner. Punk still came through, though, slipping me a twenty every few days or so, almost as though he was paying for something illicit. He would sidle over and wait for me to finish clearing or wiping down a table. With arm straight down and never looking me in the eye, he would quickly open his fingers from behind like the door of a cash register popping open. I would take the money but before I could even offer a thanks, he would walk away, as oblivious as he was generous. At first I thought his method must have something to do with income tax or not wanting to pay workmen's comp, until one day just before our clandestine transfer, I noticed his eyes catch Arlene's, his fist clench, then the nonchalant stroll back to the kitchen without giving me anything. It was then I decided maybe I should look for something else to do or, at least, consider as possibility.

"So who is this guy, Mom?"

"You never mind, honey. Hand me a tissue."

I was sitting on the bathroom counter, watching her at the mirror. I grabbed a Kleenex. "Come on. What's he do?"

She puckered her lips, blotted them. "He's an accountant."

"Where'd you meet him, at the bank?"

"No. At the diner."

"The diner!"

"Yes, the diner." She straightened, smoothing her skirt. "He started coming in a couple a months ago."

"Do I know him?"

"I don't know. He comes at lunch, usually sits at the end of the counter. Toasted cheese, side of mashed potatoes, tall buttermilk."

I shook my head, racking my brain. "What's he look like?"

"I don't know, honey." She flounced her hair, gave herself a final look-over. "Kinda tall, kinda thin, kinda sweet."

"Kinda average."

She turned toward me. "How do I look?"

"Like a million bucks."

"Oh, honey—" She kissed my forehead. "Don't look so blue. Things could be worse. It could be Redd that I'm . . . oh, there he is."

I followed her into the living room then hustled by her to the front door. "You're not supposed to answer the door, Mom. You're the date."

She smiled, shaking her head.

"Don't act too eager, either. Go in the bedroom and I'll call you."

"Henry—"

"Go."

Laughing, she turned and walked across the living room and down the hallway. I wanted a chance to check this guy out for myself. No more Redd Morgans allowed in our house.

I opened the door. "Hi—"

"Hey, what's going on? You must be Hank." A guy in a vest with no shirt, high-water corduroy bellbottoms, and leather sandals stood grinning at me. Tall wiry hair looked like it had been transplanted from his chest, frizzy chops reaching to his jaw line.

I stared at the suitcases he held in each hand. "I thought this was supposed to be your first date?"

"Come on, let me in. These are heavy."

He squeezed by, clunking the suitcases against the doorjamb. I gawked as he heaved them onto the sofa. The handle of a black hair-pick jutted from his back pocket.

"Praise the Lord, I felt like my arm was gonna fall off." Rubbing his shoulder and still smiling, he walked past me and went back outside.

I looked at the suitcases, wondering what it was about Mom that attracted these guys, when it suddenly hit me. I whipped around. "Dana!"

"Hey, Junior."

"Mom! It's Dana!"

She dropped her handbag, stretched and yawned. "What's there to eat?"

Mom came bursting from the hallway, hands glued to her face. She froze in disbelief, eyes welling. Dana had been gone almost two months and we hadn't heard from her in a couple of weeks.

The doorbell rang again. Wire-head was holding more things, paper sacks and a long dark walking stick. "Sister Dana, is this yours?" He held the cane aloft. Behind him stood two girls about Dana's age also carrying sacks, and an older short-haired man. They all shuffled in as Mom hugged Dana in the middle of the living room. Mom's mascara was running and she couldn't talk.

"Yeah, it's mine." Dana pointed at the couch, Mom still clutching her. "Just put everything over there."

The guy and two girls unloaded Dana's stuff, but the other man didn't budge, remaining in the doorway studying his shoes. He looked up. "Hi." A bouquet of daisies appeared from behind him.

"Milton—" Mom let go of Dana, wiping tears with the insides of her wrists. "Oh, Milton, I'm sorry. Let me . . . oh, they're beautiful—thank you." She took the flowers, glanced around the living room as though searching for a place to stick them, then finally dropped her hands and began crying again. Milton scanned the living room floor as wire-head with perpetually goofy grin eased the flowers from Mom's fingers.

Dana went to her and gave her another hug. "Who's this, Mom?"

"I was about to ask you the same thing." She watched her flowers disappear into the kitchen. "This is Milton—" Mom wiped her face again. "Milton Howard. Milton, this is my daughter Dana and my son Hank."

"How do you do." He held out his hand.

"Dana's been away and I wasn't expecting her tonight. Milton, could we maybe do this . . ."

"Certainly, of course. Sorry I interrupted. I'll call you."

Dana stared. "You were going on a date?"

"Yes, honey. Thank you, Milton. I'm really sorry—"

"Mom." Dana's eyes widened.

"What?"

"I'll still be here when you get back."

"No, honey, I just—"

Dana frowned, pursing her lips.

Wire-head carried a vase into the living room and set it on the coffee table, proud of himself. "There." His smile stretched wider, as if the flowers were his idea. "I'm Jay." He shook Mom's hand. "And these are sisters Tina and Rachel." They looked about as related as Peefee and Cisco, one short with brown curly hair and the other a leggy blond girl.

Mom shook their hands. "Well—" She looked at Milton.

He returned her gaze. "Really, we can do it another—"

"Dana's right. Go Mom." I gave her a little nudge. "We'll wait up for you."

"Well, if you're sure." She kissed me and grabbed Dana's hand. "I'll just be a moment." She hurried back into the bathroom, pulling Dana with her.

"I'm Jay." Wire-head thrust his hand out.

"Milton Howard. My pleasure."

"Do you know Jesus?"

Milton blushed, glancing at his shoes. "Well, I guess I'm a Christian, if that's what you mean."

"He's with us right now. You know that, right? He walks with us, sleeps with us—He's always with us."

"Yes, I suppose so."

"Praise the Lord."

Milton smiled and nodded shyly. "It's nice to see young people so passionate."

"There's no other way." Jay glowered. "Jesus is going to save us, Mr. Howard. He's coming and we've got to be ready. How can we not be passionate?"

"Well—" Milton sat on the edge of the rocker. "I guess you've got a point."

"It's my duty, Mr. Howard. I promised Jesus that I'd, you know, witness for Him. It's the least I can do after what He did for me up there on that cross, you know what I mean? Just one month ago, Mr. Howard, I was just this . . . this—what do you call it—lost soul. Smokin' and drinkin' and doin' drugs and whatnot. And a friend's sister—" He grabbed one of the twins. "—Tina here— told me about this big revival, kind of a Christian Woodstock that was goin' on down in Dallas. Explo seventy-two they called it."

"Roger Starbuck spoke." Tina smiled.

"Yeah, Roger Starbuck. You know, 'kick a touchdown for Jesus' and whatnot. So I—"

"Throw."

Jay stared at me. "What?"

"Throw. He's a quarterback." I stared back. "Roger *Staubach*—it's throw a touchdown."

"Oh, yeah—right. So anyways I decide to go down to see for myself. Drove all the way from Salt Lake in twenty-two straight hours. Only stopped to get gas and pee." The twins tittered. "Praise God. And I get down there thinkin', you know, it's gonna be in a church or something, right? Well, it's in this Cotton Ball place—"

"Bowl."

He glanced at me, licked his lips. "You know how big that thing is, Mr. Howard? So I get down on my knees right there on the ground with all these thousands of people around me cheerin' and prayin' and praisin' the Lord and whatnot and I ask Jesus to deliver me from my sins. You know, give me salvation and eternal life and all that. Save me from, like, the clutches of Satan and whatnot. That's what this preacher dude said, 'the clutches of Satan.' And now here I am, just a couple days later, standin' here before you a different person."

Mom and Dana emerged from the hallway arm-in-arm. "Okay, Milton. I guess I'm ready. Is everything okay?"

"Yes, Sally, we were just having a little discussion about, um—"

"The Lord Jesus!"

"I see." Mom looked at Dana, eyebrows raised. "I won't be late." She kissed her cheek. "I'm so glad you're home."

"Me, too, Mom. Come on, Jay. I'll fix us something to eat." Dana led him and the twins to the kitchen, Jay baring teeth over his shoulder at us.

"Have fun, Mom. Nice to meet you, Mr. Howard."

"Please, Hank, call me Milton. And it was nice meeting you, too. Don't worry about—" He motioned his head toward the kitchen. "—I'm sure he means well."

"What did he do?"

"Nothing, Mom. Have a good time."

I watched them walk to Milton's car, which was parked in the driveway behind a VW Bus. The bus was green and white but powdered red from road dust. Through the windshield I could see pukka shells and a chain with a wooden cross hanging from the rear-view mirror. A big yellow happy-face splattered with insects covered the VW insignia on the front and below it on the bumper was a new EXPLO '72 sticker. I waved good-bye to Mom and Milton then walked around to the rear. Stuck in the window on a piece of cardboard was a handwritten sign GOD IS GOOD with old travel decals plastered inside the glass—Yosemite, Carlsbad, Yellowstone, Grand Canyon, Pike's Peak. On the back bumper was another sticker, weathered and curled at the corners. WARNING: DEAD HEAD ABOARD. Cupping my eyes, I squinted inside, but dust and macrame curtains covered the windows, so I decided to write something, a message to the driver. I stood back, thinking about Jeff, wondering where he was—wondering where *Dana* was—then put finger to glass and wrote JESUS SAVES then underneath AND WHATNOT.

Back inside, Dana and her friends were sitting around the kitchen table holding hands, heads bowed. Tina was speaking and when she finished, they all said "amen." Jay started wolfing a sandwich, following it with a fistful of corn chips.

"Where's Jeff?"

"Hank—come have a bite with us." Dana scooted over, pulled up another chair.

"Did you see him?"

"Of course I saw him. We were in Hawaii for two weeks. Remember? Didn't you get my postcards?"

I walked over to the goldfish bowl. "Yeah, but I thought—"

"No, Hank. We didn't go AWOL."

Stella and Frank were hanging near the surface, lipping bubbles.

"Brother Hank—" Jay's little finger was stuck inside one cheek, stretching the corner of his mouth back, poking at a molar. "—have a seat, man. I wanna rap with you. Dana here tells me you read a lot."

"Yeah, I guess so."

"Have you read the Good Book?" He withdrew his pinkie, studying it before sucking something from the nail.

"Yeah, I've read several good books. Which one?"

"No, the Good Book, man. The one and only."

I shrugged. "Yeah. Parts of it, I guess."

"Right on." He took another bite of sandwich. "So what'd ya think?"

"About—?"

"The Book. The Bible."

"Well, I didn't actually read the whole thing, cover-to-cover."

"Yeah. Me, neither. But I'm going to. Soon as I get back." He swallowed, took another huge bite. "When I do, though, let's rap. Okay?"

"Sure."

Dana got up and came over to the fish bowl, rested her hand on my shoulder. "How they doin'?"

"I dunno. Okay, I guess."

"They been lonely?"

"Yeah, maybe a little. They don't seem to be getting any bigger though. They look any different to you?"

Dana stooped down eye-to-eye with the fish. "No, not really. Is Stella still dominant?"

"Of course."

She tapped the bowl, ran her finger over it. "Hank, Jeff's fine. But it's been horrible. His feet have some kind of fungus. Jungle-rot or something. It's under his arms, too. He says it's impossible to keep dry. And his shoulder's bothering him."

"When's he getting back?"

"He's hoping by Christmas. They've been pulling everybody out. You know, election year and everything."

I nodded. "Who's this guy?"

"Oh, Hank. I barely know him. They just gave me a ride. They're headed to Salt Lake."

"What were you doing down there, anyway?"

"It's a long story. I went down with a couple of the other wives."

"Did you find Jesus, too?"

"I don't know. It's complicated. I'll tell you later." She traced a strand of hair behind her ear and glanced back at the others sitting at the table. "Is Mom okay?"

"Yeah, I think so. She hasn't talked to Redd in quite a while. He's been mowing our lawn though. I mean a couple times every week. It's weird."

"She told me." Dana sighed. "Is she still not smoking?"

"As far as I know."

"What about Dad?"

"Dana, I think he's got somebody helping him."

"Helping him?"

"Yeah, me and Greg saw some lady leavin' the trailer a couple weeks ago. I think she's, you know, helping him with Redd."

She mulled this information over. "Did Dad pull another one?"

"Not lately, I don't think. I mean, why would he? Mom's not dating him anymore, right?"

Stella was suddenly frisky, nibbling at Frank's tail, chasing him in tight loops before coasting to their usual state of suspension.

"We need to buy them a new bowl. Maybe then they'll get bigger."

"Good idea." Dana squeezed me. "I'm glad to be home, Hank." She straightened and went back to the table and sat down.

I was glad, too, but couldn't say it, couldn't do anything but stoop there gazing into Stella and Frank's small watery world, wondering when, if ever, they were actually going to grow.

◇◇◇

Through the wrought-iron bars of Mr. Shimizu's gate we watched the backhoe scratch at earth, scooping up shrubs and trees and flowers like a prehistoric animal foraging for food. Off to one side a man was loading a pile of moss-covered rock onto a flatbed, and a couple of younger men were wrestling a round shrub into the back of a truck. Two more shrubs stood nearby on a pallet, gunnysacks of black dirt balled around their roots.

A ladder leaned against the side of the house next to a train of ivy folded over from the top where someone had begun peeling it from brick. Mr. Shimizu emerged from the back porch whistling, pulling on white cotton gardening gloves. He rounded the corner and started to scale the ladder but then spotted us and moseyed down the pebble path instead.

"'Morning. How was Hawaii? Did you get a hold of my relatives?"

"No, but I tried calling them once. We were so busy, we didn't really get a chance to see much." Dana handed him his address book. "Thanks, anyway."

"Doesn't matter. More I thought about it, they probably would've charged you same as a cab." Mr. Shimizu stuffed the gloves in his back pocket and pulled the gate open. "You were gone a long time. Come take a look."

We followed him along the shoulder-high wall that encircled his property. Holes pocked the yard, unearthed roses, miniature trees, and exotic flowers sitting here and there in ceramic pots filled with black soil. He picked up a willow branch, examined it, then stripped away the limbs and pointed it at a stream gleaming over a mossy dam of bright green rock before gurgling into a pool covered with lily pads. "I'm getting rid of that, too. My water bill's gone through the roof."

Dana lightly placed a hand on his arm. "But it's so beautiful."

"I guess." He shrugged. "What do they say—'in the eye of the beholder'? Well, this beholder's had a change of heart."

"So you're taking everything out?"

"Everything that wasn't here before. I read about it the other day in *Reader's Digest*. The vocabulary section— *Increase Your Word Power* or something. They called it xeriscaping. It's for dry climate. I've decided high desert's every bit as beautiful as all this, anyway. So why waste water?"

"So you're just going to take it out and let it go?"

"No. I'll still plant things. But just indigenous species—cactus, yucca, sagebrush—and then I'll let it go. At least until the weeds get too high."

I looked around at the ferns, the leafy carpet of ground cover, the sculpted shrubs and hedges that looked like so many poodles escaped from their groom. "How many years did it take to do all this, Mr. Shimizu?"

"Too many. The miniatures in the pots are called bonsai. They go back to the ninth century or so. It's been part of Japanese culture ever since the Edo period. But, hey, I was born in Tacoma, Washington. I haven't spoken any Japanese for years and I've even lost my taste for rice. I'm a potatoes man." He patted his belly. "Why be tied to the past when all that exists is the present? Xeriscaping is being in harmony with what's around me. Bonsai is in harmony with what went before. Twisting small trees into something they don't do in nature doesn't make sense to me anymore. I've decided it's grotesque. Look at that one." He pointed to a small gnarled pine sitting in a pot on a low wood-slatted bench. The trunk and main branch were curled to one side, almost parallel with the ground. Copper wire coiled the branch like a snake. "There's a saying—nature isn't human-hearted."

"So zeroscaping means zero landscaping?"

"Hmm." He rubbed his chin. "Maybe so. I like that, Henry—zeroscaping. From here on out I too will call it zeroscaping—zero landscaping, zero gardening, zero water. I'm going to write *Reader's Digest* a letter. 'Dear *Reader's Digest*, My friend Henry from down the block . . .'"

We laughed.

"Maybe they'll at least change the spelling." He poked the stick into a hole. "'Just as we take advantage of what is, we should recognize the utility of what is not.' Take this hole." He traced the point around the circumference, loose clods rolling into it. "A hole is zero dirt or, in other words, what is not. Right?" He tapped the stick against the side, causing more dirt to slough off. "Or is a hole the dirt around that which is not?" He scratched his head then shrugged. "Beats me."

"Maybe you can ask *Reader's Digest* in your letter."

"Good idea, Henry. Or just leave it to Confucius." He smiled broadly. "Also known as 'confused us'—confused us with zeroscaping." He plucked a purple flower from a bush hugging up against the wall. "A flower for a flower." He slipped it behind Dana's ear.

Dana smiled, cheeks deepening. "Thanks, Mr. Shimizu."

He pulled out his gloves. "How's your father been?"

Dana glanced at me. "Oh, fine."

"Bet he's happy your home safe and sound, huh?"

"Yeah, I guess."

"Is he still working the graveyard shift? I never see him drive by anymore."

"Mr. Shimizu, we better get going. Mom's waiting for us."

"Okay. I've got to get busy, too. Come over anytime. And you, too, Henry. Say hello to your parents for me, okay?"

Dana made a beeline for the gate, hopping over rocks and miniature trees and holes where plants had been. I didn't catch up with her until we were back on the sidewalk and halfway down the block.

"You mean you never told Mr. Shimizu that Dad—"

But Dana raised her hand, bit her lip, and I knew from experience not to ask her anything more.

21

*A*cross the whole of August the sun erupted, hurling solar flares toward Grand River. When I heard this I laughed, thinking Dr. McClellan was kidding, that it was from an episode of *Lost in Space* or that he was alluding to Jupiter and the myth of Phaethon and his best friend Cygnus. But then he flipped through an astronomy journal and, tracing the page with the stem of his pipe, read to us about a huge storm in the sun's northwest quadrant that was blacking out radio communications worldwide and disrupting transmission lines with erratic surges of power. Nuclear particles from a series of nine flares were reacting with the magnetic field of the earth, causing magnetic storms in the upper and lower atmospheres. The article went on to explain that these solar events normally follow an eleven-year cycle with the last being in 1969, and that having one three years later was akin to a snowstorm in July. As a result, the red, white, and green hues of aurora borealis, normally visible from more northern latitudes like Canada or Alaska, had reportedly streaked the night skies over Grand River although Dr. McClellan had yet to see them himself.

I decided that's why August had been so hot in the valley, with temperatures nudging one hundred. Maybe Jupiter really was mad. Maybe myth and science—astrology and astronomy—weren't so different after all, both man's attempt to make sense of things. When I mentioned her father's story—the mythical one, I mean—Julie grew pensive and said she'd heard it many times over the years but had never thought of it in the context of her life or of Greg and what Miss Darling had told us three months before. She was so angry with him for blowing up the Colonel that she couldn't handle being around him anymore. If he wanted to ruin his life, fine, but she wasn't going to hang around to witness it. Enough was enough, she said, and that was that.

But, as it turned out, that wasn't that. Mrs. McClellan read in the *Grand River Sentinel* obituary that Greg's uncle had died and the funeral was scheduled for the following day, the day after Greg and Lenny returned from taking their physicals for military induction.

They had met at six a.m. in front of the Federal Building downtown with fifty or sixty other "lottery winners," as Greg dubbed them. Greg was still drunk, having spent the night on the Third Sister swilling tequila and howling with Louie at the coyotes down below. He passed out near the fire a couple of hours before dawn, and Lenny'd had to drag him into the backseat of the Wagoneer and, once at the Federal Building, sling Greg's arm over his own to get him aboard and propped into a seat at the rear of the bus. Greg slept all the way to the first stop in Pinecrest, where he promptly puked—more from fumes than tequila, he claimed—and slept again until they reached the induction center at another federal building in the heart of the state capital. Lenny said he expected Greg to pull one of his stunts, maybe feign insanity or flail his arms from some mysterious nerve disorder. But once reduced to boxers and then herded like livestock from one line to the next for the better part of the afternoon, Lenny said he was docile as a lamb, being poked and prodded, cajoled and insulted as though already a member of the armed services. Greg said he kept imagining *Alice's Restaurant* and wished he too had brought some twelve-by-eighteen glossies for effect and what he called "reverse literary verisimilitude," whatever that was.

On the return, they again sat in the back so Greg could crack a window to have an occasional hit off the joint he had tucked under the seat. The nearer to Grand River, the more he puffed until the entire bus reeked of the stuff. The driver kept glancing over his shoulder, making Lenny think he was about to pull the bus over. Greg reassured him that he wouldn't. What are they going to do, he asked, arrest me? Take away my 1-A status? He insisted it didn't matter if they were classified 1-A, 4-F, or something in between because his old man was going to get them both exempted with his far-flung connections and legal wrangling. In fact, he told Lenny with a wink, the wheels of justice were already in motion.

For Lenny, the journey was just another day in his life. He had never been to Denver, and if it weren't for Greg going, he probably wouldn't have said much about it, simply shrugging or maybe commenting on the color or shape of the mountains. Passing his exam didn't seem to worry him, either. He was so tough and fit from living and running in the desert that the military may have sounded like an upgrade in accommodations. Of course, Lenny rarely voiced concern about anything. He just was.

"Here, Louie." Lenny slapped his thigh. "Come on."

"It was a beautiful service, Greg."

"Thanks, Jules." Greg took a sip of lemonade and gazed over his glass across the tenth fairway. He was wearing a white dress shirt, but it was unbuttoned, cuffs turned up and wrinkled tails hanging around Bermudas. "Thanks for coming."

Dragging fingers through waves of thick sun-bleached hair, Julie sighed. "Look, Greg, I—"

The sliding glass door opened, and Mrs. Woods stepped barefooted from the house still in her black funeral dress, a snifter of brandy cupped under her chin. "Should that dog be out here without a leash?"

Greg turned and stared at her. "*Buzhi dou. Danshi yeshu ni xuyao yige dan.*"

"Gregory, that's enough. I simply asked a question."

"I'll put him in the Jeep." Lenny started to get up, but Greg put a hand against his chest, stopping him.

"It's too hot in the Jeep, man. He'll bake."

"I'll tie him to the bumper. He'll be okay. He crawls underneath."

"Louie's fine. Relax." Greg smiled, glancing over his shoulder at his mother.

"If he gets out on that golf course, Gregory, they'll call the dogcatcher. Or worse. And we certainly can't afford any more trouble."

"Come here, Lou." Greg clapped, and the dog's tail thumped the concrete. "Come on, boy."

Louie dropped the tennis ball and licked his chops as though mustering all energy before struggling out from under the table. He picked up the ball and plodded over.

"Did you hear what I said, Gregory?"

"*Tingbudong.*"

Mrs. Woods shook her head and stepped back into the house, sliding the door closed.

"Good boy, Louie. Good dog." Louie rested his muzzle across Greg's thigh, mouthing the tennis ball and wagging his tail. Greg snatched it and Louie immediately sat, ears perked and mouth closed with just the tip of his tongue showing. Greg petted the ball. "Niiice ball. Miiine. My ball."

Louie barked, a rarity.

"Gregory!" Mrs. Woods rapped the window from inside the house.

"*Bizui!*" He threw the ball across the irrigation ditch that separated their yard from the course, Louie scrambling after it.

"How much Chinese does your mom know?"

"Not a stitch, Jules. That's what makes talking to her so much fun. Get the ball, Louie! Go on! Now the old man, that's a different story. He's fluent. Reading, writing—you name it."

"What'd you just say to her?"

Greg smiled, shrugged. "I don't know. It's irrelevant."

Julie shook her head. "No, it's not."

"Yeah, it is. She didn't know what I said. She'll never know. Come here!" Louie happily trotted back to Greg, dropping the ball at his bare feet then backing up in anticipation.

"So if I whisper something to Hank about you, it's irrelevant because you don't know what I said?"

"It's not the same thing."

"Yes, it is. Your mom didn't know what you said and you wouldn't know what I said to Hank. How's it different?"

"It's different because *no one* knew what I said."

"Wrong." Julie pointed at him. "You knew."

Greg laughed, flipping the ball in the air and catching it. "Okay, okay. Suppose I'm thinking something about you—right?"

"Yeah."

"If I don't say it, you don't know what I'm thinking."

"But—"

He held up the ball. "Wait a minute. And if I say it but it's in a language you don't understand, you still don't know what I was thinking." He threw the ball and Louie took off.

"But the difference, Greg, is this. When you're just thinking something, I don't know what you're thinking. But if you make a sound, especially if it's contextual with something I just did or said, I do have an idea what you were thinking."

Greg shook his head. "Over there, Louie!" He waved his hand toward the lilac bushes hugging up against the shed.

"So your mother knew you were saying or thinking something that wasn't very nice."

"No, she didn't."

"Sure she did. Just like at graduation. Don't you think we knew you were up there insulting everyone?"

He threw his head back and laughed, then looked at Julie with mock seriousness. "Actually, I was being very complimentary."

"Yeah, right. So what'd you say?"

"At graduation?"

"No, to your mom. When she came out."

"It's irrelevant."

"It's not irrelevant, Greg—that's my point. Tell us what you said then we'll decide."

He stood up and drained his glass. "Anybody want anything?"

Julie grabbed his shirttail, smiling uncomfortably. "Come on, Woods! Fight or flight? Where's that spirited old captain of the debate team?"

"Last call—" He held up his glass, rattling the ice cubes like dice, then walked toward the sliding glass door. Hesitating, he turned around. "You want to know where?" He crossed his eyes and saluted. "Hep, one-two-three . . ." He goose-stepped inside.

I shook my head. "Way to go, Jules."

"Come on, Hank. He was being ridiculous."

Louie brought the ball back, dropped it next to Lenny, then padded over to the swimming pool for a drink.

"No, Louie—" Lenny got up and led him back by the scruff.

"So what's the point, Julie, that you're right and he's wrong?"

"Yes, Hank! That is the point! No one else stands up to him. Not you, not Lenny, no one. You two are like a couple of puppy dogs around him. Whatever Greg says, whatever Greg does, whatever Greg . . ." She looked around, jutting fingers into her hair. ". . . whatever he screws up, that's just peachy because it's the almighty Greg Woods."

"You've barely seen him all summer."

"And for good reason, Hank. For good reason." She set down her lemonade and stood.

"You're still mad about the Colonel."

"You're damn right I am. And so should you be, Henry. The guy just threw it away. He had everything going for him and he just blew it. And now he's headed for—" Her eyes welled and she turned to leave. "And how can you not be mad?"

"Julie, come on. Don't go. What do we tell him?"

"Tell him I can't do it, Henry. I can't watch him go up in smoke like this."

"But what about his uncle, Julie? What about that?"

"And what about his mother, Henry? Her brother just died. It's not always just about Greg." Voice catching, she put a knuckle to her chin.

"Then who is it about, Jules?" Greg stepped out holding another glass of lemonade. "Cameron Pippin the turd?"

"Clever, Greg." She quickly wiped an eye.

"Queen of the castle wants a word with you."

"What?"

"My mother. She wants to talk to you." He shrugged, raising an eyebrow then screwing his mouth to the side. "So please, my dear, walk this way." Hunching his shoulder and dragging a foot, he grabbed her arm and pulled her toward the sliding glass door. "The Notre Dame way."

Julie pulled back. "I'm not going to Notre Dame."

Greg stopped, stared at her, then hunched the opposite shoulder. "I had a hunch you wouldn't." Flicking the imaginary cigar, he twisted his face the other direction and dragged the other foot. "Then walk *this* way. But please, just walk— all this humping's giving me a cramp."

Shaking her head then bursting into laughter, she allowed herself to be pulled inside, the door sliding behind them.

I looked at Lenny. "She still loves the guy." I shook my head. "Unbelievable."

Lenny was bent down digging his fingers into the scruff of Louie's neck, nose buried in fur. "Look, Hank—" He looked up from concentrating, brows knitted. "A tick." He lifted the dog's coat for closer scrutiny. "Louie's got a tick."

I nodded. "Yeah." I gazed into the sun, let it stab my eyes. "Yeah, Lenny— that's something." I closed them. Unbelievable.

And it was. It was unbelievable that Lenny could be so oblivious, that he was headed to the Army and possibly Vietnam yet seemed unfazed by either. It was unbelievable that Greg blew off the Air Force Academy and was now pointed in the same direction Lenny was. That Julie was under the influence of some political Svengali six years her senior who talked her out of becoming part of the first female class to matriculate under the Golden Dome of Notre Dame. Unbelievable that Dad was still holed up in his *Airstream*, Dana had found Jesus, Mom was dating an accountant. That Cisco was laid up with some undefined neck injury, his crazy cousin was chasing after Lenny, that Redd Morgan was still mowing our lawn while Mr. Shimizu was ripping out his. The whole world seemed tipped in an awkward direction, wheeling through space in an orbit not even Dr. McClellan could explain. It was as if all that I thought was, actually wasn't. The doors of perception Greg had always alluded to were just that: perception. I was finally starting to grasp what he and Jim Morrison and William Blake were babbling about. The sequin babe you think is behind door number two, waving in the back seat of a shiny new convertible, isn't there. In fact, she's not behind doors one or three either. She doesn't exist and Monty Hall isn't God and making a deal isn't salvation. Cause and effect are as much an illusion as Louie thinking a Green Drake Fly is something to munch on. Bite and be bitten.

My friends were going I didn't know where—*they* didn't know where—while I was going nowhere. A direction, at least, I needn't worry about altering. And the one person who seemed the most unbelievable at the beginning of the summer—Miss Darling—had, in all her wild predictions and eccentric notions, become at least as believable as anyone else.

After leaving Greg's house, Lenny and I went to Aquarius Aquariums in Teller Arms shopping center. I spent every cent from a week's worth of bussing at Sage Diner on a ten-gallon aquarium, pink decorative rock, an exotic species of water plant, and a porcelain seahorse that was on sale and looked more like a textured question mark than anything real. As we left the parking lot, Lenny's Wagoneer started sputtering, so he nursed it down Gunnison Avenue along City Park Golf Course, past the swimming pool and football stadium, then down side streets to the vacant lot across from his mom's where he popped the hood and set to work.

"Where'd you say your mom is?" I leaned against the elm, gazing across the street.

"Church."

"You mean she goes Saturdays, too?"

"And Tuesdays and Thursdays. It's the only place she goes period. Hank, get me that long flat-head, would ya?"

I poked in his toolbox splayed open on the fender well and gave him the screwdriver. "What about when Vince and what's-her-face were there. Where was she then?"

Lenny sat on the radiator, legs straddling the engine block. "In the cellar."

"What?"

He twisted the screwdriver back and forth. "She was hiding."

"Hiding in the cellar?"

He pulled it out, tossed it in the box. "Yeah." He wiped his hands on a rag. "Is there a three-eighths in there?"

I gawked at him. "Wait a minute—"

"Hank, I got to get this done before she gets home."

I rummaged around for the socket. "You mean to tell me she was hiding in the cellar that day we were in your room looking at all those knicknacks and stuff?"

"Yeah."

"Why?"

"I dunno. Why does she do anything?"

"Whoa—" I snapped on the three-eighths and handed him the ratchet. "But her car was gone."

Lenny bent over, studying the carburetor. "She hid the car, too. She wanted to know what we'd do if she wasn't there." He looked up, hands still submerged. "Guess she found out. Where's Louie?"

"Right here, sleepin'. Why didn't you tell me this before?"

"Vince just told me. I didn't stick around. Remember?"

"So what happened?"

"She caught 'em. Vince and his girlfriend."

"You mean, doing it?"

"No, but they were on her bed eating junk. And Sheila was painting her toenails."

"Oh, man."

"Guess they got Cheetos all over the white bedspread. You know, that orange stuff."

"What'd she do?"

"Vince wouldn't say." Lenny straightened and arched his back, rubbing it. "Must've been bad, though. I don't think he's been back."

Mrs. Bartelli in the cellar. Bats in the belfry. I had been in their cellar only once, after Lenny found a *Playboy* up by the brickyard on the way home from school in fifth grade. We went down there with a flashlight to take a better look. It was dank and mildewy and musty smelling. Lining the walls were fruit jars, boxes of magazines and newspapers, rusted gardening tools, an old push mower. In the corner stood the skeleton of a tall lamp with a torn shade that cast an eerie shadow against the concrete foundation when we held the flashlight to it. And cobwebs, they were everywhere. But neither spiders nor skeletons nor the threatening creak of Mrs. Bartelli walking across the kitchen floor above us could scare us away from the rain-crinkled images we ogled in the small round light beneath the house. And now the thought of her down there monitoring her sons' every movement finally confirmed it for me. As Lenny had put it, she was bent. And as she would soon prove, to the point of breaking.

"Shoot." Lenny reached deeper into the engine. "Hank, there's a Coleman's camp light in the back. Grab it, would ya?"

I crawled back, rummaged around, and set it on the manifold.

"Hold it down here. I dropped the nut to the carburetor."

I leaned into the engine, holding the light by its handle.

"Can you get it any closer?"

Lying across the fender well alongside the engine block, I worked the light downward. "See it?"

"Nope. Move it over this way a little." He tapped the grease-laden metal. I turned the light a little more, tipping it upward. Heads practically touching, we strained into the motor when suddenly everything went dark. "What the—"

We both raised up, hitting our heads. "Hey!"

Machine-gun laughter pelted the hood from outside.

"Come on!" I dropped the light, felt Lenny squirm sideways then saw his face scrunched up in the light now glowing from somewhere on the ground. "Let us out!"

"Let us out! Let us out!" Peefee Maldonado fired off another salvo of laughter. "Let us out of where, man!?! I didn' know we were in!"

The edge of the hood pinched the back of my left knee and the battery terminals poked my thigh. Someone drum-rolled their hands across the hood. I kicked my feet.

"Look at that, man! He kicks like a little *hito!*"

More laughter. Turning my head I could make out shadows moving along the crack of light between the radiator and hood. The whole gang must have been there as I heard muffled voices and shouts and snatches of laughter.

"Hank—" Lenny's nose was mashed sideways into the upturned air filter. "—I can't breathe."

More shadows cut vertically along the length of hood then the Wagoneer jounced.

"Lenny, they're . . . they're on the bumper."

The Jeep began rocking and bouncing and with every upward surge, the hood pinched my leg. To the side I could hear Louie snort, his snout pressed into the crack.

"Louie—git 'em, Louie. Go git 'em, boy."

But Louie continued to sniff and snort and I imagined his tail wagging at another game being played. Finally, the bouncing stopped and I slid my legs out, but the hood clamped down again across the small of my back and there was more drumming.

"*Pobrecito*—where you think you're going, man?"

One hand on the battery, the other on the fender well, I pushed up and was wiggling a little farther out when I felt arms wrap my middle then my pants being yanked down. I kicked furiously and to my amazement the tugging stopped. The hood released and raised open.

I staggered hopping to my feet, trying to pull my pants up. Someone pushed me from behind and I sprawled face-first into the dirt. Spitting and wiping my mouth and eyes with my sleeve, I squinted at the blurry outline of Peefee and the gang clustered around the engine and of Louie stretched out under the hood, front paws draped over the radiator. I blinked, trying to clear my vision, when what appeared to be a tree branch fell through the air. Louie yelped and jumped down. Tail between his legs, he scrambled under the Wagoneer as the branch somehow rose then fell again, glancing off the hood into the engine block.

"Homosex-u-iiils!"

I struggled to my feet, pulling my pants up and fumbling with the snap. I watched what I then recognized to be a rake lift skyward.

Lenny crawled from the engine, one forearm covering his head. "No! Don't!"

Down came the rake, striking his shoulder and staggering him backward against the grill. He slid down into a squatting position, grimacing and clutching his upper arm.

"Sinners!" Mrs. Bartelli glared around her, thrust the rake like a bayonet. "Sinners and blasphemers!" She clawed the air. "Multitudes of swine!" Lifting it over her shoulder, she began swinging in a wide arc, back and forth, scattering the gang as a dervish would so many fallen leaves. "Suffer the wrath of our Lord!"

Peefee and the gang retreated down the street into the shadows of the trees, peering over their shoulders, running backward toward the pickup as Mrs. Bartelli finally exhausted herself, the rake clanging against the curb.

"Sodomites—" She stood in the gutter, panting, feet wide, leaning against the rake as though she'd just finished weeding. Her pink wide-brim hat sat sideways on her head and one side of her black mesh Sunday dress had slipped off a shoulder, revealing her white brassiere strap. Wiping her mouth and shifting her hips, she adjusted the dress underneath her heaving bosom. She stopped, eyes widening. "Sodomites and whores!" She pointed at me then staggered forward, dragging the rake. "He who lies with another man—" The rake was lifting skyward.

Backing up, feeling my way around the trunk of the elm, I could hear the rumble of Peefee's pickup, the race of the engine, the glass-packed mufflers.

"Mom, what're you doing?" Lenny pushed with his legs, sliding up against the grillwork. From between his legs panted Louie, still under the Wagoneer, eyes and tongue just visible.

"What're you doing, Mom?"

She glared, holding the rake aloft, mouth pursed and eyes wild with religious fervor.

"Mom?" Lenny held his shoulder, rubbed it, rotated his arm back. "What're you doing?"

Mrs. Bartelli looked around, blinked, then fixed her eyes on Peefee's black Chevy pickup slowly rolling up behind her: Kenny Madrid, Silver Renteria, John Gutierrez, Jimmy Gonzales, Carl Lujan, Gabe Fuentas, Manuel Garcia, even Dan Abeyta, fresh back from reform school, all crammed in the truck bed, all staring. And up front Peefee, slack jawed, leaning over the steering wheel around the only figure not gawking: his head was locked straight ahead in a metal contraption of screws and braces and foam rubber every bit as unnatural as the woman now lowering the rake, now letting it clatter harmlessly to the pavement.

"Mom?"

That anomaly of nature, that *muy loco* woman Cisco Salazar and the gang now realized to be Lenny Bartelli's mother.

◇◇◇

Everything I bought I placed inside the aquarium to lug the six blocks home. Lenny had led Mrs. Bartelli inside, supporting her by one elbow as she shuffled across the street and up the driveway with her head back and eyes closed, as though she was an invalid or suddenly blind. I followed them as far as the carport, then leaned the rake with her hat on top against the house and hurried back to the Wagoneer.

When I got home, the sun was down, the sky was a deepening blue and a hangnail moon tipped toward Venus. Balancing the aquarium on my thigh, I fumbled with my key, inserted it, and kneed the door open. The house was dark with all curtains pulled and not a light on anywhere. I carried the aquarium across the kitchen toward Stella and Frank and set it on the table.

"Henry?"

I walked into the living room. Mom was in the stuffed rocker, the one Dad always sat in. Her feet were drawn up and she was lightly rocking. "Henry, I've told you I don't know how many times about the car."

"What, Mom?"

"The car." Her face glowed as she inhaled. "If you use the car, you hafta put gas in it."

"Okay, Mom, but I—"

"Even if you don't have money, ask me or Dana or somebody, but put gas in it. Understood?"

"Yeah, sure, Mom, but I didn't—"

She drew on the cigarette, her face pinched with intensity. "I ran out of gas, Henry."

"Oh—sorry, Mom. I—"

"I worked all day, gave Arlene a lift home 'cause Punk's not feelin' good and—" Her face glowed, the smoke curling around her hair, filling the house. "—and I run out of gas." She shook her head. "Then, when I finally get home—" She stubbed the butt into an ashtray sitting on her lap. "When I finally get home . . ."

"Mom, are you okay?" I started toward her but she held up a hand.

"I'm fine, honey. I'm fine." She set the ashtray on the coffee table and laid her head back. "Just let me rest for a while. There's some roast beef in the fridge. Make yourself a sandwich."

"Mom, I bought an aquarium."

"That's nice, honey."

"It's for Stella and Frank. I've been meaning to for a long time. It's ten gallons. It'll give them a lot more room to swim around and stuff."

"That's nice."

"You sure you're okay?"

"Let me rest, honey. Just let me rest."

I stood in the darkening living room until the rocker stopped, until her breathing slowed then deepened and there was little light seeping anywhere. I went back into the kitchen and quietly removed the seahorse from the aquarium, the plastic bag of water with the water plant, the pink rock. I set everything on the table, cracked the refrigerator open and reached in for a slice of roast beef. Taking a couple of bites, I turned around to admire the aquarium, thinking how happy Stella and Frank were going to be in their new home. The light from the refrigerator streaked the ceiling, the yellow wall, the curve of fishbowl, one leg of the barstool. Cramming the rest of the slice into my mouth, I opened the fridge wider, reached over and grabbed the lip of the bowl. I could hear the water slosh, felt it against my fingers as I brought it toward me and tipped it toward the light just inside the refrigerator door. I peered in: Stella and Frank lapped belly-up against the glass, silvery white, one against the other.

I set the fish bowl next to the plate of beef—I don't know why—shut the fridge door and sat down. Mom was lightly snoring and I could hear boxcars coupling down at the rail yards and crickets chirping in the grass outside. I thought about Dana, wondered when, if ever, Jeff was coming home. I thought about Dad and his dinosaurs and living in the desert and why people get married and have kids and build a life together and then leave and don't talk and don't see each other anymore, just go on and on as if nothing had happened, nothing extraordinary had occurred. I pictured Lenny and his wacky mom, considered whether she had reason to be the way she was. She had lost her husband early on, had to raise two boys by herself. Maybe she was sick of it all and wanted a clean break with the past. Maybe she just went about it in a messy fashion. Mrs. Bartelli went to church, baked cookies and hams for the sick, kicked her kids out of their home, wielded a rake. I got up and opened the fridge.

I slid the bowl out and carried it to the sink. Slowly, I poured the water with Stella and Frank in it gurgling down the drain. Lifting my eyes, I gazed through the small kitchen window at the paring of moon hanging over the back yard and, beyond, a spray of stars—The Milky Way—pouring across the universe. Why are things the way they are? Shaking drops from the bowl and setting it on the counter, I began to turn away, to go see how Mom was doing, if she was still asleep or not, when I caught a whiff. Just a whiff, the vague sour scent. I bent down to the sink and sniffed, picked up the bowl and smelled again. Beer. Setting it back down, I slouched against the counter. I should have known: Mom was smoking again. I rubbed my head and pressed palms against my temples. Dana was back but Mom was still upset and she was smoking again. I looked at the bowl, the empty bowl on the counter, and shook my head. Beer. Fish don't swim in beer. I dropped my hands. Redd Morgan. My jaw tightened. Redd Morgan swims in beer.

◇◇◇

"Buried sunshine."

Julie fingered the piece of coal I kept hidden under the front seat of Mom's car. "Your dad said that?"

"Yeah."

"Hank, that's so poetic."

"Feel the ridges."

Turning it over, she ran her fingers over the flat side. "Yeah. What is that?" She held it up under the dome light.

"See the little leaves and stem?" I leaned over and pointed.

"Yes!" She held it to her nose examining it. "Look at that."

"It's a fossil, Jules. A fern. This is a piece of hard coal. It's called anthracite. Dad said it's probably somewhere between two-hundred-fifty and four-hundred-million years old."

"Incredible."

"That's how coal was made, from plants and trees and stuff. Ancient forests falling on top each other then decaying and getting crushed under the earth. Layer after layer."

"Carbon."

"Yeah. It's from air, I think. But Dad says sunlight's what turns it into coal."

Julie smiled, clasping it to her breast. "Buried sunshine." She handed it back. "Seems weird it's black, though."

"Yeah." I tucked it back beneath the seat, turned off the dome light, then gazed down at my father's *Airstream*. The moon was shrouded with cloud. From the ridge the trailer's outline was barely visible, its silver reflecting what little light the stars cast down. "Dad says coal only looks black. Under a microscope it's brown and red and sometimes even gold."

"Your dad looks through a microscope and my dad through a telescope." Julie opened the passenger's door and gazed up. "Maybe they're not that different."

"It's just a matter of scale, I guess."

She got out and shut the door then leaned back in. "I meant our dads, Hank. Maybe they're not that different. Come on."

We walked along the ridge until we found a place we could slide down, holding hands so we wouldn't slip in the dark, on the loose talus and shale. Reaching the valley floor, we began zigzagging through sagebrush until finally we arrived at Dad's property. At least, I guessed it was his.

I pointed. "There's his pickup."

A couple of old tires lay here and there, and an umbrella-shaped clothesline creaked and slowly rotated in the breeze coming off Rimrock. The truck was parked where it usually was, backed up against the side of the trailer. We walked around the rusted barrels across a sheet of rain- and sun-warped plywood. The same tarp I'd seen before still covered the truck bed.

I cupped my mouth to Julie's ear. "This is where he stashed Redd's tanks."

Julie rounded her mouth and nodded enthusiastically. I had kept her abreast of all my father's actions that summer, and every time I saw her she would say "What's new?" and lift her eyebrows, at which point, if I had something, I'd lift mine; it was code for "What'd your dad do to Redd Morgan this time?" Besides Dana and sometimes Greg—though Greg rarely seemed interested—Julie was the one I confided in most about Dad's movements.

I lifted the tarp and felt around, then walked to the other side and did the same but couldn't find anything. I looked across the bed at Julie, shrugged, then motioned her to follow. A metal milk crate, serving as a step, sat upside-down in front of the door. Tumbleweeds had blown up under the trailer, and a tangle of them clung to the crate's side. I stepped up.

"What're you doing, Hank?"

A towel hung from inside one corner of the door's cracked window, half-covering it as I peered in. From the counter next to the stove a small night light glowed, illuminating a skillet and coffeepot, the canaries' cage cover, and in the middle of the floor a card table cluttered with rocks and newspaper and some kind of utensils. The backseat of a car slumped as a sofa against the opposite wall, and I could see the outline of a lampshade with some kind of hat on top.

"Hank, look."

A low rough-hewn shelf stood outside below the small living-room window. An opened can of motor oil sat on the corner next to a broken clay pot with soil spilling from it. And there underneath, stacked like missiles, lay a half dozen tanks.

"Julie! Redd's tanks!"

"Shhh!"

I hopped down from the milk crate and ran my hands over them, their smooth metallic curve, their cool length. I tipped one up, felt the broken tape. "It's empty." I grasped the next one, felt it—the one after that. "Julie, they're—" And another. "—they're all empty."

"It's probably too soon, Hank. It just happened, right? He probably doesn't even know anything yet."

"He knows."

"How?"

"Mom. I'll bet she called him as soon as Redd killed the goldfish."

"Yeah, but how? Your Dad doesn't even have a phone . . . Hank, quick!"

A light pierced the window from inside. We scrambled to the end of the shelf and squatted down against the trailer. The door creaked open as Julie clutched my shirt. I couldn't quite see his profile, only an arm, the tie of his robe and as he craned his neck and gazed up the pocked driveway to the county road, a shoulder and the back of his head. He turned toward us, but his face was blotted with shadow, hair standing on end. He stepped back and closed the door.

"Julie—"

"Shhh."

I could hear the slow fall of his footsteps travel the short length of the trailer with another sound, a companion sound of something rolling.

"What's that?"

"Let's get out of here." Julie pulled me around to the back and we started across the valley through the sagebrush toward the ridge.

"Julie, did you hear that?"

"What?"

"That sound. Like something was rolling. Wait."

We stopped. I gazed once more at my father's *Airstream*, his short-wave antenna, his truck and the umbrella clothesline that now stood quietly under the stars. A small light glowed through the thin bedroom curtain at the back of the trailer, but I couldn't see any shadows, any movement, no matter how I strained. The light finally went out, so we turned and I followed Julie all the way back across the valley, up and around boulders and loose shale to the ridge and Mom's car.

Dad had pulled another one; I was sure of it. As sure as I was that he and Mom would eventually get back together and that the Redd Morgans of the world would never, ever bother us again.

22

One month after the Green Drake was extracted from his throat, Louie still occasionally hacked, as though a chicken bone were lodged there. Molly reassured us the cough would eventually cease once the puncture completely healed. The fact that Julie and her father blunted the barbs, she explained, made the procedure less complicated, the wound smaller. Directing a penlight down his throat, she said he was lucky it had caught in his soft palate, that it could have been much worse had it reached the pharynx or gone even deeper into the esophagus or stomach, where it may have required surgery.

As she squirted something into Louie's mouth, Mr. V barged in wearing knee-high rubber boots and bib overalls, fingering a copy of *The Old Man and the Sea*. He presented it to me as prize for the biggest catch, saying now *there* was a fish, *there* was a fisherman. Maybe we're all fish, caught by fishermen of our own making; we're nothing if not fish food for circling sharks; fishermen or fish, hunters or the hunted, it matters not; and on and on and on until his beautifully pregnant wife thumped him on the chest with the end of her stethoscope. *This* is real life, she scolded rubbing her belly, *that* a story. If he wanted to play literature, he could be gamekeeper to her Lady Chatterley; otherwise, he could go tend his trees. She wanted only to enjoy these last few weeks before classes began, before the baby's arrival in late September. Giving him a whack to grow peaches on, Molly banished him from the clinic and back into the orchard.

But in the orchard is where Mr. V belonged. He had planted trees five years before and this was to be his first crop. I remembered when, in the middle of spring semester, he had arrived late to class three straight mornings wearing the same flannel shirt, these same rubber boots, and smelling of smoke. His fingernails were rimmed with soot, his beard was singed, and the wisps of hair atop his head and around his neck were even more wild and unruly than before. As he stood at the lectern, thumbing over pages to that day's lesson, we asked what had happened, expecting the worst—fire engines, sirens, smoke inhalation.

Without lifting his head, he peered over his half-moon reading spectacles and, with a grin almost as broad as his shoulders, responded with a single word—"smudging"—then commenced the class as though everything in the world was as it should be. And perhaps, back then, it was.

Soon thereafter he employed Lenny to help with the orchard, to spray and thin and mow and irrigate and then finally to pick—Bing cherries from mid-June to mid-July and peaches, Alberta's and Hale's, in late August, early September. And to document this first harvest, Mr. V commissioned him to paint—a subject of his own choosing—and gave Lenny a set of oils in a varnished box with a simple white card taped to it that read: *Ars longa, vita brevis.*

"Smell this." Lenny held the tube of paint to Julie's nose. "Like it?"

"It's okay."

He squirted blue and brown onto the palette. "Just okay?" He closed his eyes and inhaled before screwing both caps on.

"Hank, look—" Julie pointed. She sat, elbows on knees, on the end of a wooden fruit crate, wearing her straw cowboy hat and chewing a blade of orchard grass as Lenny mixed the two colors. "—it's changing to black. Lenny's an alchemist."

I looked up from Hemingway's novel. "Then it'd be gold."

"Red and green'll do the same thing. This is a kind of a smoky black. Black out of the tube's too flat." He unscrewed green and sniffed it. "How can you not like that smell, Jules?" He held the tube out. "It's déjà vu." He squeezed paint onto the palette. "Maybe from when I was a little kid. I don't know. Or before I was born."

Shielding my eyes, I looked across the orchard at Mr. V bouncing across furrowed ground on his John Deere, pulling a flatbed of bushel baskets. "You're starting to sound like Miss Darling again. I can always tell when you've been hanging out over there."

Julie watched him dab the brush in green then mute it with black.

"Yeah, I still go over there and help her out sometimes."

"Sometimes?" I slipped the paperback into my back pocket. "You're over there more than you're here."

Lenny stood back from the easel like a fencer—parrying the brush as a foil, palette to the side, canvas before him. He eyed the orchard a long while, then uncapped yellow and squeezed a smidgen into the green. "You don't know her." He stood back, clicking the wooden end of his brush against his teeth, studying the trees before stroking more color across canvas.

"After that sweat lodge thing, I think I know her about as well as I need to, Lenny."

Julie looked at me, raised an eyebrow. "What sweat lodge thing?"

"Lenny didn't tell you?"

He jammed the brush into a jelly jar of turpentine, swished it around. "Come on, Hank."

"I thought you told her."

Julie stood, grinning. "Told me what?"

"Well, Lenny and Miss—"

He lunged at me with his brush but I jumped aside, and as he set down the palette, I started running toward the house, laughing. "Lenny and Miss Darling! They were—" I just reached the lawn when he caught me, throwing me into a headlock and bulldogging me to the grass.

Julie rushed over and stood above us, giggling. "Hank! Tell me! What!?!"

Lenny bore down, squeezing my head almost as hard as Marble-head had in the tournament. I could feel Julie pile on, the smell of suntan lotion, strawberry chapstick. She was giggling, digging fingers into Lenny's armpits. "Come on, Hank! Say it!"

I could hear Lenny half-laugh, felt the hold slightly loosen as Julie continued to tickle. "They were—" I thrashed my head, pulling on his elbow and working my chin over the crook of his arm. "—naked!"

"What?" Julie peered down at me over Lenny's shoulder, eyes wide, hands covering her mouth.

Lenny let go, pushing my head into the grass and brushing Julie aside. We watched him get up and walk across the gravel to his paints and easel.

"Naked?" She stared at me, hands dropping to my chest. "Oh, my God." She wore that roller coaster look. "Oh, my God—they were naked." Still on top me, she gazed across the gravel at Lenny, who was busy cleaning his brushes and breaking down the easel. Her eyes dropped back to mine, her voice barely a whisper. "What were they doing?"

I shrugged, at least as well as you can with someone's knees on you. "Sweating."

"What?" Her eyes narrowed.

"Sweating. They were sweating."

She gazed into my eyes, turning the word over in her mind.

"You know, it was a sweat lodge so . . . they were, um, sweating."

She nodded, rolled off me, clearly understanding no more than she had when I eked out the word and possibly, though I couldn't tell for sure, not wanting to know any more—which for Julie was a first.

Lenny was loading Louie and his art supplies into the Wagoneer. He shut the back end, got in, and started the engine.

"Hey, Jules, maybe this is what green smells like."

She glanced at the grass stains on my pant legs before looking up and watching him back the Jeep up in front of Molly's clinic. As he started down the gravel road, we heard the John Deere honk.

"Hey, Lenny!" Across the orchard Mr. V stood straddling his tractor seat. "Leonardo!" He waved.

But the Wagoneer continued down the road, disappearing into dust swirling up from the gravel along the irrigation ditch.

Mr. V turned to us, cupping his mouth. "Where's he going!?!"

I threw up my hands. "I think he had to go home!"

He nodded then sat back down, grinding the tractor into gear.

Julie stared at me.

I stared back. "What?"

"'I think he had to go home?'" She shook her head, snatching the blade of grass from her mouth and pitching it to the ground. "Maybe you do smell like green."

And as usual, Julie was right. Lenny couldn't go home and, at age eighteen, I was about as green as they come.

◇◇◇

After the episode with the rake—with Cisco, Peefee and the boys—Mrs. Bartelli had fallen into a deep swoon, marked by head thrashing and incoherent babbling in foreign tongues. It reminded Lenny of going with her to the Pentecostal Holiness Church when he was little and witnessing revivals, people writhing at the altar, wailing and crying and even peeing on themselves. The latter he knew to be true because he had been one of them, but losing control out of fear rather than anything religious or transcendent.

Every few hours of the thirty-odd she spent in bed, Mrs. Bartelli would surface just long enough to glare at Lenny as though he were Satan himself, as though he had suddenly appeared like an apparition, as from a story in the Bible. She didn't realize that her son had been tending her the whole time, placing cold compacts on her neck and forehead, cradling her head to slip pieces of crushed ice into her mouth, and rubbing and elevating her swollen feet. And how did she thank him during these moments of semi-lucidity? With scripture. Until,

243

finally, in the middle of the second night when Lenny was on the verge of dialing Dr. McClellan for help, with this: "Cheetos! You!" She pointed a finger at him and then, instead of a rake, grabbed the nearest knicknack, a ceramic Easter Bunny holding a carrot in one paw and a basket of colored eggs with the other. "You and that harlot! Fornicators! And on my clean white bed!" Clutching the rabbit by the ears, she leapt from the covers and took after him as though Christianity itself depended on her clocking him with it. Though relieved his mother returned to earth with the same zeal she left it, he only wished she could see him for who he truly was—Lenny, her youngest son—not an intruder, not her eldest with whacko girlfriend and orange-stained fingers.

Yet again Lenny was forced from home by his mother, returning with Louie to the Third Sister where Julie and I found him a few days later for what was to be our final Magic Club. After watching him finish a charcoal sketch of a raven perched atop sandstone, we swung by the Woods to pick up Greg, who was on the telephone. He lay across the waterbed in paisley boxers, puffing on a joint.

"*Buzhidou! Buzhidou! Buzhidou!*" He waved us in. "*Muqin! Ni shi yige chougoushi! Hulihudu!*" He took a hit, holding the phone at arm's length, a voice crackling from the ear piece. He exhaled. "*Meiguanxi, Muqin! Ruguo ni hui shuo Zhonguo-hua, wo gasu ni yiyande qongxi—ni shi yige chuncai!*" Tossing the phone aside, he flopped back. "My mother—" He rolled onto his side, the waterbed sloshing. "She hung up on me!"

Julie sighed, shaking her head. "Passive aggression."

He wet his fingers, pinched the joint out, then reached over and balanced it on an incense holder sitting on the backboard. "It's a first." He sat back up, bobbing on the bed, and looked up at us for the first time. "My own mother— click." He hung up an imaginary phone. "What's that, Jules?" He wiped his eyes.

"You—speaking Chinese to your mom and she not knowing what you're saying. Classic example of passive aggression."

He looked at Lenny and me, rolled his bloodshot eyes. "Pray tell, Doctor."

"Shall I go on?"

"Why not? You always do."

"Well, you're developmentally stunted, partly from smoking too much dope and partly from a dysfunctional living environment. You're angry with her, which makes you hostile, but because you can't express basic human emotion— anger, love, fear, et cetera—you resort to belittling and infuriating her by speaking Chinese."

Greg rolled from the bed and grabbed a T-shirt off the floor, slipped it overhead.

"Want to hear more?"

"No, Jules. That smile on your face pretty much says it all."

I cleared my throat. "Uh, where's your mom, Greg?" From the top of his dresser I picked up an album still in its cellophane wrapper and flipped it over, pretending to read the back.

"Oh, she's been staying over at Uncle Phil's condo. It's been like musical chairs around here. She goes over there, my old man comes back. She returns, he leaves. I'm just waiting for one of them to get confused so they'll both be gone at the same time."

"Yeah, maaan! So we can, like, reeeally get twisted!"

We whipped around to Warren Dillard standing in the bedroom doorway.

"Hey, Woods, I couldn't find it, maaan. You did say in the fridge, right?"

Julie and I gawked at him, at each other, then at Greg.

"No, I said in the cooler, Dill, which is on the counter."

"Oh, oh—right. Hey, fun-seekers! Joining us on our little foray into the desert, huh? Hey, Lenny! What's happenin', man?"

Lenny clasped his outstretched hand. "Not much, Dill."

"Still doin' the wilderness gig, huh?"

Lenny shrugged. "Yeah, I guess."

"Far out, dude. I think that's, like, what I'm gonna do, too. You know, build myself a cabin up in the mountains somewhere and just, like, live up there. You knooow, live off the land and shit."

Julie laughed. "Live off the land, Dill, and the only thing you'll be shitting are rocks."

"Screw you, Julie."

"Dill, just go get the cooler, will ya?" Greg slipped into his flip-flops. "You don't want to tangle with Julie today. I think it's a lunar thing."

"You're like sooo screwed up, Julie. I never did like you, man."

"Dill, go." Greg pointed to the door. "We'll meet you outside."

Shaking his head, he turned and shuffled out the bedroom. "Freakin' Julie, maaan. What a freakin' . . ."

We listened to him mumble his way down the hallway and out of earshot.

"Sleeping with the enemy, Woods?"

"Uh-oh. Don't tell me. Another of Daddy's psychosexual theories of dysfunction."

"You can't seriously tell me that after what he did to you, ratting to the police and everything, that you're letting him go with us."

"Come on, Jules."

"I can't believe he's even here!"

"Hey, live and let live."

"Listen to you. You're turning into a bigger cliché than even Dillard."

"You guys bring your bags?"

"Yeah."

"Well, let's do it then."

Julie grabbed his arm. "Dill goes, I stay."

"Come on, Jules."

"I'm serious, Greg."

"Okay, okay. I'll tell him outside."

"Tell him now."

"Would you ease off." He pulled his arm free. "I'll tell him. Okay?"

We followed him down the hallway past the long mirror and sunken living room to the den.

Greg leaned in. "Dad, we're taking off. See you later."

"Gregor! Come in here for a minute."

"We're getting ready to go, Dad."

"Just for a second. You have to see this, son."

We stepped into the den.

"Hi, guys. Julie McClellan! How are you, dear? How are your parents?"

"Hi, Mr. Woods. They're fine, thanks."

He held his glass out, pointing at the television. "Spitz just won the two-hundred free."

"Great."

"No, not just great. He's already won the one-hundred free and he broke the world's record in both. It's remarkable. And he's got five more events to go."

"Well, his name isn't Mark for nothin'." Greg elbowed me.

"What, son?" Mr. Woods glanced over his shoulder, took a drink.

"Nothing, Dad. We're heading out."

"Okay, guys. Have a great time."

We followed Greg back down the hallway and outside. It was hot. The sun splashed off windshields, off the shimmering leaves of cottonwoods and poplars looming high above rooftops. A globe willow hung limply in the front yard of the neighbor's house, and a sprinkler was turned on low, splashing the curb and watering a scorch spot near the walk. The newspaper boy tossed the Grand River Sentinel onto the driveway at our feet.

Greg picked it up, flipped it once in his hand—"I've always wanted to do this."—and flung it back, just missing the boy's head. The paper skittered across pavement and thumped against the curb.

Julie jutted fingers into her hair and shook her head as the kid looked over his shoulder, scowling. "What on earth possesses you?"

The kid continued wobbling around the cul-de-sac, his load of papers slung over the handlebars, before pedaling away from us down the other side of the street.

Dill came out carrying a large cooler, which we loaded along with our sleeping bags into Greg's trunk. "Your old man's far out, dude. Look what he laid on me." He held out a twenty-dollar bill. "He told me to go buy some pop and chips and stuff."

"Yeah, why don't you go do that, Dill."

"What?"

"Go get that stuff."

"We'll just do it on the way, man."

"No, I have to go gas up. We'll meet you back here. It'll save time."

"Right on. Catch you cats later." Dill shambled off to his beat-up Corvair.

"Greg, as much as I can't stand Warren Dillard, how can you deceive him like that? Why can't you just tell him that this is a Magic Club outing and that he can't go?"

"Jules, believe me. He's got twenty bucks in his pocket. He's not complaining."

"Yeah, your dad's twenty."

"Are we ready?"

After listening to them argue about who was going to drive and where, Lenny and I climbed into the back seat with Louie. Like Dillard's car, Greg's was a disaster: beer cans, fast-food wrappers, opened and unopened mail, an eight-track with the tape tangled around it, golf balls and a colorful array of tees spilling from beneath the front seat across the floorboard. Stuffed in the back window behind the seat were golf shoes, two tennis rackets, an assortment of suntan lotions and analgesics, a towel, and two more eight-track tapes, their black plastic warped and buckled in the late afternoon sun.

Julie drove as compromise for going to the adobe hills north of town; she wanted to go to the potholes above Rimrock where there was water. But before going anywhere, we dropped by Retolaza Liquors, where Greg bought a case of Coors and a half-pint of Peppermint Schnapps using one of the many fake IDs he kept in the glove box. When arrested the night of his going-away party, he had two confiscated from his wallet but wasn't charged for either. His father had convinced the DA's office to drop all charges except reckless endangerment, the most serious offense. The police also found a trace of marijuana in his pants pocket—a roach clip with residue on spent paper—but they eventually dropped that, too.

With Greg's direction, Julie drove north then west along the canal toward Otto, past corn and sugar beet and alfalfa fields until she again turned north onto a maze of dirt roads that wound and dipped and climbed into the barren clay hills below the higher pink shelf of the Bookcliffs. Beer in one hand, schnapps in the other, Greg prodded and cajoled her into going faster—at least fast for Julie—over a series of roller coasters across which Greg kept shouting "Catch air, man! Come on, Jules! Faster!" We hooted and hollered and spilled beer while Julie, who despite herself was becoming progressively exhilarated and daring, drove on and on until finally she careened down an arroyo and skidded laughing to a stop in a bowl encircled by clay hills. I wondered if the hills in Hemingway's Spain were as gray and elephant-like as these, their cracked and furrowed surface in shadowy relief from a low slanting light.

While Greg and Julie hiked with Louie to the highest hilltop to watch the sun go down, Lenny built a fire. He formed a miniature pyramid of twigs, lit it with a single match, then blew it from smoke to flame. It struck me that this was standard procedure for him, that cooking out had become as ordinary as my going to the fridge for a baloney sandwich. He was in his element—the desert—while Julie, Greg, and I were mere guests, passing through with no plans to stay but a single night. We, after all, had beds and bedrooms to go home to.

From the trunk we unloaded the cooler and skillet, sleeping bags and inflatable mattresses. I set the cooler lid across my lap and pressed hamburger into patties, sliced onion and tomato and pickle spears, and uncapped the mustard and ketchup bottles. Lenny jiggled the skillet level into the coals and after dragging a piñon log over from a nearby gully, tossed a glob of burger hissing and sputtering across the cast-iron to test its temperature.

By the time Julie and Greg returned—Louie had already caught the scent of food and plodded back down the hillside—the hamburgers were done and we began doctoring our buns.

"Should have seen the sunset from up there, man. Unbelievable." Greg stretched back on his bag and took a huge bite. "Forgot my camera again."

Julie popped a beer, sat down next to him. "It reminded me of that sunset you took for the annual."

I nodded, holding out my bun for Lenny to slide on a burger. "Yeah, the one of Magic Club."

Julie harrumphed. "It would've been better had someone actually been in the picture. Like me, for example."

Greg smiled. "You were, Jules. We all were."

"Well, if I was—" She took a bite of hamburger. "—I certainly was thinner."

"Thin as air." He looked up at the night sky then over at Lenny, who was scraping grease from the skillet using the spatula.

He set the skillet on a flat rock and looked up. "What?"

"Nothin', Lenny." Greg smiled. "Come eat with us, man. We can do that later."

Leaving his bag rolled, Lenny sat down on it and began eating, tossing every third bite or so to his dog. It was dark by the time we finished and cleaned up. Then Lenny took Louie for a walk while Greg, Julie, and I spread our mattresses and bags around the fire and lay gazing into the flames, sipping Coors. Since getting sick on a quart of beer at Stankey's New Year's Eve party, I couldn't so much as sniff the stuff. But I knew that it might be a while before we were all four together again, so I gave it my best shot, holding my breath and forcing it down.

The desert was as quiet as it was barren, an occasional breeze stirring the flames and the only sounds the fire popping, an occasional plane droning overhead, a bullfrog croaking from a distant bog. Greg got up and brought something wrapped in aluminum foil from the cooler.

"Time for dessert." Julie and I groaned as he unwrapped it and bent down. "Come on, have one. My mother made them. You'll hurt her feelings if you don't."

"I'm stuffed." Julie folded an edge of the aluminum down and peered over it. "What are they?"

"Cookies. 'Specially made just for tonight."

"I thought your mom was mad at you." She chose one and studied it. "Looks like a brownie to me."

"Cookies, brownies—what's the dif'? Come on, Bartelli, have one or I'll tell her you didn't like them."

Lenny had returned with Louie, unrolling his bag and stretching out on it. He took one and I followed.

"Why are you and your mom always fighting, Greg?"

He shrugged, staring at the fire and munching on the cookie. "I don't know, Hank. Ask Julie. She's the psychiatrist."

"People who love each other always fight, Hank."

Greg burst out laughing.

Julie stared at him. "What?"

"You believe that crap?"

"It's not a question of believing. It's true."

"See, Lenny—there's hope."

"What?"

"Next time your old lady tries to bop you one, just remember it's all in the name of love. It'll keep your nose from bleeding."

"That's not what I meant, Greg." Julie glanced across the fire at Lenny.

Greg shook his head. "In families like ours, it's not because of love. Is it, Lenny?"

He gazed into the fire, chewing his brownie. "I don't know."

Julie waved her hands. "Of course it is."

Greg looked around as though the puzzle of his parents lay scattered across the vast desert that surrounded us. He grabbed a handful of brownies, stood up, and walked away from the fire.

Julie looked at Lenny and me, raised her eyebrows and shrugged. "Wrong topic, I guess."

"Hey, Sonny." Greg reappeared from the darkness, looming over Lenny, both cheeks bulging with brownies. "Hey, Sonny—" He kicked Lenny's leg. "—I'm gonna make-a you an offer you can't refuse."

No one laughed.

"Our families—we gotta this thing, Sonny, that . . . that bonds us like grapes to the twisted familial vine. You know whatta I mean?"

Lenny looked up at him.

"Yous, Michael, Fredo, and, of course, Vinnie—right?"

Lenny nodded then grinned.

"And when you give it to Vinnie's girl—that whack-a job—up against the bathroom door like in the movie . . ."

Lenny laughed, covered his ears and shook his head.

". . . you be sure you do it with *amore*. *Capiche*?" Greg grabbed Lenny by the wrists, prying his hands from his ears. "*Capiche*, Sonny?" He let him go and, stomach pooched, tottered around the fire to me, the Godfather kibitzing in the garden. "And yous, Michael."

I nodded, trying to raise my head.

"Michael, when you father talks to you, have a decency to look up. Hear what I say?" He kicked my side.

"Yes, yes—"

"You a good boy, Michael, but don't messa round with you father."

My head felt leaden as I tried to look up.

"Next time, Michael, we put the whole horse in a Redd Morgan's bed. And we do it with—" He raised his hands.

"*Amore!*"

"Ah, very good, my little meatballs."

Julie raised herself up giggling from the sleeping bag, but Greg gently tapped her on the forehead, sending her rolling onto her back.

"We gotta somethin' special here, my little bambinos." He grabbed her ankles. "And you, Jules—" He elevated her feet above her head. "—you make me want to sinka my teeth into that, that cactus over there, you make-a me so crazy."

Julie tried to rise up again but seeing his jaw-jutting face swollen up as though he'd just had wisdom teeth extracted, rolled laughing back to her bag.

"But I love you, Jules, I love a you so much it makes me wanna poop."

"Ohhh!"

"Not a necessarily on you, my little a-turtle, but poop nonetheless. And this we call—"

"*Amore!*"

He stood over her, grandly swept his hand out. "We poop, we fight, we drink, we eat, we fight, we poop, and then a-finally we die. And on and on and on and on, all in the name of a familial love." Greg turned away, bent down, and using his index and middle fingers scraped globs of brownie from inside both cheeks. "Remember—*familia amore*. Let us go in peace." Chewing the remaining brownie, he receded back into the darkness. "And let us a poop in peace, too. *Salud*, my little bambinos. *Ciao*."

The three of us lay exhausted, listening to the car door open and then the Doors—rain and thunder from *Riders on the Storm*—crackle from the eight-track. I tried to get up but my head was leaden, so I lay there with Lenny and Julie and gazed into the fire. It flickered and wavered then leapt with the breeze only to recede to a tiny fist of light before waving to life again, fingers of fire stretching skyward. Nothing else mattered, all I wanted was to lie there and watch the flame suck oxygen, enveloping and eating and consuming. I stared into the fire, aware Julie was dancing around it, around its brilliant, gnashing consumption. Lenny lay back against Louie, pointing at the sky and laughing at the spray of stars shooting up from the blaze. I listened to the thunder, couldn't understand how it was raining without clouds overhead, without our skin getting wet. The fire illuminated Julie swaying in the rain. Greg reappeared from the darkness and joined her, shirt off and his tan skin glowing orange in the heat. Head thrown back, Julie floated around him, smiling, her hair wild and unruly like Medusa's. Lenny was up now, too, arms stretched wide, gliding around the flames. I reached my hand out but couldn't feel the fire's warmth, its piercing heat. Pulling back, I stared at my palm, traced thumb and fingers, uncertain whom they belonged to if anyone.

The rain washed over us, the musical rain tinkling its song across the desert and then I was up dancing, too, tap dancing in the rain like Mrs. Woods pirouetting over the breathing hills on arthritic toes with those perfectly formed breasts, those Mary Poppins, and like Miss Darling scuttling across sand, chanting into the fire before beseeching the sky and heavens to relieve her of her pain, to cleanse her of its curse, and off to the side Mr. Shimizu digging a hole with his shovel, then stopping to lean against it, wiping his brow and waving at me as Dana sat in a lotus position nearby, holding a sweating glass of lemonade as though it were a prayer candle, and Mom and Dad dancing, too, not crazily like Greg and Julie and Lenny, but slow and fluid and elegantly, smiling at one another as if no one else existed, and Cisco Salazar, his neck healed, half dancing and half wrestling, moving and jumping and squatting and thrusting and going through all the gyrations of wrestling, with Mr. V and Coach Hicks off to the side watching, nodding and chatting amiably while Molly squatted behind with a litter of Louie's puppies spilling from underneath her skirt and Jim Morrison singing again in the background. Holding a cedar branch as a microphone, he hopped onto the car hood. Julie, Greg, Lenny, and Miss Darling were holding hands, dancing, hopping, kicking in a circle. Colonel Sanders joined in, the five of them giggling, kicking around the fire like kindergartners at recess, black puppies tumbling and somersaulting at their feet. They laughed harder and harder until they couldn't laugh anymore, until all fell away except Miss Darling, cackling like a chicken with her head . . . then the Colonel exploded. The Colonel exploded. Colonel Sanders exploded.

The rain was plastic now, coming down in sheets of white. Covering my head, I curled up on the sleeping bag, and when I thought the plastic musical rain had subsided, looked up to see Greg holding the cedar branch on the car hood, his hair engulfed in feathers of fire like an Indian headdress, dancing,

dancing, dancing and Miss Darling standing naked, erectly above him on top the car, holding a torch like the purveyor of fate and mortality, like the Statue of Fuckin' Liberty posed against a dwindling sun, against a dying echo of rain and thunder and chaos and the light brightening and then blinking, blinking, blinking, blinking until finally, thankfully blinking completely, irrevocably out, leaving us to be three out of what once had always been four.

And then it thundered and there was nothing more, nothing more remained.

◇◇◇

Ashes lay black and smoldering. I rolled to my back, shielded my eyes; the sun was high enough that it must have been eleven o'clock. Across the fire pit, Julie sat on her sleeping bag, hugging one knee, resting her chin.

"Jules." I sat up, the back of my skull exploding. "Ohhh—" I grabbed my head, rubbed my neck. "Julie. What happened?"

She turned toward me, cheek now resting on her knee. "'Morning, Hank." She tried to smile then rotated back to her chin and resumed gazing at the distant hilltops.

I looked around. "Where's Lenny and Greg?"

She shrugged.

"Where's the car?" I staggered up, circled around like a punch-drunk boxer. Lenny's sleeping bag remained unrolled and Greg's stretched empty across the sand. "And Louie." I squatted, head down, clamping my throbbing skull between my forearms. "What happened? Where is everybody?"

She shook her head. "I don't know, Hank. I don't know anything anymore."

"What do you mean?" Shading my eyes, I looked around at the barren hills. "Where'd they go?"

"Hank, I don't know where they are. They're just gone, that's all. Gone—" Her voice trailed off and her back started quaking. Slowly at first, just the fabric of her tank top moving and then faster until her whole body was shaking and a deep wrenching sob plunged from her.

"Jules—" I knelt down and put my arm across her heaving shoulders and the sob subsided, swallowed up as quickly as it had emerged before degrading out of exhaustion into a double-hitch of breathing followed by the hiccups. I brushed matted hair from her face and kissed the top of her head.

She looked up at me, eyes red and swollen. "He did it again, didn't he?" She took a breath. "I thought somehow, this time, you know, it would be different. That he'd, he'd learned something from all the crap he's been through—his uncle, losing his appointment to the academy, being arrested . . ." She shook her head, her voice trailing off. "But he'll never learn, will he, Hank? It'll just go on and on and on until he's finally—" She bit her lip. "It's coming true, isn't it?"

"What?"

"What Miss Darling said. It's finally happening—"

I looked down at my hands, smudged with soot, fingernails rimmed with black. "I don't know."

"I do." She forced a smile. "I do, Hank. And then it'll finally be over and we can go on and do whatever it is we're supposed to do in this screwed up life. It's probably already happened and here we sit. In the dirt." She reached over and handed me a milk jug of water. "Here—at least they left us some water. Unintentionally, I'm sure."

I uncapped the jug and pressed it to my lips. "Whew—thanks." I wiped my mouth and gave it back. "My head feels like a cracked melon. What happened last night? Did I just dream all that?"

"Last night?" Julie shook her head. "Last night, Hank, the Magic Club was subjected to one last little prank to send us on our way. Thanks to Greg Woods and his trusty boy-servant Warren Dillard."

"Dill was here?"

Julie shook her head. "No, Hank—" She smiled, reached out and caressed my cheek with the back of her hand. "Dill wasn't here, but his brownies were." She stretched and yawned. "I don't know how you could've slept so long. I think I got maybe an hour, two at the most. Of course, you threw everything up. Maybe that was the difference."

"I did? You mean those brownies were—"

"Hank?" Julie straightened, pointing across the arroyo at the northern ridge line. "Look. I think it's—" She stood, stepped forward, began walking then jogging, then full out running across the desert.

I trained my eyes on a figure winding its way up and down a gully before emerging from behind a slight swell on the horizon. Heat waves separated the head from its body, mantling magnetically like gravity, like drawn barbwire quivering between fence posts. Julie rushed to him, grabbed him by the shoulders, and held him at arms' length, grilling him. I grabbed the water and headed toward them as Lenny, turning, pointed into the distance at a speck appearing from behind the barren ridge. Shielding her eyes, Julie spotted him, too, then dropped to her knees at Lenny's feet.

By the time I reached them with the jug, Greg was across the arroyo with his golf bag slung over one shoulder, waving his tennis racket overhead; Julie was half crying and half laughing into her hands; and Lenny and Louie were just standing there, waiting for a drink of water.

It would be a full two hours later that a fifteen-year-old kid with his fourteen-year-old cousin seated next to him in a faded-green '51 Ford farm truck happened along and picked us up as we walked across the desert toward the canal. With Greg's direction, the kid turned the truck around and took us by a twenty-foot-high drop-off at the bottom of which sat the Dodge Swinger. As we sat dusty and parched in the back of that flatbed truck and watched Greg half-slide and half-run down the loose hillside then trudge slowly back up with an armful of eight-tracks, his golf shoes tied together around his neck, and a baggie of marijuana stuffed in his shirt pocket, no one so much as said a word. No one needed to—not at the sight of the car listing, three of its tires flat and its front axle broken. Along with Lenny and Louie, Greg had somehow escaped flying off that chopped-off hillside unscathed. The graduation present his parents had given him wasn't so lucky.

23

With September came rain. Real rain. The kind that darkens the western horizon maybe once or twice a summer, that rolls in from the Utah desert in great black loaves, pushing hot air out of the Grand Valley and streaking the sandstone ledges of Rimrock National Park. Rain that makes redolent the dusty roads and sandy clay soil, drums the metal roofs of fruit sheds and packing houses and boxcars, and floods the neighborhood gutters in town, beckoning children outside to ride bicycles in celebration of cooler days.

In those first wet days of September, the *Grand River Sentinel* trumpeted American victories both at home and abroad. Bobby Fischer defeated Boris Spassky for the world chess championship, wresting the title from the Soviet Union for the first time since 1946. The Selective Service announced that the military draft would be terminated at the end of 1972, a year too late for Lenny and Greg. Mark Spitz won his sixth gold medal and set his sixth world record, leaving Greg's dad the happiest man in the valley, while the U.S. wrestling team, led by Dan Gable, made its best showing ever with three golds, two silvers, and one bronze, making Mr. V at least second happiest. And Grand River residents successfully circulated two petitions: the first, for a ten o'clock curfew at Sherwood Park to stem drug use, underage drinking, and unwanted pregnancies, and the second, for tightening dog-leash laws, both of which were unanimously passed by City Council (before being uniformly ignored by everyone else).

But the paper reported losses, too. Russian Valery Borzov won the one-hundred-meter dash, only the second time in the last nine Olympics that an American didn't win that event. Senator George McGovern, having had Thomas Eagleton resign as his running mate a month earlier because of electric shock therapy for depression, lost his Tennessee campaign manager and then failed to gain any endorsements at the Southern Governors Conference (making Julie, in turn, contemplate electric shock therapy for herself and maybe murder for Cameron Pippin III since he was spending all his time either traveling, she said, or working at the McGovern headquarters in Denver, leaving her to man the Grand River office —not what she had in mind when passing up Notre Dame). The Grand Valley Peach Administrative Committee announced that, because of severe spring freezing, only one-hundred-twenty-one thousand bushels of peaches were shipped to market at an estimated value of one-million dollars, about a third of what was shipped the year before (but what was for Mr. V a bumper crop, it being his first). And at the bottom of page five, next to local bridge club news, it was reported that Jose Angel Gutierrez defeated Denver's Corky Gonzales for the chairmanship of the Mexican-American *Raza Unida* at the party's national convention in El Paso, Texas. This despite a local rally for Gonzales at Riverside Park complete with banners, homemade tamales, speeches peppered with quotes from *I am Joaquín*, shouts of *viva la Raza*, and the unveiling of a mural of itinerant fruit pickers painted by Jimmy Gonzales in the tradition of Diego Rivera on the outer east wall of Riverside School. Cisco, Peefee and the boys were there for the ribbon cutting, hoisting Jimmy on their shoulders afterward and parading him around Riverside Park as though he himself were the winning candidate and his artistic talent an extension of themselves, which of course it was.

It was relayed to us by Julie from "Peepee," as she continued to call him, that Cisco no longer wore a halo, that his doctors replaced it with a simple styrofoam brace. And we believed this for a while until she said Peefee began spinning another one about how Cisco had begun wrestling again, pinning his own father in a living-room brawl then taking on Kenny Madrid and Silver Renteria at the same time and pinning them also.

But early that Tuesday morning we saw for ourselves the state of Cisco's health. There had been a break in the weather and we were sitting in Sage Diner at the counter after bringing Mom to work. I was drinking Punk's iced coffee and Lenny *Earl Gray* because he had caught a bad cold from our night in the desert, when Peefee and the boys appeared bobbing down the sidewalk along Gateway Avenue. They were walking in a knot, hunched over with collars turned against the unseasonal cool left over from the storm. As they passed, one of them, Carl Lujan, noticed Louie lying at the diner entrance waiting for us to come out. He walked over with his hand extended before bending down and petting the dog's head. A few more peeled back and were quickly joined by the rest. Peefee, Frank Serrano, and a couple of others recognized Louie, so they went right to the front window instead and, cupping their hands, peered inside, their hot breath fogging the glass.

"Guess who's here." I tipped my head without looking.

Some of them were blowing into their hands, but most lined up shoulder to shoulder with Peefee, staring inside.

"They're headed to the packing sheds to work. I wonder where Peefee's truck is."

I grabbed Lenny's arm. "Come on, let's get out of here."

"No, wait." He held fast, returning their gaze. He nodded. "Look."

I glanced over without turning my head: only Peefee remained stuck to the window, the rest turned away, now huddled behind him talking. And then I looked, again. There, in the middle of the huddle, wearing the styrofoam brace, stood Cisco Salazar. Stepping through his friends, he grabbed his cousin's arm and pulled him back from the window into the circle. Then, looking straight at us, he did something I'll never forget—neck brace and all—he lifted his chin. Dumbfounded, we found ourselves lifting ours and then Cisco, Peefee and the boys were gone, disappearing down Gateway Avenue.

I looked at Lenny.

"Julie was right, Hank." He nodded into his tea and then smiled. "Cisco got his halo off."

"Yeah, and he even kind of waved at us." I shook my head. "Maybe your mom scared them."

He coughed into a napkin. "I kinda doubt that, Hank."

Maybe his mom scared me. Maybe his mom had been scaring me ever since I met Lenny in third grade when I first started going over there to play. But scare Cisco, Peefee and the gang? Cisco had to deal with a tattooed father with a penchant for tequila and backhanded how-do-you-dos. Gabe Fuentas was, at age seventeen, foreman on a cement crew with biceps the size of cantaloupes, and Kenny Madrid was afraid of nobody except maybe his overgrown sister Geraldine, who not even Cisco liked the idea of tangling with. And then there was Dan Abeyta. Dan had already been in and out of reform school twice, where he carved and crossed-out the names of three girls on the inside of his left forearm using the honed shard from a broken bedspring and then on his second visit spent the first four days in lockdown for asking the superintendent why his wife looked like Ernest Borgnine. No, Lenny was right. More than likely—and this I would ponder for many days afterward—Mrs. Bartelli had merely surprised them. At least surprised them initially with her railing, rake-swinging hysteria, then perhaps amused them when she'd found Lenny with the end of those metal tines, and finally subdued them when they realized this *muy loco* woman was, in fact, Lenny's mother. Maybe at that point an unspoken bond formed between Lenny and the gang, a shared understanding stronger than race or injury. They understood something about Lenny's life in that split-second realization that Julie, Greg, and I never could. And that's why they never chased Lenny again. Or me.

"How's the tea?" Mom walked from the kitchen with Arlene, carrying washed coffeepots in both hands. She set them behind the counter. "Feeling any better, hon?"

Lenny had spent the last two nights sleeping on our living-room couch. As his cough worsened, so too did his guilt, worrying that he was keeping everyone awake. "Maybe a little."

"Don't sound like you do." Arlene put her palm to his forehead. "This boy's got a fever."

"He does?" Mom pressed a hand to his cheek. "We better get you in to see somebody."

"I'll be all right."

"Mmm-hmm—" Arlene reached over and picked up the telephone. "I'll call ol' Doc Simpson. He'll see you."

"No, really. I'm fine." Lenny coughed. "I just sound bad."

"Feeling good, sounding bad, huh?" Punk came out from the back, tossed a packet of coffee filters on the counter. "Reminds me of a joke I heard in the Navy." He plucked off his paper hat and sat down next to Lenny, rubbing his scalp. "This guy goes into the doctor's office, see. Doctor says—"

"Punk, honey, what's ol' Doc Simpson's number?"

"How would I know? Doctor says, 'You ain't looking too good.'"

"You'd know 'cause you were just in there for that prostate trouble." Arlene reached across and grabbed the phone directory. "And doctors don't say 'ain't.'"

Punk glared. "So the doctor says, *ain't* looking too good.' Guy says, 'Well, I feel okay.'"

"I think he's feeling puny, if you ask me." Arlene licked her middle finger, flipped a few pages. "Let's see—doctor, doctor, doctor—"

"In the joke, Arlene—he says it in the joke, fer chrissakes."

"I don't care where he says it. I'm telling you, doctors don't talk that way." Her finger stopped. "Here it is." She bent forward, squinting. "'See physicians.' Oh, for crying out—"

"So's the doctor gets his big, you know, medical book out. Opens it up and says 'feeling bad, looking good—naw, that's not it.'"

"Physicians—here they are." Her finger scanned the page.

"'Feeling bad, looking bad'—naw, that ain't it either."

"Allergists, Anesthesiologist, Cardiologists . . ."

"'Feeling good, looking good'—no, no."

". . . Dermatologists—how many names do they got for themselves, anyways?"

"'Feeling good, looking bad.'"

"Simpson, Arthur." She held out a pen. "Write this number down, Punk." Her nose disappeared into the directory as though sniffing might help decipher it.

"'Yes,' he says, 'here it is.'" Punk grinned. "'Feeling good, looking bad—you're a vaginer.'"

"That's two, four, two—" She looked up. "What'd you say?"

Punk was still grinning. "You're a vaginer."

"A what?"

"Vaginer. Get it?"

"No, I don't get it, but you're going to if you don't write this number down." She pointed the pen at him.

"Here, I will." Mom took the phone book from Arlene, jotted on her order pad then ripped the number off and stuck it in her apron. "I'll call as soon as they open, which won't be for a couple hours yet. You two going to be home?"

I shrugged. "I don't know."

"Well, come by or call if you're not and I'll tell you when the appointment is."

The door dinged and the first two customers of the day strolled in. Punk picked up his hat and pulled it low over his small head. "You ruin just about everything you touch, don't you?"

Arlene gawked at him, mouth wide. "Me?" She slid off the stool, shadowed him toward the kitchen. "You're the one that can't tell a joke."

"How would you know? You didn't even get it."

"What's to get? It was stupid."

"No matter what it is, you have to go an' throw flies in the soup."

"Ha! Couldn't hurt your soup any, that's for sure."

"Keep it up, Arlene—just keep it up."

"Well somebody's got to."

"What do you mean by that?"

The customers sat in the booth, listening to Punk and Arlene argue their way into the kitchen and then clang skillets and pots around as Mom filled the coffee cups.

"See ya, Mom."

"Okay, honey. Milton's taking me to play miniature golf after work so you don't have to pick me up."

"Miniature golf?"

She smiled. "I'll talk to you two later."

"Okay, Mom."

"Go get some rest, Lenny."

"Thanks, Mrs. Kessler. I will."

◇◇◇

I awoke to a mower. Lenny and I had taken Mom's advice, returning home and going back to bed. I was sound asleep when the roar cut through my dreams, somehow fitting in for a while with the pictures in my head until it abruptly stopped, jolting me upright. I sat for a moment, reconciling the inside of my skull with the inside of my bedroom before bolting upstairs and out the back door. Reaching the end of the driveway, I just caught a glimpse of the truck disappearing around the corner.

I trudged back inside through the front door to find Dana sitting cross-legged in Dad's chair with her eyes closed. "I can't believe it, Dana. After what he did, he still comes back to mow."

She sat motionless.

I glanced around the living room. "Hey, where's Lenny?"

The couch was empty and the blanket he used was folded neatly on the armrest with the pillow on top.

"Dana, where'd Lenny go?"

She opened one eye, shrugged, then closed it again.

"Well, did you see him? Did you see Redd Morgan?" I kicked the chair. "What's wrong with you, anyway?"

Taking a deep breath, eyelashes fluttering, she opened both eyes then blinked a few times. "Hi, Hank."

"'Hi, Hank?' 'Hi, Hank?' Redd Morgan's out there mowing our lawn at—what time is it?—seven-thirty, and all you can say is 'Hi, Hank'?"

"TM." She yawned and stretched, rolling her head. "I met this guy outside the Cotton Bowl in the parking lot and he had his camper opened up with this canopy and a mat underneath. He was selling pukka shells and beaded headbands and things. Anyway, he taught me. It's easy. All you need is, like, a mantra."

"A mantra." I studied her, wondering how long this one would last. "At a Christian revival?"

"It's Buddhist, Hank." She stood and stretched again, palms to the ceiling.

"You mean now you're a—"

"Yeah. Remember you asked me if I got saved?" She smiled. "Well, I guess I kinda did."

"Great." I shook my head. My sister was clearly whacked. "So did you even hear him? Redd Morgan was out there with his mower, again."

"Not for very long."

"What?"

"Well, I think I heard him drive up a few minutes after Lenny left."

"Where'd Lenny go?"

"Said he was going over to Greg's, that there's more room over there and he wouldn't bother anybody with his coughing. He said Greg told him he could stay as long as he wants."

"So as soon as Lenny left, Redd drove up?"

"Yeah, pretty much. But I just heard him mowing for a while. I don't think he even got to the back."

I stepped outside onto the porch wondering why Redd Morgan would come back to the scene of his crime just to mow our lawn. Just part of my increasingly crazy world.

The night I found Stella and Frank belly-up in their bowl, Dana and I had gone to the grocery store, bought two dozen eggs and drove them over to Redd Morgan's. We sat in Mom's car across the street, a carton open on each of our laps, talking about Mom and Dad and trying to marshal enough courage to actually throw the things at his clapboard house. The big lava rock was still in Redd's front yard—Mom said he had actually grown proud of it—but his welding truck was gone and there were no lights on anywhere. We convinced ourselves that egging his house without his being there wasn't good enough, something about broken yolk not a fitting punishment for murdering goldfish, so we went home not sure what to do. That's when I went to Dad's with Julie to tell him about the fish and instead found some more of Redd's empty welding tanks. Somehow, Dad must have already known about our fish although I still didn't know how. All this I was mulling over, staring at the lawn, when suddenly it dawned on me: the grass wasn't cut—or rather, only some of it was.

"Dana! Come here!"

We stood at the curb in front of our house, trying to figure out what it was we were looking at mowed into the long summer grass. We gawked as children might at the sight of some circus wonder, some sleight-of-hand magic trick, then as we stepped slowly backward across the street, turning our heads this way and that, the wide swaths gradually transformed into meaning. There, cut so closely as to scorch the very ground the grass grew from, were four letters branded into our front lawn, letters Dana haltingly spelled out and I repeated then unthinkingly spouted out, stringing them together as though the word they formed was the winning answer to some TV quiz show instead of what it really was—a loser's answer meant for our mom:

S-L-U-T

◇◇◇

The rest of that Tuesday unfolded in a haze. After Dana borrowed Mr. Shimizu's mower—ours was rusted and broken down—and had him adjust the blade as low as it would go, I mowed our front lawn over and over until the word became indecipherable to anyone but us. Then, with my sister sitting silently next to me, I drove west out of town to Rabbit Valley. We parked at our usual spot on the ridge above the *Airstream* and sat on the hood, wondering whether we should go down there to tell Dad what Redd Morgan had done since he certainly wouldn't discover it on his own. After turning the problem over in our minds, examining it at different angles under the shifting slant of morning light, we decided not to tell anyone, to keep it a secret until we could decide what best to do ourselves. Dana thought that if Dad found out he might kill Redd Morgan. And though I didn't say it, I couldn't disagree, so I turned the car around and drove back to town.

We dropped by Sage Diner for a minute to make sure Mom was okay. It was almost noon by then and the place was filling up. Mom's hair was pinned back, but strands were falling around her face and she kept pushing at it with the back of her hand between taking orders, serving food, filling coffee cups and water glasses, and bussing tables. Watching her, I felt pangs of guilt for not being in there to help. I'd told Punk a few weeks earlier that I was cutting back my hours so I could look for something else to do. What that something was I didn't know, so I promised myself two things: to return full-time to work the very next day and to buy Mom a barrette or comb for her hair.

After dropping Dana off at home, I went to Greg's to find Lenny. Although

I had promised Dana not to say anything, I was certain she would understand if I told my best friend what had happened since Lenny didn't repeat anything to anybody, secret or not. When I got there it was Greg's mother who answered the door, a Bloody Mary in hand.

"Henry—what a pleasant surprise."

"Hi, Mrs. Woods. Is Greg—" I stepped inside and followed her graceful strides down the hallway into the kitchen. "Is Greg around?"

"You mean you didn't come over to see me?" She rummaged in the refrigerator. "Sit down, Henry."

"Thanks, Mrs. Woods, but I need to find—"

"Sit." Without turning she pointed at the barstool then took a bottle of mix from the fridge door and a glass from the cupboard. "I hate drinking alone, Henry. Virgin Mary, right?" She smiled, mouth closed and lips pursed.

"Uh, yeah, I guess." I sat on the stool.

She clinked ice-cubes into the glass and cut a slice of lime. "So how was your summer, Henry? Meet a lot of interesting people?"

"Oh, no, not really."

"Not really? I thought you must have, going out with Gregory at all hours." She laughed, lifting her arms. "Partying your brains out and all, right?" Taking a drink, she turned on the faucet and began washing a stick of celery.

"Sometimes I guess."

"Sometimes—" She turned off the water, toweled the celery and stuck it in my drink. "But not the night he lost track of his car?"

"Well, yeah—I mean I wasn't—"

"Save it, Henry." She raised a hand. "It doesn't matter at this point." She held out the glass. "So does Gregory still talk to you? In English, I mean?"

I reached out to take it but she kept hold. "Well, yeah."

She let go and turned with her back to me and took a long drink. "Not to me."

I waited, not knowing what to say.

She shook her head. "He speaks nothing but that deplorable Chinese." She studied her drink. "His father's always thought it was funny, even when he was little. But now he won't speak anything else." She jiggled the glass, twirling ice cubes. "Henry, can I trust you to keep a secret?"

"Yeah, I guess—I mean, sure."

"Two days after Gregory was arrested, you know, after his party and he was released and everything, I came home from the parade downtown. His father was playing cards or golf or whatever it is he does." She turned facing me, coiling a strand of long black hair around her painted index finger. "Anyway, I came home and Gregory had all his stereo equipment spread out on the lawn at the side of the house. You know, with an extension cord out his bedroom window and everything, and he had his albums there and he was playing one of them full-blast so that the neighbors were coming outside to see what all the ruckus was, all the noise. And to top it off, Henry, to top it off he, uh—" She took a drink. "—he had the sprinklers on."

"What?"

"Yes, the sprinklers—full-blast too. He was sitting there very intently, you see, not laughing or anything like he does when it's a big joke or something, just sitting, staring into space. I said, 'Gregory, what on earth are you doing?' You know, a few of the neighbors—the Bowerly's, in fact—had come over and were standing right out there in the street watching, and there was Gregory just soaking the new stereo that we had given him just last Christmas—the speaker, the turntable, the what do you call it, receiver—just soaking them and staring at who knows what. So I asked him again, screamed at him in fact, what are you doing? Finally, I ran inside and into his room and unplugged it. I didn't know what else to do. He could have electrocuted himself. And, and you know the saddest part, Henry, the absolutely saddest part was that I was afraid to go back outside. I was afraid of him. My own son." She drained her glass and set it on the counter. "So I called Dr. McClellan, Julie's father, and they came and got him and he spent his Fourth of July up there in the hospital for evaluation or observation or whatever they do. They brought him home the next day. And do you know what Dr. McClellan said Gregory had told him?"

I shook my head.

"That he was watering his music, Henry, so he could watch it grow. Can you imagine? And that—and here's the kicker—that he was watering the music and that I had come home and killed it, Henry, that I had killed his music." Mrs. Woods' finger was almost to her face, her hair twined around it. She was gazing out the kitchen window across the golf course at the Bookcliffs. Slowly, she lowered her hand, the hair unwinding and falling away. "How do you like that?"

"I don't know—I mean, I can't believe it."

"No, Henry. I mean the drink, how do you like the drink?"

"Oh, fine. It's good—thanks." I took a sip then immediately coughed, eyes watering.

She smiled. "Here, Henry, perhaps you need a bit more of the virgin." She poured more tomato juice and stirred it with the celery stick. "I'm sorry, Henry. I thought maybe just a touch of Vodka was in order. You know, give it some character. And we never did properly celebrate your graduation, did we?"

"No, it's okay."

"Your mother would probably kill me, wouldn't she?" She studied me. "You don't really look much like her, do you?"

"Everybody says I look like my dad."

"I see. Well, your mother's very pretty." She turned again to mix herself another drink. "It'd been years since I've seen her but she's still quite stunning, isn't she?"

"Yeah, I guess."

She laughed. "Don't guess, Henry. Tell me what you think. Say 'Yes, Valerie, she's quite stunning.'"

"Yes, she's quite stunning."

"Valerie."

"Valerie."

She laughed again, pirouetting with her drink. "Come. Let's go outside and enjoy the sunshine. All this rain's made me depressed." She held out her hand then led me through the sliding-glass doors. "I can't believe how much cooler it's gotten."

"Mrs. Woods, is Greg still in bed?"

"No, I don't know where he is." Kicking off clogs, she unsnapped her jean shorts and slid the zipper down. "Since his father and I split up, I can't seem to keep track." Bending over, she worked them over her hips and slid them down her legs. She stepped out, revealing black bikini bottoms. "Have a seat, Henry. I'll go fetch you a pair of Gregory's trunks."

"Oh, that's okay, Mrs. Woods. I can't really—"

She disappeared into the house.

I sat in the lawn chair. Out on the golf course, people were hitting. I remembered the opening sentence of *The Sound and the Fury*—"Through the fence, between the curling flower spaces, I could see them hitting."—and the unfettered sense of that; I *knew* that Benjy character.

A foursome piled into a cart and motored after their little white balls. Across the long fairway in the distance four others were putting on the tenth green where Greg had blown up the Colonel. It seemed so long ago; so much had changed.

Mrs. Woods walked out. "Here, Henry." She held up a pair of bright orange trunks as though in a store and she was sizing them to me. "Try these." She tossed them on my lap then peeled off her *I Love New York* T-shirt with the glittery red apple in the middle of it.

I glanced around, uncertain what to do, where to go.

"Here, put some baby oil on me, would you dear?" She turned and sat on the edge of the chair between my legs, holding hair atop her head.

I squeezed oil onto my palm, rubbed my hands together and ran them from her neck over shoulder blades, then down her spine to her lower back.

"Mmm, that feels good, Henry. How 'bout a little more down by the elastic. I get sunburned down there." She scooted forward so she was barely on the chair, the cleavage of her bottom peaking out from her suit.

I squeezed out more oil and, taking a deep breath, rubbed her lower back.

"Little lower, please."

Closing my eyes, I felt the twin dimples where spine meets hips, the rise and fall where two halves cleave.

She abruptly stood so that my palms grazed her bottom. She turned around, hands still holding her hair in place. "Now my legs, Henry." She lifted a foot and rested it on the edge of the chair between my legs.

The sun burned behind her head, her face appearing and disappearing from shadow as she shifted from one leg to the other, the sun's rays alternately stabbing at me over either shoulder as I applied oil to her calves, to those long firm thighs. She pushed her hips forward. "Can't forget my belly."

My heart throbbed, breathing ragged as I worked oil across her rib cage, around her naval. The skin here wasn't quite as tight but still warm and tan and smooth. She brought a finger up and absently twirled my bangs. "Henry—" She said my name softly, tenderly, and when I looked up, my hand froze at what I saw: her chin trembled and tears welled in her eyes. Placing her fingertips under my chin, she tried to smile. "Henry, please don't tell Gregory what I—"

"Valerie!"

She turned and looked up, wiping an eye, then waved. "Hi, Clance!"

The fat guy from the party, the guy with the green pants, raised an iron overhead out on the tenth fairway. "They're killing me today, babe! How 'bout a drink!?!"

"Come on over!" She waved then turned, picking the trunks up from my lap. She stroked my head. "Henry, why don't you go into Gregory's room and change. Clancy won't stay long, then we can go for a swim or something. Actually, why don't you just relax and I'll come get you, okay?"

Covering my lap with the trunks, I hurried into the house. Through the kitchen window I could see the guy making his way across the ditch, pulling at a white glove and yelling something over his shoulder at his playing partners. His golf bag he left lying in the rough on the edge of the fairway, and he was chomping a cigar, wearing those same ridiculous green pants.

I continued down the hallway into Greg's room and caught a glimpse of my profile in the closet-door mirror; Mrs. Woods still had my full attention. Sitting on the edge of the waterbed frame, I buried my face in my hands. I could smell the baby oil mixed with the scent of her, of that exotic aroma she always had on. I took off my shirt and rubbed my own shoulders, my own chest. My God!—if that Clancy guy hadn't shown up, who knows what would have happened, what *would be* happening. I undid my shorts, sprung from them. There I was standing in my friend's bedroom, at attention, waiting for his mom to, to, to what? The tears, her trembling chin. I glanced around Greg's room; it was in its usual disarray and I tried to clear my head, tried to remember why I was here, who I was. Lenny, that's right. I was trying to find Lenny to tell him what Redd Morgan had done. I looked around for evidence that Lenny had been there but, through all the chaos that was Greg's life, it was hopeless. I couldn't stay here—what was I thinking? What if Mr. Woods came home and there I was with his wife? What if Greg came home? Oh, God—I had to get out of there. I had to go find Lenny. I had to figure out what Dana and I were going to do about Redd Morgan. What had I been thinking, anyway?

I put on my shirt, zippered my pants and hurried back into the hall. Studying myself in the long hallway mirror, I gave myself a look of resolve and strode into the kitchen. Nobody was there so I looked out the window. No one there, either. I slid back the door and stepped outside onto the patio.

"Mrs. Woods?"

Walking around the pool, I gazed across the fairway, then checked both sides of the house before going back inside. I stood in the kitchen, listening: not a sound. She must have taken the guy back to the country club or to his car. Or maybe they were out front though I doubted it; I would have heard them. Whew, I was actually feeling relieved. What could I have told her my reason for leaving was? Would she ask me to come back? No, this was better. I would just leave.

I went back down the hallway, my image in the mirror bouncing along almost jauntily when I thought I heard something in the den. I stepped back, listened again, not sure I'd heard anything. Quietly, I cracked the door open.

Mr. Woods sat in his leather chair with his head back. I hadn't even heard him come . . . no . . . wait. A cigar was moving just over the curve of skull in tight fitful circles. The sound of leather giving, a pudgy hand kneading the armrest, sausage-like fingers drained of blood, whitening fingernails. Sliding the door a little farther, I could see the side of a thigh, a black sock pulled mid-calf, a green pant leg bunched over a white golf shoe. Then I saw the television. It was turned off and against the dark screen, its reflection: the wide chair, a head tossing back against it, arms braced as though for blast-off, white splayed legs, a bare back, and between gaping white knees, a second head of unmistakably long black hair, bobbing as though for apples on a Grand River Fourth of July.

24

*D*arin! Stop it!"

"You're not the boss of me."

Julie took a deep breath and slowly exhaled, eyes rolling and cheeks puffed out. She sat at the end of a long gray table and, closing her eyes, massaged both temples.

Her little brother leaned into the wall behind her, his tongue working one corner of his mouth. Dropping his hands and stepping back, he cocked his head at his artistic handiwork.

Arms crossed, I studied the poster as though it were one of Lenny's canvasses. "Not bad."

"Would you please not encourage him." Julie glared at me and frowned.

I smiled back then pointed. "Now, how 'bout some glasses?"

Darin raised his small fist, the blue Magic Marker jutting from it like a knife blade. "I can't. It's too tall."

Stepping over, I picked him up under the arms and elevated him as he drew two circles, one around each of McGovern's smiling eyes. "A shift in image. Might kick-start his campaign."

Julie got up and turned around and, placing hands on hips, sighed at the image of her now bespectacled, mustachioed candidate plastered against the wall. She walked over and took the marker from her little brother.

"Don't!" He grabbed for it.

"Just a minute." Bending forward, she drew in a goatee, a pair of horns, and pointy ears.

He giggled. "It's the devil!"

"Yes, his new running mate—" She blackened in the goatee, making it longer. "Satan."

"And my new girlfriend—" Cameron Pippin III stood in the doorway, a leather briefcase tucked under the arm of his Harris Tweed. "—Judas."

"Oh—Cameron . . . uh, hi. I'm just, um, we're just, well—" She put the marker on the table as if it were burning her hand. "I had to baby-sit my little—"

He walked across the room from the back entrance, a tall blond woman wearing bookish black glasses following closely behind. Tossing the briefcase on his desk near the front window, he collapsed into the chair. "Julie, Helen Fitzsimmons. Helen, Julie McClellan." The chair creaked as he leaned back and uncurled his wire-rims from behind both ears before holding them up against the fluorescent lighting. "Helen's been helping us with the west, mostly Nevada, Utah, and Idaho, but she also has great connections in Washington and Oregon." He lowered the glasses and began shining the lenses against his shirt pocket.

"Great—I mean, nice to meet you." Julie shrugged like a schoolgirl, her face crimson.

Helen Fitzsimmons stuck her hand out, shook Julie's, then pulled her in close. "Don't worry. There's always room for humor, even on a sinking ship." She winked.

"Julie, did you get those mailers out?"

"Um, no, Cam. I was going to but then Rog—I mean my father dropped Darin off, so I was, um . . . I was going to get them out this afternoon."

"I wanna go home."

"We will, Darin. But first I have to—"

"Are they stamped? I can take them over if you want. Helen and I have a meeting at the courthouse in fifteen minutes. I'll drop them off on my way."

"No—I mean that's what I was going to do, stamp them and then—"

"So tell me, Julie—" He dug in the desk drawer, pulled out a tie and draped it around his neck. "—what have you done lately? Anything?" He glanced up at the poster. "That is, anything except draw little pictures with your little brother's crayons?"

"Come on, Cam. That's enough." Helen picked up his briefcase, and grabbing both ends of the tie with her free hand, pulled him protesting toward the door. She looked back at Julie, smiling. "We'll get you some volunteers over here to help. Cameron tells me it's a staunchly Republican district, but I'm sure we can find at least a few warm Democratic bodies lying about. Nice meeting you, Julie." Pressing the briefcase to his middle, she gently pushed Cameron Pippin III out the doorway.

"Yeah, nice to meet—" Julie raised a hand good-bye then slumped forward in her chair, palms against her forehead as the door clicked shut and we heard them laughing outside on the sidewalk.

"What a jerk!" I swung wildly in the air. "Can you believe that guy? 'Have you done anything except draw little pictures with your little brother's crayons?'"

"Hank, he's not a . . ." She buried her face in her hands, then nodded. ". . . yeah, he is." She looked up. "And for this I gave up Notre Dame." She gazed around the Democratic Headquarters as though seeing the place for the first time. "I don't even know what I'm doing here."

"Come on, Jules. Let's go find Lenny."

"I can't. Who'll watch the—" She waved a hand around the large room.

"The what? There's not even anybody here."

"Don't remind me."

"Yeah, there's nobody here." Darin drew concentric circles over George McGovern's mouth and chin.

Julie stood. "You win." She peeled the poster from the wall, rolled it up, and tapped Darin on the head.

"Give it!" He jumped as she held it aloft. "Come on, Julie! Give it!"

She lowered the poster and he glommed onto it. "What do you say?"

Waving the poster overhead, he skipped toward the front door. "Thanks— Judith!"

She shook her head. "Judith." She rummaged in her purse for keys. "Judith, Judas—I don't know. Maybe they're right."

"Come on, Jules. Let's go find Lenny."

"Hank, do you realize how much time you spend looking for people? If it's not Lenny, it's Greg or Dana or your dad or me or, or—I mean, come on."

Her little brother was tooting through the rolled poster.

She ran fingers through her hair. "Look, I better take him home before I cripple him."

"I'll cipple you!"

She looked at her little brother and sighed. "Drop by later if you want." They climbed into her VW, and she rolled down the window. "Hank, I'm sorry. I just don't know what the hell I'm doing anymore."

"That's okay."

"You said hell. I heard ya. I'm tellin'!" Darin was directing an eye through the poster at his big sister.

"Darin!" She grabbed the end of the poster he was now tooting into her ear.

"Give it!" He yanked back.

Jaw clenched, she crossed one eye at me as they played tug-of-war and then, shifting into gear, abruptly jerked from the curb. "Come by!"

I nodded and waved as the Volkswagen bucked forward, Julie and her little brother struggling all the way down Main Street over the disguised and crumpling face of a beleaguered George McGovern.

◇ ◇ ◇

As soon as I saw them standing in front of our house in the middle of the street—Dana, Mr. Shimizu, Milton, Punk, and with an arm around Mom, Arlene—I knew she'd seen it.

It was dusk, and in the dwindling light Mr. Shimizu walked over to the edge of lawn and squatted. Pulling up a sample of dead turf, he held it up to examine then brought it to his lips. "Lime." He spit, pitching it to the side before brushing his hands together. "It's reacted with all the moisture we've been getting and here you have the result." He stood. "Who would do such a thing?"

"Who?" Punk rubbed his tattoo as though it were a rash. "We know who."

Arlene nodded. "And when we get hold of the son-of-a-bitch, he'll know too."

"Perhaps we should report this to the police." Milton glanced around but no one responded.

"Hank?" Mom motioned me over and clutched my arm. "Dana said Redd was over here early this morning. Why didn't you come tell me?"

I stared at the word burned into our lawn. "I don't know. I just didn't want you to . . . I just couldn't, that's all."

"You should've, honey. Then maybe we could've—"

"Could've what, Mom?"

"I just think, I just thought—" Mom's eyes searched the curb as if what she wanted to say might be written there in cement. Shaking her head, she moved from Arlene's grasp and started up the driveway.

Milton hurried over and put a hand on her shoulder. "Sally—Sally, I best be going. I'll give you a call tomorrow though, okay? Maybe we can go out to dinner or to a movie or something, all right?"

Without turning, Mom half-raised a hand over her shoulder and continued up the drive and into the house.

Milton gazed at his shoes and then his eyes flitted about as though he suddenly found himself in a place he didn't want to be. "Well, I guess I better—" He too half-waved but for different reasons, hurrying across the street to his car.

"Now there goes an ass-kickin' superhero for ya. Milton Milquetoast." Arlene shook her head as he drove away. "Punk, let's go find that Redd Morgan pig and see if we can't make a purse out of him. You two keep an eye on your mom. We'll be back as soon as we can."

Dana, arms drawn in like a pair of wings, watched Punk and Arlene bustle across the street, get in their car, and drive away. Her eyes followed them around the corner then panned across to Mr. Shimizu.

He gazed back and tried to smile. "What'd I tell you? Grass gives nothing but misery." He reached out and squeezed her arm before looking over what was left of our lawn. "But tomorrow we take it out. Okay?"

Dana nodded then she too walked up the driveway and into the house.

◊ ◊ ◊

Against my better judgment I drove back by the Woods' to see if Lenny was there. He was, sitting out front in the Wagoneer with Louie. The Jeep was running and whitish blue exhaust leaked from the tail pipe into the chilly evening air. I honked so he climbed out, his hands jutted into an old Army coat.

"Hey."

"Hey, Lenny. Where've you been?"

He shrugged and coughed.

"You sound horrible."

"Yeah." He nodded. "I've got a headache, too."

"We should've gone back by Sage Diner. I think Mom made an appointment for you. Man, you wouldn't believe what's happened today. Still haven't found Greg, huh?"

He shook his head. "He'll be here. He told me I could crash for as long as I want."

"Why don't you just come back to our house? At least until you feel better. You can have my bed and I'll sleep on the couch."

"That's okay. Greg'll be here. He promised."

"If you say so. Man, you're not going to believe what Redd Morgan pulled this time."

"What?"

"Hey, boys!" Mr. Woods stepped from the front doorway. "Come on in here! The Olympics are almost on!"

"Hi, Mr. Woods!" I waved. "When's Greg getting back?"

He raised his arms and shrugged before turning back into the house.

"There's no way I'm going back in there."

"Why?"

"Greg's mom. I think she's losing it."

"She's not here, Hank. She left a couple hours ago."

"So how long have you been out here waiting, anyway?"

Lenny shrugged. "A while."

"Come on! Hurry up!" Mr. Woods waved. "It's just starting!" He held the door, motioned us inside.

I followed Lenny across the circular drive. "Remind me to tell you what Redd Morgan did this time, okay?"

Lenny nodded as we went into the house.

Tucking each of us underarm as though we were a pair of crutches, Mr. Woods led us down the long hallway. "They're going to replay the four-hundred medley first, Spitz's seventh gold."

I could feel the weight of him across my back and could smell the pungent juniper aroma of gin mixed with stale after-shave.

"It's pre-recorded. Actually, I'm not sure myself who won because I try not to watch or read anything all day so it's like I'm watching as it happens. But who could possibly beat that team, right?" He chuckled. "Do you boys realize that Mark Spitz is probably one of the three or four greatest Olympians of all time? And that Hollywood smile! He reminds me a little bit of Greg. I mean not the athleticism, of course, although Greggy's a pretty good little athlete himself, but just that look, that confidence. The kid's got it all." He motioned to the paisley couch for Lenny and I to sit. Standing at the wet bar, he mixed himself another drink. "You boys want a cola or something?"

"No thanks, Mr. Woods." I stared at his leather chair: if furniture could only talk.

"What the hell's this?" He pointed his glass at the television. "Must've hit the wrong channel." He walked over and turned the dial one way and then the other before returning to the same channel, the same image: a man wearing a floppy-brimmed white hat standing on the balcony of what looked to be an apartment building. Mr. Woods turned up the volume and stepped back. Holding his drink, eyes trained on the screen, he slowly squatted on the edge of his leather chair. The drink remained untouched in his hand as the sober voice of sportscaster Jim McKay filled the den.

"They broke in at five o'clock this morning. They killed Moshe Weinberg, the wrestling coach when he resisted, two bullets in the head, one in the stomach. They reportedly have killed another man, unidentified. They gave a deadline first of noon, then they said one o'clock, then they said five o'clock, then they changed it back to three and finally to five. Five was the final deadline. There had been negotiations going on apparently, men going in and out of the building, the deadline past twenty-one minutes ago. It could be they're just waiting for the

guerillas to make a move, but what that move should be . . ."

"Oh, my God." Mr. Woods was standing now, the back of his hand with the glass in it pressed against his lips. "Oh, my God—no."

"The Games themselves, remember, have been suspended. Uh, as soon as the competitions that are on right now have finished, that will be all, at least until tomorrow. At ten o'clock tomorrow morning there will be a memorial service in the huge Olympic Stadium for the two men dead so far, attended by the athletes of the world."

Mr. Woods half-sat and half-fell back into his chair. "No, no—"

The white-hatted man stepped back and disappeared into the building.

I glanced over at Mr. Woods, his head resting against the back of the chair. "What *is* this?"

"This can't be. This just can't be."

"The live picture you're watching is the one, of course. That's now. We're going to bring up some videotape we want you to see. This is videotape and these are the volunteer squad of thirty-eight men, we are told, in athletic uniforms. They're actually either, either Munich police or West German border guards. As Peter Jennings indicated, the German Army, because of very complicated, uh, laws would not be allowed to participate. And there you see an athlete holding a canvas bag in which is obviously a machine gun. He's not an athlete, he's, he's a policeman. A bulletproof vest quite apparent there . . ."

"These are the Olympics, goddamnit." Mr. Woods pointed at the televison. "The Olympics!"

Elbowing Lenny, I raised my eyebrows and motioned my head toward the doorway. "I gotta get going. You want to—"

He shook his head and whispered. "I'm going to wait for Greg, Hank."

"All right. Tell me what happens, okay?" I got up and walked to the sliding den door. I looked back: Mr. Woods was draining his glass of gin as Lenny sat shivering on the couch, the man in the floppy white hat emerging again onto what I later learned was the Israeli Olympic team's dormitory balcony.

◇◇◇

I got into Mom's car and headed west through town toward Rabbit Valley. It felt even cooler now, stars standing sharp as needles against a black inky sky. Training the rear-view mirror on myself, I watched the contours of my face illuminate then fall to shadow as I passed porch lights and street lamps and neon store signs. Farther out on the edge of town, as pairs of headlights bore out of the darkness less frequently, I heard sirens whine in the distance and then what

I thought to be a sonic boom. Rolling the window down, I stuck my head out and took in the scent of cut alfalfa and sugar beets and corn fields, manure from a passing hog farm, grain elevators and tilled earth, smelled everything I could until my vision went blurry with wind and I pulled my head back inside.

Only the dash lights illuminated my face now as I pulled up to the stand of sagebrush by his mailbox and looked one last time into the mirror: "You can do this." I turned the engine off and got out. Walking around the car a couple of times, taking deep breaths, I looked up at the sky. I felt like I did before a wrestling match, chest and stomach tight, my breathing measured but uncertain. Rubbing palms against pant legs, I started up the rutted drive. The sandy ground was already starting to dry after all the rain, but I stepped on some bentonite and slipped into a puddle, caking my shoes. Trying to kick off the mud, I suddenly found myself standing there before the trailer door.

Stepping onto the milk crate, I felt the mud ooze underfoot between the metal grating. My knees quaked, hands clenching and flexing, and my eyes squeezed shut as though I had no say in the matter, as though my eyelids were shutters and a gust of wind had caught them. Finally, taking another deep ragged breath, I opened my eyes to my fist extended against the metal door, my reflection warped against the small cracked plate-glass window, against the towel hanging as a curtain by one corner. I knocked, felt the give and creak of movement, the vibration of a life within. The outside light blinked on. The knob turned and the door opened. And there he was. He stood back, still in shadow, the kitchen light shining behind him. One of the canaries chirped.

"Junior?"

"Hi, Dad."

"What're you doing out here this time of night? It's good seeing you, son. Come in."

"Thanks, Dad."

He held the trailer door as I stepped in, staring at my shoes.

"Slip them off, son, and I'll find you something dry."

And it was then, as I stooped over to take them off, my mud-caked tennis shoes, that I saw the two small rubber wheels and above them, the tank. And in the seeing, all that I had imagined about our father—about his love for our mother and their secret conversations, his ingenious pranks on Redd Morgan, about all the archaeology and dinosaur hunting he'd been doing and the million other reasons I had for his life, for his not contacting us after all those months— crystallized in my hopefully deluded mind and then just as suddenly, crumbled away.

Slowly I straightened, my eyes scanning up the tank's shiny metallic length to a handle with Dad's veiny hand gripping it and then the clear plastic tube running up along the worn lapel of his blue terrycloth robe and dividing beneath that stubbled chin along his sharp jaw line and around his ears before disappearing into each of his pinched miner's nostrils.

He was standing under the kitchen light now, leaning on the card table already straining from too much weight—broken rock, a mound of dirt, a geologist's hammer—my father, the whole of him laboring with each incumbent breath, watching me.

"Dad—"

"Yes, son?"

I lifted the shoes, lifted my eyes, saw myself for the first time in almost two years in those deep-set miner's eyes. "Where should I put these?"

"Anywhere, son. It doesn't much matter."

And it didn't. I dropped them where I stood.

"Look, Junior." He picked up a rock from the table, held it out as if he were offering me an apple. "A petrified gizzard stone."

I nodded. "Yeah." I took it from him, felt the weight of it in my own sweaty hand.

◊ ◊ ◊

Three firemen huddled on the sidewalk, talking. Their fire truck idled at the curb, its red lights turning and flashing off the big lava rock and surrounding trees, and lighting up the neighboring houses. The gutter ran white with a foam that oozed down along the street before emptying into a drainage grate at the corner. As I eased Mom's car by, a cop vigorously swept the beam of a flashlight at me across the wet pavement to keep traffic moving, which was when I saw it: the truck. It was parked in its usual spot to the side of the driveway. Its hood was up and doors were open, and I could see the exposed seat springs and blackened steering wheel, could see that even the rectangle of steel above the truck bed, the thing he'd called his headache rack, was charred. No need for throwing eggs now. Now, the whole smoldering welder's truck—the whole smoldering life of him—had become a headache. Redd Morgan's fiery own.

◊ ◊ ◊

"Do you believe in God?"

Julie sighed, gazing at the stars and hugging her knees to her dad's oversized parka. Her toes were curled inside the hem of her nightgown as she sat on the redwood bench that encircled the telescope platform.

I had come by late after going back to the Woods' to see if Lenny was still there—he wasn't—tapping on her bedroom window and, through the screen, telling her about Redd Morgan's truck and what he'd mowed into our lawn. I told her about finally seeing Dad and his being hooked up to an oxygen tank, about Mrs. Woods in the den with the guy in green pants, about Cisco lifting his chin, Lenny being sick, Mr. Woods becoming upset, Dana converting to Buddhism, Mom smoking cigarettes. I told her everything I could think of until I couldn't think of anything more. But still I talked. She sat listening, until I finally fell silent too. Then she pressed her palm to the screen and asked if I wanted to go around to the back yard and look through her father's telescope.

"Do I believe in God?" Julie smiled. "Most of the time I guess. I mean, looking through that thing is enough to convince almost anyone, you know what I mean?"

"Yeah, I guess so." I had it trained on the moon, its surface pale and pocked and cold-looking.

"When I was little, Rog would tell me that all the stars in the sky are but a twinkle in one of God's eyes."

"Your dad's a poet."

"You know how a few people just seem to know things and the rest of us have to really try and figure them out?"

"Yeah, like Miss Darling." I lifted my face from the eyepiece.

"Rog just knows things, too. It's kinda scary."

"Sometimes I feel like I don't know anything. Like tonight." I took another look at the moon and then straightened. "The whole world seems upside-down."

"Rog says that what we think to be up and down, left and right, are just reference points because we're what he calls Viewers."

"Viewers?"

"Yeah. We're just tiny lookout points stuck here against a little magnetic rock hurtling through space on the same constant orbit. Even if we could see through all the eyes of all the people on the planet at the same time, we still couldn't see much. He says when we look at the sky we should remember that it's three-dimensional, that it has limitless depth, and what we see is an extremely limited image from a very limited perspective."

"I've lost all perspective."

"Not just you, Hank. He says that most people look at the sky and see something flat, like a map. That's why early man drew pictures by connecting the brightest stars and made up stories as a way of explaining what they were seeing."

"So maybe that's why we have people like Jesus and Buddha. Maybe they're our pictures."

"I think God's much bigger than all those guys put together. Rog says that we're really not looking for God outside ourselves anyway. That what's out there is but a shadow of what exists in here. He likes to say 'a wise man sees as much as he ought, not as much as he can.'"

"We should see infinity."

"Look, Hank." She pointed. "A falling star."

I just glimpsed the tail end of it. "Even stars don't last."

Julie nodded, then leveled her gaze at me and closed her eyes.

25

Only the S remained. It snaked palely through the green lawn near the driveway, leaving Mr. Shimizu and me a ten-yard swath to dig up. We worked right to left, he cutting parallel lines approximately three feet apart with a long flat-headed shovel and I prying and scooping the grass up using a steel snow shovel. I tried to roll or flop it over onto itself, as I had seen at a sod farm, but the lawn was old and shot through with crabgrass and dandelions so Mr. Shimizu had to sever the roots underneath as I wrestled it from the top. Now our yard was littered with clumps of broken and torn earth, mounds of dirt here and there where roots from Mrs. Whitsen's ancient willow next door had surfaced like serpents rolling up out of the deep. By noon the L-U-T was gone, which was about when Greg screeched up in his father's Lincoln Towncar, jumping the curb and bucking to a stop.

He leaped out, leaving the door ajar as though drunk or on speed or both. "Hank!"

I looked up but continued to drive the shovel into the ground.

"Hank—" He hurried up the driveway past Mr. Shimizu who was leaning against the flat-head wiping his neck with a red handkerchief. I smirked as Greg—a pretty good little athlete himself, as his father once bragged—stumbled up the porch and then, without knocking, barged into our house.

"Friend of yours?" Mr. Shimizu retied his bandana.

I continued to dig but without the same enthusiasm. "Yeah—kinda." I looked up at the head of hair silhouetted through the living-room window against the kitchen light and tried to decide if it belonged to Greg or Dana.

"Your mother won't like that." Mr. Shimizu pointed to the muddy footprints smeared up the driveway.

"No, probably not." I dropped the shovel and was pulling off my gloves when Greg burst from the front door.

"Hank! Come on!" He was back behind the wheel before I could respond, before I could tell him to go to hell, that my days of following him were over. He could find some other lackey to amuse himself with hallucinogenic brownies and blowing up corporate symbols and driving around like a maniac and about a million other stunts he had pulled across the many years I'd known him. I was finished, finally and completely.

Mom stepped from the doorway, her hand cradling an elbow, a cigarette rotating nervously between her fingers. "You better go with him, hon. Dana and I'll help Mr. Shimizu finish up here."

I sat silently in the passengers seat, uneasy, but as always, wondering what he was up to now as he sped down Gateway Avenue, past Teller Arms, City Park, Sage Diner, then south down First and west again over the bridge past Riverside, over the Colorado River before turning southwest onto Monument Road toward Rimrock National Park.

By the time he jumped out of the car at the trailhead and I caught up with him across the wash through the tamarisk and sagebrush, sirens were coming from town—they seemed to follow this guy—and I knew something was wrong.

Greg ran like I'd never seen, his white tennis shoes churning up the wet clay along a fresh set of tire tracks that had recently spun and sputtered up the slippery trail. He beat me to the top, wheezing and coughing, hands on knees and his head down. Without lifting his eyes, back heaving, he pointed across the top of the Third Sister.

The Jeep was parked where it usually was, near the edge overlooking the ridges and gullies facing Rimrock National Park. I walked toward it as though it were an injured animal and I was suddenly wary of it. The windows were rolled up, and through the mud-splattered glass of the rear end I could make out an olive-green sleeping bag and a pillow case stuffed with a down parka, one sleeve protruding from it. To the side over the wheel wells lay clothes, a towel, a remnant of carpet. A bag of dry dog food was stuffed underneath against the back tire with a Coleman stove and lantern and other camping equipment. The door windows, too, were splattered, and a white plastic sack of something hung from the side-view mirror as I moved alongside it, moved as though underwater, everything wavy and blurry and dream-like. I stepped to the front bumper on the driver's side, and it was here, atop the Third Sister facing the sweep of Grand Valley beyond, that I peered through the wiper-smeared windshield and saw him.

He was sitting on the passenger's side in his army coat, one hand clutching it closed beneath his chin, the other resting against an open sketchbook tipped across his lap. His head lay at an angle against the glass above the door lock as though he were sleeping or taking a nap after one of his many runs or after a long session of painting or sketching, after taking his dog for a hike or helping Mr. VanHorn with his orchard or Miss Darling with her chores, after building a fire and cooking and cleaning up or doing whatever else he did in the course of a day, of a life. Slumped there in the Jeep Wagoneer his uncle had willed him, in the Jeep that ultimately betrayed him, my best friend Lenny looked to be resting—inexorably and forever resting.

◊ ◊ ◊

Black, Lenny said, is what's left over when all other colors are absorbed. An object is one color because it absorbs all others.

"If that's true, an apple would be every color *but* red." I was sitting with him on the old condemned railroad bridge, dangling feet, watching the river flow past.

"No, red's the color left over."

"So an apple, a whole one, is all colors but red, which is the one I can see."

"I guess that's one way to put it, Hank."

"And when every color is absorbed, black's reflected."

"Well, pure black's hard to find. Maybe in a cave somewhere. Black is what you get without light, so if there's a reflection on it, it's usually white."

"Like Peefee's truck when it's all shiny."

"Yeah, a reflection from the glare."

"So if I take the apple into a cave, does it stop being red?"

He nodded.

I craned my head and spit between my feet, watched the saliva separate into two long, looping globs before hitting the water. I thought about this, the lunacy of something being a particular color because it's the only color it actually isn't. "So people in a cave are all the same color then."

"Or no color."

We sat in silence for a while, the river surging and swirling and eddying past beneath our feet. And then I thought that maybe nothing exists. That everything is a figment of imagination from what Miss Darling called the Cosmic Trickster. And this is what she called God, Miss Darling, who said that dreams are what's real.

"Without eyes, no color. Without ears, no sound. How 'bout without sleep?"

He lifted his eyes to me. "No dreams."

"And without life, no world?"

"Maybe everything's that way, Hank. You know, inside-out. Maybe we don't really know anything until we're dead."

"Maybe."

"How 'bout without souls?"

I looked at him, afraid of what he was going to say next. "That's easy."

"Tell me then?"

I shrugged, racking my brain for something, anything. "Without souls—" I closed my eyes, tapped my fist between my eyes. "Without souls—" I opened them. "—no goldfish." Then spit into the river.

◇◇◇

Now it was I who ran yelling and windmilling my arms down the side of the Third Sister. Greg remained where he had stopped to point at Lenny's Jeep. He knelt, hands locked behind his head, rocking. He looked like the prisoner-of-war I had seen in *Life Magazine*, a North Vietnamese farmer on a dirt road between rice paddies in a like pose but more erect than Greg with elbows back, not forward, not wrapped around his head. Greg remained there rocking on his knees the entire time, through the sirens—sheriff's car, ambulance, another sheriff's car—blaring past the Three Sisters to the rangers' station at the entrance of Rimrock National Park then turning around and roaring back to where I stood in the middle of Monument Road waving my arms; through the emergency medical technicians huffing up the Third Sister carrying the stretcher; through all the sheriff deputy's questions—Lenny's name, address, age, parents' names—and the examination of the body, the note taking, the easing of his body from the front seat onto the stretcher and their carting him down the muddy hillside and across the wash through the tamarisk and sagebrush, and sliding him into the ambulance before driving him away; through the deputy pulling on plastic gloves, removing the keys from the ignition—the Jeep had idled itself to empty—and dropping them into a plastic bag as though they were somehow contaminated; through the same deputy turning off the heater fan and dome light, loading the camping equipment and locking the doors, and with help from the other, tying a yellow investigation ribbon around the Jeep as though gift wrapping it for someone else. Through all that, still Greg rocked until it was just he and I atop the Third Sister, at which point he pitched forward on all fours and vomited.

Standing, wiping his mouth on his forearm and shaking his mane of hair back, he looked bleary-eyed toward Rimrock and said what I was thinking: "Where's Louie?"

The rest of that day we shouted Louie's name to hoarseness until around dusk, Julie showed up with her father. Dr. McClellan stood to the side for a while, toeing the damp earth and gazing out over the sandstone horizon. Finally, after circling the Jeep a couple of times, he made the long trek back down to his car as the three of us remained on that barren hilltop, next to that damned beribboned Jeep, and hugged, whispering to each other that it would be okay, but knowing deep down that it wasn't okay. It would never be okay. Lenny, the best of us, was gone.

26

*E*arly the next morning Julie returned to the Third Sister by herself. As she sat knees to chin on the hood and watched the sun rise over the Colorado River between the Bookcliffs and Spruce Mesa, Louie crawled out from under the Wagoneer, rolled to his back and, with Julie clutching his mud-matted scruff to her face, repeating his name, peed like a puppy all over himself. But when she was ready to leave and the sun shone high above Spruce Mesa, the dog crawled back to the same spot, and though his tail thumped the ground when she called him, he refused to budge from underneath that Jeep.

A couple hours later, after the breakfast crowd at Sage Diner had finally thinned, I returned with Julie to the Third Sister where a couple of men were already hooking the vehicle up to their truck. They wore red coveralls with Ace Towing across the back and their names stitched in white cursive above the pockets. They weren't too much older than we, and the tall raw-boned one, Lyle, said yes, there had been a big black dog there that they'd had to force out from underneath using a long stick and finally a couple of well-aimed rocks. It was vicious, he said, snarling and snapping until there was nothing left but to drive it out with force. They didn't know if they had injured the dog, but it had finally yelped and loped off down the hillside.

Julie asked if we could take the dog food from the back for when we found him. Lyle answered no, the Jeep was being impounded and all evidence had to remain intact until it was officially released by the sheriff's office from the impoundment lot downtown. Julie and I stared at each other and didn't have to say anything; we knew what the other was thinking without actually saying the word. It was the first time we had even considered that Lenny's death was anything other than an accident.

Numbly, we watched them tow the Jeep down Monument Road toward town and then did what Greg and I had done the afternoon before, shouted for Louie while traipsing up and down all the trails and ridges he and Lenny had spent so many hours of their lives running.

As for me, over the next several days, running became my salvation. What had begun with my best friend, now continued in my search for his dog. The farther I went, the closer was Lenny. Eagle's Wing, Liberty Cap, Stagecoach, Blue Lake, Gunny Loop, Rattlesnake, Whitewater—all the runs he had taken me on were now my attempts to bring him back. A little faster and I could feel his shoulder next to mine; a little farther and I could hear his breathing. Sometimes, peripherally off the edge of my rippling cheek as I put mile after mile underfoot, I could envision him matching my every stride, encouraging me on, only to turn and see nothing but the jiggling landscape going past. Running became who I was and, in that knowledge, he became more a part of me in death than he was even in life. The memory of him was a gift and it enriched me.

But running was also my punishment. When I thought I couldn't go another step, I was at my most euphoric. Lungs burning, throat parched and cottony, joints and muscle and ligaments aching to pleasurable, grinding distraction. Every sharp pain in my side was just one more stitch in my tortured creation. I immersed myself in bone-numbing distances my brain could neither count nor conceive. And finally as I would pull up, sopping and gasping, I'd imagine Lenny standing there, waiting for me, and so I would run some more. Why I craved this pain, I never understood. Why not, seemed the better question— or answer—reducing everything I thought I knew to what Faulkner called the "reducto absurdum of all human experience." Lenny was dead, and with that as my compass, nothing else mattered or made sense.

The morning of the funeral I honored him by running the twenty-three miles over Rimrock. It was the last day of the Olympics, a hot cloudless day in Grand River. Julie picked me up in her VW and dropped me off beside the ranger's station at the east entrance. Lenny had always preferred trails, where every strike of the foot carried a little different angle over rocks and ruts, a slight variation in pitch to break the physical monotony, the constant pounding. Only occasionally would he take me on the pavement and never over Rimrock National Park; it was too far for me, he said. But now I would run it as a tribute, in yet one more attempt to conjure him back to life through running.

Julie was waiting at the other end as I staggered down the last incline toward the west-entrance rangers' station. The run was harder than I had expected, and the asphalt harder yet. As I stumbled into her arms, she pressed ice cubes from a Coke she was drinking to the back of my neck because I was shivering from heat exhaustion; it had taken me over three-and-a-half hours, and in my ignorance, I hadn't carried water. She helped me into the VW, gave me the rest of her Coke and a handful of M&Ms then drove to Ruth's Cafe in Otto where she ordered scrambled eggs and sausage and mounds of pancakes with syrup and strawberries.

While eating the food and drinking water, we watched on a fuzzy Zenith the closing ceremony of the Munich Olympics. Flag-carrying athletes somberly circled the track of Olympiad Stadium, a few waving to the crowd but most simply walking—wanting, I imagined, only to get back home to their own countries, to their families and friends. The terrorists had marred the games, killing eleven Israeli team members and one German policeman and sacrificing five of their own, but still the athletes of the world marched. And it was this, the marching, the refusal to quit, that I now understood in a way I never would have before Lenny's death.

The service began at one-thirty. Mom, Dana, and I were almost late because I was exhausted from the run and had fallen asleep downstairs. I was dreaming of Miss Darling and Lenny or, rather, in the muddled logic of a dream, a hybrid of the two. In body, it was Miss Darling, her squat crippled form, her wild wisps of gray hair, her cackle and toothless grin, but in essence it was Lenny, that calming voice, his quiet instruction on how to untether myself from the bonds of gravity, from the confines of weight and physics. "Think it," he kept saying. "Imagine you can fly, Hank, and you will." Initially, I could get no higher than what I could jump. But gradually, through the gritty dint of will, I hovered longer and longer until I was actually suspended above ground, if only for a few seconds. Slowly, with every succeeding effort, I would jump a little higher, hold it a little longer, until I was finally able to sever the magnetic ties of earth and take flight. With Miss Darling/Lenny leading the way, I was just beginning to soar effortlessly, swooping skyward over roof and treetop toward the clouds, when Dana shook me awake at a quarter after and the three of us did our own flying out the front door to Mom's car.

As we pulled into the parking lot of Pentecostal Holiness Church, I recognized the VanHorns' pickup, Julie's parents' wood-paneled station wagon, Dillard's Corvair, and Punk and Arlene's Chevy Malibu among the otherwise unfamiliar cars. The organist, a wisp of a woman, was playing a dirge as we walked into the vestibule and were escorted about halfway down to our seats. The ushers were men from this, Mrs. Bartelli's church. I didn't recognize any of them and was certain Lenny wouldn't have either. I sat between Mom and Dana, each of whom kept glancing at me, patting my leg. Toward the front on the right side sat Mr. VanHorn and Molly, and I was surprised when Coach Hicks slid in behind them, leaning over and whispering in Mr. V's ear before shaking his hand. I noticed classmates scattered here and there—Stankey back from Stanford, Margaret Kohler from the east coast, Dillard (from who knows where), Lloyd Webber, Ben Fritzland, Teddy Green, and, of course, Julie, sitting between her parents a couple of rows in front of us. Her father's arm rested along the pew behind her, his hand on her shoulder, while her mother gently bounced baby Bubby under chin against her bosom. Julie turned and raised her eyebrows at me, dabbing a pink kleenex to her eyes.

The organist stopped playing, and Carl Lujan rose from a foldout chair behind the podium next to a sprawling wreath of chrysanthemums draped over the shiny, closed casket and began playing *Amazing Grace* on his accordion. As he played, in walked—as if on queue—Cisco, Peefee and the gang. They must have been twenty strong, marching straight down the middle aisle to the front, dress shoes clicking on the wooden floor, and starched white shirts and pressed pants shushing like sandpaper against pine. They slid into the front two pews normally saved for immediate family members, their pant legs squeaking against the varnished wood before settling in as though it were they who were Lenny's ushers, not these unfamiliar men, these anonymous church members.

As Carl struck his last reverberating note, Mrs. Bartelli, Vince, and Sheila entered from a side door. Mrs. Bartelli, covered in black and supported at the elbow by Vince, tottered toward the front pew and then stopped as though to catch her breath, to take stock of the people seated before her. Then, from behind her veil, she cut loose with a wail every bit as loud and plaintive as the church organ or Carl Lujan's accordion. A ship signaling a return to harbor, she listed to starboard, Vince struggling at her side to keep her afloat and Sheila bobbing haplessly behind gnawing a cuticle. She plunged forward, mooring herself bosom-first against the pew. Vince, red-faced, strained to tug his mother upward, but it was no use, until Reverend Lujan and Kenny Madrid, who was sitting on the aisle, hoisted her upright into her seat. Vince and Sheila quickly sat as Mrs. Bartelli straightened the wide-brimmed hat that had slipped to the side and again caught her breath for another round of wailing, which lasted the entire length of Reverend Lujan's invocation and well into the service. But then abruptly, in the middle of his sermon, as though commanded, she stopped. Not another sound came from her. It was both a relief and a sorrow; her silence hung louder than any organ or accordion or set of vocal chords could muster. Mrs. Bartelli had fallen painfully, abjectly silent.

When we stood to leave, after Reverend Lujan's final prayer that Lenny's soul would gain safe passage into the kingdom of Heaven—he had said nothing about Lenny the person—I spotted Greg. He was sitting by himself in the corner of the back row. Eyes hidden behind aviator glasses, hair wild and unruly, he rested his chin on one fist clenched atop the pew in front of him. Around him sat more church members, people oblivious to the role he'd played in this death, a role I felt as keenly as the knot in my stomach yet, if asked, could barely articulate. If only he'd shown up that night like he promised, maybe Lenny would be alive and none of us sitting here at his funeral. Not me, not Julie, not Greg. I don't know if he saw me, but by the time I excused myself past our row of mourners and started up the aisle toward him, he'd left—the last to come and the first to leave our best friend's funeral.

◇◇◇

"Where's the plastic?" Julie nodded toward the pink sofa and chair, the coffee table with a bowl of glass fruit encircled by a porcelain band of winged cherubs, the china closet jammed with Hummels, a large gold vase of long-stem silk roses sitting on the piano I'd never heard played much less seen uncovered.

I took a sip of punch. "The sidewalk's gone, too."

Where the plastic runner had been was now a strip of slightly lighter pink shag leading down the hallway before forking into the bathroom and two bedrooms. The pink brocaded living-room curtains had been pulled back, the first time I'd ever seen them open, and afternoon sunlight draped across the piano, glistening off the black and white keys and glaring in the wall mirror full of people. Most were the same unfamiliar members of Mrs. Bartelli's church who had attended the funeral. They crowded into the kitchen around a long table of food, spooning up potato salad and beans, mashed potatoes and gravy, ham and turkey and roast beef, garnishes and mustards, rolls, crackers with dip and cheeses, fruit jello, and an assortment of pies, cakes, and cookies. It was as if all the food Mrs. Bartelli had cooked for church all those years had now been returned to her.

Mrs. Bartelli, herself, bustled about making sure everyone was comfortable or had enough to eat or drink, offering like hors d'oeuvres glimpses of Lenny's baby pictures or the family shots taken at the Shriners' Circus when he was in sixth grade. She was the perfect hostess, dressed in a high-neck velvet maroon dress she had changed into from the funereal black one. Relieved of the veiled hat, her hair was coifed and sprayed into stylish curls that made her appear younger than when in her usual headdress of bobby pins and rollers. Even Julie she treated with affection, hugging her when we arrived and introducing her to Reverend Lujan as Lenny's girlfriend. Julie's cheeks flushed and she gazed downward, slightly confused but not entirely displeased. As for me, she smiled curtly and shook my hand, perhaps concerned that people might think it was I who was Julie's boyfriend, not Lenny.

"Should we go in?" Julie gazed down the hallway and started toward his bedroom.

"Jules—"

She looked back at me. "It's okay, Hank." She glanced around the packed living room, people now sitting on every available piece of furniture, people standing and eating, people ringing the doorbell and streaming through the entryway. "She won't even notice."

I followed her down the short hallway, past the pictures of Mr. Bartelli in the army, with his wife on their wedding day, at a podium receiving some kind of sales award, with Vince cradled in his arms next to a lit Christmas tree, smiling. Julie took a breath and pushed open the door. It was dark, the windows covered with what looked to be butcher paper and a single candle flickering across an army of polished knickknacks standing watch across shelves tacked around the room. As our eyes adjusted, we could make out old photographs of Lenny mixed among the glass and porcelain animals, propped among the Swiss yodelers and Santa's elves, leaned against unicorns and armadillos and African warriors carrying ivory-tipped spears. Lenny in the first year of Jr. High, Lenny on a blanket as an infant, Lenny the ghost on Halloween, Lenny the little brother with Vince, Lenny on Easter Sunday wearing hat and bow tie. Lenny everywhere, but no where older than twelve or thirteen, the age he stopped going to church.

Julie knelt over the candle, the flame illuminating her face, and picked up from beneath a picture of Jesus holding his hands out a toothless Lenny of six or seven. "God, he was cute." Using the cuff of her blouse, she traced under both eyes before wiping off the glass and leaning the frame back against the wall. "I don't get it."

"Me neither." Taking a deep breath, I looked at the ceiling then turned around to all those eyes staring out at us from the bedroom walls. "Come on. Let's go home."

"I'll be just a minute." She stepped into the bathroom and closed the door.

I glanced around the menagerie, the hundreds, maybe thousands of miniature figurines, painted and polished and situated in myriad poses, stuck frozen in time around the bedroom. And for what? Posterity? Decoration?

I spotted a giraffe on the floor near the baseboard, a fairly large one, about ten inches tall. I picked it up and ran my fingers over its cool freckled neck, down its sloping back and stiff porcelain legs. Holding its head in one hand, body in the other, I brought it down and pressed it to my leg, bent my weight over it until I could feel the muffled give across my thigh.

"Hank?" Julie stuck her head in. "What're you doing?"

"Nothing." Straightening, I set the two pieces on the shelf next to the picture of Lenny on Halloween, Lenny as ghost.

She walked over and picked up the head, examined it then looked up at me. "Accident?"

I stared back; her face was blotchy and damp from being freshly rinsed. "I didn't know there was such a thing."

She set the giraffe's head down, took my hand and gave it a squeeze. "Yes, there is, Hank. I can show you."

She led me out the bedroom through the crowded living room, through the kitchen past Mrs. Bartelli who was holding court over the sink with women from church, chattering about which dish soap leaves the fewest spots. We slipped out the door to the back yard.

"There's Vince."

He was under the carport, leaning against the shed with his arms folded, watching Sheila arch back and blow bubbles she dipped from a plastic bottle.

"Vincent." Julie walked over to him and placed a hand on his arm. "Vince, I'm so sorry."

He nodded, glancing down at scuffed Beatles boots and high-water bellbottoms. "Thanks."

"Me, too, Vince."

He looked up at me. "You knew him better than me, man."

I swallowed. "Yeah, I guess."

"Not 'I guess.' You did." He unfolded his arms and pushed off the shed, kicking each boot and pulling at his pant legs. "He was a good little dude, huh?"

"Yeah."

"The old lady could never see it though. Even when we were little. Now I guess she can." He lifted his chin toward the house full of people. "I guess you have to either join the church or off yourself. Then you're in like flint, you know what I mean?"

"He didn't 'off' himself, Vincent."

He gazed at Julie then shrugged, looking around. "Doesn't much matter now, does it? Hey, Sheila. Enough of the bubbles, all right?"

Sheila dipped the plastic wand, hands out like a ballerina, then twirled in circles, liquid pearls forming around her.

"Did ya hear me?"

She stopped, bottom lip at once pouty. "It's for your little brother, Goob. It's for Lenny!"

"All right, all right—" Vince shook his head. "Hey, Sheila, what do you say we go show them what we got yesterday?"

After dipping the wand one more time then capping the bottle, she held her arms back like wings and raced under the clothesline and around the shed, the bubbles streaming behind her. "Wooooo—"

"Piece of work, man. Sheila's a freakin' piece of work."

"Wooooo—"

We followed him to the corner of the shed where Julie stopped suddenly cold: Sheila had hopped up into the driver's side window, a *Let's Make a Deal* bimbo with one hand extended overhead and the other inviting us to feast our eyes. Bare feet pointed like Peter Pan's, she threw her head back and smiled theatrically.

"They towed it over yesterday afternoon." Vince walked over and popped the hood.

Mouth open, Julie gawked at me and then at Vince. "They what? What are you—"

"They towed it. Didn't cost us a dime." He reached into the engine and pulled out the dipstick, studied it. "The old lady even told me I could keep it here 'til I get her up and runnin' again."

Covering her mouth with both hands, she stepped backward. "How can you . . . how could you—"

He rubbed oil between thumb and forefinger before sliding the dipstick back in. "Hmm, not bad. After a tune-up and fixin' the exhaust and everything, she'll be ready to roll."

"But it's, it's where . . . it's what—" Julie didn't finish; she didn't need to. Wheeling around and bumping into the clothesline, she ducked under, ran across the yard, and disappeared around the far corner of the house.

Vince looked at me. "What's with her, man?"

"You really don't know?"

He shrugged, shutting the hood before going around to the back seat. He stuck his head inside. "Here—maybe this'll cheer her up." He brought out a large sketchbook.

"Where's the rest of his stuff?"

"You mean his clothes and shit?"

"No, his paintings. His paintings and drawings."

"Oh." He scratched his head. "I dunno. The old lady's got 'em stashed somewhere, I guess."

Sliding the sketchbook under my arm, I turned to leave.

"Hey, man."

"What?"

"Her family's rich, dude. I know where she lives." He flicked his hair, licked his lips. "I ain't got squat, man. Tell her that."

By the time I circled the house, past kids playing on Mrs. Bartelli's front lawn, and down the street along all the cars to the VW, I'd flipped through the sketchbook and with each page understood something about Lenny that I never had. Something so fundamental and obvious that I hadn't seen it. It was too close to me. Or perhaps I'd been denying it all those years.

"Hey, Jules."

Her eyes were closed and her forehead was resting on her hand against the top of the steering wheel. I reached through the passenger's side window and touched her shoulder.

"He didn't 'off' himself, Hank."

"I know."

She straightened, raking her hair back with both hands. Gazing out the windshield, she reached under for the ignition.

"Look what Vince gave me." I propped the sketchbook up so she could see it. "It's Lenny's."

But I didn't show her. She was mad, and I figured she was tired of crying and better off angry. And it wasn't my place to tell or show her, anyway, so I got in the car and placed it on the back seat where she could discover it on her own like I had, discover that each page was a drawing of her and her alone—except the last one, a watercolor: Magic Club, left to right, Greg Woods, Julie McClellan, Henry Kessler, Jr., and Lenny Bartelli standing on the Third Sister against the pink, red, and orange brilliance of Rimrock National Park.

◇ ◇ ◇

As I sat in the VW waiting for Julie to come out of her house, I thought about *A Separate Peace*, a novel Mr. V lent me, about how the character Gene had agonized over whether he had jiggled the branch, causing his best friend Phineas to fall from the tree. I wondered how one slight move, one mere decision no matter how minute or seemingly insignificant, can alter lives forever. Your own, your family's, your friends'. Leave one minute earlier and you wouldn't have gotten into that accident. Stop for gas; go that route instead of this; pull off for something to eat; go to the bathroom; don't leave at all; wait till tomorrow. Choices, one piled atop another across a lifetime and here we are at a particular point in a series of points and no one knows which will be our last. Planets and stars and meteorites wheeling across the universe as senselessly as Greg Woods speeding down a Grand River avenue, choosing not to be anywhere, even if he promised. The negation of choice—abstention, which can lead just as surely and irrevocably into oblivion.

Julie finally came out carrying something wrapped in tinfoil. She got in and handed it to me. "Hold this."

"What is it? More brownies?"

"Cute, Hank."

"What took you?"

"I was talking to Rog. I told him what Miss Darling said about being careful around cars and how we thought she meant Greg not Lenny. I asked him what he thought it all meant."

"What'd he say?"

"Nothing."

"He didn't say anything?"

"No, he said it *meant* nothing. And then he said that when something happens like this, maybe it's better to ask a poet than a scientist like him."

She turned the VW off Monument Road onto the trailhead. As we got out of the car, shadows were growing long and I noticed evening primrose starting to open among the cactus and sagebrush. Julie took the tinfoil, and I followed her across the wash and a few steps up the trail to a dip where it steepened and dried tire marks creased the ground.

She squatted, pointing. "See how they slip there, Hank, and kinda slide back?"

"Yeah."

"This is where Daddy thinks it happened."

"What happened?"

She unwrapped the tinfoil and laid it out on the ground, revealing a cylindrical length of partially crumbling mud about three inches long.

"What's that?"

"You'll see." Using a twig, she gently brushed at a spot on the backside of the dip. "Now where did it—"

"What're you looking for?"

She bent lower, brushed another area a little higher. "Let's see—" She delicately picked up a couple of clods and tossed them to the side. "Here it is."

I bent down closer. "What?"

"There. See it?"

"That little hole?"

"Not just a hole, Hank." She blew into it and carefully brushed dirt from the opening. She picked up the mud cylinder but one end broke off. "It's crumbly." Taking the longer one, which was still intact, she held it to the hole. "See, Hank? See how it's the same size?"

"So? What is it?"

She looked up at me searchingly, as though waiting for the light to go on. It didn't.

"What is it, Jules?"

"The tail pipe, Hank. Lenny's tail pipe."

"What?"

"Rog found it. He showed me this morning."

I looked again.

"Daddy went by the impoundment lot. The tail pipe was completely packed. And this was jammed in there, too." She held out a small, flat piece of rock.

I took it, a piece of sandstone, and held it in my palm, staring at it, feeling its weightlessness. "A rock."

"He showed the sheriff, too. It happened when the Jeep rolled back or slid or something."

I looked at the rock, at Julie, and then back at the ground until it all grew blurry, and there was nothing left but this hole.

◇◇◇

By the time we drove back across town, the tall streetlights down the middle of Gateway Avenue were flickering, and as we made the turn onto the canal road, a sprinkling of stars were appearing over Spruce Mesa. The road was dry but rutted from the recent rain, and the canal ran a deep reddish brown from all the runoff. Julie decided to park up above near the cottonwood, where Lenny always had, rather than pull in below like a customer over the stand of kochia weeds. When we got out and walked down the embankment to the mud hovel, we immediately sensed something different: the Pomeranians, they weren't yapping.

"Where's her dogs?" I walked over to the chain-link gate. "Look, Julie." I pushed it open. "No padlock."

Inside, scraps of paper, mostly newspaper, and spent cans of soup and beans, tuna tins, and a dented milk jug littered the weeds leading up to the door, which stood crookedly ajar. Sticking my head in, I was immediately greeted with the stench of life, of rotting chicken, which brought back the memory of her so forcefully that it pushed me gagging backward and out the gate. I covered my mouth. "I guess she's gone."

"Well, she forgot her broom then." Julie pointed to a splintered broom leaning against the fence.

I smiled. "She didn't need it, Jules. Look." The Cadillac was gone, leaving a bare rectangular outline in the weeds. The oily stump where one wheel rested was still there, and faded rain-crinkled cardboard boxes were strewn about.

"That's where her sweat lodge was." I pointed across the property. "She *is* gone."

We walked over to the fire pit, scorched rocks with charred remnants of newspaper and magazines and a Montgomery Ward's catalogue with one corner burned off.

I squatted and stirred the ashes with a stick. "Looks like she just used this a couple days ago."

"Used what?"

"This fire pit for the coals." I stood, pitching the stick to the side. "Well, I guess she finally left. She finally broke the Ute curse. Maybe they're still flyin' around in their dreams together."

"Yeah, and Lenny's now a star."

But Lenny wasn't a star. And Greg's car wasn't a chariot and Miss Darling wasn't a witch, not even a cursed one. Later that night as we lay in the McClellan's back yard, gazing at the sky, Julie would reach her hand out, fingers splayed against the black universe.

"Look, Hank," she would say.

"What?"

"Lenny's everywhere the stars aren't."

And for me, that was enough.

27

We found Louie one morning under a juniper. It was growing at an angle from some rocks in the saddle between the Second and Third Sisters. We spotted him lying there on his side, barely breathing. He was dehydrated and weak, and we had to bring the VW around to load him in the back so we could take him to the clinic. On the drive there, I told Julie I was surprised the coyotes hadn't gotten to him first. But she didn't say anything, only gripped the steering wheel harder. I thought about the day Lenny and I had found him in much the same condition and, if he died now, maybe it would be okay since in a way that's how he was born, the day Lenny first took him from the desert.

But Louie didn't die. Molly got him started on an IV, and by nightfall we went out to the kennel and found him standing, his tail barely waving. And it was there at the VanHorn's that Louie spent the remainder of his life, outdistancing Huck by several years and taking over as most eligible bachelor and clinic sergeant-at-arms.

Molly had their baby that same September. It was a little girl, the first of three, and they named her Lena. Everyone thought it was for the jazz singer—Lena (Van) Horne—but it was a short "e" not a long one, and as soon as you heard her name you would've understood. At least, if you knew about Lenny and his life, and the role he'd played in Mr. V's.

As for Cisco, Peefee and the gang, they'd scattered like leaves across a fall afternoon. Kenny Madrid and Silver Renteria joined the Army, one to San Diego and the other to some place in North Carolina but neither to Vietnam. Carl Lujan won a music scholarship to the University of Tulsa, and Jimmy Gonzales became a painter in Santa Fe. And from what we heard, a quite successful one. We lost track of Dan Abeyta, but then read in the *Grand River Sentinel* some years later that he'd graduated from the state reformatory in Buena Vista to the state penitentiary in Canyon City after shoving a broken bottle into a bartender's face at a tavern east of town. *Pefe* Maldonado moved that fall also, to Denver, where he opened up a muffler shop, specializing in glass-packs, which, now that I think about it, sounded a lot like his laugh. Cisco Salazar's neck finally healed, but he traded wrestling shoes for the running model and eventually landed far from his father on a cross-country team in Alamosa. I guess, as in me, Lenny continued to run deep inside Cisco too.

And while Cisco and friends were all leaving Grand River, Jeff was finally on his way back. He made it in time for Thanksgiving and, as far as I could tell, the war hadn't changed him much. At least not as much as Dana, who by then had already dropped transcendental meditation in favor of being a Moonie. Luckily, with Jeff's arrival, that receded, too, until her lunar phases disappeared altogether when she discovered around the first of the year that they were pregnant and she'd finally have something tangible to latch onto—a baby boy.

Mom continued to date off and on, and while some weren't half-bad, none, she realized, was good enough to marry. Redd Morgan she saw only once, at the grocery store, but he didn't see her—or pretended he didn't—which is just as well; some fires, like coal, will burn forever and there's no use trying to put them out.

Dad lived two more years in Rabbit Valley until his lungs gave out and we had to move him to an assisted-living facility north of town, where he didn't last a year. Dana, Jeff, and I visited him at least every Sunday those last few years, helping him with his oxygen tanks and having barbecues outside at the trailer where he could look at rocks and watch the sun set over Rimrock. I inherited Chip and Beamer from him, along with the *Airstream*, and found canaries to be more engaging than goldfish, although unlike Dad and his father before him I never did take them with me into the mines. After my father's death, I tried mining, went to school off and on, and then traveled, all the while poking, instead of at rocks, at words, which remained my only constant.

That November, after Nixon's landslide over McGovern, Julie moved to Boulder to continue her study of politics and psychology. Despite being abandoned by Cameron Pippin III, she saw the campaign through to its bitter conclusion, closing up the county Democratic Headquarters herself and then loading up her Volkswagen and driving over the Rockies all in the same day. The Golden Dome of Notre Dame she would never see and, despite her mother's lament, she made peace with it; fly fishing, after all, would have been only marginal in that part of the country.

And Greg Woods? Well, what can you say? How do you describe someone so complicated yet so superficial, so intellectually rich but morally bankrupt, so creative but so destructive? How do you describe music or religion or color or philosophy or language or perception, when you suspect they may all be part of the same illusion? How, in your right mind, do you describe magic?

"Any holes-in-one?"

"Hank—" Greg folded the sports section across his lap. "How'd you find me?" He grabbed his sunglasses and an unwrapped Big Hunk from the top of his pack and, sticking the candy bar in his mouth, slid the pack over so I could sit.

The station was busy; a Trailways bus idled outside, waiting to be loaded for Salt Lake City while another eased up behind, brakes screeching.

"Where you going?"

He bit off the candy bar and held it out to me, but I shook my head.

"Denver. I have to report in a few days."

"They don't waste any time, do they?"

He shrugged, looking around and chewing the candy bar. "Guess not."

"I thought the Army's supposed to bus you over."

"Doesn't really matter, man. Just so you're there."

"What about probation?"

"When you're drafted all that stuff's history. Expunged, they call it."

"So if you don't have to report for a few days, why are you leaving early?"

"Oh, I don't know. So I can go hang for a while, I guess. Probably, you know, clean the pipes out one last time." He lifted his chin. "See all these people, Hank?"

I looked around at the crowded depot, people sitting and reading or napping, others gathering up belongings and heading for the double doors. "Yeah."

"They're all in transition, man. It's not like in an airport. You know, where everybody's on vacation or going on a business trip or visiting Aunt Betty in Boca Raton. No, this is the real stuff. It's like they're all in a trance, you know what I mean? With their little suitcases and things, clutching their tickets, all ready to carry their little lives off some place else—Denver, Salt Lake, Vegas. Like a change of scenery's going to make it all better. Like climbing on that bus is going to change the picture. Point A to B. Screw the journey, just get me there. Just get me there and everything'll be fine." Sliding his sunglasses back like a hair band, he scanned the depot. "What a way to live, huh? Why not just jump on any of them and see where it takes you? What difference does it make? You know, enjoy the ride and all that crap. And if you can get away with it, Hank, never, ever buy a ticket." He smiled.

I looked outside. A family of five—mother, father, and three small children—was filing through the glass double doors, stepping up onto the bus. The father handed the driver their tickets.

"How can you get on without a ticket?"

Greg stuck the rest of the candy bar in his mouth and wadded the wrapper. "Guile, man. Pure guile." He stuffed the paper in a side pocket, stood up and cinched the shoulder straps. "Well, Hank. I'm finally getting out of this valley." He stuck his hand out.

"You mean, you're getting on this—"

"Oh, shit—" Clutching both my shoulders, he swung me around, my back to the station's front doors.

"What're you—"

"Stand right there, Hank." He peered over my shoulder then looked quickly down, studying a strap on top his pack. "Just be cool—be cool. Act like we're—" He glanced up. "—like we're fixing my pack, okay?" He began fiddling with his rolled sleeping bag.

Out the corner of my eye I could see two policemen walk across the terminal, scouring the crowd. They stopped, then one stepped into the restroom while the other stood guard.

"Hank—" Head still down, Greg glanced around, slid his sunglasses on and removed a knit cap from his pack. He pulled it low and poked his hair up underneath. "Where'd you park?"

"Just down the street."

"Here—take my . . . wait." He quickly sat, elbows on knees, staring at the floor between his legs. "Take my pack. Go out that side door. Then bring your car around."

"What's going—"

"Just do it!"

I grabbed the pack and headed for the door.

"Hank!"

I turned.

"Put it on, man. Put the bloody thing—" He gestured as though hooking one arm through a strap.

I hefted it up, slung one shoulder through the straps and hurried out the door. Mom's car was no more than a block away, but by the time I reached it I was sweating and out of breath. I opened the back door and sat down with the pack, slipping it off and laying it across the seat. Turning a U, I sped back down the block and screeched up to the door, feeling like an accomplice.

Greg wasn't there. I tapped the steering wheel, my leg bouncing up and down. I squinted inside, glanced in the rear-view mirror. Just as I was about ready to jump out to go find him, there he was, nonchalantly strolling down the street from the alley behind the depot.

He got in. "Shall we?"

"What happened? How'd you—"

"It was Barney Fife and Andy, man. A couple of Grand River's finest. I cruised right by them to the back and then right out the door. A pair of geniuses. Come on, Hank. Let's roll."

I pulled out and drove down the street, my nerves still jangled. "I don't even know where we're going."

"Just head out toward the interstate."

We were approaching the on-ramp. It was mid-morning and traffic was light. Just as I crested the exit onto I-70, he was gesturing me to pull over. I stopped. He jumped out, opened the back door, and slid the pack out. Pulling off the knit hat and shaking his hair free, he stuck his head back in. "So—"

"So this is it, huh?"

"I guess. Unless you want to go with me." He smiled, stuffing the cap back inside his pack.

"To Vietnam? No thanks."

He gazed up at me, shaking his head. "Good old Hank, man. You're perfect." He stuck his hand out.

"'*Let us go then, you and I . . .*'" I shook it, waiting for him to finish the line.

He stared back, eyes vacant, then blinked and hesitated before finally shrugging. "Let's." He stepped back from the car.

He didn't know. Greg Woods didn't know the poem. Smiling to myself, I started to pull away but then braked, leaning across the seat. "Hey, Greg."

"Yeah."

"Where were you that night?"

"What night, man?"

"You know, that night at your house. For Lenny. You said you'd be there. I have to know."

Standing there on the shoulder next to his pack, adjusting the straps, he looked up and leveled his eyes at me. He looked off down the interstate, his mind working, then slowly shook his head. He brought his eyes back to me. "Some day I'll tell you, Hank. I promise. Just not now. And remember, I loved Lenny too, man." He stepped back again. "So, Hank—after we toasted the Colonel, you really thought it was Dill, huh?"

"What do you mean?"

"You know, that called the police the night of my so-called going-away party."

"You mean it was—"

He laughed. "You didn't actually think I'd let them ship me off to the academy, did you?" He pointed at me. "You're beautiful, man. Take care, Hank. And take care of that beautiful mother of yours, okay?"

I nodded, lifted my hand good-bye, and then accelerated down the interstate to where I could cross over back to town.

I probably did know; somewhere in that deepest recess of memory and thought, in the place we keep stored that which we know but refuse to acknowledge or give voice, maybe I actually knew.

As I dipped down and then up the dirt median and merged Mom's car with west-bound traffic, there he was digging in his pack. His back was to me, those long ringlets of blond hair, and he didn't see me. But it was then, as I focused on the back of his head and, whizzing past, switched to the rear-view mirror to see his face one last time, that it struck me full on. Not that he had crossed I-70 to head west instead of east—this I had expected; war was the last thing he was ready for—rather, it fully struck me that it was him, it'd been Greg Woods all along. Not my father. From stealing welding tanks to torching Redd Morgan's truck, none of it at all had been my father. None of it. And as he receded in the mirror to a single dot before disappearing altogether from my life, I realized that either way it no longer mattered.

End

CPSIA information can be obtained at www.ICGtesting.com
Printed in the USA
BVOW062323270312

286225BV00003B/1/P